By The Mud Stove

A NOVEL

by

DIVYA TOMBRAN

Tepui Roraima Publishing

Tepui Roraima Publishing
2850 Lakeshore Blvd West
P. O. Box 80036
Etobicoke, Ontario
Canada
M8V 4A1

Printed in the United States of America

Cover Design by John Mantha

ISBN: 978-1-7753482-0-7

This book is in sweet memories of my loving parents,
Reverend Richard and Nellie Sookhia Tombran

And my grandmother, my Mother's mother, and my Auntie Betty

If yuh plant plantain yuh can't reap cassava—you reap what you sow.

Guyanese Proverb

ACKNOWLEDGMENTS

Many thanks to you, Ron, for your unfailing love and support as my husband, and, as importantly, for taking a keen interest and valuable time in critiquing my work; my lifelong dream. You have sent me back to the writing desk many times to rework my manuscript and enhance my literary craft, and because of you, I feel I have done a thorough job in depicting exactly what I was envisioning as I wrote and told the story. You've not only been a critic of my work, but, also, a mentor and manager in coaching and directing me along the way to bring *By The Mud Stove* to completion. My gratitude to you will never waver.

Thanks to family and friends of mine as well as my husband's who have supported me in this challenging endeavour, and who have been very patient over the years in waiting for the completion.

A special thank you to John Mantha, the book cover illustrator, who has captured the setting by the mud stove so realistically and meticulously. He has also done an exceptional job in portraying the three main characters.

Again, thank you all.

AUTHOR'S NOTE

Since I left my homeland, Guyana, in the late seventies and emigrated to Canada as a teenager, I wanted to write a story to capture the precious memories I have of growing up in the small village of Rose Hall. I attempted this in my mid-twenties but, due to other obligations, could not follow through. I picked it back up in 2012 and completed the manuscript of *By The Mud Stove* in 2018.

I drew inspiration from watching my Grandmother and my Auntie cook on the mud stove, called a 'fireside' in Guyana, though as a little girl, I seldom saw my Grandmother as she was then living in the far off village of Crabwood Creek. In setting the main scene, I imagined my Auntie's little, old, wooden house down by a brown water river in Rose Hall Village, East Berbice-Corentyne. Many times, I escaped the modern conditions of my life to go visit my Auntie and her old fashioned way of living. I would sit in the hammock at her bottom-house and observe her doing her chores; she used to daub the earthen ground of the bottom-house with a wet mixture of cow-dung, clay, and water with a pinta broom, attended to her flower garden in the front yard and small vegetable garden in the back, and she used to cook delicious hassar and tilapia fish curry on the mud stove in her tiny bottom-house kitchen. We would sit on peerahs at the bottom-house and eat together from enamel plates, and while I ate with a spoon she provided, she would eat with her fingers. Those times —the curls of smoke from the mud stove, the crackle of the wood, the spicy smell of the fish curry mingled with the maar of rice bubbling on the stove and the aromatic smoke of the wood burning, the torrid heat of a mid-afternoon, the melancholic sound of a sitar accompanied by the alluring beat of a tabla playing on a neighbour's radio, and my Auntie's silent love—are indelibly etched in my mind and will resonate with many of my fellow Guyanese, as it did with my late mother. I had the opportunity of reading a few chapters to her, and as I was doing so, she sat at the edge of her seat with a ceaseless smile on her face, and after the reading, she commented that the story reminded her of growing up with her grandmother.

I wrote this piece of literature through laughter and tears, and in developing the story, I tried to capture that feeling of enchantment I felt then, playing it out through Nani, a widowed grandmother. I've also assembled a cast of characters of six friends who represent the six peoples of Guyana, weaving a story that depicts the good times through love, food, music, humour, and in the setting of the scenes and moods, encapsulating the culture as I experienced it back then.

As I mentioned earlier, in Guyana the mud stove is called a fireside, but because in many parts of the world the term fireside refers to the area around a fireplace or a hearth, I've chosen, instead, to use 'mud stove' in the title and body of the book.

As for the cover of the book, I had a vivid vision and designed a detailed pencil sketch for illustrator John Mantha to execute. He brought the entire scene alive in colour, depicting the three main characters, Nani, Indira, and Francine. The stools or peerahs they are sitting on are lower in my original sketch, which is a more accurate version of a peerah. However, I like the artist's rendition and decided to go with that. Every detail of the cover can be found in the description of the kitchen in Chapter One, and the scene itself relates to Chapter Seventeen, in which Nani is clearly having a talk with Indira and Francine.

The reader should not surmise that this is the story of Guyana in whole, but, rather, part of a story as seen through my eyes, in growing up there, which I've portrayed through fictitious characters and incidents.

Divya Tombran

CHAPTERS

PART ONE

PART TWO

PART ONE

1

Nani And Indira Go To The Market

Like a typical night in Guyana, tonight was warm and a gentle breeze was blowing. The sky was adorned with millions of twinkling stars and the sleepy little village of Rose Hall was faintly lit by the sliver of a crescent moon. The electric lights were out in the sparse, colourful, wooden houses built on stilts, and the kerosene oil lamps of the old shacks were long extinguished. *Candleflies*—fireflies were about, flickering in the dark corners of the bushes, and the *crapos*—frogs were croaking loudly as the crickets were chirring. Dogs were heard barking as two cats were having a fight, while the other animals were sleeping in barns, yards, and out in the fields. Chickens were perched on ladders in their coops, and the birds were roosting in dense trees, while the bats and owls and the sly mongooses were out on the hunt. In a distance, the ocean churned like a rhapsody ever so soothingly.

A green mosquito coil repellant was burning in a little wooden house on stilts down by a flowing brown water river, emitting a sweet incense-like scent. Indira, a little five-year-old Indo-Guyanese girl, woke to the crowing of the *fowlcocks*—roosters, and she laid there in the dark for a moment beneath the white mosquito netting, staring through the mesh at the mosquito coil on the bedside table as it was burning slowly at the glowing red tip, emitting curls of smoke. When it was all burnt down to ashes, she

9

rolled over and shook her snoring *nani*—grandmother, and she said, "Wake up, Nani, wake up." It was three-thirty in the morning and it was time for Nani to wake up and cook on the mud stove, called a *fireside* in Guyana, and, she also had to prepare to go to the market to sell her produce; vegetables, fruits, and chicken eggs.

Nani woke up and rubbed her eyes with the back of her hands in an effort to wipe the heavy sleep from her lids, then she said, "Good morning, child. Have you said your prayer, as yet?"

"Good morning, Nani," Indira returned, "I haven't said my prayers, as yet. I will do so now." And she crawled out from beneath the mosquito netting and knelt beside the bed and started saying her usual prayer: "Now I wake and see the light. God has kept us through the night. Make us good, oh Lord, I pray. Keep and guide us through this day. Amen."

Nani, after kneeling at the bedside and saying a prayer herself, got up and said to the child, "Find me the matches, child." Indira foraged through the bedside table drawer and found the box of matches and handed it to her, and Nani took a matchstick and fired it up and lit the wick of the kerosene oil lamp that was sitting on the bedside table, for she had no electricity.

The light of the lamp revealed a small and tidy room with ragged, unpainted greenheart wood walls and bare floor that was worn but scrubbed clean. In the middle of the room was a single bed with a coconut fibre mattress covered in a pink cotton sheet, with a matching pillow made of feathers. Above the bed cascaded a white mosquito netting from the low corrugated zinc roof, and beneath, was a white enamel *posey*—chamber pot, which Nani would empty in the latrine in the backyard everyday just before the break of dawn. Resting on the small bedside table was the kerosene oil lamp as well as the mosquito coil. In one corner of the room was a clothes-horse, and next to that was an old wooden trunk. On a miniature dresser, backed against a wall, was a fine-tooth comb, a tin of Yardley perfumed talc, and a bottle of fresh, home-made coconut oil, which Nani used on her skin and hair. An old wooden window overlooked the front yard and beside the one that faced the backyard was an armless wooden chair, as worn as everything else. The early morning wind was now gently blowing through the windows and it tossed the maroon lace curtains about playfully.

After Nani lit the lamp, she hung up the mosquito netting and Indira helped her to make up the bed, then Nani sat on the bed and said to Indira, "Fetch me the fine-tooth comb, child." Indira got the comb from the dresser and handed it to Nani and Nani combed her long, silver hair and fixed it in a bun, then she put on her faded brown headkerchief and got dressed in her tattered work dress. She left her feet bare for she went everywhere as such. But, she always made sure that Indira wore some sort of footwear.

Indira slipped on the pair of rubber slippers Nani handed her and she hurriedly got into her work dress, as well, eager to get going with things she found fascinating in her little world. "Please let me help you to milk Rani this morning, Nani," she pleaded with much exuberance. "And can I get the warm eggs from under the chickens, also?"

Nani did not answer right away but picked up the kerosene lamp and held it up to Indira's face, and she smiled benevolently, admiring the child for a moment. Indira was a pretty little girl with light golden-brown skin that was soft and tender at her age. A head of coal-black locks framed her delicate, oval-shaped face, and her large, luminous black eyes were fringed with long lashes. The child was not only blessed with ethereal beauty, but was also endowed with the cutest dimples that, depending on the mood she was in, made her look mischievous sometimes, sweet most of the time, and on the occasion when she threw a temper tantrum, made her look adorable. With her looks, smile, and sweet ways, it was hard for Nani to say no to the little girl. "Okay, child," Nani eventually answered, "I will let you help me to milk Rani and get the eggs from under the chickens, but this is not the kind of work for a five-year-old girl. I want you to focus on school and having an education. I don't want you to end up farming and selling at the market like me, breaking my back under the blazing hot sun and struggling to make a living. When you grow up I want you to work at the bank, and marry someone who works at the bank, also. So put your head on your schooling."

"I like going to school, but school work is hard, Nani," Indira said.

"I know, child, but always remember this . . . " Nani went on to quote an old Guyanese proverb, *Slow fire ah boil hard cow-heel,* meaning, if you persevere you will succeed, and she explained, "In other words, if you put your head on your school work and study hard you will pass your exams, and you will be able to get a bank job someday."

"I will do as you say, Nani, but I also like to help you with your work," Indira said, precocious for her age. "I like to milk Rani and I like to get the warm eggs from under the chickens. I like the smell of the earth and I like planting seeds and watering plants. You're getting too old now, Nani, and you need help. Please let me help you."

Nani was touched by the kindness of the child and she pinched her lovingly on the cheek and said, "As you wish, my dear child. Now, come on, let's go." And she took Indira by the hand and, with the lamp in her other hand, made her way out of the bedroom into the tiny sitting room, the old floor creaking as they walked.

Like the rest of the house, the greenheart wood walls in the sitting room were devoid of paint, and the floor was worn and bare, as well. As in the bedroom, the place was immaculately kept, and the furnishings were scanty. A decrepit rocking chair was positioned by the small wooden window facing the street, a faded jade-green sofa was backed against a wall, and in a corner was an obsolete treadle Singer sewing machine. In the centre of the room was a wicker table, on which rested a green glass vase of fresh hibiscus flowers, and a conch shell, which Indira would often place against her ears to listen for the sounds of the ocean, as Nani had told her to do. A doormat made of colourful strips of scrap fabrics threw some brightness in the room, and so did the green and pink floral-patterned curtains hanging from the two small wooden windows. On one wall was a picture of the Kings and Queens of England, flanked by a pair of praying hands carved of mora wood, and on another wall was a picture of Jesus in a lily white robe, ascending into heaven.

Nani guided Indira around the corner of the sitting room leading to the kitchen, saying as she did, "We will first have a cup of coco tea before we do our chores, child."

The slim entrance to the kitchen was partitioned by long strands of shiny, colourful glass beads, which Nani had strung herself, and they made a jangling sound as Nani parted them to enter the kitchen, Indira close at her heels. Nani hung the kerosene oil lamp on the hook from the chain dangling from the low corrugated zinc roof, which had a thin layer of soot that had accumulated from the smoke of the mud stove, which was in one corner, above which always hung a black iron pot of cow's milk. The kitchen was tiny and sparsely furnished like everywhere else, the walls and floor bare and worn. At the foot of the dish sink, protruding from one side of the wall, was a green barrel filled with water, where Nani kept live *mullet* and *tilapia* and *hassar* fishes whenever she fished. A couple of *peerahs* or low stools were situated in a corner next to the barrel. Above the narrow kitchen counter was tacked a map of Guyana, and on the counter were all of the utensils that Nani possessed, including, a *masala brick* used to grind spices for cooking. In an Amerindian straw basket, which was under the counter, were *cassava, breadfruit, plantains* and other vegetables, and spices. By the window facing the backyard was a scarred wooden table with four chairs. And a door with upper and lower sections led to an outdoor backstairs.

Nani opened up the window to let the early morning breeze in and then shoved some wood in the mud stove and started a fire with a matchstick. She took down the black iron pot hanging over the mud stove that contained cow's milk from the previous day, and she scooped the cream that had settled on top and gave it to Indira to eat—a real treat for the child—then she put the milk on to boil and got the tin of cocoa powder and made a pot of coco tea. She poured some in a white enamel cup for Indira and gave her a couple of sweet biscuits to nibble on, then poured a cup for herself, and both she and Indira sat on the peerahs in a corner of the kitchen and sipped on the hot coco.

The kerosene oil lamp shed a dim and comforting light in the kitchen as the burning wood in the mud stove crackled and emitted a sweet smoke, making the place feel warmer than it was. Through the smoke-filled room, Nani watched Indira, her countenance being the picture of innocence, and she was suddenly moved with profound compassion for the child. Indira was not her only grandchild for she had two grandsons, Ajay and Ajit, from her only son, Ram, but her son and his wife, Nita, were alive, and Indira's mother, her only daughter, Geeta, had died in a car crash a year ago, in 1965, so did her father, Sameer, leaving behind Indira, who was their only child.

Indira was left with her grandparents fighting to get custody of her. Her father's parents, Dr. Ramesh and his wife Shanti, were wealthy, for Dr. Ramesh had inherited a great deal of land from his parents and he was making a good living being a doctor in the village, and he held out that Indira should be given to his care because he was educated and rich enough to raise her properly. Nani, a little, old Indo-Guyanese woman who was now a widow, and who had never set foot in a classroom, argued with him that though she was uneducated she was a wise woman with good moral values and a strong faith in God, and though she was poor she still had enough food to share with the neighbours, therefore the child would be better off in her care.

In the end, Nani won the custody battle, for Indira cried and cried and held out that she wanted to stay with her Nani. Indira knew her father's parents were rich and if she went to live with them she would have any fancy thing her little heart desired, but, she knew, too, that she would be happier with her poor Nani for she was fond of the old woman. When her parents were alive, her Nani used to drop by their house every day on her way home from the market and bring her treats; sweetie and sweet drinks and fruits. Her Nani would allow her to play with the fluffy yellow ducklings by the pond in her backyard and she would let her climb the tamarind tree and other trees in her orchard and pick fruits, and, whenever she went to visit her on the weekends, she would let her stay up late in the nights and tell her stories. The old woman would pick pretty shells at the beach whenever she went fishing and would give them to her, and Indira had fun painting them with pink nail polish. And Nani always bought her picture books. But, mostly, Indira loved watching her Nani cook on the mud stove. It was the most enchanting of things. And the most enchanting place where she wanted to be. There was nothing Dr. Ramesh could have done to stop Indira from crying to stay with the old lady and it broke his heart to hear her cry, so he gave up the fight for her custody, and Indira went to live with her poor Nani in the little, old house down by the riverside in Rose Hall Village.

In the first few months Indira had cried incessantly for she missed her parents. Nani told her there was no need for her to cry because her Pa and Ma were alive and living with the angels in heaven, and she also told her that someday she would also go to heaven and she would meet them there. Indira believed it and, eventually, she stopped her crying. It helped, also, that Nani would buy her sugar-coated *blood-drop* sweetie and make her *sugar cakes*, and sew fancy dresses for the dolls she bought her. Life with her grandmother was a bowl of sweetie and nice things that made the young child happy again. A year had gone by and Indira had ensconced herself in Nani's humble abode, and it was now a new beginning for the child, as it was for Guyana—formerly, British Guiana—as the country gained independence from Britain that same year; 1966.

Nani finished her cup of coco tea and sat quietly for a moment longer and cherished the child's company as she was finishing hers, and once Indira was finished, Nani got the lamp and beckoned her to follow her.

It was still dark outside when they made their way out onto the verandah and down the front stairs. The light from the lamp illuminated the sun-bleached greenheart wood house which was held up by spindly stilts, and it revealed a garden of chameli, hibiscus, roses, and *jump up and kiss me* or *jump & kiss* flowers in the front yard, which had a narrow dirt pathway leading to a ragged gate. As they made their way to the *bottom-house*—the space beneath a house built on stilts, the lamp shed light on the earthen ground, which had been daubed the previous day with a wet mixture of cow-dung, clay, and water, and was now dry and smooth and grey and swept clean. Tied to a pair of stilts was a hammock that was gently swaying in the wind. Rani the cow and Solomon the donkey were laying on the earthen ground beside a donkey-cart that had been loaded the day before with straw baskets full of vegetables and fruits, and was ready for the market.

With Nani still holding the lamp, she guided Indira to the back of the house. At the bottom of the backstairs was a pipe, by which was a stone slab used to *beat* soiled clothes on, and a washboard to *rub* clothes. Just beyond here was a fowl coop to the left, in the backyard. A pond was in the middle, on the surface of which floated water lilies, and *shame-baby* weeds—so called because the tiny leaves would close up when sprinkled with water or touched, thus, shying away in shame—and beneath the pond swam fat tilapias and hassars, which Nani raised mainly for consumption. A green crapo—frog was now sitting on a lily pad, and beside the pond a Muscovy duck and her five ducklings were sleeping on a bed of grass. Beyond the pond was a vegetable garden, flourishing with *bora* and *karela* and *callaloo* and *ball-of-fire*—Scotch Bonnet hot peppers. Further back there was an orchard, the trees loaded with mangoes and *guavas* and *guineps* and coconuts, and a great tamarind tree towered above the other fruit trees. In the very back, where *crabgrass* bush grew around the edges of the paling, was a small cubicle for a bathroom, made of corrugated zinc, and not far from there was an old wooden latrine. From here, you could hear the gushing of the river which flowed beside the house next door, and in a distance the ocean tossed restlessly.

Nani led Indira to the fowl coop, where some chickens were roosting on the ladders and others were sitting on straw nests, and she hung up the lamp on the hook of a chain hanging from the low zinc ceiling. Indira was excited as they went around collecting the brown and white eggs from under the chickens—some still warm from just being laid. They placed them into two empty paint cans, altogether two dozens and two—Nani would boil a couple for breakfast and take the rest to the market to sell.

Nani grabbed the lamp as they left the fowl coop, and after she loaded the paint cans of eggs onto the donkey-cart, she got the aluminium milk bucket and let Indira help her to milk Rani, much to Indira's delight. They milked half a bucket of thick, rich milk, which Nani took upstairs and poured into the black iron milk pot and hung that up above the mud stove.

Nani then stoked the fire in the mud stove and put the fresh eggs on to boil, then she made *roti* and *saltfish* with tomatoes for breakfast, with hot chocolate from chocolate sticks and fresh cow milk. Indira got the enamel plates and cups from the kitchen counter and Nani served her as well as herself, giving thanks to the Lord for the meal.

While Indira sat at the table having her meal, Nani sat on the peerah and ate, the light from the kerosene oil lamp falling on her brown face, revealing her noticeable wrinkles. She was now in her early sixties, a petite woman, with skin that was weather-beaten from the many years of labouring in the garden beneath the scorching rays of the sun, just to make a meagre living. Her face, showing traces of a faded beauty, was thin, her cheeks hollow, and her deep-set brown eyes, once sparkling, now bore a dull appeal. Her once full lips were now shrunken and she had two gold-capped teeth in the front of her mouth which were very conspicuous whenever she smiled, a smile that had not lost its attractiveness with time. Age, though, had turned her once long, lustrous black hair to silver-grey, streaked with yellow, which she now always kept tucked away beneath her headkerchief.

The past few years had been tough on her. She lost her husband, Amar, a few years ago, and severe grief over the loss had deteriorated her health, causing her to feel depleted of vigour. Then when her only daughter, Geeta, died, she thought she would not be able to endure life much longer. But having to care for her granddaughter, Indira, alleviated much of her suffering. The child brought her such abundant joy and refreshed her life so much that she now kept looking forward to each new day. Indira reminded her of Geeta when she was her age, and she loved the child dearly. Being her only granddaughter heightened her affection, and she felt great compassion for her because she was an orphan.

Her son, Ram, contrarily, had no empathy and could never understand her feelings for the child. He would always accuse her of favouring Indira over his two sons, and because of this, he kept her two grandsons as well as her daughter-in-law away from her, something that grieved her soul immensely. Her son was a wayward and belligerent man, and her relationship with him was often trying. She always prayed for patience and compassion to cope with him for she loved him much more than his bitter mind could comprehend, and she prayed he would change his ways. As she sat there having breakfast, she thought of her grandsons and she longed to see the children, and hoped that her son would realise her deep love for them and bring them around someday.

Nani was so lost in thoughts that she might have sat there for a while longer after she finished her breakfast, but Indira interrupted her, saying, "Nani, it's time to empty the posey before it gets bright outside and the neighbours will see you carrying it."

"Okay, child, I'll empty the posey," Nani said. "And while we're downstairs we'll bathe. Go and get your toothbrush and my chewstick and bring along a towel and let's go."

While Indira hurried off to get the things, Nani washed the dishes and tidied the kitchen then went to the bedroom and got the chamber pot—so called posey—and they headed downstairs. After emptying the posey in the backyard latrine, Nani scrubbed it with some ashes by the pipe at the foot of the backstairs. She then chewed on the *black-sage* chew stick to clean her teeth while Indira used a toothbrush, and they had a quick wash in the backyard cubicle before heading back upstairs.

As Nani was replacing the clean posey under the bed, Indira, with much impatience, said, "It's time to go to the market, Nani."

"I know, child, I know," Nani said. As it was Saturday morning and not a school day, she would take Indira to the market with her, something Indira always looked forward to. "As soon as you get ready, we'll leave."

They quickly got dressed in their worn but clean market clothes, then Nani got her old cloth money bag—dark green in colour—and put it in her dress pocket and, without further delay, they hurried back downstairs. Nani harnessed

21

Solomon the donkey and helped Indira onto the loaded donkey-cart, and she mounted it herself. Given her affinity with her animals, she gently tapped Solomon on his backside with a stick instead of whipping him, and she jerked the reins and they started off for the market, Solomon trotting slowly as he hauled the heavy load along.

A tinge of darkness from the night lingered in the early morning air and the stars were fading as they made their way up the street to the narrow dirt road, passing houses that were just beginning to stir. Dogs were heard barking, and cats and chickens and cows and pigs and goats and donkeys were wandering the street and road sides as marketeers were on their way to the market. Some ladies were carrying large straw baskets of live fishes and fresh fruits and vegetables on their heads. Others were on donkey-carts, trotting alongside the few people on bicycles.

Soon Nani and Indira arrived at the market. The market was situated at the archway to the main road which was sparsely lined with little shops—with people living above, a couple of banks, a restaurant or two, and other businesses. The marketeers took up their places on both sides of the road, spreading old rice and flour bags on the dirt ground and laying out their copious amounts of fishes, fruits, and vegetables. Indira was fascinated with the fishes because the hassars and mullets and tilapias were still alive and jumping, even the shrimps. She loved the smell of the fresh hassars and produce, and the earthy smell of the warm early morning air. The chatter of the marketeers and the hustling and bustling excited her. She just loved coming to the market with her Nani this early in the morning. There was something enchanting about the ambiance of the place at this time: the sapphire-blue of the sky, the feel, the sounds, the smell, the energy.

She eagerly helped Nani to unload the straw baskets of produce from the donkey-cart, and she unfolded the old rice bag and spread it out on the dirt ground, taking her seat on a peerah beside Nani's. She assisted Nani to lay out the vegetables and fruits and sprinkled them with water. She even helped to get the brown and white chicken eggs from the paint cans and wiped them before parcelling them in four. She felt important that Nani let her hold the old cloth money bag, for Nani put her in charge of collecting the money from the customers as Indira was good at counting, exceptionally competent at her tender age.

Soon the sun was up, bright and hot, and the market quickly became crowded, with mostly Afro-Guyanese and Indo-Guyanese, and other Guyanese, including, Amerindians, Chinese, Portuguese, and a few other Europeans. Most were in western attire, but there were a few Indian women wearing colourful *saris*—Indian garment, and a couple of Indian men were in *turbans*—headwear, and *dhotis*—Indian pants, and some black men and women were in African-influenced attire, and *head ties*—head scarves.

The market was now very noisy with buyers bargaining with marketeers and marketeers hollering to the top of their voices: "Fresh shrimps for sale . . . " "Big *hassa* for sale . . . " "Nice mullets for sale . . . " "Come taste my guineps, sweet like sugar . . . " "Come buy my ball-of-fire peppers. I'll make you a good deal . . . " "How about some sweet potatoes and cassava and plantains . . ." "I have some nice callaloo here . . . " "Ripe and delicious mangoes for sale . .

. " "I have many kinds of apples here, from *star apples* to *sugar apples* to *monkey apples* to *golden apples* to *pineapples* . . . and I have *five-fingers*, too . . ." "Come buy my fresh beef and liver and I'll give you a little extra . . . " Nani was as vociferous as the others in beckoning her customers to buy her produce.

Mrs. Ramsammy, a regular customer of Nani, came over carrying a large straw basket in her hand, and she said to Nani, "I'm making a big cake for a birthday party and I want to buy all of your eggs, give me all of your parcels. And give me four bunches of bora and a squash, a couple of *baigans* and five bunches of *chorai callaloo*, and six karelas. I'll also take a dozen mangoes and six guavas, and four bunches of guineps. And give me three parcels of *wiri wiri* hot pepper."

Nani loaded up Mrs. Ramsammy's basket, giving her a little extra of this and that, and she worked out a good price for her. Indira was quick to collect the money from Mrs. Ramsammy, and she counted it and untied the string from the green money bag and put all of it in the bag. Others came as the morning sun grew hotter and hotter, buying up Nani's produce and, by midday, Nani sold everything she had.

Indira stuffed the money bag full with bank notes and coins and, with a beaming face, handed it to Nani. Nani put the money bag in her dress pocket and smiled as broadly as Indira, showing off her glittering gold teeth, because she had a good day at the market and could afford to buy some meat, and other foods. As she was packing away the empty straw baskets onto the donkey-cart, she turned to Indira and said, "Come now, child, let's go to the butcher and buy some meat to cook for lunch."

Indira was happy that Nani made a bag full of money but the smile on her face suddenly ceased, for she was not looking forward to going to the butcher, and that was because she found his demeanour to be intimidating, and he was often times obnoxious to his dog. The butcher was a strapping Indo-Guyanese man with very pale, oily skin, and dark hair that was saturated with oil, as well, and his blood-stained apron and hands would scare the little girl. He always brought his old dog with him to the market and he barked at the dog and kicked it whenever it was in his way. This would annoy Indira but she was forced to keep quiet because she was scared of him and afraid that if she were to say something to him that her Nani would become austere and scold her, for Nani would think of her as being disrespectful to an elder. Nani would not tolerate her disrespecting the butcher for he was one of her friends at the market.

Indira's sulking and reluctance to accompany Nani to the butcher only caused Nani to haul her by the hand over to his stall. The butcher smiled when he saw Nani approaching with Indira now clutching at her skirt, and he asked, "Why is the little gal hiding her face behind your skirt?"

"Never mind her," Nani said, "she's playing the fool."

The butcher shrugged it off and turned his attention to doing business with Nani, and he asked, "What can I get you today, old lady?" And he kicked away his old dog who was hanging around him for a scrap of meat.

"One pound of beef for me today," Nani said, and added, "and be generous, boy."

The butcher cut off a chunk of fresh-smelling beef and placed it on the scale, and he added a sizeable extra piece. "I'm giving you some extras for the little gal," he said, amused by Indira's behaviour, and he went about wrapping up the beef in brown paper. Indira did not find her situation amusing at all, though, neither was she bought over by the butcher's generosity, and she was happy when Nani paid him and collected the beef and they left.

Nani then went to Mrs. Surjeet, her friend who also sold at the market. Mrs. Surjeet was half Nani's age, in her early thirties, a light-skinned woman of medium stature, who wore her long, black hair in a single plait down her back. She had five young children, and was in a troubled marital relationship, often turning to Nani for support. Mrs. Surjeet had some schooling as a young girl and knew how to read and write, unlike Nani, so she would write up Nani's grocery list for her. She did so this day, for Nani planned on stopping in at the little grocery shop on her way home. As always, Nani would not only stop for groceries, but, also, to get treats for Indira for helping her out at the market. Before Nani headed off to the shop, Mrs. Surjeet asked her to accompany her to the bank so she could square up some bills and pay back the small loan she had taken from her.

The bank happened to be just around the corner, on the main road, and Nani and Indira followed Mrs. Surjeet there. Nani had only been to a bank a couple of times prior to this, only to accompany Mrs. Surjeet, for she always kept her money at home, and she found the bank to be something of a dream. She was taken by the fresh coolness of the place and the beautiful women who worked there, with their soft, clear skin. As she was waiting by the door for Mrs. Surjeet, she said to Indira, "Someday you will grow up and be as beautiful as those girls working here, and you, too, will work here, child." So was her dream for Indira.

When Mrs. Surjeet was finished at the bank, she settled up the loan with Nani. Nani and Indira then said ta-ta to her and mounted the donkey-cart, and Nani got the stick and gently tapped Solomon on the backside then jerked the reins, and they headed off.

The sun was now at its peak and boiling hot, and people took shade from its scorching rays under umbrellas of all different colours and patterns. Indira had her little pink parasol that Nani had bought her and she clutched it tightly as Solomon, with a lesser load to carry, trotted along the bumpy dirt road, jostling her and Nani about.

In the bright daylight, they passed colourful houses on stilts along the way, mostly of medium and small sizes, except, for three, which were large houses, where the rich people lived. One was owned by Mr. Gopu, a wealthy businessman by inheritance of land and gold, who lived with his wife, Chanda, and two young daughters, Nadia and Raaka. Another was owned by a successful Afro-Guyanese surgeon, Dr. Lawrence Fraser, who inhabited the place with his wife, Phyllis, and their only teenage daughter, Roxanne. The other house was owned by Mr. Ramal, a high school principal, who lived with his wife, Banita, and a teenage son, Vishnu, and two young daughters, Aashi and Babita.

All those wealthy men and their families were friends of Dr. Ramesh, Indira's grandfather, but Indira had never met any of them because whenever she visited her grandparents they would spend the time alone with her, giving her their undivided attention to make up for the seldom times they saw her. So she was left to wonder about the rich people in the big houses.

Whenever she passed those beautiful, painted wooden houses, which stood tall on silts, she would stare in fascination at the glass windows and the concrete-paved bottom-houses. She was impressed with the big, lovely yards, and the colourful flowers and palm trees that flanked the pathways, and the brand new cars in the driveways.

As she was passing by now, all the rich men and their families were gathered in the front yard of Mr. Ramal, their teenage children playing volley ball in the baking hot afternoon sun. There were two white children, Peter and Karen, playing, as well. Both were around Indira's age, and they had golden hair and blue eyes just like their parents, John and Nancy Patterson. John and Nancy were teachers from Canada, teaching at the same high school where Mr. Ramal was principal, and they were friends of Mr. Ramal and his friends. As much as Indira was fascinated by the rich people, she was also intrigued by the white family.

The houses in which the affluent people lived were like Indira's grandfather's house. Dr. Ramesh lived out on the main road in a beautiful, big, yellow house, with a big yard lined with flowers and trees, and he also had a car in his driveway; a shiny blue Studebaker. When Indira's father, Sameer, was alive, he used to take her only on special occasions to visit her grandparents. This was because of an on-going quarrel between her grandfather and her father: her grandfather wanted her father to become a medical doctor, just like him, but, instead, her father had chosen to work at a bank, pushing papers and counting numbers, and her grandfather would harp at her father over this whenever he saw him, causing them to argue. So, her father had chosen to keep away from him as much as he could to avoid the arguments, and, for that reason, Indira saw very little of her grandfather back then.

But now she still saw very little of him. The reason for this was because Dr. Ramesh worked seven days a week and did not have even a second to scratch his head, for he attended to the sick all day long and was sometimes called upon at any hour of the evening, and he would, at times, be woken from his sleep in the wee hours of the morning to care for those stricken with infirmities.

Indira was aware of this and she felt sorry for her grandfather that he had to work so hard. As for her grandmother, Shanti, she was a sickly woman who suffered from high blood pressure and other ailments, and she was often confined to bed, wanting to be left alone with her sufferings. Indira felt sorry for her sick grandmother, also. She had no doubt, though, that her grandparents loved her, for whenever she visited them they made her feel special.

Dr. Ramesh had not taken a day off work in years, since before Indira was born. In his younger years he used to throw parties and invite his friends over to his house for pig roasts. At the recent prompting of his friends, he agreed it was about time to consider a day off to entertain them again, and he thought he would have Indira there, and told her so, much to her delight And, now, as Indira was traveling along the dirt road on the donkey-cart, in the searing sun, she was dreaming about going over to her grandfather's big, yellow house for the pig roast and meeting all of the rich people and the white family with whom she was so fascinated.

Indira was so caught up in her little world that she had not been paying attention to Nani as Nani was prattling on about this and that along the way, but, when Nani said, "We'll stop off at Mr. Wilson's shop and I'll get you some treats," her ears perked up and she said, "Treats! Treats! Hurry up Solomon and take us there as fast as you can!"

Solomon picked up speed when Nani nudged his behind with the stick, and soon they arrived in front of the little grocery shop. As soon as the donkey came to a halt, Indira quickly hopped off the cart and ran inside, with Nani taking her time following in the heat.

The owner of the shop, Mr. Wilson, a stout, black-skinned Afro-Guyanese, affable in nature, was standing behind the small wooden counter when they entered. He greeted them with his characteristic pleasant smile, displaying his impeccable white teeth, and he said, "Good afternoon, ladies, what I can get for you today?"

"Good afternoon," both Nani and Indira reciprocated, and Nani handed him the grocery list that Mrs. Surjeet had helped her to write up, smiling at him as she did and showing off her gold teeth.

Mr. Wilson took the list from Nani and looked it over: 1lb of flour, 1 bag of rice, *garam masala* spice, curry powder, split peas, a piece of saltfish, barley, 1 tin of corned beef, a couple of onions and a garlic, 1 cake of *salt soap* and 1 *sweet soap*, *laundry blue cubes* and starch, a stick of *soft grease*, and a bottle of Limacol. He got the items from the shelves behind the counter and loaded them

30

into Nani's straw basket. Then he smiled down at Indira and asked, "And what can I get the little gal?"

Indira returned Mr. Wilson's smile with a broad smile, her dimples deepening as she did, and she thought for a moment. She loved all the sweet things there in the glass case and her eyes danced from the sugar-coated blood-drop sweetie to the Bulls-Eyes sweetie to the red sugar cakes made with coconut, and tamarind sugar balls, and she could visualise the frozen *custard block* and Fudgesicle ice cream bar in the refrigerator, and cold lemonade, as well. But Nani would not let her have them all at once; she was allowed to have three choices for her morning's hard work. "I will have some blood-drop sweetie, Uncle Wilson, and a sugar cake, and a bottle of lemonade," she decided.

Mr. Wilson handed her a cold bottle of lemonade and then bagged the treats, throwing in some extra sweetie for her like he would always do. He then totalled the bill and gave Nani a substantial discount, for Nani would always bring him vegetables from her garden and would not charge him for any of it. Once Nani paid him, Mr. Wilson gave Indira a custard block to have while he and Nani discoursed for a while. Mr. Wilson filled Nani in on the news in the Guyana Chronicle Newspaper and, after they talked about the happenings in the village for a little while longer, Nani and Indira bid Mr. Wilson ta-ta and they left for home.

When they reached home, Nani let Indira sit in the hammock at the bottom-house and enjoy her treats while she went about cooking up stewed beef and potatoes and rice on the mud stove and, when she was finished, she and Indira had a late lunch. Nani, feeling lethargic from the heat of the day, then took a nap in the hammock while a warm breeze was blowing as lazily, and Indira sat beside her, on the earthen ground, and played with her dolls for a while, then she went about chasing after the butterflies in the flower garden in the front yard.

When the old lady woke up, she worked in the vegetable garden under the hot sun for a while, with Indira close by her side, insisting on helping. They tilled the soil and planted seeds, and pruned and watered the existing plants. When they were through with that task, Indira helped Nani scrub the front and backstairs, and sweep the bottom-house with a *pinta* broom, which Nani had made herself from the spine of coconut leaves. Nani then taught Indira how to make a mixture to daub the earthen bottom-house; she collected cow-dung from Rani and placed it in an aluminium bucket and then added water and clay. With the pinta broom, they daubed the earthen ground with the mixture and left it to dry. Nani then gave Indira a cake of sweet soap and sent her to the cubicle in the backyard to bathe, while she merely rinsed her skin by the pipe at the bottom of the back stairs, as she would bathe after cooking dinner.

It was now around four in the afternoon, and as Nani sat on the front steps thinking what to cook, Mrs. Surjeet came by with a fresh catfish her husband had just caught. Indira had finished bathing and, dressed in clean home clothes, she came down the stairs just in time to see Mrs. Surjeet deliver the live fish. This excited her for this meant that Nani would cook fish curry, and there was nothing better Indira loved than to watch her Nani cook fish curry on the mud stove in the afternoon.

She hurried back up the stairs and got a peerah and sat down in the corner of the kitchen and waited for Nani to begin. As much as Indira loved watching Nani cook, the old lady just loved the little girl's company. It was here, by the mud stove, that the two of them would share many precious moments together.

As Indira sat with her elbows on her knees, propping her face in the tiny palms of her hands, she quietly eyed Nani's every movement. Nani first shoved some wood in the mud stove and started a fire and placed a pot of water on to boil to make rice, then she went about cleaning the catfish in the dish sink, setting the sac of fish eggs aside, and washing the fish with lime until the skin was almost white. After cutting it up into thick portions, she got the masala brick and sat on the peerah and ground up some curry powder and garam masala and fresh onion and garlic, and ball-of-fire peppers she had picked from her garden. She placed the spicy mixture in a *calabash*—the dried, brown shell of a calabash fruit, used as a bowl; Nani would also often use this for her meals instead of eating from a plate. She then put the *carahee,* a cast iron, bowl-shaped frying pan, on the mud stove and heated some coconut oil and started cooking the catfish curry.

The late afternoon sun now cast its golden rays over the village, seeping through the cracks of the old greenheart wood walls of the kitchen. Somewhere in the distance someone was playing Indian music on the radio, and the silky voice of Lata Mangeshkar, accompanied by the sweet melancholic sound of the *sitar* and the alluring drumming of the *tabla,* sailed through the old wooden kitchen window. The flames in the mud stove leaped around the boiling pots on the mud stove, creating a layer of soot, and the burning wood crackled softly, emanating heat and making the place even warmer than it was in the late afternoon heat. The aromatic smoke of the burning wood filled the air and mingled with the spicy, delicious smell of catfish curry cooking, and *maar*—water from the boiling rice. As Indira sat there on the peerah, she was lost in the enchantment of the moment.

As soon as Nani finished cooking, she gave thanks to the Lord for the food and then dished out some steaming rice and hot catfish curry with fish eggs on an enamel plate for Indira. She gave her a silver spoon to eat with, and the child immediately started devouring the spicy, mouth-watering meal. Nani then dished out some for herself in a calabash and sat down on the peerah and ate with her fingers, just as hungrily.

After the scrumptious supper, Nani washed the dishes with salt soap and scrubbed the *blackpat*—soot on the pots —with the ashes from the mud stove with a rag, and she cleaned up the kitchen then lit the kerosene oil lamp and placed it on the bedside table in the bedroom. She then got a cake of sweet soap and a dried *nenwa* vegetable—a loofah—and went downstairs to bathe. While she was doing so, Indira changed into her nightie, after which, she fluffed the feather pillow and jumped up onto the bed and lowered the mosquito netting, tucking it under the coconut fibre mattress. She then straightened out the clothes on the clothes-horse before she went and sat on the old wooden chair by the window overlooking the backyard, like she would usually do in the evenings.

The sapphire-blue hue of dusk had now settled across the firmament and the birds were flying in large flocks to their evening roosts. Soon night enveloped the village and innumerable stars began to emerge, sparkling like diamonds in the sky. A patch of clouds obscured the light of a crescent moon and, in the darkness, the blinking yellow lights of the candleflies were conspicuous as they swarmed about the corners of the bushes. It was not as hot now as it was in the daytime, just pleasantly warm, and as Indira sat by the window listening to the sounds of the night creatures, a slight wind blew her curls about, and she quietly observed the neighbours' homes.

Beyond the backyard, through a clearing in the dense orchard, Indira could see a tiny wooden house on stilts, where an old, dark-skinned, small-statured Indo-Guyanese lady lived. Her name was Pyari and she wore a gold nose ring and always had on a red headkerchief. Indira could not fathom her ways and found her to be mysterious and always wondered about the strange life she lived. Pyari was now sitting by her window in the sitting room, and the light from the gas lamp was bright enough for Indira to see that she was smoking a pipe and talking with a young man, who was sitting just opposite her with a drink in his hand. Pyari kept the company of lonely men who often times visited her in the evenings for a free glass of strong drink. The other company this peculiar woman kept was a parrot, whom she called Raj. Raj was quite a talker, and a good listener, too. He would listen to the secret stories the men would divulge to Pyari, and when the men were gone he would prattle and talk out loud their personal affairs. And, he would swear just like them. His swearing greatly annoyed Nani, and she warned Indira not to visit Raj because his mouth was too filthy. As it was, Indira could now see that Raj was sitting in his cage on the table, listening intently to Pyari and the young man as they were discoursing, and he was repeating every swear word he heard.

While still staring at Pyari and her company, Indira tuned her ears to the cry of the baby girl coming from the broken-down house next door to the left, which, from that viewpoint, was obscured by Nani's kitchen. It was along this house that a brown water river flowed. An Indo-Guyanese Muslim family of eight lived in this dilapidated house on shaky stilts. Shazam's wife, Fazeela, a beautiful, fair-complexioned woman with long, curly, black hair who captivated everyone in the village, was only twenty-five years old and already had six children, the last of whom was just a baby, and she was now pregnant again. Their only source of income came from Shazam's job at a movie theatre, where he worked as an attendant. He had too many mouths to feed and too little income, so the family lived a very impoverished life. Indira would go over and play with the baby girl and the other siblings, and the children would show her strips of film that Shazam would bring home from work, and Indira would hold up the film strips to the sunlight and see the images of the beautiful and exotic film stars from India and be star-struck. She always thought that Fazeela looked like those film stars in the negatives, only that she did not have the beautiful clothes and makeup they wore.

Fazeela's baby girl always cried whenever Fazeela put her to bed at nights, and once her cries subsided tonight,

Indira shifted her focus to the right, where, in a modest house on stilts, lived an Afro-Guyanese family. George Williams was a respectable high school teacher, who bore a striking resemblance to the handsome actor Sidney Poitier. His wife, Joan, a voluptuous, brown-skinned woman, was a seamstress, who worked from home and made all of Nani and Indira's clothes. The Williams' were a middle-aged couple who were blessed with an only child, Francine, a baby-face, chocolate-skinned girl, who was the same age as Indira.

Indira sat there remembering the first day she met Francine. The Williams' had moved next to Nani the same day that she had moved in with Nani a year ago, and on that very first day Francine was sitting on their verandah looking at her as she was playing hopscotch by herself at Nani's bottom-house. She called out to Francine, saying, "Would you like to play with me?" Without hesitation, Francine had skipped down the stairs and came over and joined her, and they played hopscotch and with their dolls all that day. Very soon, they became friends. When Francine started kindergarten recently, Indira held out that she wanted to go to the same school as Francine, and Nani arranged it.

It did not matter to Indira that Francine was an Afro-Guyanese girl, neither did it matter to Francine that Indira was Indo-Guyanese, the two were best friends, and Indira always looked forward to going over and playing with her. Francine's parents were mostly away on the weekends visiting both their parents who were living in New Amsterdam, and taking along Francine, so Indira would see Francine only during the week. As Indira sat there thinking fondly of her best friend, she could not wait for Monday morning to arrive when she and Francine would go to school together.

Indira's beautiful thoughts were suddenly interrupted when, from the corner of her eye, she saw something moving on the old bedroom wall. She turned to see a reddish-brown centipede, thick and long, crawling up the wall, the light of the kerosene oil lamp revealing its numerous legs, and she shrieked in fear. Nani, who was just on her way up after bathing, heard her cry, and she rushed into the bedroom and saw the centipede on the wall. A bite from that, she knew, could cause extensive pain and swelling, and even, in rare cases, death to children. Without hesitation, she quickly grabbed the old cricket bat she had in the corner of the room and hit the centipede, killing it before it could cause harm to the child. Nani then tried to reassure Indira that the centipede could not hurt her now, but Indira was more scared of it than she was of snakes, and even though Nani had killed it, she was still petrified.

To distract her, Nani took her over to the clothes-horse and told her to pick out her favourite dress for Sunday School in the morning, one that Francine's mom, Joan Williams had sewn for her. At the mention of Francine and her favourite dress, Indira soon forgot the old centipede. She picked out the pink dress with frills and was now looking forward to wearing it to Sunday School.

Nani then got the kerosene oil lamp and took Indira to the kitchen, and she got out the coal iron and loaded it with coals and lit it. When it was hot enough, she spread a clean cotton flour bag on the bare kitchen table and ironed Indira's dress, and hers, as well. Her white headkerchief, she handled with special care. She had prepared it for ironing previously; washed and rinsed it in laundry blue and dipped it in starch, and when it was dry she had sprinkled it with water and rolled it up tightly. Now that it was ready, she took her time ironing it until it was smooth and crisp. She then draped the ironed clothes over the clothes-horse for the morning.

The chores of the day were all done now and it had been a long day. By the time Nani and Indira were ready to retire to bed it was late in the evening. Just before they did, Nani lit a mosquito coil repellant and placed it on the bedside table. She then blew out the kerosene oil lamp, and she and Indira crawled under the mosquito netting and laid back on the single coconut fibre mattress, sharing the feather pillow, also.

Nani then said to Indira, "Now, you say your prayer before you go to sleep, child."

Indira clasped her little hands, and said, "In my little bed I lie. Heavenly Father, hear my cry. Lord, protect us through the night, and bring us safe till morning light. Amen."

Nani said a bedtime prayer, also, and then she and Indira went to sleep to the sounds of the crapos croaking and the crickets chirring and the soothing flow of the nearby river, and the distant churn of the restless ocean.

2

Going To Church On Sunday Morning

Indira heard the fowlcocks crowing around four in the morning and she woke up and quietly lifted the mosquito netting and crawled out of bed, not wanting to wake her grandmother who was fast asleep. It was Sunday morning and they did not have to wake up until six o'clock, but she liked waking up this early while most of the villagers were still sleeping as it was quiet and dark and somewhat mystical outside at this time. She tip-toed over to the chair by the window overlooking the backyard and sat there and looked out at the starry, moonlit sky as a warm morning breeze was gently blowing.

While she waited for dawn to break, she passed the time thinking about all the wonderful things and people that made up her young life; yellow ducklings, sweetie, flowers, Solomon and Rani, the neighbours, her grandfather Dr. Ramesh and her grandmother Shanti, the rich people and the white family, her best friend Francine, the mud stove and her Nani. It was her usual routine to sit by the window in the evenings and most mornings and engage in such pleasant and innocent thoughts. The moon and the stars gradually began to fade as she sat there relishing her thoughts, and just as the golden sun began emerging over the horizon, she went over to the bed and shook her Nani and woke her up.

Nani hauled her old bones out of bed and they both knelt by the bedside and said their morning prayers before changing their nighties, then Nani put on her brown headkerchief and they headed straight to the kitchen. Nani first opened the window facing the backyard to let in some of the soft morning light, then she reached for the iron pot of milk hanging above the mud stove and let Indira stick her fingers in and scoop up the layer of cream that had settled on top. While Indira sat in the corner on the peerah savouring the cream, she went about cooking breakfast. She started the fire and put on a pot of water to boil then went down to the garden and picked some lime leaves, and she returned and put them on to boil to make tea, then she began cooking *dosa*, known as *dosea*—Guyanese style pancakes, and fried eggs, as curls of smoke from the mud stove drifted about the dimly lit kitchen, tinting it a pale blue.

Indira, now with her elbows on her knees and her face cupped in the palms of her hands as she sat on the peerah, watched through the smoky room as her grandmother was cooking and reverently humming the hymn *Amazing Grace*. The ambience was one that emitted a pleasurable loneliness, like Sundays usually make one feel, and there was a sense of serenity in the soft air of the early morning, a tranquility that her Nani exuded. The sweet, contagious peace washed over Indira like she was bathing under a warm waterfall, putting her in a state of contentment as she sat there listening to her Nani. Flames in the mud stove swayed about as the wood crackled and spouted sparks as the dosea sizzled on the *tawa*—flat iron pan, and the delicious smell mingled with the fried eggs and lime tea and scent of the burning wood, pervading the air, and adding a sense of comfort to the place. Indira was entranced by the dreaminess and mystique of the morning.

She moved over to the table when Nani was finished cooking, and Nani served up the hot breakfast and took her seat beside her and asked her to bless the meal. The child clasped her hands and closed her eyes, and said, "Lord, thank you for this food and bless it to our bodies. Amen."

Not too long after they began eating, Nani began cautioning Indira, saying, "Remember to behave yourself in Sunday school, child."

"Okay, Nani, I will," Indira complied.

"And be respectful to Miss Chandra." Miss Chandra being Indira's Sunday school teacher.

"I will be."

"And pay attention when Miss Chandra is teaching. Don't be distracted or do anything to interrupt her."

"Okay, Nani," Indira said, used to the same words of caution from Nani every Sunday morning. Before Nani went on to the next thing, she said, "And I will try not to fall asleep during church service."

Nani smiled and said, "Good, child."

With that, Nani fell silent and sat there enjoying the child's company as they continued to eat. By the time the wood in the mud stove burned down to ashes and the smoke dissipated, they were finished, and it was time to do the absolute necessary chores.

Nani first washed the dirty dishes then she and Indira went downstairs, where Nani hooked up a green hose to the pipe by the stone slab at the bottom of the backstairs and left Indira to water the flower plants in the front yard, while she went and took care of feeding the chickens and the fishes and loosed Solomon and Rani to graze on the grass alongside the house.

Watering the flower plants was one of Indira's favourite things to do, for the fragrance of the flowers would rise and fill the air like sweet perfume. This morning she would have liked to just sit on the front steps and breathe it all in for a while, but Nani finished her chores and sent her in the backyard to bathe, for Sunday School was at ten o'clock and the church service was at eleven, and they had just enough time to get ready and get to church.

After Nani finished bathing herself, she rubbed fresh coconut oil on her skin and oiled and combed her long, silver hair and fixed it in a bun, then she put on her crisp, white headkerchief and green, floral cotton dress. She left her feet bare, as usual, which looked incongruous with her neat attire, but Nani would not even wear shoes to church. By the time she was finished dressing so was Indira, in her pink frilly dress and pink socks and white shoes, and all powdered up with sweet Yardley powder. Nani tied the sash in the back of her dress for her and she turned her around and fixed her black curls. After giving the child an affectionate kiss on the forehead, she picked out a white lace-sewn hat for her to wear.

Indira did not mind wearing hats to school but never liked wearing them to church, and she asked, "Why do I have to wear a hat in church all the time, Nani?"

"A lady should dress decently in the house of the Lord so she should cover her head at all times," Nani replied as she placed the hat on Indira's head and tied the ribbons below her chin.

Indira looked down at her grandmother's bare feet and, with the innocence and humour of a child, asked, "And shouldn't you be dressed decently, also, and cover your feet in the house of the Lord, Nani?"

In response, Nani just pinched her dimpled cheeks and smiled in amusement at the wittiness of the child. She then went about getting the green money bag and took out a five dollar bill to give as offering to the church, and she tucked it in the fold of her headkerchief. After closing the windows and bolting the doors, she and Indira left for church, on foot.

By now the heat was beginning to rise as the sun crept higher in the bright blue sky, and puffs of soft white clouds were drifting by in the warm breeze. Being Sunday and a day of rest, villagers were few in the streets. It was just another day for the animals, though, and they were roaming about; dogs, cats, goats, donkeys, cows, and pigs, and chickens were pecking at the grass along the street sides.

As Nani and Indira made their way up the dirt street to the narrow dirt road, walking hand in hand, and with umbrellas to shield themselves from the glaring sun, Nani looked down at her granddaughter and thought how beautiful she looked in her pink frilly dress and white shoes with her white, lace-fringed parasol, and she wished someone would come along so she could show her off.

Within moments, Mrs. Surjeet, Nani's friend at the market, who would always write up her grocery list for her, came walking up the road.

Nani squeezed Indira's hand, and said, "Remember your manners, child."

When Mrs. Surjeet approached them, Indira held herself properly and smiled, and she politely said, "Good morning, Auntie." Mrs. Surjeet had no biological connection to Indira but Indira was taught to address the elders as such out of respect.

Mrs. Surjeet did not respond to Indira, for she seemed preoccupied and sorely distressed, fidgeting with her long, black plait which was draped in front of her bodice.

"What's the matter, gal?" Nani asked, sensing that something was awry.

Mrs. Surjeet's light face turned pink as she began crying, and between sobs she blurted out, "A thief man broke into my garden last night and dug up my potatoes and stole the whole crop. Now I have nothing to sell at the market tomorrow, which means I would have no money to buy food for my children. That good-for-nothing husband of mine left me again. He's gone to drink *bush rum* at the *backdam* and he'll stay there in the back woods for a few days until he finishes the illegal spirits. Now, I don't know what to do."

"Stop crying, gal, I will help you out," Nani said to her, and consolingly patted her on the shoulder. "I have a few dollars I've put aside for a rainy day. Tomorrow I will lend you some of it so you can buy some food and feed the children."

"But you're a poor woman yourself and I hate to bother you for money again."

"I may be a poor woman money-wise but I'm rich otherwise, in my spirit, and my heart is full with treasures," Nani responded. "Don't feel bad about borrowing money from me. It makes me happy to be able to help you out in your time of trouble and need. Meet me at the market tomorrow morning and I will lend you a few dollars. I will also give you some vegetables from the garden to cook for the children, and I'll bring you some fruits."

"You are too kind and generous," Mrs. Surjeet said, "to both me and my children." And she wiped away the tears from her eyes with her fingers, taking comfort in knowing that her children would not starve the next day. "I will repay you as soon as I can, I promise."

"First, make sure the children are taken care of before you do," Nani said. "My Lord will provide for me in the mean while."

"Oh, woman of great faith," Mrs. Surjeet said, "thank you. I will forever be grateful to you." She now looked down and noticed Indira, and she said, "Your granddaughter looks so pretty today in her pink frill dress."

Indira looked up at the lady and she blushed and said, "Thank you, Auntie. Auntie Joan, my best friend Francine's mother, sewed it for me. And Auntie Joan made the same dress for Francine, also. Francine looks pretty in hers, too."

Indira put a smile on Mrs. Surjeet's face, and Nani smiled broadly at Mrs. Surjeet's compliment to her granddaughter, thinking that Mrs. Surjeet had already re-paid her, even more than she knew. Mrs. Surjeet went on to reassure Nani, though, that she would repay her and, again, thanked Nani, effusively, for her kindness in offering to help her out in her predicament, and then she said ta-ta and went on her way.

Next, Mr. Jackson, another one of Nani's friends, came walking up the dirt road.

Mr. Jackson always made Indira nervous and scared because he was a strapping Afro-Guyanese who was a soldier and he prowled around the village at times in an ugly green army jeep, and his uniform was an ugly green, too, and his boots were gigantic and sounded thunderous to her when he walked. His voice also sounded like thunder to her.

When she saw him approaching, she tilted her parasol downwards to avoid looking at him, but she could hear his big boots pounding the dirt road as he was walking. As he drew closer and closer, she could feel her heart starting to beat fast. From behind the rim of the umbrella, she looked down with apprehension as his big boots came into sight and stopped at an abrupt halt, and her heart accelerated even more. She knew she would have to greet him properly and not sullenly or else Nani would think she was being disrespectful, and she tightened her tiny grip around her grandmother's hand and almost choked on her words when she said, "Good morning, Uncle Jackson."

"Well, good morning!" Mr. Jackson greeted in his loud voice. "You sure look like a princess today!"

She said nothing in response but kept her face covered with the umbrella and tried to steady the tremor in her legs. Mr. Jackson only smiled because he long sensed she was scared of him, as were other children, and that only amused him at times.

Mr. Jackson was an innocuous man. His intimidating looks contradicted his benevolent and gregarious disposition. He was the kind of man who would gladly give the shirt on his back to a stranger if he needed it, and he would even put his own life at risk to save someone else's.

47

He was well liked by everyone, except, of course, for the children. When there was political rivalry between Mr. Forbes Burnham and Mr. Cheddi Jagan, Mr. Jackson was bold in voicing his political views. He did not give a damn whether the country was ruled by an Afro-Guyanese or an Indo-Guyanese, as he believed that both races were equally competent, and he found it despicable and distressing that there was racial tension between citizens to the point where acts of violence were committed, at times. Mr. Jackson was an honourable man, and he treated the Indians as he would his fellow blacks; as comrades. He would frequently preach to whomever would give a listening ear: "Why should it matter who rules the country? All of *we* is one family, man. May God bless the land of the original people—the Amerindians, and the Indians and the Africans and the Chinese, and the Portuguese and other Europeans." Then he would bellow the national anthem of Guyana: *Dear land of Guyana, of rivers and plains. Made rich by the sunshine, and lush by the rains. Set gem-like and fair, between mountains and seas. Your children salute you, dear land of the free* . . . Whenever he walked down the road, he would also sing *Hail The Man*, a song by Ken Lazarus, and he would literally hail every citizen he passed on the way.

Now, once Mr. Jackson turned his attention to Nani, he chatted with her for a little while. "How are things going with you, my old friend?" he inquired.

"Good, by the grace of God," Nani replied.

"And are you doing well at the market these days?"

"Some days are good and others are not so bad, but I'm making a living, boy."

"Do you have any chickens for sale now?"

"Not until next weekend. The chickens need a little more time to fatten up some more. I'll also have a good crop of vegetables by then."

"Good," Mr. Jackson said, "I'll be by then to buy a couple of chickens, and I'll purchase some vegetables, as well." To this Indira cringed. Mr. Jackson went on to say, "By the way, did you hear that there's a thief man in the village stealing people's fowls and vegetables from their fowl coops and gardens?"

"Mrs. Surjeet just told me she got broken into last night and had all of her potatoes stolen," Nani said, perturbed since she heard the news.

"I must caution you that if you hear anything strange in the night, if *them* chickens start clucking loudly and you suspect the thief man is in the coop, scream at the top of your lungs. That will scare him away. Until we catch the culprit everyone must be on the alert. Beware!"

Nani thanked him for the warning and his good advice, then she nudged Indira to say ta-ta to him, and Mr. Jackson went on his merry way, whistling the national anthem of Guyana as he did, and hailing everyone passing by on the road.

Indira was relieved to hear his footsteps fade away in the distance, but now she was even more frightened. She had overheard the conversations of Mrs. Surjeet and Mr. Jackson about the thief man and she was afraid of him, and tears began welling from her eyes as she said, "Oh, Nani, I'm scared of the thief man."

"Don't be scared of him, child," Nani said, and bent down and gave her a kiss on the cheek. "Everything will be all right. If he comes, Nani will holler and scare him away.

49

Now, wipe your tears and let's go to church and I will pray for God to protect us."

The thought of God protecting them gave Indira a sense of relief and comfort, and she dried her eyes. She and Nani then continued up the road, stopping occasionally to say good morning to the few villagers passing by, and soon they made it to the church.

The church, painted white, was a small wooden structure on stilts, with corrugated zinc roof and glass windows which were now open. The bottom-house, paved with concrete, was where Sunday school was held in the open air; a few benches were already arranged for the class. The yard, vast and grassy for the most part, with dirt patches in some areas, served as a playground, where children and teens and adults participated in volley ball, cricket, and tennis. All games took place during the week only, for Sunday was reserved for religious observances; the sabbath.

Observing the sacredness of the day, the Sunday school children were on their best behaviour today. And they were in their Sunday best; all freshly bathed and immaculately dressed in ironed clothes, and socks and shoes, with hair oiled and neatly combed. They were gathered at the bottom-house when Nani and Indira arrived, some already seated on the benches. Nani hugged and kissed the children and left Indira with them, and she went upstairs to assist with decorating the church with fresh flowers, while they waited for Miss Chandra to begin Sunday school.

Miss Chandra was a young woman in her late teens with clear skin and long, shiny-black hair that was down to her ankles. She fascinated the children and was loved by them because of her gentle and kind ways, and for making Sunday school fun. She taught them Sunday school songs and gave them colourful picture books to follow along as she told them of miraculous stories from the Bible. Last week she told them about Daniel in the lions' den and, this week, as Indira and the other children were now sitting in class, she was telling them about the story of Lazarus whom Jesus brought back to life from the dead. The stories kept Indira wide awake for she found them to be fascinating and could assimilate the simplicity of the rudimentary storytelling. This was not the case when she was in church service, though. She could not quite comprehend the pastor's convoluted sermons and had no interest in what he was saying and would often times fall asleep, not only from being apathetic, but, also, due to hunger and thirst and the heat of the day. The only part of the church service she really liked was the singing for it was lively with the clapping of hands and the beat of the instruments.

The church congregation's capacity was merely about forty, with approximately a dozen newly carved pews, six on each side to seat everyone with extra seating for special occasions drawing larger crowds. The mahogany wood floor was polished, the walls painted lily white. Fresh hibiscus flowers and palm plants decorated the area between the altar and platform. In the foreground of the platform was erected a wooden pulpit, back of which were a few armless chairs reserved for the pastor, musicians, and song leader.

Indira was now in service, seated on the pew in the third row, to the left, beside Nani, by an open window. A slight, warm wind was blowing while her grandmother had her eyes closed and her hands clasped as she was praying inaudibly; only her lips moving. Indira looked around, observing the members as they reverently entered the church and took their seats. She watched as the musicians and song leader arrived and got seated. A handsome guitarist in his early twenties took his place on the platform and began fine tuning his guitar, a youth, wiping a mouth organ against his shirt, took a seat next to him, and a teenage girl with a tambourine in hand came and sat on the other side of them. Moments later, the song leader, a spirited young man, arrived and joined the others on the platform, followed by a middle-aged woman, who took her place at the church organ on the main floor and started playing a hymn very softly. Next to enter the church were two white American missionaries, a handsome couple in their early forties, who generated inquisitive looks from the congregation as they took their seats on the first pew to the right. Soon after to arrive was Pastor Delford, a young, well-dressed, fine-looking Afro-Guyanese, who was known as the 'fire and brimstone' preacher. He took his seat on the platform beside the musicians and song leader.

Indira stood up when the song leader invited the congregation to join him in singing a fast-tempo song, and she clapped along as the hibiscus flowers and palm plants that decorated the church picked up the lively rhythm of the instruments—or that of the breeze coming from the open windows—causing their reflections to dance on the polished floor. A few more lively songs were sung, followed by a selection of solemn hymns, and the offering was collected. The missionaries then went up to the platform and spoke of missionary work and the progress they were making in reaching out to save souls in the country and around the world.

Indira did not understand much of what the missionaries were saying in their American accent, not that it mattered much to her anyhow. She was more taken up with the colour of their skin, which appeared like fluorescent tube light, and hair that looked like it was on fire, and she was particularly captured by the pretty peach dress and the white high-heeled shoes the lady was wearing. She sat quietly and listened, nevertheless, like the rest of the congregation. The talk went on for a while and by now she was beginning to feel peckish. Then an embarrassing thing happened to her; her tummy started rumbling. She placed her little hands over it and squeezed it to silence it, becoming increasingly self-conscious from thinking the people around her must be hearing the noise it was making. She sat there in discomfort for what seemed the longest while, wishing the service would be over soon, but she knew that would not be until Pastor Delford was finished with preaching his fiery sermon, and not a succinct one.

Pastor Delford eventually took to the pulpit and started preaching. She was kept alert for a while by his feisty voice reverberating throughout the church and the flinging about of his arms and his vigorous movements in emphatically expounding the precious word of God. As he continued on, the place grew hotter and hotter, with not even a stir of breeze coming from the windows now, and her eyelids started to feel heavy with drowsiness. Hunger and thirst compounded her situation, and she fought to stay awake because she had promised her Nani she would try to do so, but she soon leaned against her grandmother's arm and succumbed to nodding off.

Enveloped in the heat of the day, she was enjoying her doze and could have slept through the rest of the service, but it was not the gentle nudging from her grandmother that jerked her back to a wide wake, it was the preacher's bellowing voice saying, "*And those who slumber will not make it into the kingdom of heaven . . .*" She sat up straight to find the preacher was looking directly at her, or so she thought, and she started feeling ashamed of herself, so much so that she wanted to cry.

Indira never slept during church services after that embarrassing incident. She had no choice but to listen to the sermons on abominable sins, prophecies, miracles, promises, atrocious wars, and a fiery pit—for the wicked—that burns somewhere far in outer darkness, and a city—with mansions and pearly white gates and golden streets—that shines brightly somewhere far, far beyond the sun and moon and stars, far beyond human life, where good souls and archangels and angels and cherubims live in eternal peace and love and harmony with God.

Those were the beliefs instilled in Indira at that tender and susceptible age. Her grandmother also impressed upon her to love and have compassion instead of hating, to overcome evil with good, forgive those who hurt you, and love your enemies.

After Indira listened to what seemed like the longest sermon Pastor Delford had ever preached, there was an altar call, and Nani went up to pray, a prayer that was almost as lengthy as the sermon, and one that Indira had to endure with patience and wide eyes.

Nani's prayer derived from a prayer that her late father had taught her, a man who was a staunch Hindu and who was a sagacious and enlightened old man, who had sought the knowledge of all the great faiths, including, Buddhism, which his own father, who was from India, had passed on to him. Even though Nani's father used to ritualistically pray to numerous deities and worshipped many idols, he chose to ultimately believe in one Supreme Being. He composed a meditative prayer out of the insights he had gained from the great religions, and unfailingly said that prayer each morning, a prayer he passed on to Nani. Nani had been a Hindu for most of her life, during which time she always said that prayer. She converted to Christianity just a few years ago when her husband Amar passed away. It so happened that she was selling at the market one day and was crying with grief over her loss when a white American missionary lady approached her and told her about A Comforter who would bear her sorrow for her, and the nice lady persuaded her to seek Him. Although Nani did so and found great relief in her new path of faith, she would still say the same meditative prayer her wise Hindu father had composed and taught her.

Kneeling at the altar, Nani meditated as she prayed.

Nani's Prayer
Cleanse my heart, oh God, and make me as pure as the white of lily,

Remove from me all fears, worries, anger, bitterness, and conflicts,

Fill me with peace, love, happiness, compassion, and contentment,

Let wisdom guide me along the way, and protect me from all harm,

Help me to give up attachments of all things that I crave and desire,

I pray for You to remove or ease all manner of human sufferings,

If I am stricken with illness, give me the strength and will to endure,

Give me perseverance to handle any other challenges life may bring,

Hear the cries of all Your children, of all faith, colour, and culture,

Enlighten us to know that goodness is the only path that leads to You,

Help us to do the best we can each day that You grant us earthly life,

Thank You, dear God, for everything that You have blessed me with.

Amen

Indira, who had just about ran out of patience waiting for Nani to finish her meditation and prayer, was relieved when Nani rose from the altar and joined her back on the pew, and soon the church service was dismissed. Nani stopped to chat with a few people for a while, and then she and Indira unfurled their umbrellas and started walking home, the baked dirt road now feeling like hot coals on Nani's bare feet.

Once they were back home they got changed into their home clothes and Indira went and sat on the steps of the backstairs overlooking the backyard. Nani got a green coconut and chopped the top off with a cutlas and gave it to her to drink the cool coconut water to quench her thirst from the scorching heat of the day. Nani had one, also, then she chopped the coconuts in halves and left them for Indira to snack on the coconut jelly, and she went about cooking lunch, leaving Indira on the back steps.

Indira took a piece of husk that Nani had chopped off the top of the coconuts and she scooped the sweet white jelly and relished eating it. Once she was finished, she went downstairs and wandered around the backyard. She stood by the pond—not too close as her grandmother had cautioned her—and observed the hassars and tilapias swimming amongst the lily pads and shame-baby weeds. The mother duck, standing on the grass beside the pond, seemed cross today and chased her away when she tried to play with her yellow ducklings, so she went and checked on the fowls and chicks to make sure the sly mongoose had not snatched any of them. She then went and climbed the tamarind tree and picked some green tamarind. She wanted to go over to the river and sit on the bridge and eat the tamarind there, but Nani had warned her to stay away from the precarious river because she could fall into it and drown, so, instead, she went back upstairs to get some salt and hot pepper sauce to eat with the tamarind, and she ended up sitting on the peerah in the kitchen and ate the tamarind there while she watched as her grandmother was cooking on the mud stove.

Nani fried up a tin of corned beef and had a pot of water boiling to cook rice. As she was washing the rice in the dish sink, she was keeping a steady eye on Fazeela's kitchen to see if smoke from her mud stove was coming from her kitchen window. Nothing. No smoke was an indication that Fazeela had no food to cook, which meant that she and her children would go hungry that day. As would always happen, whenever Fazeela's children had no food to eat, a relevant Guyanese proverb ran through Nani's mind: *Baby who ah cry ah house and ah door ah same thing*, meaning, treat someone else's child as well as you treat your own for they are the same. Nani left off washing the rice and dried her hands on her apron, and she got a straw basket and packed some plantain, cassava, breadfruit and, being as magnanimous as she was, included a big piece of saltfish, and she said to Indira, "Come and take this basket of provisions over to Auntie Fazeela, child."

Indira would run this errand at least a couple of times a week, for Auntie Fazeela would run short of food that often, and she took the basket from Nani and started heading out the kitchen door.

"Wait a minute," Nani said, and looked over at the windup clock on the kitchen counter to check the time; it was now 1.30 pm. "I want you to be back by 2 o'clock." Indira had failed to be back on time when Nani had sent her last Sunday to run the same errand and Nani had scolded her, so Nani explicitly added, "You will know when it's 2 o'clock because Uncle Shazam will come home from work for a break then."

"Okay, Nani," Indira was quick to promise. This was a fun errand for her because whenever she dropped off a basket of food to Auntie Fazeela on Sundays, Nani would allow her to play with Auntie Fazeela's children for half an hour. Any other day she could play until the sun went down, but not on Sundays for it was a day of rest and worship, her Nani told her. Besides playing with the children, she always looked forward to holding Auntie Fazeela's baby. With that in mind, she made another start for the door.

"What time have I asked you to be back by?" Nani asked.

Indira stopped again and turned around and answered, "2 o'clock. And that's when Uncle Shazam comes home from work for a break."

"Lunch will be ready by then, so don't be late!" Nani warned, and she resumed washing the rice and put it on to boil.

"I promise I wouldn't be," Indira said, and she turned and skipped down the backstairs before Nani could stop her again.

Indira took the basket of provisions straight up to Auntie Fazeela's kitchen, where Auntie Fazeela was pacing around, holding the baby girl on her hip, her other hand on her large belly, worried sick as to where she would get the food this time to feed her unborn child and all of her children. Auntie Fazeela broke out in a smile when she saw Indira with the basket of provisions, and she lifted her head and exclaimed, "Thanks be to Allah!" As she took the basket from Indira, she found herself thinking that the God of Nani had provided for her, and she could not help but wondering whether she and Nani served the same God, after all, she thought, God is God. And she gave thanks to Nani's God, as well.

Auntie Fazeela's film star beauty captivated Indira, like it would do with everyone else in the village, and Indira stared at her and her fair skin and long, black, curly hair for

59

a moment, then she eagerly asked, "Can I hold the baby for a little while, Auntie Fazeela?" The baby being the picture of what Fazeela must have looked like as a baby.

Auntie Fazeela carefully handed the half-naked baby girl —clad in just a white cloth napkin—to Indira to hold for a moment, and she smiled at the pleasure it brought to Indira. Then she took the baby back and said, "Now, go downstairs and play with the other children." Auntie Fazeela then went about cooking, unaware that Nani had told Indira to be back by 2 o'clock.

Indira hurried downstairs where Auntie Fazeela's other five children were gathered at the bottom-house; beneath the broken-down house. They were two older boys and three younger girls, dressed in ragged but clean clothes, and they were barefooted, and freshly bathed with their hair oiled and neatly combed. The children were hungry but ignored the hunger pains, for playing was foremost on their minds. When Indira joined them they were excited and gave her the first turn to play hopscotch on the earthen ground. After a few minutes of that they started playing *banga* with *wara awara* fruit seeds, where three holes are dug in the dirt ground and players aim to get the golf-ball-size black wara seeds—called banga—into the holes. They all played for a short while, then the girls wanted Indira to join them in making doll-size cups and plates with wet clay, and the boys got them some clay from the streamlet in front of the house to do so.

Indira was having so much fun with her little fingers in the wet clay that when Uncle Shazam got home at 2 o'clock she wanted to stay for a while longer, but she remembered the sound scolding she received from Nani just last week for being disobedient for not returning home on time, and she dropped the clay cup she was moulding and made a mad dash for home.

Nani smiled pleasingly at her when she showed up with her fingers all muddied, and she gave her an affectionate kiss on her forehead and sent her to wash her hands by the pipe at the bottom of the kitchen stairs.

When Indira returned, they sat down and had lunch, after which, Nani went to take a nap in the hammock. While Nani was doing so, Indira got some pink bubble gum and chewed it, then she went in the backyard and pasted the gum on the barb wire fence to catch a blue saki bird. The blue saki would come around from time to time, and every Sunday while Nani would nap, Indira would try and catch the bird, but, so far, she had no luck in doing so. She sat on an aluminium bucket in the shade of a mango tree and patiently waited for the bird this day. The blue saki came around but did not land on the pink bubble gum, much to her disappointment. It perched on a tree branch for a little while, then flew away.

While waiting for it to return, Nani woke up, and Indira had to abandon the idea of catching the blue saki this time, hoping she would next Sunday. Nani got her to pick a couple of eggplants in the garden, and Nani roasted them on the mud stove to make *baigan choka* to go with some hot roti, for dinner. After dinner, they bathed and got dressed and went to church in the evening.

When they returned, they both got into their nighties and settled in to their Sunday night routine. Nani took a seat in the old rocking chair in the sitting room and was relaxing in the cozy light of the kerosene oil lamp, while Indira sat in her usual place in the bedroom, on the chair overlooking the backyard, and was thinking that her best friend Francine should be home soon from her usual weekend visit to her grandparents in New Amsterdam. She was looking forward to seeing Francine in the morning, and was thinking of them going to school and meeting up with their other friends.

3

Indira And Francine Go To School

It was now Monday in Rose Hall Village, a school day for
Indira and a day at the market for Nani. They both woke up
in the dark of the wee hours of the morning to the crowing
of the fowlcocks and took the kerosene oil lamp and went
about doing their chores; milking Rani and collecting the
eggs from the chicken coop. Today, Nani would only take
the eggs to the market to sell because yesterday was
sabbath and she did not harvest fruits and vegetables like
she would normally do during weekdays, and it was too
dark outside now to do so. She managed, though, with the
aid of the light from the lamp, to pick a few vegetables in
the garden to give to Joan Williams and Mrs. Surjeet. She
already had a basket of fruits she had picked last Friday,
which she would also give to Mrs. Surjeet, and she loaded
those onto the donkey-cart along with the vegetables. After
also loading up the two paint cans of eggs, she went up to
the kitchen and made breakfast and fed Indira well with
fried cassava, plantains, and saltfish, and a hot cup of cow's
milk. Once she was finished eating herself, she got out the
coal iron and began ironing Indira's school uniform; a
pleated green skirt and white short-sleeved blouse, which
Joan Williams, Francine's mother, had sewn for Indira.

After she finished ironing, Nani got ready for the
market. She remembered she had promised Mrs. Surjeet
that she would lend her a few dollars from her meagre

savings, which she kept under the mattress, and she got the money and put it in her green cloth money bag and placed it in her dress pocket. She got Indira's uniform from the clothes-horse and gathered up her socks, shoes, brown beret, and her floral-patterned cloth school bag, in which were a slate board and slate pencil, and, after she put out the kerosene oil lamp on the night table, she said to Indira, "Come now, child, let's go over to Auntie Joan. Are you ready?" On school days when she had to leave for the market in the mornings she would take Indira over to Joan Williams, and Joan would take care of Indira until it was time for her to go to school.

Indira was too eager to go over to Auntie Joan to see her friend, Francine, and she said with great excitement, "Yes, I'm ready, Nani!" She was clutching a girl baby doll in her hands, ready to play, and asked, "Can I take my new doll to show Francine and play with?"

"Sure, child," Nani said as she was closing the bedroom window.

Being granted permission, Indira quickly placed the baby doll in a cloth bag, along with a toy feeding bottle and cloth napkins, and she went on to ask, "And can I take the doll to school to play with my other friends?"

"No, you can't," Nani firmly answered this time and stopped as she was about to exit the bedroom to look at Indira. "Don't just think about playing. When you go to school I want you to put your head on learning, so pay good attention to Miss Watson." And, rather regretfully, she added, "Poor me, I don't know how to read and write, and I don't want you to end up like me. Your grandfather, Dr. Ramesh, is paying for your private schooling, so show him how well you can do. Be a good child in class and learn all you can."

"Okay, Nani," Indira promised, but precociously complained, "School work is hard and I'm afraid I wouldn't succeed."

"Remember the song Miss Watson taught you, 'If at first you don't succeed, try, try, try again.' Never fail to try and you will succeed." And Nani also reminded Indira of the Guyanese proverb: *Slow fire ah boil hard cow-heel*—if you persevere you will succeed.

In spite of Indira's complaints, she was a bright student and was way ahead of her class, as was Francine, because Francine's father, George Williams, a high school teacher, started tutoring the girls a year before they commenced kindergarten a few weeks ago. And by now, Indira as well as Francine knew how to count and read and write. Indira was now Nani's little bookkeeper, counting the money Nani made at the market and recording them in an exercise book, and she just finished reading *The Elves And The Shoemaker* and *Snow White And The Seven Dwarfs* and *The Princess And The Pea*, books that a friend at school had lent her.

"You're doing very well, my child," Nani complimented her, and encouraged her, saying, "just keep on persevering."

"I will do so just because you told me to, Nani."

Nani smiled and pinched her cheeks. Indira returned Nani's smile then went and foraged through the bottom drawer of the dresser for the treat she had put aside for Francine, and after placing the folded brown paper in her dress pocket, she slung the bag containing the doll over her shoulder, ready to go over to Auntie Joan. Nani handed her

her school belongings to fetch, and she went to the kitchen and got the basket of fresh callaloo and karela and bora vegetables she had picked for Joan, and they left.

By this time, the darkness of the night had lifted and the sky was the shade of sapphire-blue tinged with pink, and a soft morning light was upon the village causing the dew that had settled on the green grass to glisten. The villagers were beginning to stir everywhere now, and Fazeela's baby girl was heard crying. The neighbour down the street, who had a pig farm, was rounding up some pigs for the butcher, and the pigs were squealing as the dogs were barking and the cats meowing, and the moos of the cows and the hee-haw of the donkeys and the bleating of the sheep all added to the early morning clamour. Smoke was seen coming from the kitchen windows of those who had mud stoves as people everywhere were cooking breakfast, some making curry, rice, and roti to eat this early in the morning, the piquant and delectable whiffs drifting about in the air.

There were no activities happening at the Williams' residence at the moment for they were still asleep, their house—modern but modest and painted lime green—still in darkness. Nani and Indira managed to climb over the broken paling and entered their yard, and as they made their way to the front stairs, Jacko, the Williams' little, brown pet monkey, a Capuchin, was on the verandah feeding on a banana. When he saw them he began to chatter out of sheer excitement of seeing them, and he dashed inside to alert Joan and Francine, as was his habit.

Within moments, Francine came rushing down the stairs in a powder blue nightie, her soft brown cherubic face radiating happiness at the sight of Indira. She quickly greeted Nani with a good morning kiss on the cheek, then after Indira handed Nani her school belongings, she hugged Indira. The two of them then hurried off to the backstairs, with Jacko the monkey accompanying them.

Within moments after the girls took off to play, Francine's mother Joan, a curvaceous, brown-skinned woman, still in her long, pink nightie and wearing a matching African-influenced head tie, made her way down the stairs in her bare feet, rubbing the sleep from her eyes and yawning as she said to Nani, "Good morning, Auntie."

"Good morning, gal," Nani returned and, before handing her Indira's school belongings, gave her the basket of vegetables she brought for her. "Here, take this. And don't make a fuss about taking it this morning."

Joan hesitated a moment before saying, "But, Auntie, don't feel that you have to bring me something every time you drop off Indira in the morning. No need to do this because I take care of her for a couple of hours for you. Take the basket of vegetables to the market and sell them and make some extra money for yourself."

"This is the least I can do for you for being so kind to me, gal," Nani said. "Allow me to do this for you. I have plenty of vegetables to take to the market to sell tomorrow. Take the vegetables, I insist."

Joan always felt bad about taking food from poor old Nani but Nani would never let her refuse it, so Joan took the basket of vegetables and thanked her. Then she said, "I will make sure that Indira is fed again before going to school. And I'll see to it that she bathes and dresses neatly."

"Thank you, gal," Nani said and, before turning to leave, asked, "Can I ask you to do me another favour?"

"What is it, Auntie?"

"As you're at home all day long, please keep an eye on my fowl coop and garden. A thief man is going around stealing people's fowls and vegetables."

"Oh, my God!" Joan exclaimed and widened her eyes at the news. "Who did you hear this from?"

"Mrs. Surjeet told me she got broken into and had all of her potatoes stolen a couple of nights ago, and Mr. Jackson warned me yesterday to be on the lookout for the thief man."

Joan, who was known for her fiery temper at times, said, "That scamp! Why can't he go and make a living from the sweat of his brows instead of stealing, especially, from poor people. This makes me so angry!" And her nostrils began flaring.

"Don't upset yourself with this, gal," Nani said. "Calm yourself down."

"Calm down! Well, I'll tell you what, Auntie, I'll keep an eye on your place but with a cricket bat in hand. And, God have mercy on him if I encounter the scamp!"

"It would be better to holler at the top of your lungs if you see him," Nani said, repeating what Mr. Jackson had told her.

Joan let out a heavy sigh and collected herself and said, "You're right." But then she added, "What the thief man needs is some good cuffing up and boxing on the ear to bring him to his right senses. That will teach him a good lesson."

"Pray for his wretched soul," Nani said, then echoed the same caution Mr. Jackson had told her, "and be on the alert." With that, Nani turned to leave for the market, and as she did, she could hear Joan sucking her teeth as she made her way up the stairs.

Once Joan settled down somewhat, she went about cooking breakfast. She boiled some green plantains on her gas stove, and pounded them with a mortar and pestle and made *fufu*, and she ground up parched shrimps on a masala brick and made *shrimp chutney* to go with it, which was one of Indira's favourite dishes. All the while, she was anxious to tell her husband, George Williams, about the thief man, but George was still sleeping, so she decided to wait for an opportune moment and continued on with her cooking, while the girls were playing outside.

Indira and Francine were now sitting on the back steps, which overlooked a bushy backyard of crabgrass, and Jacko was sitting with them as the early morning sun was beginning to rise.

Francine adored Indira as much as Indira adored her. Today she had a treat for her best friend, and she dug into her nightie pocket and pulled out a folded brown paper and said, "Look what I have for you today, Indira."

"What?" Indira asked as she took the brown paper and unfolded it. "Blood-drop sweetie!" she exclaimed when she saw the red sugar-coated sweeties, about half a dozen.

"Grandma got me a bag full yesterday and I saved some just for you."

"Oh, thank you, Francine," Indira said, and gave Francine a kiss on the cheek. "I brought you something, too." And she pulled out the folded brown paper from her dress pocket and handed it to Francine.

Francine unfolded the brown paper and exclaimed, "Blood-drop sweetie, also!"

69

They both laughed, and Indira said, "Nani got them for me on Saturday and I saved some just for you, too." And she went on to say, "I brought something else to share with you." She reached into the cloth bag she had and got out the golden hair, blue-eyed baby doll and handed it to Francine, who reacted with delightful fascination.

The two of them remained there on the backstairs in the golden rays of the sun and had their treats and shared some with Jacko. Then they combed the doll's hair and pinned on a cloth napkin, and fed it with the toy bottle, and burped it and put it to sleep, just like Indira would see Auntie Fazeela would do with her baby. They then went and played hopscotch on the earthen ground of the bottom-house and skipped with their ropes, while Jacko sat and watched contentedly.

By this time, the look-alike of Sidney Poitier, George Williams, was up. Being as charming as the actor, also, Indira took a special liking to him, especially, because he would make her laugh a lot. George Williams taught at a local high school and he would usually leave for work an hour before class commenced, and before he did he would have breakfast with Joan and the girls, and he would tell the girls funny stories.

At breakfast this morning, while they were having the fufu and shrimp chutney, he told the girls about a foolish bee that got caught in a honey jar, and a smart fish that talked its way out of the frying pan and back into the pond, and a crazy chicken that had a fancy for another chicken's bottom and picked at it. And the girls laughed until their little bellies ached.

The girls wanted him to stay longer and tell them more of his hilarious stories this morning, but he had to get ready for work. Joan caught him as he was getting dressed in the bedroom and she broke the news of the thief man to him.

In response, George Williams said, "I would strongly urge you to go up the road and stay with your friends for now."

"I wouldn't do such a thing," Joan said adamantly. "I'm not going to let that scamp scare me away from my home!"

"You're stubborn at times, Joan. For your own good, stay with your friends for now."

Joan shook her head and said, "I'm staying right here!"

George Williams threw his hands up in the air and said, "Okay then, have it your way. I'm going to work." And he gave Joan a quick peck on the cheek and left.

Joan put the thief man out of her mind momentarily and went about getting the girls ready for school. She sent them to bathe before they got dressed in their uniforms and socks and Yatin—sports footwear, and she braided their hair and put on their brown berets. She then took a moment to admire her only daughter, for Francine was to Joan what Indira was to Nani; the apple of her eye. After kissing both girls, she walked them to the gate. The girls slung their cloth school bags over their shoulders and headed off for school, hand in hand, walking up the dirt street as the sun was shining warmly at this time.

Some ladies carrying straw baskets and umbrellas in their hands were on their way to the market now, and some were heading to the main road to shop at the stores there and do their banking. Students, of all ages, neatly dressed in uniforms, were making their way to school. Cyclists, the odd car driver, people on donkey-carts and animals were all passing by, but Indira and Francine paid them no mind for they were caught up in their own little world.

"I hope Laliwa is not late for school today," Francine said. Laliwa was an Amerindian-Guyanese girl. She was one of the four classmates whom Indira and Francine kept as close friends, and for the whole of last week Laliwa was late for school.

"Miss Watson will be upset with her if she is," Indira responded. "And I hope Ling doesn't get into trouble today." Ling was a Chinese-Guyanese boy who was always skylarking and getting into trouble with Miss Watson for bringing crapos and snakes and other creepy, crawly creatures into the classroom and scaring the little girls.

"He might get licks this time if he brings anything scary in class," Francine said. "I wish he could be as nice as Afonso." Afonso was a black-haired Guyanese boy from Portuguese descent who had bright blue eyes. His father was a successful businessman, who owned a white mansion on the other side of the village, and he would often travel and bring back Afonso children's books. "Afonso told me that he'll bring a couple of books to lend us today."

"He told me that, too," Indira said. "And Sally said she'll bring us some *cheese rolls* that her mother will bake especially for us." Sally was a red-haired, freckled-face Guyanese girl from European, specifically, English background. Her father managed a sugar estate and her mother loved to stay at home and bake pastries.

The two friends continued to chat about their friends at school as they kept on walking up the street to the narrow dirt road, and soon they reached the school.

The school was operated on the ground floor of a big, old wooden house, which was owned by a Miss Hillary Watson, and it was privately run by her. The schoolyard was spacious and unpaved. In front was a guinep tree, and in the back were cherry and tamarind trees, all loaded with fruits. Just outside the school entrance, a couple of ladies were sitting on the roadside selling sweet and savoury treats, and a lady in a stall had a big slab of ice on a counter with a shaver to make balls of *crush ice*—shaved ice, which she would drizzle with cherry syrup and sell to the children.

Ling and Afonso were presently standing in the shade of the guinep tree in the front yard, both dressed in crisp, white, cotton shirts and khaki pants, with hair oiled and neatly combed, and with their school bags slung over their shoulders. Sally was with them, also, and she was smartly dressed in her school uniform and beret. Besides the school bag hanging over her shoulder, she was also carrying a bag of cheese rolls in her hand.

When Indira and Francine joined them, Afonso, all excited to see them, dug into his school bag and quickly got out the books he had promised to lend them, and he handed *Beauty And The Beast* to Indira and *Cinderella* to Francine, saying as he did, "Bring them back next week and I'll bring you two more." He then reached into his pants pocket and took out a five-dollar bill. "See," he said as he showed off the bill, "daddy gave me this for doing well in school. I'll buy you all some treats and sweet drinks after school."

"My Mom has sent some cheese rolls for you all," Sally interjected. "We'll have them after school, also."

Indira and Francine reacted with verbal gratitude, but Ling was quiet and acting suspicious, and the friends immediately guessed that he must be hiding something in his pants pocket.

"We know you have some creepy, crawly creature in your pocket," Indira said. "So whatever it is, get rid of it," she urged. "You'll only get into trouble with Miss Watson if you bring it in class."

"Yes, you better get rid of it," Francine concurred, to which Afonso nodded his head in agreement, also.

Ling obstinately said, "No, I wouldn't get rid of it! I'll keep it hidden from Miss Watson."

Sally, not at all timid as the other girls were over creepy, crawly creatures, said, "I'll get rid of it for him!" And she launched forward and made an attempt to shove her hand in Ling's pants pocket.

Ling grabbed his pants pocket and pulled away, and as Sally made another attempt to seize whatever he had, they heard Miss Watson ringing the school bell, and they all hurried inside the classroom with the other children and took their seats. Ling and Afonso and a couple of other boys sat in the front row to the right, and on the left side, also sitting in the front row, were Indira, Francine, and Sally, and a space was there for Laliwa, who had not arrived, as yet.

The small, unpainted wooden classroom, with shutters now open, consisted of six desks with benches—three on each side—to accommodate four students each. The walls were bereft of decor and the floor was bare and worn. In the front of the blackboard were an old wooden chair—now occupied by Miss Watson—and a desk, on which were chalk, eraser, some books and papers, the school bell, and a *wild cane*—bamboo whip.

Shortly after the students were all seated in their respective seats in the classroom, Miss Watson got up from her seat and stood in front of the class. She was a middle-aged, black-skinned Afro-Guyanese woman, tall and slender, with a face that bore the beauty of a black pearl and was devoid of makeup except for a soft touch of mahogany lipstick, and her hair was pinned up nicely in the sixties fashion. Today she was dressed in a bright yellow skirt suit and had on a white pair of high-heeled, pointed shoes, and she was wearing rectangular-shaped, gold-rimmed spectacles.

Miss Watson was educated in England and returned to Guyana to start up her own private kindergarten school. She was a single woman who had no children of her own but felt that she owned all the children in her school; she loved them all and taught them well. She wore an air of strictness to keep the children in line, but she really was a soft-hearted woman. She did not like using the wild cane on the children, but sometimes it was necessary for her to do so in disciplining bad behaviours.

As she was standing in front of the classroom now, with her yellow skirt suit conspicuous against the blackboard, she lowered her gold-rimmed spectacles and scanned the small room, across which was blowing a slight, warm breeze, coming from the open shutters. Her students, mostly Afro and Indo-Guyanese, were all there, except, for the Amerindian girl, Laliwa, she noticed. The girl had not arrived, as yet, again, and it was now going on to the second week that she was being late.

Miss Watson began the class without her, and greeted the children with: "Good morning, children," wearing a serious look on her face though she was happy to see the children after the weekend.

"Good morning, Miss Watson," the children promptly returned.

"How is everybody this morning?"

"Fine, Miss Watson," everyone answered.

"Did you all behave yourselves while you were away from school on the weekend?"

"Yes, Miss Watson," they all answered, except, for Ling, which Miss Watson noted.

"Good, I'm glad to hear that," Miss Watson said. She then took up the attendance sheet and started calling out each name on the list, ". . . Indira."

"Present, Miss Watson," Indira answered.

". . . Francine."

"Present, Miss Watson," Francine answered.

". . . Sally."

"Present, Miss Watson," Sally answered.

Miss Watson went down the list and all the children answered 'present' except for Laliwa. She started teaching, however, and got the children to get out their slate boards and slate pencils and instructed them to practise writing the alphabet, and she went around assisting and checking on each child.

Fifteen minutes into the class, Laliwa—a reddish-brown, tiny girl with high cheekbones and straight black hair in pigtails—walked into the classroom, and there was a hush for everyone was scared for her. When she was late all last week, Miss Watson had asked her why that was so, but the girl did not answer, even when Miss Watson threatened her with the wild cane. Miss Watson had not lashed her, as yet, but the children, especially, her five friends, were sorely worried that she would get licks today if she did not speak up.

When Miss Watson saw her entering the classroom she left off assisting a student and went up to her desk in front and picked up the wild cane, and she called Laliwa up to the front of the classroom and, rather sternly, said to her, "If you don't tell me this time why you're late again, Laliwa, then I will have to use this wild cane on you."

Laliwa lowered her soft black eyes to the floor and said nothing, too shy to speak in front of the class. Miss Watson, knowing that Laliwa was bashful, waited patiently for her to speak, and when Laliwa still would not say anything, she began brandishing the wild cane. Her friends thought for sure now that Laliwa would be whipped.

Sally, desperately wanting to save her friend from the sting of the wild cane, jumped up suddenly, and boldly asked, "May I speak to you, Miss Watson?"

Miss Watson turned her attention to Sally, and in return asked, "What have you to say, Sally?"

"I know why Laliwa is late again."

"You do? Then go on and tell me why."

"It's because of a lamb," Sally said.

"A lamb?" Miss Watson said, puckering her eyebrows in bewilderment.

"Yes, Miss Watson," Sally said, "it's because of a lamb." Sally went on to tell Miss Watson what she had learned from Laliwa last Friday as the two of them were walking home from school, that Laliwa's neighbour's sheep had given birth to a lamb '*with fleece as white as snow*', and Laliwa would stop by on her way to school and play with the lamb, which she fancied being the little lamb in the nursery rhyme *Mary Had A Little Lamb*. "And that's why Laliwa is late again today, Miss Watson," Sally said.

"Is that so?" Miss Watson said. "Well, isn't that a story." And she turned to Laliwa and asked, "Is that true, Laliwa?"

Laliwa, with her eyes still lowered, nodded her head.

Well, Miss Watson was charmed by the story of the lamb and Laliwa, and she softened her voice and said, "Okay, Laliwa, I will excuse you this time and spare you a good licking. But, from now on, don't be shy to speak to me about such things. Now, I want you to promise me that you will play with the lamb after school and not on your way to school. Can you do that?"

Laliwa nodded her head, and Miss Watson asked her to take her seat, and her five friends let out a quiet sigh of relief as Laliwa took her seat beside Sally.

Soon after Laliwa was spared the wild cane, Ling got into trouble, inevitably so.

Miss Watson was sitting at her desk up front and was scanning the class to see if any one of the children needed her help, and it was then that she saw it; the face of a crapo poking out of Ling's pants pocket as he stood up for a second. She jumped up and grabbed the wild cane and said, "Naughty, naughty boy!" The little girls, realising that Ling must have something scary in his pocket, shrunk back in fear. Miss Watson had warned Ling a number of times not to bring frogs and scary creatures into the classroom and frighten the girls, but he just would not listen and kept on testing her patience. She had spared him the wild cane so far, but the child was incorrigible, and now she would have to discipline him. "Come up here right now, Ling!" she summoned, and when Ling did, she said, "I've warned you many times not to bring anything in the classroom to scare the girls but you're hard ears. Now, stretch out your right hand." Afonso jumped up at this point in an attempt to try and save his friend, but Miss Watson said to him, "Sit down, Afonso!"

The five friends, unable to save Ling, watched helplessly as Ling got two lashes across the palm of his right hand. Ling took the lashes bravely even though they stung, never wincing but held a straight face lacking contrition. After the licking, Miss Watson sent him outside to dispose of the crapo. He did so but returned with a salamander in his pocket this time. At recess, he was skylarking and went to a nearby stream and caught a baby alligator. Afonso took it away from him and threw it back into the stream before he could take it into the classroom and get into trouble with Miss Watson again. Ling then made an attempt to climb the guinep tree to pick the fruits, which Miss Watson had expressly forbade the children to do. This time, Sally apprehended him and brought him to play with the group of friends to save him from being caught by Miss Watson.

All the children were in the sand-brown, dirt-packed backyard now, and while some took shade under the cherry and tamarind trees, others were playing hopscotch and banga. The six friends started playing and singing *Ring Around The Rosie* under the hot sun, then *London Bridge Is Falling Down,* and *Rick, Chick, Chick, Chick.* Then they broke out singing *Hear Auntie Bess* and *Bamboo Fire* and *Missy Loss She Gold Ring,* and the song that Miss Watson had taught them '. . . *If at first you don't succeed, try, try, try again . . .*'

Afonso then sang Laliwa his song: ". . . Laliwa would you like to dance with me in a beautiful garden of roses, hibiscus, and jump & kiss flowers, under a palm tree . . ." Laliwa, who was not the least bit shy in front of her five friends, smiled and promised Afonso that she would do so someday when she grows up, and Afonso picked a purple jump & kiss flower in the yard and stuck it in her hair.

When the children returned to class after the recess, Ling still had the salamander hidden in his pocket but he was not caught with it, and Miss Watson went on to teach sums with no other interruptions in class this time. At lunch time, Joan Williams brought Francine and Indira fried callaloo with shrimps and rice for lunch, and a mango each, and she gave them some sugarcane juice to drink. After all the children had their lunch, they played again under the blazing sun and then cooled down to balls of crush ice with cherry syrup, which they bought from the lady at the stall near the school entrance.

Back in the shade of the classroom, Miss Watson asked the children to get their slate boards and slate pencils out again and she gave them sums to do and left them momentarily to work on the exercise while she went to her office, which was in the house, right outside the classroom. Indira, Francine, Laliwa, and Sally finished their assignment before anyone else did, and if Afonso was not so distracted by Ling fishing in his pocket for the salamander that had apparently escaped during lunch break, he and Ling would have finished as fast, also.

Once they were all through with the assignment, they sat and waited for Miss Watson to return. It was now roasting hot and uncomfortably still in the classroom with not even a light breeze blowing through the shutters. Indira and friends whispered among themselves, talking about the treats they would have after school, and the others whispered, too. And then the room fell completely silent for a moment.

Suddenly, a fight broke out between an Indian girl, Satie, and a black girl, Sandra, over Sandra accidentally breaking Satie's slate pencil. They were sitting beside each other in the second row, right behind Indira and her girlfriends, and they started clawing each other and pulling each other's hair. Things escalated from there and they began calling each other racial names. Just then Miss Watson walked in and heard them and she picked up the wild cane and summoned them both up to the front of the class, for this made her quite furious.

"I'm not going to tolerate any such behaviour in my classroom!" she admonished them in a stern voice, as the rest of the class sat in silence and looked on. Addressing the girls as well as the class, she continued on with saying, "This lesson I will teach you all today, children: We are a country of six peoples, and whether you are Amerindian or African or Indian or Chinese or Portuguese or any other European, we are all humans, and no people or race is superior than the other. In other words, children, no people or race is better than the other. We have the same red blood flowing in our veins, and we're all related, all brothers and sisters. Now," she said, turning directly to Sandra and Satie, "you must be punished for such name calling. I will make an example of you so no such thing ever happens again in my school. Stretch out your hands." The girls stretched out their hands and were both given two stinging lashes. "I want you to say sorry to each other now," Miss Watson then said. The girls, with tear in their eyes from the stinging lashes, did so. "Take some time out now and go and play seesaw together in the backyard, and when you hear the bell ringing, return to class."

Miss Watson watched as Sandra and Satie left the classroom, apart and not looking at each other. When they got to the backyard, she resumed class but kept an eye on them through an open shutter. She noticed that they kept up their distance and stared at the seesaw for a little while. Then Sandra made the first move and sat on one end of it. After a few moments, Satie took her seat on the other end. Soon they were bouncing up and down, and they looked at each other and started laughing. When they returned to the classroom at the ringing of the bell, they were as gleeful and friendly with each other as they were before the incident. A lesson well learnt, Miss Watson thought with a certain pride, and she smiled at them.

Class then resumed with no other incidents. When school was dismissed for the day, Indira and friends left the classroom together and they stayed in the schoolyard for a while and snacked on the cheese rolls that Sally brought to share with them. They then stopped by the ladies selling sweet and savoury treats on the roadside and, as promised, Afonso bought them all some pink *badam lacha* sweets, *bara* and *pholourie* savouries with hot tamarind sauce, and some sweet drinks with the five dollar bill his father gave him. They began their journey home then, having their treats as they walked up the dusty dirt road, and stopping to take in the sounds and sights along the way. They momentarily listened to a *steel band* playing *reggae* and *calypso* tunes on the roadside, and as they moved on from there, were captivated by a *Sadhu* who was passing by in a saffron-coloured gown and matching turban, with a garland of flowers hung around his neck, a Hindu holy man who was said to live in a temple. After the man disappeared down the road, Laliwa led them all to her neighbour's house and they dropped in and played with the little white lamb, over which she had gotten into trouble with Miss Watson.

As the friends continued on, they came upon a field where a few men—dressed in white shirts and pants—were playing cricket, and the children stopped under a great mango tree and looked on as the men were batting under the sharp sun. They would always stop and watch whenever a game was going on, but it was not just the game that they enjoyed, for they also loved to watch the players' friends and families *bush-cook*—outdoor cooking with wood. A bush-cook was currently taking place under a great tamarind tree; a huge iron pot—placed on two stones with a pile of wood in between—was bubbling over a vigorous fire, and the mouth-watering aroma sailed across the field to where the children were sitting under the mango tree.

"We can do a bush-cook ourselves," Ling said as he looked on, always thinking of ways to skylark.

"We'll only get into trouble if we do," Afonso responded.

"No, we wouldn't," Ling argued.

"Yes, we will!" Sally said feistily.

Ling knew better than to contend with Sally, so he shifted his attention to the cricket players. "When I grow up I want to become a famous cricket player," he said.

"If you stay out of trouble and instead practise the game you may become just that," Sally said precociously.

Indira then butted in and said, "Nani wants me to work at the bank when I grow up." And she turned to Francine and asked, "What do you want to do when you grow up, Francine?"

"I want to sew pretty dresses like my Mom does," Francine answered.

Sally then said, "When I grow up I want to go to England and study to become a nurse. And I want to see the Queen!"

"I want to go to America and become a film star," Laliwa chimed in, dreamily.

"But you're too shy to be a film star, Laliwa," Ling argued.

"When I grow up I wouldn't be shy," Laliwa retorted.

Afonso then said, "I don't have to work at all when I grow up because my father is rich. But I want to become a policeman and ride a motorcycle!"

The six little friends, representing the six peoples of Guyana, sat there and continued to converse as they watched the men play and the bush-cook taking place, and as soon as the game was over and the men started to eat and drink, the friends left for home, going their separate ways, all except for Indira and Francine, who walked home together hand in hand, chatting and giggling as they did.

4

Bag Of Gold And The Thief Man

A week elapsed since Nani encountered Mr. Jackson on her way to church and, as she had promised him, the chickens were now ready for sale. It was Saturday morning and she decided not to go to the market to do any selling, instead, she would stay at home and sell off some of the chickens, eggs, and a few vegetables she had picked just this morning. It was barely seven in the morning now and she and Indira were in the semi-dark fowl coop going around collecting eggs, and they filled up three paint cans; about three dozens or so. Nani inspected the chickens as they fluttered around and went "cluck, cluck" and she counted the ones that were round and fat and ready to eat; half a dozen altogether. She would sell those off today, and those along with the eggs and some vegetables would fetch her a few good dollars, she thought.

A call at the gate sent her and Indira rushing out of the fowl coop. By the bellowing sound of the voice it was no other than the intimidating Mr. Jackson, Indira figured, much to her displeasure. Nani, on the other hand, was pleased because her innocuous and gregarious friend, her first customer had just arrived.

"Good morning, old lady!" Mr. Jackson roared, "I've come to buy some chickens!"

"Good morning, boy, come on in," Nani called out as she made her way to the gate to meet him. Indira, tensed and scared, clutched on to Nani's skirt and tried to hide her face behind it as she reluctantly went along, surreptitiously stealing askance glances at Mr. Jackson's ugly green soldier's uniform and big, scary boots.

Amused by her behaviour, Mr. Jackson smiled down at her and said, "No need to hide from me, little gal. I don't bite."

"Don't pay any attention to her, she's just playing the fool," Nani said as she led Mr. Jackson down the narrow dirt pathway—flanked by the aesthetically pleasing garden of sweet-smelling flowers—and brought him to the bottom-house, where Solomon and Rani were laying on the earthen ground beside the hammock.

Ignoring Indira now, Mr. Jackson went on to comment, "It sure is a very warm morning." And he took out his handkerchief from his jacket pocket and wiped the perspiration from his forehead. "It's going to be a blazing hot day, I tell you."

"A reason why you should not be wearing your uniform today," Nani said.

"I feel like I'm on duty all the time," Mr. Jackson responded.

After exchanging the usual pleasantries, Nani got down to business and asked, "What can I get you today, boy?"

"I'm doing a cook today for some friends and I want three chickens," Mr. Jackson said. "Get me your biggest ones. Make sure they're nice and plump. I'm going to curry two and fry one."

Three chickens on the first sale, this made Nani very happy, and she flashed her gold teeth at Mr. Jackson and asked, "And would you like some eggs, also?"

"Yes," Mr. Jackson replied. "I will take half a dozen browns ones and half a dozen white ones."

"And how about some vegetables? I have some fresh chorai callaloo and ripe tomatoes and a whole lot of wiri wiri hot peppers that I picked just this morning. I'll work out a good price for you."

Mr. Jackson thought for a moment then said, "I'll take some chorai callaloo for sure." He then took a tomato that was in a straw basket on the donkey-cart and bit into it. "Fresh and sweet," he said, "give me a few of these. And give me a pound of wiri wiri hot peppers, also. I'll make some pepper sauce with them."

Nani took the straw basket Mr. Jackson brought and left it on the donkey-cart intending to pack the eggs and vegetables after she selects and weighs the chickens, then she turned to Indira and nicely said, "Come, child, help me to catch the chickens for Mr. Jackson." When Indira insolently flouted and would not move, still clinging on to Nani's skirt, Nani nudged her and now spoke in a stern tone of voice, "Stop misbehaving, and let's go and catch the chickens for Mr. Jackson." And Nani pulled her along.

"Let me help," Mr. Jackson offered, which only irritated Indira even more, but there was nothing she could do or say but quiver in her little rubber slippers as she heard Mr. Jackson's boots pounding the dirt ground as he followed her and Nani into the fowl coop.

Once his eyes got adjusted to the semi-darkness of the fowl coop, Mr. Jackson keenly looked over the chickens and pointed to a fat fowlcock, and he said to Indira, "Help me to catch that one, little gal."

Indira did not make a move but kept on clinging to Nani's skirt.

"She's stubborn at times," Nani said, trying to cover up Indira's aversion to him, and she elbowed Indira to get her going as she herself was not as swift in catching the chickens, but Indira refused to budge and clung on even tighter to her skirt.

Mr. Jackson figured that the girl was not being obdurate, and benignly said, "She's just scared of me. Leave her alone, I'll catch the chicken myself." And he went about chasing the fat fowlcock around the coop.

Still holding on to Nani's skirt, Indira eyed him steadily as he did, darting from here to there and going in circles as the chickens ran around the coop and hollered and fluttered their wings. To her, Mr. Jackson looked as big and clumsy as the fat fowlcock that was running for its life, and she found the scene to be funny and suddenly a little smile broke out in the corners of her lips. Mr. Jackson managed to catch the fat fowlcock and he handed it to Nani to tie its feet and he went around chasing the second one, a fat hen this time. Just as he was about to catch it, it slipped out of his hands and made him look silly, Indira thought. Finding this even more amusing, she broadened her smile. When Mr. Jackson attempted to go after the chicken again, he stumbled and fell, with his big buttocks sticking up in the air, making him look even more funny to Indira. She could not contain herself now and burst out laughing with deep dimples, saying as she did, "I'll help you to catch the chicken, Uncle Jackson." And she released Nani's skirt and joined him.

Soon, the two of them were chasing the fat hen around the fowl coop. Indira was having so much fun that she was laughing her little head off now, and she soon forgot about Mr. Jackson's ugly green uniform and his big, scary boots. He became her friend that morning, which greatly pleased Nani. She helped him to catch the fat hen and the other plump one he selected. The three of them then carried the three chickens to the bottom-house to be weighed, and Indira, with her new found amity towards Mr. Jackson, was now walking right alongside of him, laughter still imprinted on her face.

Nani placed the fat fowlcock on the scale and said to Mr. Jackson, "This one weighs ten pounds and six ounces. But I will only charge you for ten pounds." She then weighed the two fat hens. One was exactly eight pounds, and the other, eight pounds and five ounces, and she said, "And I will not charge you for the five ounces for this one."

"Thank you," Mr. Jackson said appreciatively. "Now give me a good price also on the vegetables and eggs."

Nani packed the chorai callaloo, a few tomatoes, and a pound of wiri wiri hot peppers in Mr. Jackson's basket, throwing in extras of each, and she packed fourteen eggs instead of a dozen. She had a few mangoes and star apples which she had picked the day before, and she included two of each for free. She then totalled everything, including the price of the chickens, making Mr. Jackson a good deal. Mr. Jackson took out a bundle of crisp Guyanese dollars from his pants pocket and paid her right then.

Before making a move to leave, he asked Nani, "Did you hear that Mrs. Ranga got broken into?"

"She did?" Nani said, raising her eyebrows in fear as she tried to assimilate the news.

"I think it's by the same thief man who stole Mrs. Surjeet's potatoes."

"When did this happen?"

"Just last night. The thief man stole three of her ducks from her fowl pen, and he cooked them up. Just this morning some boys went to the seashore and found stones and burnt wood and duck feathers and, not only that, also some empty bush rum bottles scattered about. Apparently, the thief man had a bush-cook last night with company, and they had the theft food and drank the illegal spirits."

"You mean there's a gang of thieves out there?" Nani asked, alarmed.

"No, I don't think so. I think the culprit acts alone. He steals food and takes it to his friends, and they cook and eat and drink rum."

"I'm an old woman, how would I protect myself and my poor granddaughter if he comes to steal from me?" Nani asked, worried more for Indira than herself.

"Keep your doors bolted at nights because he does his wickedness in the dark of the night, never in bright daylight," Mr. Jackson answered, and to quell Nani's fear, added, "He has never broken into anyone's house so far, just their gardens and fowl coops, and he has never hurt anyone, so you don't have to worry about the little gal and yourself being harmed. As I mentioned to you last week, if you hear the chickens making funny noises in the night and you suspect he's in the coop, yell at the top of your lungs for help!"

With that, Mr. Jackson tucked the chickens under his arms and grabbed the basket of vegetables, fruits, and eggs and left, whistling his favourite songs, the national anthem of Guyana and *Hail The Man*, hailing everyone passing by on the street.

Indira had conquered her fear of Mr. Jackson, but now there was the thief man. Echoing Nani's own fear, she said, "I'm scared, too, Nani. I'm scared that the thief man might come to our house to steal our chickens and vegetables."

Nani gave her a hug and a kiss in trying to pacify her, even though she was also scared, and she said, "I don't want you to worry about the thief man, child. Remember what I told you on Sunday? God will protect us from him."

Before Nani could try to further assuage Indira's fears, Mrs. Surjeet came calling at the gate. Nani let her in but refrained from talking about Mrs. Ranga's break-in so as not to further scare Indira. It just happened that Mrs. Surjeet was not aware of the theft and had other things on her mind. She thanked Nani for the money she had lent her last Monday, and said that she bought some food for the children with some of it, and with what remained, she bought some fish from a local fisherman and sold them at the market and was able to make a good profit. She could now repay Nani fully—partly because her husband had returned home and went to work cutting sugarcane and made some money himself—and she could now also afford to buy a chicken and some eggs. Nani gave her a discount price, and threw in some vegetables and fruits for free, and Mrs. Surjeet went on her way. Joan Williams then came over and bought one chicken, also, and a dozen eggs, and she insisted on paying the full price without taking anything extra from Nani. Nani made good money on the sale of the five chickens, and she decided that instead of selling the sixth one, she would give it to Fazeela to cook for the children for lunch. And so after she took the chicken over to Fazeela, she returned home and began her chores.

The bright morning sun was high in the clear, azure sky now, and it was growing hotter and hotter by the minute. The village women were busy with Saturday domestic drudgery; scrubbing and cleaning their homes, and some gathered at the communal well to wash their clothes. Nani washed her and Indira's clothes with salt soap on a wooden washboard at the bottom of the backstairs by the stone slab and pipe, *screeching*—washing by hand the delicate ones, and she beat the white sheets with a clothes *beater*—a wooden paddle. She soaked the sheets in laundry blue cubes to whiten before wringing and hanging them out to dry on the clothesline in the backyard, along with the other clothes. Indira helped her to sweep and scrub the upstairs floor and front and backstairs, and they daubed the earthen ground of the bottom-house with fresh cow-dung, clay and water mixture and left it to dry.

Nani then took a break and sat on the front stairs, and as she was wondering what to cook for lunch, she was knitting a *cast-net*—fishing net she was making to sell. While she was doing so, a lady dropped in to see if she wanted to buy some fresh, live shrimps she was carrying in a straw basket on her head. Nani purchased two parcels and went about cooking shrimp curry and rice for lunch.

She had lunch with Indira in their respective places; Indira at the table, and Nani on the peerah, eating from a calabash with her fingers while Indira used a silver spoon.

When they were finished, Nani went over to the dish sink and rubbed some salt soap on a dried nenwa and scrubbed her fingers clean, and while drying her hands on her apron, she turned to Indira and said, "I have something to show you, child." And she went in the bedroom and came back with a faded brown cotton bag that had a string tie.

"What's inside the bag?" Indira asked curiously as she was still sitting at the table overlooking the backyard.

Nani pulled up a chair right opposite her and said, "You'll soon see, child."

As they were sitting in the somewhat dimly lit kitchen while the embers in the mud stove were now burning softly, emitting wispy curls of smoke, Nani untied the brown bag and emptied the glittering contents onto the scarred table upon which a sharp ray of sunlight fell. Indira let out a gasp at the sight of the twelve thick gold bangles, six heavy chains with matching earrings, and six finger rings, dazzled by the shine of the gold in the streak of sunlight. She had seen some women in the village decked out in gold but she never knew that her Nani had such treasures for she had never seen her wearing any jewellery.

"These were all given to me by my mother, Raajee," Nani explained to Indira. "My mother got it from my grandmother, Chaaya. And my grandmother, Chaaya, got the jewellery from a rich Englishman who was an overseer for a sugar plantation. She worked for him as a housekeeper and he was smitten with her beauty and would buy her jewellery whenever he travelled to India. And so you see, the jewellery has been passed on from generation to generation, and someday, child, it will all be yours."

"All mine!" Indira exclaimed as she reached out and touched the glittering gold jewellery that felt warm and smooth. "And what would I do with it, Nani?"

"When you grow up you will wear it," Nani replied. "And someday you will marry and have children and you will pass it on to your children." With that, Nani put the precious gold back into the faded brown bag and tied the string, and she went and hid it away in the bedroom.

Indira could not get the glitter of gold from her head long after Nani put the jewellery away. When Nani later had her siesta in the hammock at the bottom-house, she sat on the earthen ground beside her and daydreamed of wearing the bangles. She had seen women in the village with *tikka*—a black dot between the eyebrows, wearing saris and bangles almost up to their elbows, and she loved the jingling sounds the bangles made and could not wait to grow up to wear them. It was not until Nani woke up and told her that they would go fishing that her thoughts shifted from that to the hassars and tilapias in the pond in the backyard.

The sun was beating down on the village now, blazing hot in the middle of the afternoon. In Nani's fowl coop the exhausted chickens—panting for breath—were resting on the ladders. The fruits trees in her backyard were still for not even the slightest breeze was blowing, and the vegetable plants drooped wearily, thirsty for a sprinkle of water. The lily pads and shame-baby weeds floating on the surface of the pond were fortunate for they caught splashes of warm water as the hassars and tilapias were jumping periodically.

The fishes were now fat and ready to eat, so Nani decided she would catch some for dinner today. She could not drag a hand seine fishing net through the pond because of the water lilies and shame-baby weeds, neither could she drain the water in the pond to catch the tilapias in the mud, so she resorted to using a fishing rod.

She was now standing by the pond with her bare feet on the hot dirt ground, holding the fishing rod in hand, while Indira was standing close by. Beside was a big, aluminium bucket filled with water to keep the fishes Nani would catch. Nani got the tin of worms she had and put the bait on the fish hook and she cast the line into the pond. As soon as she did, a fish took the bait and she jerked the fishing rod back and caught her first fish; a dark, fat tilapia, twisting and glistening in the sharp sun. She unhooked it and dropped it into the bucket of water, and she fastened another worm on the hook.

Indira, all excited about the catch and thinking it was so easy to do, asked, "Oh, Nani, can I catch a fish, too?"

Nani hesitated a moment then said, "Okay, child. I'll let you catch just one." And she handed the fishing rod to Indira. "Stand up straight and hold the rod tightly and cast the line into the water, and when you feel a fish biting, I want you to quickly pull the fishing rod up and backwards. Think you can do that?"

"Sure I can," Indira said optimistically, and she clutched on to the fishing rod and cast the line into the pond and waited for a fish to bite. Within moments, she felt a slight tugging at the end of the line, and she exclaimed, "The fish is biting, Nani, the fish is biting!"

"Pull back the fishing rod quickly!" Nani said, smiling and totally enjoying watching the child having fun.

Indira, with all of her strength, jerked the rod back, but there was no fish on the hook. "It got away, Nani," she said, disappointedly. "And there's no worm on the hook."

Nani put another worm on the hook and said, "Try again." When Indira tried this time, she pulled back the fishing rod too hard and fell back and found there was no fish on the hook, and she made a face like she wanted to cry. "Get up, child," Nani said and put another bait on the hook. "Try again. Don't give up now."

Indira got to her feet and dusted herself off and tried for the third time, and this time she caught a hassar, and she cried out with excitement, "See, Nani, I did it! I did it! I caught a hassa!"

"Good gal," Nani said and smiled pleasingly as she unhooked the fish and placed it in the aluminium bucket of water.

"Can I catch another one?"

"I only promised to let you catch one," Nani said firmly. "Now go and pick some water lily nuts for us to eat."

Indira handed the fishing rod back to Nani with a bit of reluctance, then she got a stick with a hook and, under the protective glances of Nani, hauled out some water lily pods from the pond, which she and Nani burst open and had the seeds. Nani then resumed fishing, catching one fish after the other, much to the thrill of Indira. Indira's fun was interrupted when she caught a mongoose sneaking around the yard, and she left Nani to go and chase it away before it could get into the fowl coop and steal a chicken. After the mongoose was gone, she stopped to look at the beautiful peacock that visited the yard from time to time, then she went running after the mother duck and her yellow duckings. A turkey made its way into the yard and distracted her then, and she followed it around, mimicking its gobbling. By the time she returned to Nani, the aluminium bucket was filled with live, shiny fishes, splashing about in the water.

Nani took the bucket to the stone slab by the pipe at the bottom of the backstairs and cleaned some of the hassars and tilapias, and she washed them and wrapped some up in brown paper for Joan, Fazeela, and Pyari. She sent Indira to take the parcels over to Joan and Fazeela, and she went herself to deliver a parcel to Pyari in an effort to keep Indira away from Raj the parrot and his foul language. When she returned, she sliced and salted some of the tilapias and hung them up on a line in the backyard to dry. She then took the live fishes that remained in the bucket up to the kitchen and placed them in the green barrel of water, for cooking over the next couple of days, and she went about cooking the cleaned hassars for dinner.

Indira delivered the parcel of fishes to Auntie Fazeela, whose belly was now even larger with her seventh child, and Indira lingered there a moment to stare at her fair beauty and play with the baby girl, then she went over to Auntie Joan and delivered her parcel. She returned home with Francine, who brought along Jacko and a bag of toys. Francine was rarely at home on a Saturday because her parents would often visit their parents in New Amsterdam, but this week they stayed at home and Indira jumped at the chance of playing with her friend.

They both went up to the kitchen to see Nani, and Indira begged, "Can Francine stay and play with me, Nani? Auntie Joan said it's all right for her to do so."

"And my Mommy said I can sleep over if that's okay with you," Francine chimed in.

Without hesitation, Nani said, "Then that's all right with me. Now go and play, children, and don't get your clothes too dirty."

While Nani continued with cooking the hassar curry, Indira and Francine went to the bottom-house and played house with their dolls and clay cups and plates, while Jacko, Solomon, and Rani looked on. The girls played until the glowing red sun slipped below the horizon and the sapphire-blue of dusk enveloped the village, bringing about a pleasantly warm breeze, and by now, flocks of birds had taken to the sky and were making their way to their evening roosts.

Before the black of night set in, Nani sent the girls to the cubicle in the backyard to bathe, and after they did, she gave Francine one of Indira's dresses to wear. Nani then went and bathed and oiled her skin and hair with coconut oil, after which, she lit the kerosene oil lamp and seated both girls at the kitchen table and served the hot hassar curry dinner, providing them both with spoons. She had hers in her usual place on the peerah, in a calabash, eating with her fingers, while Jacko sat in a corner and ate a cashew fruit and struggled with breaking open the nut.

After dinner, Nani washed the dirty dishes and tidied the kitchen. While she was cleaning the mud stove she realised she did not have enough wood to cook breakfast in the morning. She decided she would leave the girls alone for just a few minutes to go and get some from Mrs. Surjeet, who was living just up the street. When she got to Mrs. Surjeet, she ended up staying longer than anticipated, for Mrs. Surjeet's husband had left again and she was crying on Nani's shoulder.

Indira and Francine were thrilled to be left alone to play. Before they started, Francine helped Indira to let down the mosquito netting and straighten out the clothes on the clothes-horse in the bedroom. They then sat on the bare bedroom floor with Jacko and, with the kerosene oil lamp on the night table shedding light on them, they played Chinese Checkers and Snake and Ladder, and they chatted.

"I think Afonso likes Laliwa," Francine said.

"I think so, too," Indira responded.

"On Monday, he sang her a song and picked her a purple jump & kiss flower and stuck it in her hair."

"I think Laliwa likes him, too. She promised him she will dance with him when she grows up."

The girls both giggled then and said, "Ha, ha, Afonso likes Laliwa. Ha, ha, Laliwa likes Afonso."

They went on to talk about their other friends, Sally and Ling, then moved on to themselves, Francine, rather sadly, saying, "You know, I have no sisters to play with."

"Neither do I," Indira said and, as sadly, added, "My Dad and Mom died and left me all alone." Then she asked, "Would you like to be my sister, Francine?"

Without dithering, Francine answered, "Sure, Indira, I'd like to be your sister."

"Then put your little finger around mine and let's make a promise that we will be sisters from now on and forever," Indira said.

Francine wrapped her little finger around Indira's and said, "From this day I will be your sister forever."

"And from this day I will be yours," Indira said. "Now we can play like sisters."

After making the pact, the girls carried on with playing, this time with marbles and beads. In the midst of playing, they were suddenly interrupted by the sound of loud voices coming from outside, and they rushed to the window overlooking the front yard to find out what was happening. Through the dark of the night, they barely made out a young couple quarrelling in the street, carrying on in a blackguard manner, low-rating each other.

The couple was known in the village for their tempestuous relationship and were often heard arguing in the street in the dark of the nights. Tomorrow, in the light of day, they would be seen walking down the street and carrying on as if nothing had happened. Indira and Francine had heard them other times before and thought it was just another argument they were having and did not take them too seriously.

Once the couple's voices subsided as they disappeared down the street, the girls moved over to the window facing the backyard. Indira gave Francine the chair to sit on and she stood by the window with her hands on the sill, and they looked out.

Tonight it was pitch black and eerie with no moon or stars in the overcast sky, and the fruit trees in the yard appeared like clusters of dark shadows. The pond was still, and the fowl coop was dark and silent for the chickens were roosting on the ladders. The only sounds heard now were those of the crapos croaking and crickets chirring and the dogs barking, and the faint whistle of a warm, lackadaisical breeze blowing through the black night.

Pyari, the strange old woman who lived beyond the backyard, was entertaining a young man at her house the light of her gas lamp revealed, and they were both sitting by the window smoking pipes and drinking hard rum and talking and laughing, while Raj the parrot was in the background mimicking them. Over at Fazeela's house, the children had all gone to sleep for the cry of the baby girl had long ceased. Joan and George Williams had apparently gone to bed for the lights were out in their house.

The girls sat there silently observing Pyari and the young man as they listened to the sounds of the night, both thinking of how frighteningly dark the night was. Then, suddenly, the chickens started to go "cluck, cluck" and the clucking became louder and frantic, and the girls got scared.

"I think the thief man is in the fowl coop," Indira whispered to Francine, and they both ducked and peeped out of the window at the dark fowl coop.

Francine, who had learned about the thief man from hearing her mother talking about him, began to tremble, and she asked, "What shall we do?"

"I don't know," Indira said, as she also started to quiver. Then she remembered what Mr. Jackson had told Nani and she said, "I think we should scream at the top of our lungs."

"No," Francine objected, "the thief man will know that we're alone at home and he can come after us."

"But if we scream then someone might hear us and that will scare the thief man away," Indira said, trying to persuade her friend to do so.

"I don't think we should," Francine held out.

They did nothing for the moment but peeped out into the darkness and listened. For a moment the chickens became silent, then they started clucking again, even louder this time. In spite of Francine's objection, Indira took deep breaths and started screaming at the top of her lungs, "Help, help! The thief man is in the fowl coop! Help, Uncle Policeman! Help!" Francine now acquiesced and went along with Indira and started screaming for help, also, and Jacko started shrieking. Rani heard the noise and began mooing, and Solomon joined them all and began hee-hawing, causing quite a commotion.

Just then Nani arrived home in the pitch black of the night and was coming through the gate when she heard the uproar, and she dropped the fire wood she was carrying and started screaming herself, adding to the clamour.

The noise woke up the neighbourhood, and soon George and Joan Williams came rushing over, so did Shazam, with a torch light in his hand, and the young man with whom Pyari was drinking, jumped over the paling and came, also.

Indira and Francine rushed down the front stairs, meeting Nani and the others at the bottom-house, and they cried, "The thief man is in the fowl coop! The thief man is in the fowl coop!"

"Quick!" Nani said to the men and Joan, "Let's go and catch him before he gets away."

"I'm not letting him get away!" Joan swore. "Just wait till I get my hands on him!"

"I can't wait to get my hands on him, either," Pyari's young friend added. "When we're done with him, I bet he would never steal in this village again!"

Indira and Francine were sent back upstairs and were told to bolt the doors and stay inside with Jacko, and Nani and Joan and the three men rushed to the fowl coop, with Shazam leading the way with the torchlight. The scared chickens were now even more frantic, clucking louder as they entered the coop. Shazam shone the light around and there in a corner was the culprit, crouching beside a ladder, caught red-handedly.

He was recognised as a young *dougla* man—of Indian and African descent, who was from the village. He was tall and skinny with skin as black as tar, and he wore all black to camouflage himself in the night, with only the white of his eyes looking conspicuous.

Joan, who had been waiting to confront him ever since Nani had told her about him, launched at him right away and started cuffing him up and boxed his ears real good, roughing him up before Pyari's friend got a chance to clout him. Nani and George Williams had to pull her away from the cowering thief man, much to his chagrin. Once they freed him from Joan, they hauled him out of the fowl coop and brought him to the bottom-house and held him captive there until the police—whom George Williams went to fetch—came to take him down to the police station.

The next day, the news that the thief man was caught spread like wild fire throughout the village, and the fear of the villagers subsided and life returned to normal.

5

Day Of The Pig Roast

Indira woke up this Saturday morning to the crowing of the fowlcocks with a smile on her face for the day of the pig roast had finally come and she would be going to see her grandfather, Dr. Ramesh, and her grandmother, Shanti. She crawled out from beneath the mosquito netting—careful not to wake her Nani, as yet—and she went and sat on the chair by the window overlooking the backyard and enjoyed the warmth of the gentle morning breeze as she looked up at the stars twinkling against the black sky. She was overcome with excitement at the thoughts of seeing her grandparents and the beautiful, big, yellow house they lived in and all the beautiful things therein. Her grandfather would be sending a chauffeur to pick up her and Nani in his luxury Studebaker and she sat there dreaming about riding in the blue car. She wondered what kind of gifts her grandparents would give her this time, and she was looking forward to giving them the gifts she had made for them; a fish for Grandpa and a flower for Grandma, which she sculpted out of clay and painted with the help of Miss Watson.

She sat there for a while lost in the dreamy anticipation of the day, and it was not until the sky turned from black to sapphire-blue and the stars began fading that she went and shook her Nani and said, "Wake up, Nani! Wake up! We have to get ready to go and see Grandpa and Grandma

104

today. Let's go over and get my new dress from Auntie Joan."

Nani slowly opened her eyes and wished she could lay there and rest her old bones for a bit longer, but in the faint morning light coming through the mosquito netting she saw the excitement on Indira's face, and she said, "Okay, child, I'll get up now." And she hauled herself out of bed.

Once Nani got on her feet she wasted no time in first taking care of the early morning chores; collecting the eggs, milking Rani, feeding the chickens, watering the plants and flowers, letting Rani and Solomon loose to graze in the yard, and making breakfast. Soon after cooking, she and Indira had *sago* porridge with fresh cow's milk, and roti with saltfish and tomatoes, some of which she set aside for Joan. As soon as they finished eating, they left to go over to Joan with the basket of breakfast, and by now the village was stirring with Saturday morning activities; cooking, scrubbing floors, beating clothes, and sweeping and daubing bottom-houses. Some were heading off to the market, stores, and banks. And some animals were roaming about foraging for food.

Nani and Indira were now in Joan's sewing room, a small room packed with fabrics of all kinds and colours, with the most modern fashion catalogues from America, Canada, and England strewn about.

"Mommy got up very early this morning to finish your dress for the pig roast," Francine said to Indira.

"Can I see it now?" Indira asked eagerly, more concerned about the dress than about Auntie Joan getting up early to get it done.

"I hope it wasn't too much of an inconvenience, gal," Nani said to Joan.

"Oh, no, Auntie, I had to get up early anyway to prepare to leave for New Amsterdam for the weekend to visit my parents as well as George's," Joan said and held up a purple lace dress, A-line with satin sash and puff sleeves and strands of pink beads on the round neckline. "Come and try it on, babe," she said to Indira.

Indira got out of her clothes as quickly as she could and put the dress on and stood in front of the full-length mirror beside the sewing machine. "I can't wait for Grandpa and Grandma to see me in it," she said, pleased with the pretty dress.

Joan looked over the dress and said, "It's a perfect fit. I don't have to make any adjustments." She then glanced over at Francine who was leaning against the chair beside the mirror, and she noticed the forlorn look on her face. "What's wrong, my love?" Joan asked her.

"I want to go to the pig roast too," Francine said, almost at the brink of tears.

"Can Francine come with me to the pig roast?" Indira was quick to ask.

"Not this time," Joan answered, and she reached over for Francine and placed her on her lap. Placating her with a tender hug, she said, "Don't start crying now, babe. We promised your grandparents that we'll visit them today and if you don't go they'll be terribly disappointed. They'll be waiting for you with all kinds of treats."

At the mention of 'treats' Francine lightened up and said, "Well, then, can I go with Indira another time?"

"Sure you can," Joan said, and fondly kissed Francine on her forehead.

Indira was now disappointed that Francine could not go along with her, and she said, "I'll tell my Grandpa to have another pig roast just for you, Francine." Francine smiled and got up and took Indira's hand, and they went in the corner of the room and sat, whispering to each other.

Nani then asked Joan, "How much would you charge me for the dress, gal?"

Joan never liked to take money from Nani and would much prefer to trade her service for other things, and she thought for a moment and said, "Never mind the money, Auntie. Just give me a couple of eggplants so I can roast them and make baigan choka for breakfast before we leave. I'll make some dosea to go with it."

Nani did not bother to object for she knew it was futile to do so because Joan would refuse any money for making clothes for Indira—Francine's sister as Joan would call her —so Nani went on to say, "No need for you to make breakfast, gal. I've brought you some. I made some saltfish and tomatoes, and roti for breakfast this morning, and put aside some for you." And Nani handed her the basket of food.

Joan did not know how to make roti and was delighted to hear that Nani had made her some. "Oh, thank you, Auntie, no need to get me the baigans then," she said. "You'll have to teach me how to make roti someday. It's not only a treat for me to have some for breakfast, but George would enjoy it, too, and so would Francine."

"I've made enough for all three of you," Nani said, and asked, "Where's George?"

107

"He's bathing to get ready for the trip."

"We have to get going ourselves to get ready for the pig roast," Nani said, and, without further ado, she and Indira left for home.

As soon as Nani returned home, she bathed, scrubbing herself with a piece of dried nenwa, then she oiled her skin with coconut oil, leaving her silver hair clean just as it was, without oiling it. She then sent Indira to bathe, after which, Indira puffed on Yardley sweet powder all over and got dressed in her purple lace dress and pink socks and white shoes. Nani tied the satin sash for her and combed the child's long, black hair and made ringlets, then she looked at her and said, "Well, look at you. You're looking as pretty as a jump & kiss flower."

Indira fluttered her lashes and smiled and said, "That's because I don't have to wear a hat today, so everyone can see my long curls."

Nani pinched her cheeks, and said, "But you will have to do so tomorrow for church."

Indira then asked, "What would you wear today, Nani?"

Nani, in her bare cotton slip, flopped onto the bed and let out a frustrated sigh. "I don't know what to wear, child," she said. Dr. Ramesh had mentioned to her that he would be having some big shots over for the pig roast—the wealthy and educated people and their children—and she did not have a frock that was good enough for the occasion. Besides, she had no shoes to wear and was afraid she would embarrass the doctor in front of his friends by going barefoot. "Maybe it's not a good idea that I go," she decided.

"You must go, Nani," Indira said, feeling let down. "I'm sure you can find something to wear."

Seeing the disappointed look on the child's face, Nani said, "Okay, child, I will find something to wear." She went over to the old wooden trunk which was in a corner of the bedroom and opened it and the smell of moth balls gushed out of it. Inside, she had stored away a few precious, sentimental clothing, which included a yellow silk sari ensemble she had gotten married in, as well as her late husband's yellow *sherwani*—a knee-length coat, with a matching dhoti and turban, three other saris; green, blue, and white, with corresponding bodices and petticoats, and, at the very bottom of the trunk was a red silk sari, embroidered with gold threads and beads, with matching bodice and petticoat.

Indira had never seen these clothes that her Nani had kept hidden from her; she would learn the secrets of them and Nani's life as the day would unfold. "Wear the red one," she urged, for it was the prettiest of them all.

Nani clutched the red silk sari to her breasts and said, "This, your grandfather, *Nana* Amar had given to me when I had turned seventeen, a year after we had gotten married. I had worn it for him yearly up until he passed away," and she paused with trepidation before saying, "but I don't know if the bodice and petticoat would fit me now."

"Just try them on, Nani," Indira said.

Nani tried them on and, much to her relief, they did fit, for she was still petite and slim. She went on to wrap the red silk sari around herself, and it fell softly about her, making her look graceful.

"You look beautiful, Nani," Indira commented admiringly. "When I grow up I want to wear a sari."

Nani kissed the child on her forehead, then she went about combing her long, silver hair in front of the mirror, letting it cascade down her back, and as she was doing so, she thought of when she had first worn the sari when she was seventeen and how her husband had asked her to dance for him, and she smiled as she stood there remembering the days of her youth.

Indira could not understand why Nani was smiling to herself, and taking her time in doing so, while she was growing impatient, and becoming more and more excited at the thought of getting into the car. Interrupting Nani, she said, "Hurry up, Nani! The car will be here soon!"

"All right, child," Nani said, snapping out of her reverie. She then finished combing her hair and did not put on her headkerchief but let her wavy, silver hair hang loose in the back, and she oiled her little feet and left them bare. "Now, don't forget your presents for your Grandpa and Grandma," she reminded Indira.

Indira rushed to the sitting room and got the sculptures which Nani had helped her to wrap in gift paper and place in a pink cloth bag, and she came running back to the bedroom, and asked, "Are you ready now, Nani? The car will be here soon!"

"Yes, child, yes," Nani said. "Go and look out the window and tell me when you see the car coming up the street." She had only been in a car a few times in her life and she was also getting excited about the car ride.

Indira scurried back to the sitting room and stood by the rocking chair by the window and anxiously watched for the car. To the left of her, a milkman came riding down the street on a bicycle, carrying bottles of fresh cow's milk, and stopping at the neighbour across the street to make a delivery. A donkey-cart rolled by in the opposite direction, passing children playing banga on the dirt street as it was heading with a cart full of produce to the market. A jeep sped past it, leaving a trail of dust behind. Once the dust settled, the blue Studebaker came glistening in the white sunshine. "It's coming, Nani! The car is coming!" Indira shouted, wild with excitement. And she clutched her pink gift bag in her hand and rushed out the front door onto the verandah and down the stairs, waving to the chauffeur as she did.

Nani shut the windows and bolted the doors, and followed quickly behind. By the time they walked through the ragged gate, the Studebaker had pulled up in front of the house, the revving of the engine causing quite a stir among the neighbours, who were peeping out of their windows to see the beautiful car.

The chauffeur, a fine, young Indian man, named Sahil, dressed in a white uniform with a white cap and matching shoes, got out of the car and greeted Nani and Indira, saying, "Good morning, ladies. I'm here to fetch you both to Dr. Ramesh."

"Good morning," they both returned. And Indira added, "Dr. Ramesh is *my* grandfather."

Sahil smiled at her then opened the back door of the car and let Nani in the back seat, and he went around and let Indira in on the left side of Nani. He then got behind the wheels, turned the car around and headed up the street.

Indira had been looking forward so much to the car ride that she was beside herself now, shifting around on the plush blue leather seat and feeling the smoothness of it and inhaling the fresh, new scent it emitted. The car seemed so luxurious and cool and dreamy to her. She peered out of the clear glass window as they drove along the bumpy dirt street and smiled at the passersby staring at the car, and she even waved her hand as if she belonged to Britain's imperial family.

As they continued up to the road, they encountered a truck that was carrying a house on its back, and Sahil veered off to the side and waited for it to pass, for it took up almost the entire width of the narrow dirt road. Once it passed, they continued on through the noisy market and came to the main road where they passed stores and banks, busy with villagers doing business, and then they came to Dr. Ramesh's big, yellow house.

Sahil drove through the tall iron gate and entered the big, beautiful yard, aesthetically lush with colourful flowers and palm trees. The house itself was a mansion on stilts with glass windows and many rooms, encircled by a verandah, and it had a concrete-paved bottom-house. Unlike Nani's old-fashioned house, the opulent home was furnished with modern amenities; electricity, a gas stove, a refrigerator, upstairs bathroom, a dial-up telephone, and it even had a record player with stereos, and a chandelier. The great house was serviced by Aaja, the servant who took care of the house chores as well as cooking. A personal attendant was hired to strictly take care of the needs of the sickly Shanti.

Dr. Ramesh, a brown-skinned, distinguished-looking gentleman with a head of well-groomed grey hair, looking smart in a beige *shirt-jack* and khaki pants, was sitting on the front verandah toying with his black-rimmed spectacles, impatiently awaiting the arrival of his granddaughter. When he saw the Studebaker entering the gate, he hurried downstairs to greet her and scooped her up in his arms as soon as she alighted from the car, and he kissed her on both cheeks and exclaimed, "My Granddaughter, oh, my Granddaughter, what a pretty purple dress you have on, and how pretty you look!"

"And how handsome you are, Grandpa," Indira returned with a sweet smile, displaying her cute dimples. "How I missed you!" And she hugged him tightly. Then she showed him the gift bag she had in her hand and said, "See, Grandpa, I brought you a present. And I brought one for Grandma, also. Where is Grandma?"

"She's having a *puja*, her morning prayer ritual, and we cannot disturb her now," Dr. Ramesh said. "You will see her when she's finished, and we will exchange gifts then."

"I can't wait to see what you and Grandma have bought for me!" Indira said, her beautiful, dark eyes luminous with excitement. Then her expression changed to that of a child's cute appeal as she went on to say, "Oh, Grandpa, my friend Francine can't come to the pig roast today. Can we do another one for her sometime?"

Dr. Ramesh, struck by the beauty and sweetness of his granddaughter, could not say no to the child, even though he was overloaded with work. "We'll do another one for your friend sometime, my dear Granddaughter, I promise," he said, and fondly pinched her cute nose.

Lost in the excitement of seeing his granddaughter, Dr. Ramesh did not notice Nani until she got out of the car and came and stood beside him, and he said to her, "Well, it's good to see you, Nani. That sure is a beautiful red sari you're wearing. You're looking very nice today I must say." Then he looked down at her feet and saw that she was not wearing any shoes. Nani's eccentric appearance—as well as her behaviour—would be an aberration among his elite coterie of well-dressed, well-spoken friends, and he instantly thought her bare feet would cause him an embarrassment. "I have invited some special guests today as I mentioned to you before," he said to Nani, "and it is not fitting for you to be seen in your bare feet. Shanti has many pairs of shoes and I'm sure she will be glad to lend you a pair to wear just for today."

Nani expected this and thought his vanity was preposterous, but, not wanting to cause the doctor any embarrassment, she agreed that she would wear a pair of Shanti's shoes, knowing that Shanti's feet were a size bigger than hers, and her shoes had high heels and she would take a risk of wearing them and perhaps cause a bigger embarrassment if she were to stumble and fall in them. With that apprehensive thought in mind, she went and sat at the bottom-house and waited for Shanti to finish her puja.

Dr. Ramesh took Indira by the hand and led her to the backyard where, under an enormous guinep tree, a couple of men were tending a pig that was already roasting on a spit for the feast, the mouth-watering aroma filling the morning air, and the exuding heat causing the place to feel like an oven.

They lingered there for a while and looked on as the men were basting the pig. Then Dr. Ramesh lifted his granddaughter and held her close, secretly wishing the girl would stay and live with him and Shanti. If she did, she would have a luxurious life with a servant to attend to her and she would have anything her little heart desired, he thought. But he knew that was just wishful thinking and regretfully dismissed the thought, for the girl loved living with her Nani, and he could not take her away because it would cause her a great deal of distress, and he could not bear the thought of that.

He set her down on her feet and decided to take her upstairs and wait for Shanti to finish her puja. They went up the backstairs to the big, blue kitchen, which was very hot from the flurry of activity of the two cooks he had hired for the day. They were busy making spicy *black pudding* from the pig's blood, and curried *iguana,* and fried *bush-hog* and *watrash* wild meat delicacies, and *shark choka* and cook-up rice and *pepperpot*, and savoury and sweet treats of bara and pholourie and *gulab jamun* and *mithai* and *vermicelli cake.* The delicious aromas of the foods mingled in the kitchen and permeated the entire house, stimulating everyone's appetite.

While Dr. Ramesh stopped to instruct the cooks, Indira slipped away to check if her grandmother was finished with her puja. She passed the large, green dining room to the left where Dr. Ramesh's hired servant, the plump, middle-aged Aaja, was busy setting the enormous dining table with silver and china wares for the feast and, in between, dashing back and forth to the kitchen to assist the other cooks. After returning Aaja's friendly greeting, Indira proceeded to the huge, yellow sitting room, furnished with bright-red leather sofas, where she stopped for a moment to observe the young woman, Daksha, Shanti's personal attendant, as she was assisting Aaja the housekeeper in dusting the furniture and cleaning the glass windows. Daksha smiled happily and waved at her, and when she got down on her knees to polish and shine the wooden, mahogany floor, Indira moved out of her way and hurried off. She went along the hallway, passing the many locked rooms on the right side of the house, until she came to the first room in the very front, the interior of which was painted the colour of crimson, where her grandmother had a holy shrine.

Dr. Ramesh claimed to be a man of no religion though he believed in a God, and his wife was a staunch Hindu, and out of respect for her religious beliefs, he let her have this room solely to have her pujas. The door to the crimson room was now locked, so Indira went outside on the verandah where she could catch glimpses inside through the flimsy, white, lace curtain flapping in the warm wind. The room was dimly lit by brass *diyas*—little lamps lit with *ghee* soaked cotton wicks—that were placed around the altar and in a brass tray. On the crimson walls were gold-framed pictures of the god Vishnu—the Preserver of the Universe with his blue skin and four arms—and his avatars, Krishna and Rama, decorated with garlands of flowers. Lotus flowers, a favourite of Shanti, were placed at the feet of the brass *murtis*—idols at the altar, and incense was burning, the aromatic wisps of smoke sailing through the window to where Indira was standing.

Shanti—once fair and beautiful and exuberant but now looking old and frail in a light-green sari—was seated in a lotus position in front of the altar. She had just finished reading the Bhagavad-Gita and was now performing an *aarti* or fire offering to the deities. Indira watched intently as she was circling the brass tray of ghee-lit brass lamps around the murtis and chanting the mantra, *Hare Rama Hare Krishna.*

Indira continued to look on in silence until her grandmother was finished with her ritual, and as soon as her grandmother got up to leave the room, she rushed back inside and met her at the door entrance and wrapped her arms around her waist and exclaimed, "Oh, Grandma, how I missed you!"

Her grandmother, pale and decrepit as she was, bent down and hugged Indira and kissed her cheeks, and a tear of joy fell from her eyes when she said, "I missed you, too, my dear Granddaughter. You do look as lovely as a doll in your purple lace dress."

Indira fluttered her eyelashes then held up the pink gift bag she was carrying and said, "I have a present for you, Grandma, and one for Grandpa, too."

"I cannot wait to see what you brought us," her grandmother said and smiled. "Come to my bedroom and we'll open them there. Daksha!" she called out in a weak voice to her personal attendant, "tell Dr. Ramesh to come to our bedroom."

While Daksha ran off to fetch Dr. Ramesh, Shanti took Indira to her bedroom, which was huge and imperial, painted in white and decorated with custom-made hububalli wood furniture, including, the four-poster bed—covered in

117

royal blue satin sheets with a white mosquito netting draping over—the bedside tables, wardrobe, and dresser. Against a wall was a blue leather chaise longue, on which Shanti reclined, and while she waited for Dr. Ramesh, she cuddled Indira with the warmth and tenderness of a grandmother.

Dr. Ramesh rushed in shortly after, thinking something was wrong with his wife, but her sunken green eyes had a glimmer of joy and he knew it was because of their granddaughter. Shanti had been bed-ridden for the last few days because of her high blood pressure and he wanted to cancel the pig roast for her to convalesce, but she would not hear of it and found the strength to get up today to be a part of it.

"Come," Shanti said to her husband, "and see what our granddaughter has brought for us." Dr. Ramesh came and joined them on the chaise longue, sitting on one side, with Indira in the middle.

"I made the gifts myself," Indira said proudly to her grandparents as she opened the pink bag and took out the wrapped gifts. "Let me give Grandma hers first." And she handed Grandma Shanti her gift.

Shanti took the gift and opened it up and found a flower sculpture painted in pink, and she exclaimed, "What a lovely pink rose! You said you made this yourself?"

"Yes, I did. And Miss Watson helped me to paint it," Indira said as Grandma Shanti gave her a hug and a kiss.

"Now let me see what you brought for me," Dr. Ramesh said, amused by his granddaughter.

"Here, Grandpa," Indira said, handing him his present, "I hope you like it."

"I hope so, too," Dr. Ramesh said and took the gift and opened it. "A blue fish! Well, I'm hungry now. Can I cook it for lunch?"

"Oh, don't be silly, Grandpa," Indira said and smiled, showing off her cute dimples. "It's made of clay and you can't cook it. It's an ornament."

"I know, I know, dear child," Dr. Ramesh said. "Thank you very much for the beautiful fish. I will put it in my office for everyone to see what my granddaughter has made for me. Now, your grandmother and I have some gifts for you." And Dr. Ramesh got up and walked over to the dresser on which were three gift boxes.

"What? Beads?" Indira asked as her beautiful, dark eyes lit up.

"And that, too," Grandma Shanti said, as Dr. Ramesh brought the gift boxes and handed them to Indira and sat back down beside her.

Indira excitedly opened the first gift and found a clear tube filled with colourful, shiny, glass beads, and she said, "Oh, thank you Grandma and Grandpa." Then she opened the second gift and it was a Barbie doll, and she said, "Oh, thank you Grandma and Grandpa." She then opened the third box and her dark eyes widened at the pair of small gold bangles, and she exclaimed, "Bangles! I don't have to wait until I grow up to wear bangles! Oh, thank you Grandma and Grandpa!" And she put them both on one hand and shook her hand to hear them jingle. She then turned to her grandparents and hugged and kissed them both and said, "I have something to tell you Grandpa and Grandma."

"What is it?" both Dr. Ramesh and his wife asked simultaneously.

"Miss Watson told me that I'm doing very well in class."

"I'm so happy to hear this," Grandma Shanti said, and gave Indira a peck on the head.

"Well, that's great. We're proud of you, dear child," Dr. Ramesh said. "And your Nani must be, also."

"She is. And she wants me to work at the bank when I grow up and finish high school."

Just then there was a knock on the door and it was no other than Nani. Dr. Ramesh beckoned her to join them, and after Indira showed off her gold bangles and her other gifts to her, the issue of the shoes came up.

"I agree with Dr. Ramesh that it is not fitting for you to be seen without shoes in front of our guests," Shanti said to Nani. "I'd be more than happy to lend you a pair of mine to wear just for today." She then sent Indira to get Daksha, and when Daksha came, she told her to bring a few pairs of shoes for Nani to choose from, shoes which she had accumulated in her younger years when she was known to be flamboyant.

Since Dr. Ramesh presented the idea to Nani for her to wear Shanti's shoes, she became apprehensive, and now that Shanti was insisting she should, it made her even more anxious. Nevertheless, she acquiesced, complying with Shanti, also, to save them both any embarrassment. She went ahead and tried on a few pairs and they were all about a size too big for her feet, which she figured they would be, and she ended up settling for a gold pair of shoes that had a two-inch heel, lower than the rest of them but still too high for her. Daksha helped to fix the problem of the size by stuffing the front of the shoes with newspaper, and she gave them to Nani to try on again. Nani did and tried walking in them and felt strange and unbalanced, so she decided she would sit with them on when the guests arrive so she would not have to walk and stumble and make a fool of herself. She took the shoes off and carried them in her hands to the bottom-house and selected a bench, where she sat and put them back on, ensconcing herself there, in her inextricable situation.

It was nearing noon now and Shanti began getting ready. Daksha assisted her in putting her hair up in an elegant bun and getting her dressed in a pink silk sari, completing the outfit with a pair of silver slippers. She decked her out with gold bangles, necklace and earrings, and applied makeup on her, also, for even though Shanti was ill that did not stop her from being stylish. When Dr. Ramesh saw her he told her that she looked resplendent and he could not tell that she was ill, for the rouge on her fair skin made her look rosy. After giving her an affectionate embrace, he led both her and Indira to join Nani at the bottom-house to wait for the guests to arrive. Aaja had the bottom-house all set by now; benches arranged, a bar stocked with a large selection of hard liquor and wine and beer and *ginger beer,* and a table of delectable appetisers and fruits was laid out.

By now, the hot sun was beating down on the village and a warm wind was blowing gently, swaying branches of the palm trees in the front yard and spreading the aroma of the pig roasting in the backyard, tantalising everyone's appetite.

Indira was filled with ebullience more than anything else, anticipating the arrival of the guests who would be attending the feast. It was not long before the first car drove through the gate, and Mr. Gopu, the wealthy man by inheritance, alighted with his wife, Chanda, and two teenage daughters, Nadia and Raaka. Indira was beside herself now for these were some of the rich people with whom she was so fascinated. She was especially taken with Nadia and Raaka who were dressed in western fashion of the day in shift dresses and slingback, high-heeled shoes, and hair flipped up above their shoulders with *limzee*— fringe that fell right above their kohl-lined eyes, dark eyes which made their fair skin more pronounced. The glitter of the gold jewellery that adorned them and their glossy makeup dazzled her, and she was mesmerised by the pink bead purse that one of the girls was carrying.

Right after Mr. Gopu and his family arrived, Dr. Lawrence Fraser, the Afro-Guyanese surgeon, pulled up in his car, and along with him came his wife, Phyllis, and their teenage daughter, Roxanne, whom Indira stared at in admiration for she was in bell-bottoms and slick, platform shoes, her hair in cornrows with shiny beads at the ends, and her face was also attractively made up; pink lipstick conspicuous against her velvet-brown skin.

Next came Mr. Ramal, the high school principal, and his wife Banita, with their teenage children; their son, dark-skinned Vishnu, was dressed sharply in white shirt and matching pants with his black hair all groomed and looking handsome, and the daughters, Aashi and Babita, with their sun-kissed skin, were in mini dresses and high-heeled slippers, and they wore hair bandos in their flipped up hair, which fascinated Indira and made her long to grow up just to wear a bando.

Next to arrive was the white family with their blue eyes and golden hair, John and Nancy Patterson, the Canadian teachers, with their two young children, Peter and Karen. Indira just could not believe her eyes to see all the people who so intrigued her.

Dr. Ramesh greeted the guests and brought them to the bottom-house. Indira immediately aroused curiosity among them. They had never seen the girl because she lived with Nani and was rarely around the doctor, and when her father was alive he lived an estranged life from Dr. Ramesh, so Indira had remained obscure. Dr. Ramesh took the opportunity to introduce her, and he lifted Indira and proudly flaunted her, saying, "This is my granddaughter, Indira, my late son, Sameer's daughter."

"Well, what a pretty little thing she is," Dr. Lawrence Fraser commented.

"Isn't she a doll," Mr. Ramal said.

And Mr. Gopu came up and pulled on her long, black ringlets and said, "*Blackilocks* is who she is."

"Where does she live?" one of the girls asked.

The answer to that may not go over very well with some, Dr. Ramesh knew, and a twinge of embarrassment seized him momentarily, but when it passed, he answered, "She lives with her late mother, Geeta's mother, Nani, down by the river," And he pointed to Nani, who smiled and remained in her seat.

The mature folks did not react, for they did not even know who Nani was—Nani looking dignified and unrecognisable in her finery today—but the young people snickered contemptuously at Nani for they recognised her as being the poor, old woman they had seen going to the market on her donkey-cart. They had never taken notice of the girl she took along at times. They began to *su-su*— whisper and gossip, condescendingly among themselves, obviously thinking of the girl and Nani as being inferior to them.

Indira did not like the attention she was generating, besides, she sensed the bad vibes of ostracism from the youngsters and asked her grandfather to put her down, and while the guests went about mingling and drinking and nibbling on the appetisers, she went by the gate to observe the out-of-town guests as they were arriving.

From New Amsterdam, came a young Chinese doctor, Dr. Allan Chung, and his beautiful Asian wife, Sophie, and they arrived on a motorcycle. Then came another young, and debonair doctor, an Afro-Guyanese from Georgetown, Dr. Delroy Johnson, and his ostentatious wife, Aileen, and they arrived in a brand new jeep, Aileen in hot pants showing off her fine, brown legs, and wearing a skimpy halter top. And, lastly, an aristocratic-looking Englishman with a cane and round spectacles, a professor from Georgetown, Henry Barlow, arrived in a car with his young American wife, Barbara, accompanied by their teenage son, Jimmy, a redhead with stunning green eyes just like his mother's.

Well, Indira was so taken by the diverse group of guests that she wandered around quietly observing them. She noticed when the young people went up to the verandah and hung around in the hot afternoon sun, talking and laughing and drinking and flirting. She took notice of the wives of the men who took to the shade of the bottom-house, and they sat around talking and sipping wine, while

Nani sat quietly and looked on with much discomfort in her gold shoes, confined to her seat. Indira was especially fascinated with the white children, Peter and Karen, and she tried to befriend them but the children were more interested in the delectable goodies on the table. She left them alone and wandered in the backyard where the pig was roasting under the great guinep tree, in the shade of which a table was set up where her grandfather and the men were drinking El Dorado Rum on the rocks, and cold bottles of Banks Beer while they were playing dominoes and *gaffing*—conversing.

Dr. Ramesh noticed her and called her over to him, and he lifted her and placed her on his lap. And then he called out to Aaja to play some music, and soon there was calypso music and the Mighty Sparrow was singing *Jean And Dinah*, followed by a reggae tune by Bob Marley and the Wailers, *Maga Dog*. The men continued their conversation while Indira looked on and listened, trying to make sense of the *man talk*.

Mr. Gopu was now preparing for another round of dominoes, having won the previous round, and he was vigorously shuffling the pack of ivory tiles on the bare, wooden table, which made a clashing sound as he did, and after the four players—namely, himself, Dr. Lawrence Fraser, Dr. Ramesh, and Mr. Ramal—selected their tiles, raising his voice above the sound of the music, he asked, "Who's got the double-six?"

"I have," Dr. Lawrence Fraser said, and he slammed the double-six tile on the table. While he waited for the next player to cast his tile, he went about saying, "Man, it's a joyous time for our country now that we've gained independence from Britain. Guyana, *land of many waters*, the name as derived from the indigenous Amerindian language, is no longer British Guiana."

"It truly is indeed a joyous time for our country, comrade," Dr. Ramesh responded as he put his tile down next, while holding Indira on his lap with the other hand. "We've been under the rule of the British for too long, and too many others. Now we are free indeed, man."

"Indeed you are," said the Englishman Henry Barlow as he took a swig of rum and tapped his cane on the dirt ground as he looked on at the game.

Mr. Ramal slammed his tile down next and said, "We are now a free people in a land rich in gold, diamonds, bauxite, and timber, and we will work in the sugarcane and rice fields, and fisheries, and become prosperous. So is my vision for this beautiful land of many waters and plains and pristine rainforest. Let's all have a drink in celebration of our freedom." All the men lifted their glasses and toasted. And Indira joined them, holding a glass of ginger beer aloft and making a toast, much to the amusement of the men and the hearty chuckle of her grandfather, but she did not find it funny that the men were laughing at her for making a toast herself, for Miss Watson had told the class all about the independence of the country, and she thought the men were acting silly.

What she found funny, though, was the English professor's accent. Henry Barlow had moved on to the subject of literature and was talking about people she did not know of: James Joyce, Joseph Conrad, Edgar Allan Poe, and then as he was tapping his cane to the rhythm of the reggae music, in somewhat of a dramatised voice, he loudly said above the sound of the music, "*'If music be the food of love, play on . . .'* Who is like unto the great William Shakespeare!"

The latter of the authors she had heard of, and Indira was quick to echo, "Yes, who is like unto the great William Shakespeare!" The men laughed at her again, which she did not find to be funny, for she knew of William Shakespeare because Miss Watson was always reading his books in her spare time and she had told her that he was the greatest English writer of all time.

Mr. Gopu then just had his turn in playing and turned to Dr. Fraser who could not play either of the numbers next, and he said to him, "Draw from the pack, man." Dr. Fraser went in the pack and picked out a tile that did not hold the number he was looking for, same thing with the second, third, and fourth tiles, and Mr. Gopu laughed and said, "While you're at it, take all the bones, Fraser. Pile them up and I'll win the game." But on the next try, Dr. Fraser got lucky and the game continued.

By now the sun was blindingly bright and the heat of the day had risen to a peak and the place was even hotter with the pig roasting on the spit nearby as it emitted appetising wisps of smoke, and the men already had a number of drinks and were getting loud.

The next subject they touched on was dear to Indira's heart, and it started with Dr. Delroy Johnson saying, "I think of how far we've come in medicine since prehistoric times when medicine men incorporated plants and animal parts and minerals and used them in rituals to cure ailments. I wish Hippocrates and Suśhruta were alive today to witness our advancement."

"Delroy, who are these people you're talking about, man?" Mr. Gopu asked, as he slammed a tile down on his turn.

"Gopu, the only thing you know about is money," Dr. Delroy Johnson facetiously said as he took a shot of rum.

This offended Mr. Gopu but before he got a chance to react, Dr. Ramesh intervened and said, "Men, let's not start an argument. But I will agree with you, Delroy, we have indeed come a far way in medicine, and with technology advancing at the rate it is, who knows what we will be capable of doing in the future. Bringing a dead person back to life almost seems conceivable to me. That brings me to the subject of life and death and the afterlife, and it makes me wonder about the notion of the existence of God as portrayed by the great religions."

"There is no God," Henry Barlow said bluntly as he puffed on a cigar now.

"There is a God!" Indira suddenly interjected, and all the men laughed out loud at her seriousness and the passion with which she spoke. "That's not funny!" she retorted, and added, "He's living in heaven."

Dr. Ramesh wiped the smile from his face and, in trying to placate her, wrapped his arms affectionately around her as she sat on his lap, and he said, "My dear Granddaughter, yes, there is a God in all men who do good. And the devil exist in those who are bad." The answer sufficed and quieted Indira.

Professor Barlow then adjusted his round spectacles and took another gulp of liquor and persisted on, quite candidly, expounding, "The majority of people today believe that the creator of human is the God of their religion, but the ancient Greek philosopher, Anaximander, hypothesised the evolutionary descent of man from some kind of fish-like creature, and Charles Darwin added to this through his theory on natural selection."

"Rubbish! Rubbish!" Dr. Ramesh expostulated, waving his hand. "I am by no means a religious man, my dear professor, but I choose to believe in a supernatural being who created the universe and all of life therein."

"Barlow," Mr. Gopu said, "how can you possibly believe that we actually came from a fish-like creature? Are you out of your mind, man? And who are these men who came up with these ridiculous theories? This is not what my religion has taught me."

Indira did not know what to make of this complicated conversation. She believed what she was taught by Miss Chandra in Sunday school; that there is a God living in heaven somewhere beyond the blue skies, and He created Adam and Eve, and we all came from them. It was as simple as that for her. But she remained quiet this time because she was afraid the men would laugh at her if she were to chime in again.

"I don't know what your religion is, Mr. Gopu, and I don't want to know, either," Henry Barlow said flatly in an abrasive and acerbic manner. "Dogmatic devotees of the great religions will all tell you that their religious path is the right one because of some reason or the other, and that causes conflicts among men. Religions have caused, and are still causing, many, many wars."

"Stop talking about all this nonsense, Barlow," Mr. Gopu said, and he turned to the players and said, "Don't bother with this man. Let's continue to play the game, boys."

"But it's a fact," Professor Barlow insisted emphatically. "Religions are causing too many conflicts and wars in the world."

"Ah, wars, wars. Bloody wars!" Dr. Ramesh said as he took a drink. "You are absolutely right, professor, that religions have caused many wars, and still do."

John Patterson then said, "War over anything is senseless, I think. Whether it be over religion or land or ethnicity or anything else, for that matter. Why must we fight and kill each other over anything? What is so honourable about that, that we should be awarded with medals? We can act civilised and reason instead of fighting and mutilating and killing each other. Nothing, absolutely nothing is more precious than life itself. To spill blood is to drain away life. To take one's life is a tragedy, for it is indeed a miracle to live and behold life itself."

Dr. Chung then said, "I think of all the money that was spent on wars and we still pour millions into doing so. Money that goes into building weapons to kill ourselves. It is senseless, I agree. Imagine if we use part of that money to feed the hungry, then there would be no starving children in the world! Or if we provide the less fortunates with shelter with some of that money, then there would be no such thing as homelessness. And the sick will surely benefit if some of that money goes into helping them to live healthier and longer lives. Better yet, part of that money should be used to educate people and help us to evolve into a peaceful people, thus a peaceful world."

"How do you educate people to be peaceful?" Henry Barlow asked, sarcastically. "This brings us right back to the teachings of religions, which brings us right back to wars," he added with skepticism.

"We seek peace through the art of meditation, not religions; it's all about purging and calming the mind," Dr. Chung said placidly. "My ancestors, as well as Dr. Ramesh's, have practised this art for many centuries, and, numerous generations later, people still do. I must admit I do so myself, and I find I'm able to live a peaceful life because I always resort to peaceful resolutions to life's conflicting challenges. I also find that peace is a balm for stress and that is partly why I meditate. It really works, believe me."

"I heard of the art of meditation being introduced to the western world through meditation centres to alleviate stress and pain, and if this concept is as good as you make it sound, Dr. Chung, then I'm willing to give it a try, because, quite frankly, I need a good dose of peace in my life!" Henry Barlow said as he laughed, intrigued by the whole idea.

John Patterson then said, "I hope that someday we would all live in a world of peace where wars would be a thing of the past; obsolete. In addition to meditation, which I embrace myself, I believe that we can attain amity among all people if we go back to the fundamental things in life and live to eat and drink and be merry."

"I totally agree with you, John," Dr. Fraser said. "Let's all drink to world peace." And all the men agreed on this and lifted their glasses and toasted.

Dr. Ramesh then said, "Today we will indeed eat and drink and be merry!" The pig roasting on the spit was promising a real feast to come as it continued to release mouth-watering aromas into the hot afternoon air.

The players then continued on with the game, and it ended when Dr. Fraser slammed his last tile on the table and said, "Game over! I've won!"

"*Shucks*, man, I lost!" Mr. Gopu said in accepting defeat.

Dr. Fraser then turned to Dr. Ramesh and said, "Well, old chap, let's plan a day to go hunting sometime soon. God knows we haven't done that in a long while. Remember those quails we used to shoot?"

"Yes, yes, I remember. We will plan a day to do so," Dr. Ramesh said, and thought of how he missed hunting in the bush. "Perhaps we can invite our dear friend Patterson to come along."

"Well, I wouldn't miss such an adventure for anything," Mr. Patterson said. Indira found herself staring at his blue eyes and golden hair and white skin as he spoke, and she noted that he spoke funny, too, but different from Professor Barlow.

Dr. Chung then said to Dr. Ramesh, "We haven't been to a cricket match nor to horse racing in a long, long time, Ramesh."

"We will arrange to do so sometime soon, bloke," Dr. Ramesh said in response.

By this time, Indira had heard enough talk about politics and literature and medicine and religion and evolution and wars and peace and meditation and sports, and she also had enough of the men finding her funny whenever she spoke. So she hopped down from her grandfather's lap and left the men to continue their banter and enjoy their camaraderie, and she went and joined the ladies gathered at the bottom-house and sat between her grandmothers, Nani and Shanti.

Well, Nani was in a predicament now as she sat in one place and would not move to even get a drink or some appetisers for herself because she feared walking in the high-heeled shoes. And to make matters worse, she could not understand what the loquacious American woman Barbara, Professor Barlow's wife, and the Canadian teacher, Mrs. Patterson, were saying as the women were conversing, for they spoke with a twirl of the tongue and she wondered what the devil they were saying. So she sat there in one place with much unease, and in silence, which the guests mistook for her being aloof.

Indira, on the other hand, could not sit for long in one place and she soon left the bottom-house and wandered upstairs to the verandah where the young people were still hanging out in the sun. They did not seem to notice her for they were caught up with themselves, and she stood in a corner and watched as the girls—in their glossy makeup and jewellery and pretty, fresh clothes and perfumed skin—stood around with drinks in their hands and fluttered their eyelashes amorously as the young men, Vishnu and Jimmy, winked at them. She could not help staring at Jimmy with his red hair and green eyes, and she thought he looked like the men on the covers of the Mills & Boon books that Miss Watson also read occasionally in her spare time.

She was not there for long observing the teenagers, for the afternoon sun became unbearably hot to remain on the verandah, and she followed the youngsters as they made their way to the bottom-house to seek shade, where the men were now gathered with the ladies. And it was now that Nani's troubles really began.

Nani had managed to sit in one place for the longest time but now she needed to use the upstairs toilet badly, which meant that she would have to get up and walk in the high-heeled, gold shoes in front of all the guests, and she was now even more afraid she would stumble and fall. She sat there breaking out in a cold sweat, wondering what to do. She thought of removing the shoes and going barefoot, but Dr. Ramesh was right there with his friends and she did not want to embarrass him and herself in front of all the people there. She had to act quickly, though, before she pee herself and cause a greater embarrassment, so she gathered her nerves and stood up in the high-heeled, gold shoes. It seemed as though everyone was watching her as she did, and she took a couple of steps on the concrete ground and her legs began to wobble. This caught the attention of everyone indeed, and the teenagers started laughing at her for they found it to be funny. Things got even more hilarious then, for Nani's worst nightmare occurred when she stumbled and fell over with her bottom sticking up in the air, and the young people took to fits of uncontrollable laughter.

Indira was angry at the young people for laughing for she did not find it funny that her Nani fell over, and she went and helped Nani up. Dr. Ramesh, on the other hand, had been dreading Nani would embarrass him in some way, and he was indeed embarrassed and he scratched his head and wondered what she would do next.

Nani smiled next out of nervous discomfiture, exposing her two gold teeth, and the youngsters erupted in another fit of laughter, finding it funny that she had gold-capped teeth.

"Stop laughing at my Nani!" Indira reprimanded them this time, having had enough of their insolent behaviour. She had been so enamoured of them, and had such high expectations of meeting them, but she was now beginning to feel disappointed. None of them attempted to give Nani a helping hand, leaving her to take Nani's hand and help her up the front stairs to the toilet as Nani was still wearing the high-heeled, gold shoes.

Dr. Ramesh scratched his head again and wondered what Nani would do next, and it was when the sun turned to orange-gold and everyone had moved upstairs that the telephone would ring, and the next embarrassing moment came. Dr. Ramesh had answered the phone and it was one of Nani's cousins on the line, Mari, now living in New York, who said she had an important message for Nani. Mari had called a few times before and he had taken messages for Nani because Nani had never been around, but this time she was and he told Mari so and said she could speak directly to her, and he made the mistake of handing the phone to Nani.

Nani, who had never used a telephone before, held the receiver upside down and began hollering at the top of her lungs, "Mari, can you hear me! Can you hear me, Mari? I can't hear you, Mari. I can't hear a thing you're saying. Hello Mari! Mari! Mari!"

The young people burst out laughing again, and Indira scolded them again, and Dr. Ramesh scratched his head yet again and was now regretting that he had invited Nani to the pig roast.

Nani hung up the phone on Mari, frustrated that she could not hear a thing that she was saying, and feeling more embarrassed than ever she went and sat alone in one of the many rooms, and she wondered what she should do with herself now. The young people had laughed at her and made a silly old fool out of her. How would she face them again? She knew that they would do it again if she were to act the slightest bit awkward for she was now a laughing-stock to them. Just then a classical Indian instrumental was playing on the record player, and an idea struck her, and she swore that after the next act they would never laugh at her again. She wandered into Shanti's dressing room and picked out a red nail polish and she painted her toe and finger nails, and she sat in front of the mirror and combed her long, silver hair until it looked shiny like that of an angel's hair. And she smiled to herself.

While she sat there hatching a plan to get back at the youngsters, everyone was having a good time and was looking forward to the feast, which was due shortly; Aaja and the cooks were working diligently, heaping hot foods on the long dining table, the scrumptious aromas filling the house.

With Nani out of the way, the ambiance was relaxed, and the guests, now in the spacious sitting room, were socialising and wetting their appetites with piquant savouries and drinks as the golden rays of the late afternoon sun streamed through the open windows and a tepid breeze was blowing about. Suddenly, Nani emerged and made her way to the centre of the room. Everyone immediately stopped chattering and looked at her, for in the golden sunshine Nani's brown skin glowed and her long, silver hair shone, and the red silk sari she was wearing, shimmered. She had abandoned Shanti's gold shoes and her small feet were now bare and appeared pretty in the red nail polish.

Indira held her breath for she was afraid that Nani would do something fatuous again and cause the young people to laugh at her again. The youngsters themselves were wondering what foolishness Nani was up to this time and were poised to break out in laughter again at the slightest mishap. And Dr. Ramesh scratched his head yet again, thinking another embarrassment was imminent.

As if on cue, just then another classic Indian instrumental started playing on the record player, and Nani began dancing in her bare feet on the polished floor to the sound of the sitar and tabla drums. What Nani would reveal to everyone later that day, was that she was a barefooted Indian Classical Dancer in her early teens, and that would explain to Indira the clothes that she kept hidden away in her trunk—attires from when she was a performer—and why she chose to go barefoot. As Nani danced to the part of the Hindu goddess, Sita, she thought of the times when she had danced when she was only sixteen and charmed the audiences with her beauty and grace, and she moved her head and bust and torso in soft flowing movements, letting her long, angelic, silver hair cascade about her. She softly glided across the polished floor, and her hands with fingers in red nail polish were exquisite as she formed the different *mudras*, and as she danced, her red silk petticoat showed, and Nani appeared young and radiant.

137

Everyone watched in stunned silence, including, the young people, who were quite taken by the enchanting dance, and when Nani was finished dancing they all clapped vigorously and shouted, "Dance again!"

Indira was happy that the young people were not laughing at her grandmother this time but were pleased, and she also clapped her little hands and cried, "Dance again, Nani! Dance!"

Professor Barlow, very intoxicated by now, changed Shakespeare's quotation and instead said, "If *dancing* be the food of love, *dance* on, Nani!"

Dr. Ramesh, impressed by Nani's performance of great virtuosity, did not scratch his head this time but he called out to Aaja to play the music again.

Nani gladly gave an encore to more cheers from the guests. When she was finished, the young people gathered around her and started asking questions about the dance, and she told them about her life and showed them some of the dance moves, which the young girls were quick to emulate. Nani's cousin Mari then called back and Dr. Ramesh positioned the phone so Nani could speak into it, and Nani learned the important news that Mari's granddaughter had given birth to a robust baby boy.

After Nani shared the joyful news, everyone took a seat in the dining room and the feast began and the music played, and the pièce de résistance—the pig roast was succulent, and the guests ate of all the different foods piled on the table, and they drank wine copiously. Nani ate with her fingers while everyone else used cutlery, but Dr. Ramesh did not scratch his head over this, nor did the youngsters laugh, for that matter.

Now that her Nani was no longer a laughing-stock, the atmosphere was one of harmony, and Indira enjoyed the fellowship of the youngsters and everyone there, and the feast, as well. She ate until her little belly was stuffed full, then she snuck outside to wander around in the front yard, thinking about all the happenings of the day that she would tell Francine. Dusk was beginning to settle in by now and it was semi-dark out, and as she stood by the iron gate and was looking out through the bars, she noticed a beggar man passing by. He stopped when he saw her and threw her a gooseberry over the gate, and then he lingered there and started singing the song *Irene Goodnight*.

Indira found herself wondering why the old black man was singing so sadly with tears in his eyes. What she did not know was that Irene used to be the beloved wife of this beggar man, who used to be a prosperous businessman in his younger years. Irene had tragically drowned years ago and because of that the man had slowly lost his mind and lost all that he had owned. Often, in the nights, he would roam the streets and people would hear him singing goodnight to his beloved Irene. He begged for food in the daytime, and early in the evening he would walk the streets and throw gooseberries to the children, and no one knew where he got the fruit from or even where he slept at nights.

Indira studied him through the iron bars as he stood outside the gate singing mournfully, and she noticed that his clothes were tattered and he wore a hat and shoes that had holes in them, and the cane he leaned on was simply a stick from, perhaps, a tamarind tree. He looked so frail that she could not help but wondering if he had any food to eat for dinner, and she asked him, "Are you hungry, old man?"

The beggar man stopped his singing and answered, "Yes, my dear child." He knew, though, that he would not be invited in to sit at the table of the rich, so he said, "But don't you worry about me, child. I will go on my way now."

"Wait, don't go just yet," Indira said, feeling sorry for the beggar man. Her Nani, she knew, would never turn away a beggar man and would offer food to the hungry even if she had to go without, but her grandfather, she knew, would find it embarrassing to have anything to do with the beggar man. She thought she would have to secretively do something to help the poor, old man, and hope that her grandfather would not catch her. "Stay here. I will be right back," she promised him.

She snuck back in the house and peeped in the dining room and noticed that her grandfather was busy talking with the guests, and she went to the kitchen—where the cooks and Aaja were too busy to notice her—and she got a brown paper bag and filled it up with some appetisers. She went back outside to the beggar man, not knowing that in trying to be secretive that her grandfather had noticed when she had left the table earlier, and noticed when she had peeped in on him, and, wondering what she was up to, he furtively followed her and concealed himself in the shadow of a palm tree, and was secretly watching her.

"Take this," she said to the beggar man and handed him the brown paper bag of food through the iron bars of the gate, "and eat it so you don't have to go to bed hungry tonight."

Dr. Ramesh saw what his granddaughter did and heard what she said to the beggar man. He had seen the man a number of times begging at his gate and had never given him even the crumbs from his table, or a penny, for that matter. Now, elucidated by the compassion his granddaughter had shown to the beggar man, he was moved. He realised then that he could not have taught her what her Nani had. He swallowed his pride and humbled himself and stepped out of the shadow and went and opened the gate for the beggar man, and to both Indira and the beggar man's pleasant surprise, he said, "Come on in, old chap, and sit at my table and have a feast, for there is plenty of food to eat in my house."

The beggar man entered and sat at the lavish table with Dr. Ramesh and his affluent guests, none of whom snickered—not even the youngsters, after having learned a lesson from poor Nani—but they all rose to the occasion, respecting Dr. Ramesh for such a humble and compassionate act, which he openly attributed to his granddaughter. Dr. Ramesh saw to it that the beggar man was well served, and as the man ate and drank he told them anecdotes about his beloved Irene. Inspired by the bona fide benevolence of his granddaughter for another less fortunate, Dr. Ramesh opened his heart and offered him a job as caretaker of his yard. No one had ever given this destitute man such an opportunity, and he effusively thanked Dr. Ramesh. By the time he had eaten and drank until he was satisfied, it was dark outside, and he was ready to leave. Dr. Ramesh excused himself and escorted him to the gate.

"Thanks for the food and drinks, doctor," the beggar man said.

"No need to mention it," Dr. Ramesh said. "Call me Ramesh, man. *You* never mentioned what your name is, sir."

"Call me Gilbert, Ramesh," the beggar man laughed and said.

"Do you have shelter for the night, Gilbert?"

"I live like the birds of the air, Ramesh. Don't you worry about that."

"Okay then," Dr. Ramesh said. "I expect to see you bright and early on Monday morning for work."

"For sure, friend," the beggar man said then disappeared into the dark of the night with the bag of food Indira had given to him, singing sadly as he went, *Irene Goodnight*.

The feast continued way into the night long after the beggar man left, and there was more eating and drinking, and music, and the young girls were doing the *wine* dance, *wining* to calypso and reggae music; they even got Indira to join them in doing so. When the men drank themselves into oblivion, Dr. Ramesh decided it was time for them to go home. Those who lived in the village were driven home by their wives, and the guests from New Amsterdam and Georgetown were given rooms at his mansion for the night.

Indira wished the feast would never come to an end for she was having so much fun now that no one was laughing at her Nani. She was sad when she kissed her grandparents goodbye at the gate before Sahil took her and Nani in the blue Studebaker back to their little, old house down by the river.

6

A Storytelling Night By The Mud Stove

It was late on a Friday afternoon and the crimson sun was now setting, casting reddish-gold rays over the village of Rose Hall. Indira and Nani had just eaten supper, and while Nani remained in the kitchen and was washing the soiled dishes, Indira retired to the sitting room. She stood by the rocking chair looking out the window as the cane cutters—with cutlases in their hands—and the rice field workers were walking home from work, the men looking dark and haggard from working all day under the blazing tropical sun. The neighbours just opposite had just finished cutting grass in their front yard, and Indira took in deep breaths of the sweet grassy scent from the freshly cut grass as it drifted about where she stood lingering.

She had not been there for too long before Joan and Francine showed up at the gate, and she hurried downstairs to meet them.

"I've brought a *katahar* for you and Nani and Francine," Joan said, carrying the huge, green jackfruit under her arm.

Indira immediately became excited, for whenever Auntie Joan brought a katahar fruit that meant that Nani would roast the seeds and tell stories, and that also meant that Francine would be allowed to sleep over for a storytelling night. "Nani is in the kitchen," she said happily and led the way up the backstairs to where Nani was now sitting on the peerah in the kitchen.

After greeting Nani with a kiss, Joan said, "George and I are not going to New Amsterdam this weekend to visit our parents, Auntie, can I leave Francine with you for the night?" And Joan handed Nani the katahar.

"Yes, gal, you can. She can stay all weekend if you like," Nani said and got up and took the jackfruit, and she looked at both Francine and Indira, and added, "though I might run out of stories to tell them both."

"I'd love to stay all weekend," Francine was quick to say, "and if Nani runs out of stories to tell, then Indira and I can play *kai*," the game also known as Jacks, only played with stones and not plastic jacks.

"That's all right with me. She can stay all weekend," Joan said to Nani, happy to get Francine off her hands for a couple of days. "That would allow me to get caught up with my sewing. I have to get three dresses done for a customer by Sunday and, besides, I can catch up with some other chores around the house. Now, do I need to bring over a change of clothes for her?" Joan asked.

"No, gal," Nani said.

"Francine can wear mine!" Indira was quick to offer.

Joan smiled at Indira and bent down and gave her a kiss on the cheek, and said, "Thanks, babe. I'm glad you both wear the same size."

"We wear the same size slippers, too. I can give her a pair of mine to wear," Indira said, as Francine nodded, both girls filled with exuberance.

Joan then said to Nani, "The girls are excited to get ready for storytelling, and I should get going myself." And before leaving, Joan turned to Francine and gave her a hug and kiss, and she said to her, "Behave yourself, Francine, and don't give Auntie any trouble." And with that Joan went on her way.

As soon as Joan left, Nani started preparing for the storytelling night. Firstly, she took the girls in the cubicle in the backyard and bathed them, and while she sent them to get dressed, she had a bath, also, then went upstairs and oiled her skin. After the three of them got dressed in clean, fresh nighties, they gathered again in the kitchen.

By now, dusk had crept in, bringing a dense darkness over the village, conducive to a night of storytelling, and Nani lit the kerosene oil lamp and hung it up in the kitchen. Nani then took her seat on the peerah, and the girls sat on the bare floor beside her, and they watched as she cut up the ripe katahar on the floor. Nani gave them the succulent yellow fruit to eat and a bowl to place the white seeds in, and the three of them indulged and ate the whole fruit. After, they all went down to the pipe at the foot of the kitchen stairs and rinsed their hands and mouths, then Nani told the girls to play kai while she began to prepare to roast the katahar seeds, and she went about lighting the wood in the mud stove. The girls took turns and scattered the ten small stones on the floor, having fun throwing a stone up in the air and trying to gather the others in their hands before catching the falling stone, vying to be the first to catch them all. Nani enjoyed watching the game while she sat at the table waiting for the wood to burn down to embers, and by the time it did, the girls had enough of playing kai, and they put the stones away as Nani tossed the katahar seeds in the mud stove and left them to roast.

The warmth emanating from the mud stove gave a cozy ambiance to the old kitchen, along with the soft light of the kerosene oil lamp, and as the wick burned slowly, the flame danced, casting shadows on the old greenheart wood walls. The eerie shadows, the crackling of the wood, the menacing darkness of the night, along with the oscillating action of a brisk wind slamming the old kitchen window, all invoked a sense of mystery and fright, and the delicious nutty aroma of the katahar seeds roasting all added to the mood for a night of storytelling.

"Tell us some *jumbie* stories tonight, Nani," Francine said when Nani took her seat on the peerah—low stool.

"Aren't you afraid of hearing about evil spirits, my dear child?" Nani asked.

"No," Francine answered, even though her demeanour was contrary.

"I like to hear jumbie stories, also," Indira said, though she was afraid, also.

Both girls had a penchant for jumbie stories, and they sat side by side on the bare floor, in the crossed-leg position, with hands on their laps, poised to listen.

"Okay, children," Nani said, "I'll start by telling you the story about the *bacoo* and the fisherwoman."

"What's a bacoo, Nani?" Francine asked.

"A bacoo is a spirit trapped in a corked glass bottle, a spirit that people seek to fulfil their wishes and bring them prosperity. The bacoo fulfils the wishes of its owner once it is fed with banana and milk, but if the owner fails to do so, it makes bad things happen to the owner." Nani tightened her headkerchief and began telling the story by saying, "There once was a fisherwoman who lived in the village a long time ago, and she was doing poorly because she couldn't catch enough fish to sell at the market, and so she decided to purchase a bacoo to help her to prosper and become rich.

"As the story goes, this fisherwoman fed the bacoo daily at first with banana and milk," Nani continued, "and the bacoo started to fulfil her wish to become prosperous, and soon her fishing net was overflowing with fish, and she indeed became a rich woman. The fisherwoman then became so caught up with her riches, showing off her thick gold bangles and heavy gold chains, and she soon forgot to feed the bacoo. This made the bacoo very angry and it got out of the corked glass bottle somehow and started to torment her.

"People said they witnessed when she was cooking roti one day that as soon as the fisherwoman cooked the roti and placed it in a bowl that the roti would disappear just like that, and everyone believed it was the bacoo who stole the food because it was hungry. Then one day the fisherwoman's mattress was suddenly caught on fire, and everyone thought it was the bacoo who did it. Not only that, in the nights the bacoo would pelt the fisherwoman's house with stones, tormenting the woman both day and night.

"The woman then began to realise that she had forgotten to feed the bacoo and that was why it was tormenting her. So the fisherwoman went to feed it, and as she was climbing the ladder to get to where it was kept on a shelf in her bedroom, she fell and broke her neck!"

Both Indira and Francine gasped, and Francine asked, "Was it the bacoo who killed her, Nani?"

"So it is believed to be," Nani answered.

147

Indira then asked, "And what happened to the bacoo, Nani?"

"Someone lured it back into the bottle and corked the bottle and threw it into the ocean. They say if you ever find a corked glass bottle on the seashore never to open it for it may contain a bacoo!"

Both girls, though feeling frightened, were captivated by the story, and they insisted that Nani tell them another jumbie story. Before doing so, Nani went and checked on the katahar seeds and poked them around in the embers with a stick, and as they continued to roast, she came back and sat down and tightened her headkerchief again before she began the other story. "Many years ago, there was an old woman living among the people in the village who was said to be an *ole higue*."

"Is that the same as a *fire rass* or a vampire, Nani?" Francine asked.

"Yes, child," Nani answered. "As the story goes, in the day time this ole higue or fire rass used to live like a quiet old woman, but at nights she would remove her skin and place it in a calabash and hide the calabash under her bed, and she would travel the sky in a ball of fire and go to people's homes and sneak through their keyholes and enter the homes and suck the blood of their newborn babies."

Another gasp from the girls, and Indira asked, "Did the quiet old woman really do that, Nani?"

"Yes, child, that's what people said," Nani replied, rather seriously, and she continued with the story, saying, "One night this ole higue went to a young woman's home, and while the young woman and her husband were fast asleep, the ole higue sucked the blood of their newborn baby, and

148

the baby died. That night, the couple woke up and found the baby drained of blood and they figured it was the ole higue who did it. While the ole higue was still out on the prowl on that dark night, the husband quickly woke a few men in the village and they took their lamps and went to the ole higue's broken-down shack, searching for the calabash that contained her skin. They found it where she usually kept it, hidden under her bed, and they rubbed ball-of-fire pepper on the inside of her skin, and they left. And, as the story goes, when the ole higue returned home and put her skin back on, the hot pepper burned her to death!"

Indira glanced out the old wooden kitchen window into the ominous black night, looking for a ball of fire in the sky, and she was terribly scared now and asked, "Would the ole higue come to suck my blood, Nani?"

"No, child, as long as you say your prayers before you go to bed and ask God to send his angels to protect you."

"I always say my prayers before I go to bed, Nani," Indira said.

"So do I," Francine said.

"Then you don't have to worry your pretty little heads, children," Nani said.

"Tell us some more jumbie stories," Francine urged, frightened as she was.

The katahar seeds now began to crackle as they were roasting, and Nani went on to tell of the *Massacooramaan* that prevents people from exploiting the country's natural resources, the legendary hairy river monster that lurks in the black rivers and seas of Guyana, the malevolent spirit that preys on and devours people travelling in small boats. Then Nani told of the pernicious *Bush Dai Dai*, a succubus, protector of mineral and natural resources, a spirit who takes the form of a beautiful woman and, in the nights, enters the camps of miners in the dark jungles of Guyana and sleeps with them, then turns into a wild animal and eats the miners as they sleep. Nani went on to tell the story of the malicious *Churile*, the witch of East Indian origin, a woman who died at childbirth and whose evil spirit cries dolefully and roams at nights and haunts pregnant women.

Nani stopped her storytelling, momentarily, to check on the katahar seeds. By now, the seeds were well roasted and highly fragranced, pervading the kitchen, so she scooped them up with a pot spoon and placed them in a large enamel bowl and brought the bowl over to the girls and set it down on the floor to allow the seeds to cool. The girls, though still frightened, were enthralled by the stories, and they begged Nani to continue to tell them more tales of the jumbies.

Nani resumed her seat on the peerah, and then told the girls of the *Canaima*, the diabolical spirit of revenge that can change into a jaguar or any other wild animal, or possess the body of a human and drive him insane, and, having taken form, kills its victims in retaliation for injustice. Then Nani told the story of the much feared jumbies of the *Dutchman*, who once owned slaves in Guyana, whose evil spirits now attack and torment people both mentally and physically like they did when they were slave owners, sometimes even breaking the necks of small children; people are cautioned not to pass by a Dutch cemetery during the midday or midnights for fear that these jumbies would take hold of them. Nani then told the story of the nefarious *Moon Gazer*, the tall, white, misty shadow, who stands with his legs spread apart on either side of a road, with his hands on his hips, gazing at the moon, and if anyone walks between his legs he would crush them, or if he even senses the presence of anyone, he would suck their brains out through the palm of his hand. Nani then told the girls of the vitriolic *Fairmaid* or *Water Mama*, a female water spirit that lives in Guyana's rivers and seas, that falls in love with humans and blesses them with riches if they visit her regularly and take food and leave it on the river banks and seashores for her, and if they fail to do so, she punishes them; the ones who live in the dark oceans of Guyana would pull their victims to the depths and drown them.

When asked to tell them even more jumbie stories, Nani —sensing the children were getting very scared now and thinking it was imprudent to continue—said, "No more jumbie stories for the night. The katahar seeds are now warm and ready to eat. Let's eat, children."

"Tell us some other stories then," Indira pleaded.

"Okay," Nani said and, as the three of them sat around shelling and munching on the roasted katahar seeds, Nani began her next story by saying, "I'll tell you the story of my grandmother Chaaya and the jaguar."

Francine could not fathom the lore Nani had told so far and that left her wondering if they were true or not, and she asked, "Is this one for real now, Nani?"

"Yes, child," Nani answered, and she went on saying, "My grandmother used to live in a small village called Skeldon in an old house near the jungle, and on a bright moonlit night she heard a purring noise outside and she looked out her window and saw a jaguar sitting on her verandah."

"A jaguar on her verandah!" Indira exclaimed. "She must have been so scared."

"Yes, she was very scared she said, but she also said that the wild cat was so beautiful that she couldn't take her eyes off it, and she stood by the window and just watched it for the longest time, admiring its smooth, yellow-tan, black-spotted coat. She said it got up suddenly and looked at her with its golden eyes as though it wanted to say something to her, and then it turned and went into the jungle and disappeared.

"The next night she stayed up and watched for it and it came back, but it wasn't alone. Apparently, it was a mother, and she brought her newborn cub with her, carrying the tiny thing in her mouth, and she put the cub down on the verandah and then went away, leaving the helpless cub behind.

"The little thing seemed malnourished and it was obvious it hadn't been nursing. My grandmother figured that perhaps the mother couldn't nurse it for whatever reason, and maybe she brought the cub there to get some help. So my grandmother opened the door and brought the scrawny cub inside. My grandmother said she lit the kerosene oil lamp and sat on the rocking chair by the window with the little cub in her lap, and she immediately noticed that it had blue eyes, and she named it The Little Blue-Eyed One. She warmed up some fresh cow's milk and fed it with a bottle, and she took the cub back out on the verandah and left it there, and she locked the door and looked out of her window to see if the mother would return for it."

"And did she, Nani?" Francine asked, fascinated by the story.

"Well, yes, she did, and she took her cub and carried it back into the jungle. The next night the mother jaguar returned with her cub and she left it again on the verandah and went away. Grandma Chaaya said she took the cub in and fed it some milk again.

"The mother jaguar brought The Little Blue-Eyed One night after night, and my grandmother fed it with more milk, then she started to give it raw meat to eat, and soon the cub grew and was strong. Then one night the mother jaguar took The Little Blue-Eyed One away and they did not return the next night, or the next, and my grandmother, up until she died, watched for The Little Blue-Eyed One and her mother night after night, but they never returned again."

Both the girls were touched by the story and their countenance was now sad. Indira cast Francine an oblique glance and noticed that she was at the brim of tears, and she turned to her and said, "Don't cry, Francine, or you'll make me cry, too." She then reverted her attention to Nani and said, "Tell us another story, Nani."

In the dim light of the kerosene oil lamp, Nani puckered her eyebrows as she thought of another story to tell, then she asked, "Did I ever tell you the story about the lady dancer and the boa constrictor?"

"No, you never did. Tell us about it, Nani," Indira said, though she abhorred snakes, yet eager to hear of snake stories.

"There once was a beautiful white-skinned Indian lady who lived alone in a shack in the village, who had long, flowing, black hair and eyes as black as coal," Nani began, "and she was a dancer who performed on stage with a yellow red-tail boa constrictor. They said that she had found the snake in the bush when it was just a baby, just fifteen inches long, and she brought it to her shack and fed it wild pig and bird's meat and milk until it grew to be ten feet long, and over the years she danced with the snake on stage.

"As the story goes, the beautiful lady used to feed the snake everyday, but one day she forgot to do so, and she took the hungry snake out with her to perform. She came out on stage, as usual, with the yellow red-tail boa constrictor hanging around her neck and she started her dance and the people cheered. The snake started coiling itself around the beautiful white body of the scantily clothed Indian dancer, and everyone thought it was an act and began clapping even louder. But then the snake started constricting itself and it tightened its squeeze around the dancer and her bones were heard crushing as she began screaming for her life. The people, realising what was happening, stopped clapping their hands and rushed to save her, but it was too late, for the beautiful dancer had suffocated to death, and before the snake could have swallowed her, the people killed it. And so it was said that because she had not fed it that day, that the snake had killed her."

"And what did they do with the dancer and the snake then?" Francine asked.

"They buried the dancer alongside the snake," Nani replied, "for the dancer would have wanted it so."

The girls then fell silent, shelling more of the roasted katahar seeds to nibble on as they were assimilating the poignant story of the morbid and tragic demise of the peculiar, white-skinned Indian dancer. Before they asked Nani to tell them another story, Nani voluntarily said, "Now I will tell you about my mother Raajee and the alligator."

"I'm scared of alligators," Francine said, "but I want to hear the story."

"I'm scared of alligators, also," Indira said, "but tell us the story, Nani."

"Okay," Nani said and tightened her headkerchief once again before she began. "Ma told me once that not too long after she and Pa had gotten married that they went fishing one day in a black water river. She said she remembered that it was a bleak day and it was raining, and as she and Pa went into the water with their hand seine net, Ma said she stumbled upon something she thought was a car tire. She said she stood on the tire and, like a little girl, playfully started bouncing up and down.

"Well, Pa told her to stop fooling around and to help him to haul the seine so they could catch some fish to take to the market to sell. Ma said she reluctantly jumped off the car tire and took one pole of the hand seine net while Pa took the other, and they began dragging the net in the water. Soon the net felt heavy, and Ma said that Pa thought they would have a good catch that day. Expecting this, she said that they hurriedly hauled the seine net out of the water and onto the bank of the river, where their baskets were, but instead of a load of fish they were shocked to find a big alligator trapped in the net!"

"And was it the alligator that Great-grandma Raajee was jumping on?" Indira asked with eyes wide with astonishment.

"Yes, it was, child. It wasn't a car tire as she had thought."

"And what happened to the alligator?" Francine asked.

"Some fellas came along and killed it, and one of them took it home and stuffed it and kept it in his house."

"Tell us more about Great-grandma and Great-grandpa, Nani," Indira then said.

Nani did not respond right away, but she glanced over at the old wind-up clock on the kitchen counter and noted that it was past midnight, and she said, "It's getting late now and you should both go to bed, but I will tell you a little more about Ma and Pa." And Nani went on to say, "Ma and Pa got married when they were very young and both their families were very poor and couldn't help them out much. However, my grandmother Chaaya, Ma's mother, had a small piece of land and she gave it to Ma and Pa and said for them to stay with her in her old shack and sleep on the floor until they could find a way to build a little house on the land for themselves.

"Pa came from a family of fishermen, and that was all Pa knew to do, for ever since he was just a boy he used to go fishing with Grand-pa and Grand-ma in the wee hours of the morning. Pa taught Ma how to fish when they got married, and that's how they made their living. They would catch fish and Ma would carry the basket of fish on her head to the market and sell them.

"Poor Ma, in those days she used to wear dresses she made herself out of the cloth from flour bags, and she had just two, which she always washed and kept clean, just like she kept herself. She had no shoes for she couldn't afford a pair and she went barefoot everywhere. Poor Pa, too, had only two sets of cloths, one he wore to go fishing, and the other he wore everywhere else, and he washed those as often as Ma, and bathed as often as her. He, also, went barefoot.

"Anyway, Pa and Ma couldn't come up with the money to build a wood house, and Ma had become pregnant with me and they needed a house of their own, and so Pa got some of his friends in the village and they dug up some clay and built a mud house with a thatched roof, on the piece of land Grandma Chaaya had given to them."

"And what was the mud house like, Nani?" Indira asked curiously.

"It was one room and I remember it being kept clean and it was always cool. All we had for furniture was a cot to sleep on. We used to sit on the earthen ground and eat, for we had no table or chairs. And we ate from calabashes with our fingers, for Pa and Ma couldn't afford to buy enamel plates and silver spoons."

"And did they have a mud stove too?" Francine asked.

"Yes, child, they had a fireside," Nani answered. "I remember it clearly. I used to sit by the fireside while Ma would cook and Pa would tell us stories of his life."

"Just like we're doing now?" Indira asked.

"Just like we're doing now," Nani said, and continued with: "Pa and Ma were very poor, but no money in the world could have bought us the happiness we had, for Pa and Ma loved each other and adored me, and they were grateful for just salt and rice to eat if that was all we had to eat." Nani fell silent now, reflecting on the poor, yet happy days of shillings and pence.

"Tell us more stories, Nani," Indira begged, her voracious appetite for storytelling keeping her wide awake and wanting more, as was Francine's.

"I'm getting tired now, children, and the two of you should go to bed," Nani said finally, too tired to be cajoled into continuing on.

The glowing embers in the mud stove had now diminished, burned down to ashes, and the roasted katahar seeds were all gone. Nani got up and closed the kitchen window and bolted the door, and she took the kerosene oil lamp and led the children to the bedroom. She spread a couple of rice bags on the bare wooden floor and covered them with a blanket for the girls to sleep on, and she gave them the only feather pillow to share. She then lit a mosquito coil and placed it on the bedside table and lowered the mosquito netting over her bed. After she made sure the girls said their bedtime prayers, Nani, being the solicitous person she was, pacified them with hugs and goodnight kisses to dispel any lingering fear. She then blew out the lamp and retired to her coconut fibre mattress bed, and she laid her head down, and they all soon drifted off to sleep.

And so ended a night of Guyanese folklore and storytelling.

7

Uncle Ram, A Big Catch And A Bush-Cook

It was high noon and another bright and sweltering day in the village of Rose Hall, and the air was motionless for not a breeze was blowing. Indira, who was off school on this Friday, was sitting in the hammock at the bottom-house watching Solomon the donkey and Rani the cow grazing on the grass alongside the house. Nani was sitting on a peerah on the earthen ground beside her and was finishing up with knitting the cast-net—a fishing net she was working on for Shazam.

Nani had told Indira that Uncle Ram, Nani's only son, would be coming to visit, and Indira's little stomach was feeling queasy over this, because Uncle Ram would always say mean things about her and get into a row with Nani because of it, upsetting both her and Nani. Indira was desperately hoping his plans to visit would somehow be foiled, but that was not the case. He arrived shortly, and Indira could see him coming through the ragged gate, a lean and ruggedly handsome black-skinned man of medium stature, with thick black hair and skin glistening with perspiration from the heat of the day.

Without even greeting Nani, he looked at Indira with angry obsidian-like eyes and shouted, "Don't just lay around in the hammock while your Nani is working! Go feed the chickens or water the plants, you little wretch!"

Well, straight away this started a row with him and Nani. Nani reprimanded him, saying, "Don't you call my sweet granddaughter a wretch!"

Nani's defence of Indira only made Uncle Ram more irritable, and he resentfully said, "You do favour her, don't you, Ma? You do favour her over my two boys."

"That is not true!" Nani retorted. "I love my two grandsons just as dearly as I love Indira. Try to understand that she's an orphan child and my only granddaughter and I care a great deal about her well being."

"So you do favour her, Ma," he insisted scornfully. "Is it because her skin is lighter than my sons?"

"Don't be ridiculous!" Nani said, raising her voice and feeling a sudden surge of anger that only her son could bring out in her. "How could you stoop so low and say a thing like that?" She tried to restrain herself but a deluge of hurt feelings seized her and she continued on to say, "You keep my grandsons away from me for that reason, filling their heads with this rubbish, like you do with my only daughter-in-law, also. You don't know how much it hurts me not to see them."

Indira would hear this same argument from Uncle Ram whenever he came over for a visit, always accusing Nani of favouring her. She could not fathom how he could talk about her in such a mean way, but, then again, he was mean to other people, also. And he would hurt her Nani and make her angry. Unable to bear seeing her Nani so upset, she daringly said to him, "Leave my Nani alone, Uncle Ram!"

Uncle Ram's black glass-like eyes flashed with darker anger at Indira for speaking to him as such, and he shouted, "How dare you talk to me like that, you rude little wretch!"

And he reached to clout her. But Indira jumped out of the hammock in time to avoid it and ran in the backyard, with Uncle Ram chasing after her.

Nani dropped the fishing net she was knitting and grabbed the wild cane she always kept on hand whenever her son visited; the bamboo whip was the only thing he was afraid of, for he had developed that fear because he used to get licks from her late husband when he was a child. With the wild cane in hand, she ran after him and said, "Don't let me use this on you, boy!" Just the sight of the wild cane was enough to cause Uncle Ram to back off immediately, let alone, the threat. By this time, though, Indira had climbed up the tamarind tree and was hiding in the thick foliage, out of his sight.

And so started Uncle Ram's visit, with a row over Indira, as usual.

Once he settled down somewhat, he took a seat in the hammock, and while Nani resumed working on the cast-net, he told her that his wife and the boys had gone to visit his mother-in-law for a *Jhandi*, or a Hindu religious ceremony, something that Nani did not begrudge his mother-in-law, but only salted her wound. He went on to tell her that his rice field in Number 63 Village, where he lived, yielded a good crop. Then he complained about his rice field workers and his neighbours and just about everyone he knew. Nani just listened without saying much, for she did not want to get into another row with him. And that was how they communicated for the most part.

Nani did not know what made her son so cantankerous for she had brought him up with such love and good values. For whatever reason, when he grew up, he became mean and greedy and argumentative, a blackguard and belligerent drunk who always got into fights with others, and it broke her heart to see him turn out that way. She suffered day and night, in secret, thinking about him, and she constantly and fervently prayed and hoped that he would change his wicked ways someday and find peace and happiness. That was all she could do, for trying to talk to him proved futile. In her life, he was her cross to bear. She was manacled to a burden that she carried incessantly, that at times seemed too heavy and drained the strength from her, testing her faith and causing her to wonder why her God was not answering her prayers. She felt emasculated because she could not control her son's behaviour, but she still chose to have hope and kept on praying for him day after day, night after night, unfailingly.

Even though she loved him in spite of himself, she could barely stand his presence at times because of his bad attitude and ill temper, and she was happy when he said he would go fishing with Shazam today. Shazam came over just as she had finished knitting the cast-net for him, and she told him that she would settle the price later, knowing that her son would get upset with her because she would charge Shazam only for the twine and not for her labour. She thought the little money that Shazam worked for would be better used to feed his wife and children. She was happy to provide a means for him to feed his family by making the cast-net for him, something her son could not comprehend because of avarice and a lack of empathy for those in unfortunate situations.

When Uncle Ram left with Shazam to go fishing, around mid-afternoon, Indira came out from her hiding, and Nani told her not to be afraid of him for she will protect her. They both then carried on with the day. Nani had put some coconut fibre out the previous day to dry in the sun to make a single mattress, and Indira helped her to fetch them to the sitting room. Joan had previously sewed a sack for the mattress, and Nani and Indira stuffed it with the coconut fibre. Nani then showed Indira how to hand-stitch the opening of the sack, and they stitched it closed. They both then took the old mattress and discarded it in the backyard for burning later, and they dressed the bed frame with the new one, much to the delight of Indira. Nani then pottered around tidying the old house, and she daubed the mud stove with a clay wash and left it to dry.

By the time they were finished with the chores, early dusk had crept in, and the cantankerous Uncle Ram had returned with Shazam, and they were now at the bottom-house. They brought back a big catch, of live mullet and *bangamary* fishes in a large, round, straw basket, another basket of just shrimps, and a netted bag full of live *sheriga* crabs. Right away Uncle Ram started an argument with Shazam over the division of the catch, wanting to rob Shazam of his fair share. But, Nani, being the fair and generous person she was, took control of the situation and gave Shazam his fair share and some extras for all the little mouths he had to feed, and of what was left, she took a portion out for Pyari and Joan Williams, much to Uncle Ram's whining with greed. Nani, unable to tolerate his behaviour, sent him to the backyard. He reluctantly went, taking with him a bottle of rum, and he sat under a tree and started drinking and smoking and cursing.

Indira stayed close to Nani for protection. She went with her to deliver part of the catch to the neighbours, and, after, followed her as she took the rest upstairs to the kitchen to clean. The only good thing that Indira liked about Uncle Ram was that whenever he came for a visit he would go fishing and bring back a big catch, and she loved watching her Nani clean the catch.

She was now in her usual place, sitting on the peerah in the corner of the warm kitchen, which was faintly lit by the soft light of dusk streaming through the old wooden window, and the back door, which was wide open. She watched as her Nani emptied the netted bag of live crabs into a large aluminium tub, and she laughed as the crabs were trying to climb over the rim. Nani responded with laughter over the sweet laughter of the child, knowing how excited and happy this made Indira, to watch her clean a fresh catch. The excitement in the air was accompanied by the sad sound of Indian music playing on the radio somewhere in the village. As the music sounded, Indira looked on as Nani sat on the floor and shelled the crabs and cleaned the mullet and bangamary and shrimps, the freshness of the catch enticing and promising a real seafood feast.

When Nani finished cleaning the catch, she took it over to the dish sink, and as she was washing it, noticed that smoke was coming from Fazeela's kitchen window, which made her happy to know that Fazeela had plenty to cook for her children that day. She then went about lighting the mud stove and put some coconut oil in the carahee—frying pan to heat, and she fried the crab and shrimp and bangamary and mullet, the delicious fried smell of the seafood permeating the kitchen.

As soon as she was finished cooking, she set aside a good portion for her son for whenever he was ready to eat, and she put the rest of it in a large enamel bowl, and she and Indira sat on the peerahs on the floor and had a fried seafood feast, eating with their fingers.

By the time they were finished the scrumptious meal, the birds were flying in flocks across the sky, heading to their evening roosts. The moon and stars now started to appear, and Nani lit the kerosene oil lamp. By now, Uncle Ram had finished the whole bottle of rum, and Nani and Indira could hear him cursing at someone from the bottom-house.

Nani told Indira to remain upstairs and she took the lamp and rushed down to see what kind of trouble her son was making now. Indira peered out the window and saw Uncle Ram staggering to the gate, and saying to an innocent man passing by, "You wanna fight, man? You wanna fight?"

Well, Nani picked up the wild cane and went after him and gave him a good whack on his bottom, and she said, "You've come to my house to make trouble with the neighbours? I wouldn't tolerate such a thing. I want you to leave now! Go on home!"

"I'm not going anywhere," he said adamantly in a drunken drawl, too drunk now to even notice the wild cane. "I'm staying right here tonight."

"Then you will have to behave yourself and not fight with anyone," Nani said emphatically, and she hauled him to the hammock and laid him down, where he passed out immediately. With the kerosene oil lamp in hand, she looked down in pity at her handsome black-skinned son as he was sleeping, and in a voice encumbered with sorrow, she said, "I'm ashamed of you, son. I'm ashamed of your behaviour. You're such a disgrace to me." And Nani stood over her son and wept bitterly, the Guyanese proverb running through her mind as she did, *Nobody wants dutty powder*, meaning, people would not want anything to do with you if you have a dirty reputation. "Nobody respects you because of your bad reputation and nobody wants you around, son," she said. And Nani went on to say another Guyanese proverb, *Seven years nah too much fuh wash speck off ah bird's neck*, meaning, years may pass yet some people would not change their ways. Both proverbs Nani would often say to her incorrigible son.

While still in tears, Nani went and got a sheet and covered her son, and she lit a mosquito coil repellant and placed it nearby. She brought the food she had set aside for him and placed it on a stand beside the hammock, then she kissed him on the forehead and left him there to sleep for the night.

* * *

Early the following morning, Nani went to check on her son and found him still sleeping, and the plate of food that she had left for him was empty with just the fish bones remaining. Not too long after, he woke up, sober and crotchety, and had another row with her over Indira again, saying the same thing, that she favoured her. Nani decided to ignore him this time for she thought it was useless to argue with him. She wished that he would go home soon, especially, because she planned to have a bush-cook for later that day and had invited the neighbours and some friends and she was afraid that he would start drinking and fighting with them and cause her trouble. But when he learned about the bush-cook from her, he insisted on staying for it, and there was nothing she could do about that but live with the fear of him misbehaving and causing a disgrace to her, a fiasco that was imminent.

She warned him, though, not to be a nuisance but to behave himself when the folks arrive, but she knew her warning was just like pouring water on a duck's back; it just falls away without sinking in. But she warned him, nevertheless. And just to get him out of her sight, she asked him to go to a friend in the neighbouring village of Williamsburg to buy some ducks for the bush-cook, and she also made a list of things she wanted for him to purchase at the market. After he had breakfast, he left, and she was relieved that he would be gone for a while. Indira secretly wished he would not return for fear that he would make her Nani upset and cry again.

By now it was mid-morning, another hot and sunny day in the village of Rose Hall, and the villagers were busy with Saturday chores, washing and scrubbing and cleaning. Somewhere nearby a sheep was heard bleating and pigs were squealing and dogs were barking and fowlcocks were crowing, amongst the other sounds of animals and birds. And the happy voices of children playing in the dirt streets rose above.

Nani and Indira worked together and finished their Saturday chores, making the old house spic and span. Nani

167

then started preparing some sweet and savoury treats for the neighbours and friends she expected at the bush-cook, frying plantains and *channa*—chick peas, and making fudge and sugar cakes. The men she invited to the bush-cook would be doing the cooking, and all she had to do was prepare the sight for it. She and Indira went in the backyard and set up some stones and wood under the big tamarind tree, and they arranged a small table with dishes and spices and condiments, and spread some rice bags on the ground for people to sit on.

They then bathed and got dressed. Nani got out her crisp, white headkerchief and wore it with a fresh, floral polyester dress and, as usual, she wore no shoes. She fixed Indira's curls and dressed her in a pink cotton dress, and she made sure Indira wore a pair of slippers. They both then went down to the bottom-house, where Solomon and Rani were laying around on the smooth earthen ground, and they waited in the hammock for the neighbours and friends to arrive for the bush-cook.

Shortly after one o'clock, the first to arrive was Francine, and she brought Jacko the monkey with her. "Good afternoon," she greeted Nani and gave her a kiss, then she went over and hugged Indira, and said, "I've brought my skipping rope. Let's go and play." Indira got her skipping rope, also, and the two began skipping barefooted on the earthen ground of the bottom-house, talking as they did about the pig roast that Dr. Ramesh had just for Francine last week, while Nani looked on and smiled as Jacko jumped around and chattered.

George and Joan Williams arrived soon after, bringing a bunch of sugarcane and a cutlass to chop them up with.

168

After they greeted Nani, George turned to Indira and pinched her cheek and said, "Did you hear the story about the talking donkey?" And he went about amusing the girls with his funny stories and made them laugh their little heads off.

Next came the gregarious Mr. Jackson, who came through the gate bringing a radio and a couple of bottles of rum, and he laughed out loudly and said, "Good afternoon to you all! Good afternoon! We're going to play music and cook and eat and drink and be merry today!" Indira was quick to notice that he was not wearing his ugly green uniform and big boots today but was in casual clothes and sandals, not that it mattered anymore, because she was no longer afraid of his soldier's attire, nor, his loud voice, and she was happy to see him.

Fazeela came over next, carrying a cute, curly-haired baby boy in her arms, her seventh child whom she had given birth to just a week ago. Shazam followed, with the baby girl on his hip, and the other five children trailed behind him. He brought along cards and dominoes, and some fresh corns, and he happily said, "I'll roast the corns for us to eat right away, and today my children will eat well."

Next came Mrs. Surjeet, and she brought a big bottle of ginger beer and a *black cake*—made from aged, rum-soaked dried fruits. She had not seen Nani for a couple of weeks because she had not been to the market to sell, and she called Nani aside to explain the exciting reason why that was so. Apparently, her husband had become a changed man. He found religion and started going to church and had given up his vices, and had become almost as righteous as the God he now worshipped, a miracle that seemed too good to be true, but it was. No more drinking illegal spirits at the backdam, instead, he spent his days working to take care of her and support the family, so she now stayed at home and took care of the children. Mrs. Surjeet's fair skin glowed as she talked about her husband's transformation and all the loving he was now giving her. The news came as a pleasant surprise to Nani, and she could not be happier for her friend. The two stayed in a corner and enthused over it, Nani now thinking that there was a chance that her wayward son could also change someday.

Finally to arrive, was Pyari, wearing her famous gold nose ring and red headkerchief. She dropped off a bottle of rum and said she had an errand to run in the village and will be back a little later, and she took off in a hurry.

Now that everyone was there, except for Pyari and Uncle Ram, Nani gathered the children and women at the bottom-house and spread a few rice bags for them to sit on, and she served up the treats she had made, giving the children candies and bubble gum she had purchased for them, also. The men, Mr. Jackson, George Williams, and Shazam went in the backyard, where Nani had set up the stones and wood under the great tamarind tree for the bush-cook, and while they waited for Uncle Ram to return with the ducks, Mr. Jackson tuned in to the radio and played an eclectic mix of music, from reggae, calypso, Indian, and country. As the music was playing, the men poured themselves some rum, then lit a fire and put on a grid and roasted the corns. When the corns were finished roasting, the men brought them to the bottom-house, and everyone, particularly the children, had a feast of roasted corns and melted butter. George Williams then got the cutlass and cut up the sugarcane into small sticks, and everyone sat around chewing on them. After, Nani got out her wooden tub ice cream maker and she hand-cranked a tub of ice cream, much to the children's delight.

As the children sat around indulging in the delectable treats, the roaring engine of an aeroplane was suddenly heard, and everyone rushed to look up at the clear blue sky to see the silver plane glistening in the bright sunshine as it was flying by. The excited children waved at it, thinking the people in the aeroplane could see them down below. After that bit of excitement, Mr. Jackson amused the children, particularly, Indira, when, looking awkward with his big self, he climbed the coconut tree in the backyard to pick some green coconuts. George Williams collected the coconuts and chopped off the tops with a cutlas and gave them to the children to drink the sweet coconut water to quench their thirst, and he distributed some to the ladies who were still gathered at the bottom-house.

The exuberant children then went about climbing the fruit trees and playing hide-and-seek in the yard. After, they picked sour gooseberries and ate them with salt and hot pepper sauce. Indira showed them the cotton tree that was growing in the very back of the yard, then they went about chasing after the butterflies and birds. They lingered by the pond for a while and observed the hassars and tilapias splashing about in the sun-sparkled water, and then stopped to peer through a crack in the fowl coop, amusing themselves with watching the chickens laying eggs.

Suddenly, Francine realised that Jacko the monkey was missing, and a frantic search for him ensued. The elders joined the children and they all looked for Jacko in the house and in the fowl coop and in the trees, but he was nowhere to be found. George Williams had a hunch Jacko was up to some kind of monkey business, and he was absolutely right in thinking so.

When Jacko was wandering around the yard earlier, he spotted a banana tree in Pyari's yard, and he jumped over the paling and climbed up the tree to pick a banana. Pyari had gone out and left her sitting room window wide open, and from the tree top Jacko saw Raj the parrot in a cage on top of a table, and he abandoned the banana and snuck into Pyari's house to see the parrot.

Raj met him with a cold stare, and exclaimed, "Intruder! Intruder! Intruder!"

Jacko, thinking Raj was saying something friendly to him, went over to the cage and stuck his finger in, and Raj pecked him. Well, Jacko quickly got the hint that Raj was not being friendly, so he began to ignore him and went about exploring Pyari's house. He opened this drawer and that one then found Pyari's liquor cabinet. He began opening one bottle of liquor after the other, tasting each, and he spitted out the liquor because of the pungent taste. He then found a bottle of liqueur that tasted sweet, and he guzzled down half the bottle.

Raj, who was keenly eyeing him all this time, called out, "Thief! Thief! Thief!"

Jacko continued to ignore him, now too busy enjoying the sweet taste of the liqueur, and soon he became tipsy and started to prance around with the bottle in his hand.

"You rotten drunk!" Raj yelled, for Raj had seen many drunks at Pyari's house, playing the fool, just like Jacko was, and Pyari would call them so.

Jacko continued to pay him no mind. Looking around, he found a cigar laying on the table, and he began chewing on it. And he continued to prance around, making a clown of himself in front of Raj.

Raj did not find his drunken act amusing in the least bit, and he fluttered his wings and started cursing Jacko to the top of his voice, calling him so and so, and he shouted, "Get your backside out of here! Get your backside out of here! Get your backside out of here!" The same thing Pyari would say to her drunk buddies.

Jacko, now finding Raj to be annoying, flapped his arms about in trying to imitate Raj, and he jeered Raj, babbling some monkey talk, while Raj continued to curse him, even louder now.

The two of them became so loud that Francine and the others heard the commotion and rushed over to gather in Pyari's yard. Pyari, who had just arrived back home and heard Raj calling out, "Thief! Thief! Thief!" rushed upstairs and caught Jacko red-handed, stealing another bottle of liqueur and drinking it, with her cigar in his hand. She chased him around the house to catch him, but he clutched the bottle and cigar tightly and jumped out the window and onto the corrugated zinc roof of her house. There he began monkeying around, causing everyone to stare up at his drunken antics.

"Come down, Jacko," Francine pleaded with him repeatedly, but he refused to do so.

All the others tried coaxing him down but to no avail. George Williams even got a banana to entice him, but Jacko stood on the roof drinking liqueur and chewing cigar and dancing around, continuing to make a clown of himself, seeming to enjoy the attention from the children who were now laughing at him. The news that a drunk monkey was on Pyari's rooftop spread down the street like wildfire, and others from the village soon gathered in front of Pyari's yard to witness the spectacle.

The spectators were completely enthralled by the scene as they watched and waited for Jacko to come down. After waiting for a while and Jacko still would not climb down, George Williams decided that he would just have to go up and get him, so he got a ladder and situated it on Pyari's verandah and jumped up onto the roof. Trying to catch a drunk monkey on a rooftop was not an easy thing to do. George chased him from one end of the roof to the next but he could not catch him. Just when George was about to give up, Jacko stopped to take another swig of liqueur and it was then that George grabbed him, much to the cheers of the spectators. He took away the bottle of liqueur and cigar from him and brought him down, and Raj cursed him up some more before George took him home and put him in his cage to avoid further trouble between the two of them.

Jacko and Uncle Ram could have been drinking buddies, for as soon as Uncle Ram returned with the ducks for the bush-cook he started drinking, and Uncle Ram could have been a partner to Raj for he cursed the same way. And being the crotchety nuisance he was, he began picking on Indira and the other children who were now playing under the fruit trees in the shade from the sun.

"Think I've forgotten how you were disrespectful to me yesterday?" he said to Indira, referring to when Indira had told him to leave Nani alone, and he reached to clout her. Indira ran away, and he then turned to Francine and said, "Your hair looks all puffed up and awful. Go home and comb it." Then he turned to Fazeela's children and said, "Why aren't you wearing any shoes? Go home and dress properly instead of wearing those ragged clothes." And he bullied the children and took their candies and bubble gum and sugarcane sticks away from them, badgering them and dampening their exuberance.

Indira went and told Nani that Uncle Ram was bothering them. Nani immediately came to the children's aid, once again seized by a rush of anger that only her son could bring out in her, and she lost her temper and said, "You brute! Stop troubling the children or I'll get the wild cane!" At the mention of the wild cane, Uncle Ram withdrew, cursing as he did and accusing Nani of now favouring the children.

Nani assuaged the children by giving them more candies, and she kept them away from her son and gathered them under the tamarind tree to watch the bush-cook, which was now underway. A pot of rice had just finished cooking and a big pot of water was boiling on the stones over the fire, for use of stripping the feathers off the ducks.

The three fat ducks were now ready to be plucked, and Nani placed them in a large aluminium tub and poured the boiling water over them, and she got the children to assist in plucking the feathers. The men then put a metal grid over the fire and roasted the ducks' skin, the fat sizzling and letting out a mouth-watering aroma in the air. After the skin was roasted nice and brown, Shazam got a board and chopped up the fresh meat and washed it by the pipe at the bottom of the backstairs, and he brought it back under the tamarind tree to be curried.

It was past mid-afternoon by now, and the heat from the bush-cook fire only intensified the tropical temperature. The children fanned themselves with pieces of folded paper as they sat around on the rice bags watching the men curry the ducks as they were chatting and cracking jokes and playing music and drinking. While the duck meat was now boiling, emitting a bubbling sound and releasing wisps of delicious piquant spices, Pyari came over and joined the gathering. She opened a bottle of rum and shared it with the men, while Nani, Joan, Fazeela, and Mrs. Surjeet were busy catching up on the village gossip, Mrs. Surjeet euphorically sharing the miraculous news about her husband's transformation.

All of a sudden, Uncle Ram was heard cursing out loudly. Nani and the children ran to the bottom-house to see what the palaver was all about, and there was Uncle Ram sitting on Solomon and fighting with the donkey, saying, "You dumb mule! Bloody jackass! Go, jackass, go!" And he hauled Solomon's ears and beat him with a stick. Solomon did not move but just stood there. And Indira and the other children looked on silently, too scared to say anything.

"Leave the donkey alone!" Nani yelled at him. "Get off my donkey right now, I say!"

Uncle Ram ignored Nani, and he continued to shout at Solomon, saying, "You stubborn jackass! Move, I say. Go, donkey, go!" And he lashed the donkey again.

Well, Solomon was not used to this kind of brutal treatment, so when Uncle Ram lashed him again, he bucked and Uncle Ram slid off the donkey's ass, and as he was getting back up, cursing and swearing as he did, Solomon let out a loud fart in his face. The children burst out laughing, and said, "The donkey farted on Uncle Ram! The donkey farted on Uncle Ram!" Nani, in spite of trying to refrain, also started laughing. Solomon grinned and showed his big white teeth, also. Then Rani the cow got in on the action and started chasing Uncle Ram around to butt him. The children laughed even louder as Uncle Ram cowardly ran for his life, cursing and swearing as he did, his handsome dark face distorted with fury. Rani chased him all the way to the gate, and Uncle Ram opened the gate and fled out of fear and embarrassment, and Rani stood by the gate and guarded it.

After the deep belly laughter from the children subsided, the bush-cook resumed without Uncle Ram, much to Nani and the children's relief. Soon the hot and scrumptious curried duck was ready and everyone sat on a rice bag and ate heartily out of a calabash, under the great tamarind tree. The men and Pyari then drank more and played dominoes and cards, and when dusk began to fall and the birds were heading to their evening roosts, everyone went home.

It was not until late in the night that Uncle Ram returned, from the rum shop where he had been drinking even more, and he was now too drunk to have a row with Nani and fell asleep again in the hammock. Nani left him some food again and covered him with a sheet and lit a mosquito coil beside him. And she sat on the peerah beside

177

him for a long while, silently praying that he would change his bad ways, and she wept again.

At the crowing of the fowlcocks, Uncle Ram woke at the same time Indira usually did, and Indira heard him coughing and went by the sitting room window and looked out. In the dark shadows of the early morning, she saw him leaving through the gate, and though she was relieved to see him go, a certain sadness took hold of her to see him leave this way, for she knew how much her Nani loved him, and when Nani wakes up and finds him gone she will stand by the mud stove and, while cooking, she would weep.

Indira watched as he walked up the street and disappeared in the darkness of the morning. She then closed the window and went back to the bedroom and sat by the window overlooking the backyard, waiting there for Nani to wake up.

PART TWO

8

A Day At Laliwa's

Many, many full moons had gone by, the year was now 1976, and Rose Hall Village had since risen to the status of a small town. It was now very early on a Saturday morning, around dawn, and it was warm and raining heavily, the raindrops like fat drops of liquid crystal beating down hard on the corrugated zinc roof of Nani's old greenheart wood house.

Nani was sitting on the peerah in the kitchen looking at fifteen-year-old Indira as the smoke from the mud stove scattered about her while she was leaning against the side of the old wooden kitchen window, quietly watching as the rain was falling copiously on the trees tops in the backyard. Nani smiled and silently admired her in her pink cotton dress that accentuated her blossoming young figure and light golden-brown skin, her gaze falling on her innocent, oval-shaped face as a few strands of her curly, black hair, tossed about by he wind, escaped the clutch of her bun and played about her velvet-smooth cheeks, blowing across her mysteriously attractive dark eyes. Nani could not believe that the child was now a beautiful young woman.

So many things had happened over the last ten years since Indira had grown up: Indira had long finished kindergarten and elementary schooling, and she was expected to commence Fifth Form the next term, which would be her last year in high school; Grandmother Shanti had passed away; Dr. Ramesh had retired and had grown older with grief over his late wife; old age had also caught up with Nani and she was now dim-sighted, and with age also came debility, aches and pains, and her inability to work like she used to. As she deteriorated over the last few years, Indira had gradually assumed most of her responsibilities, cleaning, cooking, and gardening, plowing the earth and planting seeds for their livelihood.

As Nani sat there looking at Indira, she wondered where the waves of life would take the young woman, what shore she would be washed up on, a rocky or smooth one, but she could not predict her fate. All she could do was ride the waves of life with her for now and try and steer her in the right direction.

Bringing her attention to her present situation now, she said to Indira, "I hope the rain stops soon so I can go to the market to sell my produce."

Indira looked up at the ominous dark clouds in the firmament, and she responded, "Doesn't look like it would stop anytime soon, Nani." She had loaded the donkey-cart with produce the day before, and if the deluge of rain prevented Nani from going to the market today, the produce would not be as fresh by Monday, the next time Nani was scheduled to go to the market, and that meant that Nani would not be able to sell much of it. They could not wait until next week, though, for they needed money immediately for bare necessities. Very little was put away for a rainy day, because Nani had given away a lot of her fruits, vegetables, eggs, and chickens to the less fortunate, instead of selling them and making some extra money. So Indira thought she would have to do something right away.

She could not bear the thought of her old Nani struggling in the rain with the donkey-cart in the muddy streets to go to the market, so she said, "If the rain continues to fall then I will take the produce to the market myself and sell it."

"No, child, I will never let you sell at the market," Nani objected. "Your grandfather, Dr. Ramesh, is paying for your education so you can someday work at the bank. With whatever little strength I have left in my old body, I will go to the market and sell, in   sunshine or in rain, for it is not fitting for a young, educated woman to do so."

"I'm not ashamed to be seen selling at the market," Indira said, and widening her long-lashed black eyes, added, "What's going to happen if you were to get sick and can't do it? Then I will have to do so or we wouldn't have money to live on, and I wouldn't have money to take care of you."

"You need not worry your pretty head, child, for your grandfather and I have discussed such a situation," Nani said calmly with the assurance that a greater power, her God, would provide and take care of her in some way, through others. "Dr. Ramesh will see to it that you are well taken care of should anything unfortunate happens to me, and he has promised to take care of me, also. God bless him."

Indira sighed with a sense of relief, not for herself so much as it was for Nani, for as she grew and watched her Nani get older by the year, she would often times worry about her. "Okay," she said to Nani and smiled, her dimples even more conspicuous now that she was grown up. "I'm glad that Grandpa has offered to help in the event of an unfortunate situation. I should have known that he would.

But at the moment you're not sick and I wouldn't want to go to Grandpa to ask for money because, unfortunately, it's raining, so then let's make a compromise. If it continues to rain, I'll drive the donkey-cart and take you to the new market and set you up at a stall, and you do the selling while I do the shopping."

"I will not let my granddaughter be seen driving a donkey-cart!" Nani objected again, adamantly.

"But why, Nani?"

"As I said to you before, because it's not proper for a young, educated woman to do so. The people in our town would start wagging their tongues and that would hurt your character. Now, no more talk about driving the donkey-cart or selling at the market."

Indira really did not care about what anyone had to say about her driving a donkey-cart or selling at the market, for she had long conquered pride through Nani's own teachings and found no shame in providing for both Nani and herself in an honest way; she thought of the situation as just helping out Nani on a rainy day. She understood, though, Nani's concern to protect her reputation as a young woman. But she decided not to expostulate with her any further, for Nani could be as stubborn as Solomon the donkey at times.

"How did you do in your exams this week?" Nani asked Indira, intentionally changing the subject.

"It was difficult but I did my best and I'm feeling good about it," Indira replied confidently, for she had been consistent with high marks ever since she started high school.

"You sure make me proud of you," Nani said and smiled, flashing her gold teeth. "And so is your Grandfather."

"I'm glad school is closed now until September, though," Indira laughed and said, "I'm glad to have a break from it. Oh, by the way, I made plans with Francine for us to visit Laliwa today. As soon as I'm finished with my chores, we'll leave."

"Okay, child," Nani said, and cautioned, "Just make sure you're not out too late."

The enormous raindrops were pounding the zinc roof even harder now and the wicked wind was threatening to rip it off as the thunder crashed ferociously and the lightening flashed across the dark and angry sky. The fresh, earthy breeze forced its way in through the open window into the dim kitchen, fanning the flames of the mud stove and making the place warmer than it was as Indira was now cooking breakfast, the comforting smell of the roti in ghee and fried saltfish and tomatoes filling the air and mingling with the aroma of a pot of coco tea. Through the smoke-shrouded room, Nani watched silently as she was cooking and singing an Indian love song, and she thought that Indira could be any one of the film stars from India whom she so adored, she was so attractive. But she knew the girl had no desires for fame or fortune. There were those who thought that life as it was for her was a misfortune, having to live in a little, old house down by the river, and farm for a living. But Indira was content living in her simple and peaceful world, grateful for the little things in life; values that, no doubt, she learned from her, Nani thought. Nani could not help but smiling when she thought of how Indira would light up whenever she would buy her a little bottle of perfume or a bottle of chameli body lotion, which she would use unfailingly to make her skin soft and glowing and smelling sweet. It did not take much to make Indira happy, she loved laughing, and hearing her sweet laughter was like the sound of the sitar to Nani's ears.

As Nani watched her, she was reminded of her deceased daughter, Geeta. Now that Indira was all grown up, she resembled her late mother even more so. She looked like her, talked like her, laughed like her, even her gait and gestures were just like hers. Grief took hold of Nani at the thought, jabbing at her heart and threatening painful tears which she managed to restrain. The death of her young daughter was the kind of hurt that would never go away, that she carried with her ever since Geeta's tragic death in a car crash. But she now took some comfort in Indira; a reincarnation of Geeta it seemed like.

While Nani was lost in thoughts, Indira finished cooking, and then she sat down with Nani for breakfast, and they ate while it continued to rain and thunder outside. When they were finished, Nani said to Indira, "Make us another cup of coco tea, child, for it looks like we'll have to sit this storm out for a while."

Indira got the tin of cocoa powder and made another pot of tea, adding extra thick, fresh milk that she had milked from Rani just that morning, and she poured Nani another cup as Nani remained seated on the peerah, and she poured herself a cup and resumed her seat at the table. As they sipped the coco tea from the enamel cups, they listened to the rain as the embers in the mud stove burned slowly, warming the cozy kitchen.

186

Loving the company of her orphaned granddaughter, Nani found herself thinking about her once again and felt blessed that Indira was such a good-natured, congenial young woman. She took partial credit for the way Indira turned out, for she taught her well over the years, impressing her wisdom and values upon her. She realised, though, that she was too strict with her sometimes, and she justified that as being for Indira's own good. But, luckily, Indira grew to understand that Nani was just being protective of her. Indira would sometimes just laugh at the absurdity of her strictness in attempting to keep her from becoming depraved; like prohibiting her from listening to love songs, or wear makeup, or wear sleeveless dresses or pants, and preventing her from going to the matinée. She even prevented Indira from going barefoot anywhere, when she went everywhere in her bare feet. Indira would never argue with her out of respect over the things she wanted her to desist from, though being as fallible as a typical teenager but not as pliable, Indira would listen to love songs behind Nani's back, and paint her nails when she was out with her friends, and she would sneak off to the matinée with Francine and Laliwa to look at Indian movies. Nani would catch her sometimes, but she never fussed with her, for Nani, being pragmatic, was sagacious enough to know that her beliefs or guidelines were preposterous at times and that Indira was just a curious young woman fascinated with life, as she had been in her younger years.

The relationship between Nani and Indira evolved over the years to being one of love and respect. Nani counselled the young woman on the rudimentary ways of the world, the heart, and on the intimate subject of man and love, and like a good protégé, Indira listened and learned from the wise old woman.

"I will tell you something about the world out there, child," Nani said. "You have been fortunate in that you have so far been exposed to the good of life, but there is a lot more to the world than what meets your eye. There is good and bad in it, or light and darkness, heaven and hell, sickness and wellness, suffering and gladness. The world is like a giant pot where everything is thrown in it, love and sex, hate, anger, malice, happiness, sadness, pain, loneliness, restlessness, jealousy, greed, grief, violence, crime, a pot of corruption, if I may say. How does one maintain focus and calm with so much happening all around?"

"Tell me, Nani," Indira said, trying to picture the convoluted portrait of a world she did not know.

"It all has to do with the heart. The naked heart is a sad and lonely place to be, and it's like a restless ocean, tossing and turning. Out of the heart springs all of the things that I mentioned. One can temporarily appease the heart with happiness through wealth, things, food, drinks, music, dance, lovers, even drugs, but the heart will return to being sad and lonely and restless, and it will resort to all manner of recklessness and harm the soul."

"Where are you going with this, Nani?" Indira asked, trying to decipher what Nani was saying.

"What is it that you and I have in common, child?"

Indira deliberated for a moment then answered, "Peace."

"You're right. The only way to please the heart and calm its restlessness is to constantly seek peace. Wealth cannot do this, greed cannot do this, hate cannot do this, love

188

cannot do this because it hurts to love sometimes, anger certainly cannot do this, only peace can. And what is peace in this sense? It is simply the calming of the mind. If for one moment one takes his hands off the reins of peace, the heart goes back to being sad and lonely and restless, resulting in recklessness."

Indira was quiet for a moment, trying to assimilate what Nani had just said, then it became clear to Indira that on this rainy day that Nani had taken her hands off the reins of peace, for at the moment sadness and loneliness and a restlessness had come upon her heart, as seen through her contorted countenance.

"I'll now tell you about my affair with your Nana Amar," Nani said, sipping on her hot cup of coco, while looking out the window at the rain falling.

Indira instinctively knew now where Nani was heading. It seemed that only on rainy days that Nani would talk about her late husband for it was obvious that she missed him at those times. She pulled up a peerah and sat beside her, intrigued by the subject of an affair, and, attempting to assuage Nani's feelings, and commiserate with her, she said, "I'd love to hear about it, Nani, go on and tell me all about it if this would take away the sadness and loneliness and restlessness of your heart and bring you happiness for the moment." And she sipped on her hot cup of coco and waited for Nani to begin her story.

Nani quickly found solace in her granddaughter and a glitter of happiness now shone in her eyes as she began by saying, "Your Nana was a local farmer from the village who used to come and watch me perform on stage when I was a young woman of only sixteen. He came up to me one night after I had danced and told me that he loved me. Well, many men had professed to love me at that time and I quickly learned that it was my body they loved, so I put your Nana to the test and told him to prove his love for me."

"You made it hard on Grandpa, Nani," Indira said, "poor Nana."

"Well, I had to do so, my child," Nani said, "for I wanted to make sure that he really loved me like he said he did." For a moment Nani's dim eyes seemed faraway, pensive, lost in thoughts of the only man she had ever loved, and then she continued with saying, "And so your Nana came night after night trying to woo me and prove his love by showering me with food and flowers and gifts." She paused now and chuckled before saying, "The first night after I told him to prove his love for me, he brought me a fowlcock to cook and a bag of rice from his farm, and a basket of *sapodilla, simitoo, padoo,* and *jamun* fruits from his garden. The second night he brought me a guinea pig for a pet. The third night he brought me a Canje Pheasant, and on the fourth, he brought me a pink Victoria Regia Lily. By the end of that week, he brought me some silk fabric to make a sari and he gave me a pair of gold bangles. Your Nana thought that all his gifts proved that he loved me. Well, I refused him and told him that he hadn't proven a damn thing but had mistaken his attraction to me for love."

"I don't understand, Nani," Indira said. "When a man brings a woman flowers and gifts, doesn't that show that he loves her?"

"Not necessarily," Nani answered. "That only proved to me that he wanted to buy me over!"

"I see," Indira said. "And what happened then?"

"Your Nana was greatly insulted that I refused him. I hurt his pride and he disappeared for a while. I thought I would never see him again, but one day he returned and just brought himself, and he took me aside and admitted to me that he was merely attracted to me, and that he did not know me, and how could he love me if he did not know me? You see, he came to his senses!" Indira laughed at the term Nani used, and Nani laughed over the sweetness of the young girl's laughter, then Nani continued with saying, "And from then on he took the time to get to know me, my likes and dislikes and passions and desires, and he soon fell in love for real after knowing me. And through that I got to know him, and I started falling in love with him for the man he was. I learned that he was a sincere and decent man. He promised to love and respect and take care of me, and he was true to his promises, for when we had gotten married he treated me with utmost respect, and he took care of me in health and illness, and he loved me so dearly up until he died of a heart attack." Tears then fell from Nani's eyes for she missed her late husband.

Indira brushed away the tears that had welled up in her own eyes, for she was moved by Nani's poignant tears of sadness, and she said, "Oh, Nani, what a beautiful love story that is."

Nani wiped away her tears with the back of her hand then, with much solemnity, said, "The lesson to learn here, my child, is to not mistake attraction for love. Get to know someone before you speak of love, for you cannot truly love someone if you don't know him. And if someone professes to love you then let him prove it, only then give your heart to him. Then accept him in your heart and zip up your heart and let no other man enter. I'm telling you these things because you're now at the age when boys will show interest in you, my dear child, and I don't want to see you end up in a wrong situation and get hurt and ruin your reputation and life. And when you marry, marry someone who works at the bank."

Indira laughed again, at the latter, finding it funny that Nani wanted for her to specifically marry a bank employee, that was obviously important to her. Then she thought of all the boys in school who, with their silver tongues, professed with flowery words to love her. She understood now that their feelings were mere attraction and not love, for none of them really knew her. "Thank you for making sense of it all. I'll make sure to take your advice," she said, and laughed again when she added, "And, hopefully, I'll marry someone who works at the bank." She then leaned over and hugged the old woman and kissed her forehead, and she whispered, "I love you so dearly, Nani."

"I love you, too, child, more than you'll ever know," Nani said, and added, "And, Indira, thank you for everything."

"For what, Nani?" Indira asked as she looked into the faded brown eyes of her Nani.

"Thank you for bringing me out of that sad and lonely and restless place of my heart. Thank you for being a good granddaughter. And for helping me to clean and cook and work in the garden, and, especially, for taking such good care of me."

Indira reached for Nani's old, withered hand and kissed it, and said, "I will take care of you as long as I can, Nani, just like you have taken care of me for so many years."

With that Nani reached into her dress pocket and pulled out her green cloth money bag and untied the string, and she took out the few dollars she had in it and said to Indira, "Take this pocket money and go to the store sometime and buy yourself something nice, child, maybe a bottle of sweet chameli lotion."

Indira took the paltry sum of money and put it back into Nani's old money bag for she knew that was all the money Nani had, and she said, "If you do well at the market today, then you can give me some pocket money. Save the few dollars for now." She then looked out the window and noticed that the rain had subsided, though the sky remained dark and heavy. "I don't know how long the rain would stop for," she said, dreading the thought of Nani going out in that weather.

Nani put on her faded brown headkerchief and, with determination, said, "I will take a chance of leaving now. Come, child, help me down the stairs."

Indira did not try to stop her this time for she knew it was useless, and she took Nani by the hand and helped her down the backstairs and onto the donkey-cart.

As Solomon was hauling the loaded donkey-cart on the muddy pathway through the ragged gate, Nani looked back and said to Indira, "I hope you and Francine have a nice visit with Laliwa. And don't be too late, child. Make sure you come home before nightfall."

"I will," Indira promised, and she stood by the gate and watched as Solomon hauled the donkey-cart down the muddy street and disappeared. She then spent the rest of the morning cleaning and scrubbing the old house, and she daubed the mud stove with a clay wash. After, she fed the chickens in the fowl coop and picked up the freshly laid eggs, and she fed the fishes in the pond, and then she daubed the earthen ground of the bottom-house and left it to dry. She then went and bathed and creamed her skin with her favourite chameli lotion and got dressed in a floral cotton dress, with black background and small pink flowers, which Joan Williams had sewn for her. And she waited for Francine to arrive.

Francine came over shortly after. She had also grown into a lovely young woman with an attractive figure and soft brown skin. She was sporting a big Afro hairstyle, that accentuated her beautiful baby face and big, brown eyes and full lips, and was wearing a tiger-patterned polyester dress. Over the years, she and Indira stayed best friends, and she was now in the same class in high school as Indira and, for that matter, so were Laliwa, Afonso and Ling, all except for Sally. Sally had moved to England upon the demise of her mother; her father sent her there to live with her Aunt, his sister, for an undetermined time after Sally expressed the desire to do so, as was her childhood dream, particularly, to get to know her family there and to see the Queen.

Indira and Francine were both looking forward to visiting Laliwa, and they wasted no time in trying to get to her home despite the fact that it started raining heavily again and they had to walk through the muddy streets in their slippers and fight to hold on to their umbrellas in the brisk wind. On the way, they passed children frolicking in the rain in their yards, some naked and others clothed, euphorically jumping up and down in barrels of rain water and on the muddy ground and the grass. Laliwa's little home on stilts was a few streets away from Nani's house and was situated right opposite a high school, and she was standing on the front steps with an umbrella in hand, anxiously awaiting the arrival of her school friends.

Laliwa had long since grown out of some of her shyness and had grown up to be a petite young woman, with slanted eyes, and cheek bones more pronounced. Her complexion was now more of an olive tone, lovely against the pale peach cotton dress she was wearing, and she still wore her silky black hair in pigtails on both sides of her head, like she did in kindergarten. She descended from the Arawak Amerindian tribe and had two other siblings, both boys younger than her, and they lived a poor life with her parents, for her father worked as a rice field worker and her mother weaved baskets for a living. Though they struggled to make ends meet, Laliwa always wore a smile, for she was a contented young woman who thought there were others in the world who were less fortunate than her, who did not even have a home to live in.

And there she was standing on the front steps of her home, smiling in the rain as she was looking up the street for her friends. When she saw them coming she rushed to the gate and let them in. The girls washed their feet and muddy slippers by the pipe at the bottom of the stairs before she led them upstairs.

Laliwa's humble abode was just a two-bedroom, old wooden stilted house, unlike the rounded thatched huts other Arawaks lived in along the rivers. The dim sitting room had a couple of wooden chairs, a cotton hammock and a mat made of banana leaves, where her two brothers slept, respectively. On a wall was a faded black and white photograph of her people, in which the men were dressed only in loincloths and the women were bare-breasted in just diminutive skirts, the males in feather headdresses and females in strands of shell necklaces, with some of their faces and bodies painted. The other photograph beside that one, depicted a scene of the Pomeroon River, long inhabited by the Arawaks, and the map of Guyana tacked beside it, was titled 'Guyana, Land Of Many Waters', the name and meaning as derived from the Amerindians. On a shelf were art and crafts—painted ceramics and wood carvings—and religious artefacts made of stone, as well as, a bow, an arrow, and a spear. And, in a corner of the room was a decrepit dugout canoe now used as storage.

The beating of a drum called Indira and Francine's attention to Laliwa's father, who was sitting in a room in front of wood-carved gods, dressed in the Arawaks' traditional garb of only a loincloth and feather headdress. He had been a shaman in his younger years when he used to live down by the Corentyne River, and he still communicated with the world of benevolent and malevolent spirits, consulting the gods for advice and healing. He had some *piwari* earlier and appeared in an inebriated, trance-like state and did not take notice of the girls at all.

Laliwa's mother, who was in western attire and only spoke the *Lokono* language, briefly emerged from the kitchen and greeted the girls with just a broad smile, then she hurried back in the kitchen and went about finishing the cassava bread and pepperpot she was cooking on a mud stove. Laliwa's two younger brothers were sitting on the bare wooden floor in the kitchen, helping her mother to weave baskets to sell.

When Laliwa's mother finished cooking, she offered Indira and Francine some pepperpot and cassava bread, though there was barely enough for the family. The girls sat on the kitchen floor and ate with Laliwa and her family, and after they were done, Laliwa took the girls to her bedroom, a very tiny space with a single coconut fibre mattress bed, a small mirror on the wall, and a clothes-horse in a corner.

"The school is having their Fifth Form class party today," Laliwa said to her friends as she opened the old wooden window overlooking the school, which was a flat, u-shaped wooden building, unpainted, with corrugated zinc roofing, the upper half of the building without walls and wide open so that one could clearly see inside.

"I wish it was us celebrating our end of high school," Francine said as the three of them took their seats at the edge of Laliwa's bed, propping their hands on the window sill and looking over at the flurry of activities taking place in the section of the school building facing them.

"I know you don't mean that, Francine, because we do have too much fun at school and I know you will be sad for it to end," Laliwa said.

"What I really meant to say is that I wish I was part of the celebration that's going on right now at the school."

"We have only one more year to go," Indira said. "Before you know it, we'll be having our Fifth Form class party at our school."

The girls were all too excited to sit there and watch as the preparations for the Fifth Form class party were underway, especially, Indira, who so far had lived a sheltered life, for Nani kept her away from what she called 'worldly social functions', school parties being classified as such, also. Indira did not particularly care to attend these worldly social functions, but she was curious about the goings-on at these parties.

As the scene unfolded in front of them, the rain and the hot temperature added a certain mystery and enchantment to the amorous ambiance of the day. Loudspeakers spouted out the melancholic sound of the sitar and the sweet voice of Lata Mangeshkar, that permeated the rainy tropical air as a few students and teachers were busy rearranging the classrooms and decorating the place for the party. With the upper part of the school building being without walls and wide open, the zinc roof held up by posts, the girls could clearly see as they crisscrossed and strung colourful crepe paper streamers from one post to the other, and they blew up bunches of balloons and tied them to the posts, placing on each table a vase with straw pompom flowers and flowers made of colourful nylons and wire. In one section, they set up a stage, and a few young men started practising on the *steel pans* and fine-tuning their guitars for special performances.

In the shelter of a tent in the schoolyard were little old ladies from the town lending their hands in cooking. Some were mixing spices and others were chopping up fresh meats and picking spoiled grains from large bowls of rice, while huge iron pots set over stones were heating up over flames from chopped wood. And as they began cooking, the aromatic smell of the wood burning and the scent of the spices drifted in the rain-laden wind across to where the girls were sitting.

Around early afternoon, everything was all set for the party and the students were beginning to arrive. They came carrying colourful umbrellas to protect their fresh, immaculate finery and beautifully groomed hair from getting soiled. The Indian girls, with their heavily kohl-lined eyes like the exotic film stars from India, and the black girls, in their stylish, big Afro hairstyle and glamorous makeup, stiffly tiptoed around puddles of muddy water in the street in their delicate high-heeled sandals and slim dresses. And the ones who were wrapped in exorbitant silk saris, lifted their saris as they walked, showing off their brown and fair jewelled ankles. The black boys, resplendent in the latest style of clothing of the disco era, with their big Afro hairstyle and kickers shoes, swaggered down the street, smelling sweet and looking quite charming, and the Indian boys with their well-groomed black hair and conservative white cotton shirts and black trousers, strutted along, their polished shoes now sprinkled with rain.

Indira and Francine were enthralled by the scene as they intently looked on, but there was something about Laliwa's demeanour that made her seem absent-minded and apathetic. Indira sensed this strangeness about her and asked, "Is there something you're not telling us, Laliwa?"

Laliwa did not prevaricate, but smiled and without hesitation got up and got the Nancy Drew book that she had under her feather pillow, and she opened it and found the letter she had hidden between the pages. "Afonso wrote me a letter," she said excitedly with starry eyes.

"A love letter?" Francine teased.

Laliwa blushed and nodded.

"Can we read it?" Indira asked.

"Only if you promise to keep it a secret," Laliwa said. "My parents must not find out about this."

After both Indira and Francine swore to keep the secret, Laliwa took her seat in the middle of them, and as they sat at the edge of the bed, she unfolded the letter, Indira and Francine both leaning close to her to read it as she held it up.

The letter, meticulously written with a fountain ink pen on fine paper, read:

Dear Laliwa,

There's something I've been wanting to tell you for the longest time and never had the courage to do so, but I must tell you now because I can no longer contain myself. Ever since we were little children in kindergarten school I liked you, and as I watched you grow into a young woman and I became a young man myself, my feelings for you have also grown. Now there are times when I cannot eat or sleep from thinking of you. I dream about you day and night and long to have you. I'm in love with you, Laliwa, and there's nothing in the world I wouldn't do just to be with you.

You are so beautiful, sweet Laliwa. How I long to caress your silken black hair and whisper sweet words in your ears. Oh, Laliwa, I love you so and I must know if you feel the same way about me.

Remember the time when you were a little girl and we were playing in the schoolyard one day and I picked a purple jump & kiss flower and put it in your hair and sang you the song 'Laliwa, would you like to dance with me in a beautiful garden?' You said then you would when you grow up. If you love me too, Laliwa, and you still mean it, then write to me and say you'll dance with me someday in a beautiful garden, and I'll sweep you off your feet and steal you away.

Affectionately,

Afonso

"And are you going to dance with him someday in a beautiful garden?" Francine asked Laliwa, rather teasingly.

Laliwa laughed and held the letter close to her bosom and, with a blushing smile, said, "I think I will."

"Then you love him too," Indira said.

"I must admit that I truly do," Laliwa said, but even without a verbal admission it was plain to see that Laliwa was in love, for she had that faraway look in her smouldering dark eyes.

Indira thought of the conversation Nani had with her earlier on the subject of man and love, and she knew with Afonso and Laliwa it was not just attraction, they truly loved each other for the longest time, though it was only now that Laliwa would admit it.

"You must keep this a secret," Laliwa urged again. "If my parents find out they would get angry with me. You see,

201

my father wants me to marry a man from my tribe when I finish school. He has already chosen a husband for me."

"But you should only marry someone you truly love," Indira said, sad that Laliwa would have to marry someone she did not love out of deference to her parents and not her prerogative.

"It's not up to me to decide that," Laliwa said.

"What would you do then?" Francine asked.

Laliwa had been thinking hard about this ever since she received the letter from Afonso last week, on the last day of school, and she said, "There's only one thing I can do. Afonso figured that my father would never let me marry anyone outside of my tribe. I'm sure that's why he mentioned in his letter that he'll steal me away. Afonso and I would just have to elope someday."

With that the girls fell silent, Indira and Francine not knowing how to respond to such a thing, and they turned their attention back to the school. By now the students and teachers were safely sheltered under the school roof from the rain, and they were now seated at the tables, and the stage was set. As they were being regaled with piquant foods and drinks, they were serenaded by various singers, singing hot calypso and reggae tunes to the rhythmic jerk of guitars and the smooth, rippling sound of the rubber-tipped drum sticks on steel pans. An attractive, black-skinned black girl, dressed in a shimmering, tight-fitting gold dress and matching high-heeled sandals that accentuated her long, bare legs, captivated the audience by reciting a succinct poem, then there was a lengthy performance by a light-skinned Indian dancer who graced the stage in a flimsy blue sari, her wrists and ankles decked out in shining gold jewellery, and she danced enchantingly as the men whistled and the women applauded.

The girls looked on and listened for a long while as the various performers took to the stage, as the audience continued to be regaled with food and drinks. When they were replete, it was time for the dance. Indira had been waiting patiently for this moment for she had never been to a school dance before and was curious about it. The band stopped playing and the turntable stereo system was turned on and the students gathered in the middle of the floor and started dancing to Ernie Smith singing *Pitta Patta*. Rainy lovers' music on a late, rainy, tropical afternoon, and young people moving to the rhythm. It was purely dreamy, magical, and mysterious, Indira thought.

She watched along with Laliwa and Francine as steamy romance played out in cozy corners, and soon dusk began to fall dusty-blue and purple and black over the little town, and it was too dark to see the fires burning. Indira had seen enough that warmed her thoughts and innocently fascinated her, but what she did not know was that it was all a guise of something far, far deeper than what met the eye.

Francine, who had been silently observing the scene herself, spoke, and she said to Indira and Laliwa, "I have a confession to make."

"Don't tell me you're in love, too," Indira said jokingly and laughed, for if that were the case, Francine had imperceptibly camouflaged her feelings very well.

"I have a crush on Albert Briggs!" Francine blurted out. Albert Briggs was a fine-looking Afro-Guyanese, who was in Fifth Form and had just completed his last year in school.

This came as a surprise to both Indira and Laliwa, and Indira, being a bit annoyed at her friend for not letting her in on it any sooner, asked, "And when and how did this begin, Francine?"

"It started just this week while we were doing our exams at school. I bumped into Albert at the library and dropped my text book at his feet," Francine said, her brown baby face suddenly taking on a radiancy as her eyes sparkled with excitement. And she went on to say, "When he picked up the book and handed it to me, he smiled at me and I thought I would melt in front of him, he was so handsome. Ever since then he had been waiting under the mango tree after exams each day and had been watching me as we were leaving school."

Indira then clued in that was why Francine was acting distracted when they were leaving school for the last week. "How come you didn't mention anything to me?" she asked Francine.

"I knew Albert would be leaving school as he just completed Fifth Form, so I thought it wasn't necessary to do so," Francine answered.

"But if he likes you, too, he will come after you," Laliwa said, and added, "just like Afonso does."

"And if he does, let him prove that he loves you before you give your heart to him," Indira echoed Nani's wise words that she had spoken earlier that morning.

"How does he prove his love for me?" Francine asked.

"Let him first get to know you for who you are, your likes and dislikes and your passions and desires," Indira said, repeating Nani's very words. "And if he falls in love with you then, only then give your heart to him. My Nani says not to mistake attraction for love. She said to get to know someone before you speak of love, for you cannot love someone if you don't know him."

"It sounds like very good advice," Francine said, although, at this stage, she could not tell the difference between attraction and love; all she knew was that she was feeling euphoric and light-headed over Albert Briggs. "Now that Laliwa and I have told you about our love interests, now you tell us who you're interested in," she then said to Indira.

Indira thought of the many boys in school and she said, "I'm sorry to disappoint you both but I have no confession to make. No one has captured my attention, as yet."

"Not even Kabal the irresistible?" Francine teased.

"Not even him," Indira said, and diverted the conversation by asking Laliwa, "Have you heard from Sally lately?" Since Sally left for England she had been corresponding with Laliwa and Laliwa would update the girls on her. "And does she have a boyfriend?"

"I just received a letter from her and she's doing fine in high school," Laliwa said. "And, no, she doesn't have a boyfriend, as yet. She wants to go to nursing school to study to become a nurse and then she'll return to Guyana to work in a hospital here. She says she very much enjoys being in England with her Aunt and other family." Laliwa paused then before continuing on to say, "Remember when she was a little girl she used to say that she wanted to see the Queen? Well, her wish did come true. She said she saw the Queen in a parade in London, and she was all too thrilled over that."

After that the girls talked more about boys and love, and then they talked about going back to school in September. They could not believe that would be their last year, and they talked about what they would do after school. Laliwa no longer dreamed about going to America to become a film star, like she did in kindergarten. All she wanted now was to run away with Afonso. Francine was building a citadel in the air and wanted to marry Albert and have many children, and stay at home and become a seamstress, just like her mother. And all Indira planned on doing was to work in the garden to make a living, and, most importantly, take care of her Nani.

It was still raining when Indira and Francine left Laliwa's house, and by now it was pitch black. Only then Indira remembered that Nani had told her to come home before nightfall, for she had gotten carried with her friends and the school party and the girl talk and had forgotten all about it. She hurried home to find Nani sitting in the old wooden rocking chair by the sitting room window, in the darkness, anxiously looking out for her.

"I warned you to come home before dark," she said to Indira when she got in. "You had me worried, child."

"I'm sorry I worried you, Nani," Indira said apologetically, and gently squeezed Nani's hand in the dark. "To be honest with you, I was having fun and forgot about the time. But it's just a little after dark now and there are other people walking the streets. There was no need for you to be worried." And she went and lit the kerosene oil lamp and placed it on a corner table and sat on the worn jade-green sofa and wiped the rain off her legs and feet with a flour bag towel.

"I can't help but worrying about you sometimes, child," Nani admitted as she rocked nervously in the rocking chair, the light of the kerosene oil lamp illuminating her puckered brows. Then she sat silently for a moment, settling her nerves, as the creaking of the rocking chair was heard above the pitter patter of the rain on the corrugated zinc roof. Once she collected herself, she asked, "What were you and your friends up to?"

Indira thought for a moment before cautiously replying, "We just hung around at Laliwa's, and her mother served us up some pepperpot and cassava bread." She left out the school party, however, and that Francine and Laliwa were dizzy with love over Albert and Afonso, respectively. She knew too well that would set off a fire and brimstone sermon from Nani, on temptations and transgressions. And Indira was not in the mood for that tonight.

Nani then suddenly stopped her rocking and fished in her dress pocket and pulled out her old cloth money bag, and she smiled, the light of the kerosene oil lamp causing her gold teeth to glitter, and she said, "I did well at the market today." And she untied the string and reached into the green money bag and pulled out a few dollars. "Come, take this little money and spend it on something nice for yourself, child."

Indira got up and took the money from her and hugged and thanked her. "Kickers are in fashion now," she said, "I think I'll buy myself a pair. I'm almost out of chameli body lotion, so I'll get some, also." And she went and put the money away in the bedroom. Then she fetched the kerosene oil lamp to the kitchen and got some wood and started the mud stove and roasted an eggplant and made baigan choka

207

to eat with roti, and she boiled some lime leaves and made tea.

She served Nani first as Nani sat in her place on the peerah, and she sat at the table and she and Nani ate dinner. Then Nani told her old time stories while the embers in the mud stove burned and the rain pelted the zinc roof. When Nani got tired of talking, she went to get ready for bed. As she was doing so, Indira went downstairs and bathed in the dark of the outdoor bathroom while it was still raining, and, after, she went back upstairs and creamed her skin in her favourite chameli lotion and put on her white cotton nightie, then she went to help Nani into her bed.

She brought out the cot that was stored in the bedroom and unfolded it in the sitting room, and said, "Let me sleep on the cot tonight, Nani. You sleep in the bedroom under the mosquito netting."

"No, child" Nani said. They had gone through this conversation almost every night since Nani gave up her bedroom to Indira ever since she became a young woman a couple of years ago, and the answer was always the same: "You're a young woman now and you need your private space."

"But I hate to think of you sleeping out here on the cot while I sleep in the comfort of the bed," Indira said.

"Don't worry your little head, child. Just make the cot up nice and soft for me."

Indira, knowing this was a situation she could never win with Nani, gave up. And she went about spreading extra quilts on the cot to make it as soft and comfortable as possible for Nani to sleep on, even fluffing up the feather pillow. She then combed Nani's thinning silver hair before she tucked her into bed. After, she lit a mosquito coil and placed it nearby and placed the white enamel posey—chamber pot under the cot, and she kissed Nani goodnight and put out the kerosene oil lamp and retired to the bedroom for the night.

The rain was still falling when Indira opened the old wooden bedroom window overlooking the backyard, and she sat on the chair and listened to the sound of the pitter patter on the corrugated zinc roof and that of the crapos croaking in the pond below. And she combed her long hair a hundred strokes to make it soft as she dried it in the vigorous breeze that was blowing, then twisting it into numerous ringlets.

In the darkness of the rainy night, the scenes of the school party played out in her mind. She thought of how the students moved to the rhythm of the music while the rain was falling and how dreamy and magical it seemed. Then she thought of Laliwa and Francine being in love and she wondered what that felt like for she had never been in love before. And she dreamed of being in love.

The warm rain and the mysterious night was conducive to such innocent fantasy, and adding to the charm, somewhere down the road a neighbour was playing love songs on a turntable stereo system, and the words sailed through the night and reached her ears. She was carried away to another world as Roberta Flack seduced the night with *Killing Me Softly With His Song*, and Wendy Alleyne made it blue with *Midnight Blue*, and when Indira crawled into bed and tucked in the mosquito netting and laid on the soft feather pillow, she dreamed along with Patsy Cline when she sang *Sweet Dreams*. She dreamed about the handsome Indian film star, the young Dharmendra from India, singing a deeply sad love song, and she dreamed of wearing a blue silk sari and running through the flowery gardens of India in the sultry monsoon rain, and dancing to the rhythm of the pitter patter.

And she drifted off to a fantasy sleep.

9

The Flood And A Day Of Fishing

Indira was greatly anticipating the break from school before returning in September, but it rained incessantly for days and a flood came, bringing about a time of disaster and hardship.

It was now another gloomy, rainy day and she was standing on the backstairs of Nani's old house, holding up an umbrella in the downpour, surveying the disaster in front of her. The water had risen up to the third step and had flooded the bottom-house and the whole yard. She watched sadly and helplessly as the hassar and tilapia fishes in the pond swam away in the deluge, and her heart sank when she looked over at the vegetable garden and all she could see was water; all the crops were now submerged, the fruits of her labour and livelihood lost. The fowl coop was also flooded. Fortunately, though, Nani had sold all the mature chickens, but she had bought a new batch of chicks, and, luckily, they were in an elevated cage. Indira's concern now was not only for the chicks who were growing fast and needed space, but Solomon and Rani were standing for days at the flooded bottom-house and they had not eaten, and Indira thought she had to do something before the animals were to become sick and die.

She went upstairs and found Nani sitting in the old wooden rocking chair in the sitting room, rocking back and forth and looking out the window at the rain falling with a sense of peace about her as though the sun was shining and all was well. Indira, on the other hand, was in a flustered state, troubled by the predicament facing them. With a sense of urgency, she said to Nani, "We must do something about Solomon and Rani and the chicks right away."

"Yes, I know that, child," Nani said as she continued to rock back and forth while looking out the window.

Nani had been like this for days, practising equanimity, but appearing as being apathetic in the face of calamity, and Indira grew frustrated with her and asked, "Don't you care at all about what's happening around us, Nani?"

Nani did not answer but kept staring out the window.

"What shall we do?" Indira asked, growing more and more anxious about the situation.

Nani now turned to her and said, "Don't worry your pretty head, child. The Lord will take care of everything." And she began humming the song *Nearer My God To Thee*.

"But Solomon and Rani have been standing in the flood for days now!" Indira snapped, her frustration boiling over. "We must be practical about the situation and do something about it at once." And she paced around and wrung her hands in apprehension.

"It's no use in getting yourself all upset about the situation, child," Nani said. "It would not help a bit but only make matters worse. Take a few deep breaths and relax yourself."

Indira flopped onto the worn, jade-green sofa and let out a frustrated sigh, and after collecting herself with a few deep breaths, asked in a more unperturbed tone, "What shall we do about the situation, Nani?"

"I've been seriously thinking what is the best thing to do. And I think we will have to build a barn on stilts for Solomon and Rani, and the chicks will need a bigger cage."

"How are we going to do all that?" Indira asked, pessimistically. "We have no money to buy wood and hammer and nails. And I wouldn't know how to build a barn on stilts, or a chicken cage, for that matter."

"Have some faith, child," Nani said, and she closed her eyes for a moment as though praying and seeking an answer from above, and when she opened them she said, "I suggest we call on your Uncle Ram to help us."

Uncle Ram could not be a divine answer to a prayer, Indira thought, rather dreadfully. But they were now in a crisis and needed him. "Okay," she reluctantly agreed. "Then we'll have to get him here soon before Solomon and Rani get sick and die."

"Go over to Uncle Manil right away and tell him to give your Uncle Ram an urgent message to come immediately with his big truck, for we have a flood and we're facing a disaster." Manil was a bus driver who drove the route to Number 63 Village where Uncle Ram lived, and Nani would send messages to her son through him whenever she needed to. "Tell Uncle Manil to also tell your Uncle Ram to fetch some hay to feed Solomon and Rani."

Without hesitation, Indira put on her tall rubber boots and made her way in the flood across the street to Uncle Manil. Unfortunately, he was not at home, so she left the messages with his pregnant wife.

When she returned home she was faced with another problem; since the flood had wiped out their crop, Nani had nothing to sell at the market, and with no income they had been frugal with the little food they had, but it was now running out. "All we have left are just a tin of corned beef, a piece of salfish, some flour, rice, and yellow peas," she said to Nani. "What are we going to do when this is all gone? We don't even have eggs now that the laying chickens are all sold out."

"The Lord will provide for us," Nani simply said.

Indira wished she had faith like her Nani. Unlike her, she could not help but worrying for they were in a grave situation. She acted sensibly though and skimped on the little food they had left. That day, she cooked *dhal* with the yellow peas, and rice, and she fried up the tin of corned beef. Nani blessed the meal, and she and Indira ate it contentedly with just salt and hot pepper. In the evening, they had *dhal puri*—roti stuffed with yellow peas, and saltfish for dinner. Now all that was left to cook was a little flour, rice, and yellow peas.

With very little food left and no sign of Uncle Ram, as yet, Nani still maintained her calmness and optimism, and she laid her head on her feather pillow that night and went to sleep peacefully. Indira, on the contrary, laid in bed that night and worried about the situation, and she barely slept from dreading the arrival of Uncle Ram.

* * *

A little before dawn, while it was still dark out and the rain was still pouring down, Uncle Ram arrived with his big truck with a pile of hay. From the bedroom window, Indira could barely make him out as he got out of the vehicle and came through the ragged gate, carrying a hunting rifle. She watched as he waddled through the water, feeling his way on the flooded pathway—the flower garden on both sides now sunken—and when he removed his boots and left them on the stairs below and started making his way up, she quietly withdrew from the window and went about making up the bed and putting back the mosquito netting in place. And she stayed in the bedroom.

At this time, Nani was in the kitchen frying *floats*—fried bakes on the mud stove, and as she was cooking, the smoke from the boiling oil in the carahee and the wood burning clouded the kitchen. At the sound of her son's footsteps, she lifted her head in time to see him parting the colourful strands of beads in the kitchen doorway and entering the kitchen.

From the bedroom, Indira heard Nani saying to him, "I'm glad you've come to help me out in this crisis, son."

As always, Uncle Ram was moody and petulant, and in response, he contemptuously said, "Why couldn't you get Indira to help you?"

"Indira would do so if she could do construction," Nani said, quick to defend Indira. "I need a barn for Solomon and Rani, and a bigger cage for the chicks, and she cannot build those."

"Is she some kind of princess that she cannot do that?" Uncle Ram asked. "She's just a lazy wretch! I'll go and get her to help you out." And so started a row between him and Nani, interrupting Nani's peaceful state.

"You just leave my granddaughter alone!" Nani raised her voice at him as her temper suddenly flared, like it always did when she had to defend Indira against him. "She's a good girl, and she takes good care of me."

Uncle Ram got even more angry because Nani was shielding Indira, and he went on an acrimonious tirade, a glint of avarice in his eyes as he said, "What are you going to do with your house and land when you die? Give them all to her, right? What about me, Ma? And you tell me you don't favour her?"

"How could you be so greedy and selfish?" Nani asked. "You have enough money and you have a big house and land, and a flourishing rice field. What would you do with my old house and land? My grandsons are well provided for, for you have seen to that, but my poor granddaughter has nothing. Isn't it reasonable for me to leave my house and land for her?"

Uncle Ram went on to be even more preposterous, saying, "Now that she's a woman, you have to watch her closely so she does not run around with boys and bring a disgrace to the family!"

Well, Uncle Ram had now pushed Nani too far, attacking Indira's unblemished reputation, and Nani chased him with a pot spoon, saying, "Go on back home, you beast! I will get George Williams and Shazam to help me."

Choosing to be unobtrusive, Indira remained in the bedroom and quietly listened to the row. Every time Uncle Ram came over, the first thing he would do was to pick on her, reviling her, and she had heard his rubbish so many times that it did not hurt anymore, nor did it matter to her now, except, that she felt awful that her Nani had to go through all that antagonism and hell for her.

Nani composed herself and said, "I'm sorry I lost my temper, son. For Pete's sake, free yourself from this bitterness that you carry for Indira. It's only causing you much suffering, and you're harming your soul by doing so."

What Nani said did not sink in or even settle on the surface of his mind, but, nevertheless, Uncle Ram settled down. And Nani then went on to make him a cup of tea and she served him up some hot floats with butter. And then they went down to business. Nani told him she had no money to buy supplies for the barn and cage, so Uncle Ram took out his wallet—thick with cash—and he agreed to buy the supplies and build the barn and cage, after all that fuss. Soon after having breakfast, he unloaded the pile of hay onto the donkey-cart and took off in his truck into town to get the supplies.

Indira still kept out of his way when he returned. George Williams and Shazam, who noticed him, came over to lend him a helping hand. Without taking a break, the men finished building the elevated barn by late afternoon, which they situated right beside the bottom-house, and they helped Solomon and Rani up from the flood and onto it and gave the starving animals the hay to eat. They also finished constructing an elevated cage, big enough to hold the chicks for a while.

At dinner, Nani cooked up the last of the yellow peas, making dhal with it, and she also cooked up the last of the rice to go with it, and they had just that. Uncle Ram stayed over that night, and he sat on the donkey-cart at the flooded bottom-house and drank rum all evening, and he cursed and sang and cried himself to sleep. Nani woke him up the next morning for breakfast—the last of the flour used to make dosea— and after another row with her about Indira again, he took off with his rifle to go hunting for food, for even a morsel of food was now gone.

When he returned, he brought back watrash and bush-hog wild meats and a couple of Muscovy ducks he had shot down, and he chopped and cleaned the meats to cook, some of which Nani, being magnanimous, shared with the neighbours, much to his greedy objection. Nani advised Indira to remain confined to the bedroom to avoid him, and she curried and fried the meats and fed him dinner.

After dinner, he gave Nani the few dollars he had left in his wallet, and Indira watched from the bedroom window as he slipped away into the darkness of the rainy evening and was gone. Though she always dreaded his coming, she was always sad to see him go, and, instead of feeling antipathy towards him, pitied him because he was just a troubled man, she thought.

* * *

The inexorable rain continued nonstop for the next week, during which time Nani used up the little money that Uncle Ram had given her, and she and Indira were left with just dhal and rice, which they ate for a few days until that ran out and they had nothing to eat, leaving them in a predicament again, though Nani remained sanguine.

With no food and money, and unable to bear the pain of hunger, Nani was impelled to do something she would not normally do: "I think I should sell off some of the gold I have and buy some food for us," she said to Indira.

It did not sound like a viable idea to Indira, though hungry herself, so she did not acquiesce but rejected it,

218

saying, "No, you mustn't do that, Nani. The gold has been in our family for generations and it's something we should hold on to. We will find another way of getting some food."

Nani then remembered the hand seine net she had buried in a straw basket in the kitchen, and she went and got it and said to Indira, "Come, we're going fishing by the seaside for food."

Indira did not like that idea, either, and protested, "You're too old to go fishing by the seaside in this weather."

"I'm not too old to do such a thing!" Nani argued, and she stated the Guyanese proverb, *When dog hungry he ah nyam calabash*, meaning, when you are in need of something you do not have, you make do with anything.

Indira had never been to the seaside to fish, only heard about the arduous and treacherous trip, and she was apprehensive about it and tried to dissuade Nani by saying, "We would have to walk a far ways in the bush, water, and mud to get there, and we would have to cross the river and the shaky little bridge must be flooded over. It's still raining and it's dangerous for us to do so. You are too feeble to undertake such a journey, Nani."

"Hush, hush, child," Nani said, and for a moment she almost changed her mind, but not because she thought it was precarious to do so; she was worried that Indira would have to go barefoot. Then a pang of hunger hit her again, and she said, "Go and put on some old clothes, and don't wear any shoes for we will have to fish barefoot." And she muttered, "I don't like to do this to you, child, having to let you go barefoot in this terrible weather."

219

"Then maybe we should call on Grandpa for help," Indira suggested.

Nani shook her head and said, "Your grandfather is presently sick and I don't want to bother him now. I am not sick and we can provide for ourselves. Go on and get dressed. We will leave now."

"But you can't go out in this weather, Nani," Indira insisted.

Nani got up and got her headkerchief and, rather resolutely, said, "Yes, I can. You go and get dressed now." And Nani put on her headkerchief and tied it tightly.

Indira capitulated, giving up the argument for she figured all the persuasion in the world would not deter Nani for she had her mind made up. So she went and put on a faded pink cotton dress and put her hair up in a ponytail, and she left her feet bare.

The midday sky was dark and gloomy and it was still raining when they left, and it did not take very long for their clothes to get soaked as they made their way through the flooded yard to Pyari's house and beyond to the swamp, Indira carrying the hand seine in one hand and holding on to Nani with the other, as Nani clutched on to the straw basket she was carrying to hold the catch.

They trudged through mud and water and bush, the sharp blades of the *razor* and *busy-busy* grasses cutting Indira's bare legs in places, causing a stinging burn and making her very uncomfortable. To add to her discomfort, the place was overbearingly hot and her faded pink cotton dress was clinging to her in the rain, and her bare feet quickly became bruised and sore. She was irritated by the buzzing sound of the swarming mosquitos, the beat of the rain, and the splashing of the water as she ploughed along. Even the innocuous and lively cacophony of the chirping yellow-breasted kiskadee, blue saki, and scarlet curi-curi birds, among the others, perched on the branches of the trees, annoyed her. Nani, on the other hand, with her tough old skin, intrepidly trudged along, not seeming to mind the dreadful conditions, nor the dangers that lurked in the water surrounding the mangrove roots.

"Alligators live in the water among the mangrove roots," she said to Indira, rather nonchalantly, as though talking about a harmless fish.

"Alligators!" Indira exclaimed, a bout of fright immediately seizing her, and she stopped in her track. "I'm scared, Nani, let's turn back and go home. Instead of us catching food for ourselves, we may end up being lunch for the alligators."

"All of God's creatures, including, humans, birds, animals, and fishes have to eat, and it is as such that we eat each other to survive," Nani said in trying to make light of the situation. And becoming more considerate of Indira's fear, added, "When your Nana Amar was alive, we had taken this route many, many times to go fishing and nothing has ever happened to us. Now, come on, let's continue on, child."

Indira reluctantly proceeded, jittering as they struggled through the mangrove roots in the water, and soon they came to the river, the expansive banks strewn with young dead sharks, and *buck crabs* crawling madly in every direction. Indira hesitated here again. They had to cross the bridge over the river to get to the seaside, and the bridge was merely ten inches wide and about thirty feet long and it

221

had no railings and was flooded over. "I'm not crossing this bridge, Nani," she tremulously protested again. "I can't swim, neither can you, and we will surely drown if we slip and fall into the river."

"Don't be afraid, child," Nani said, "just take my hand and we'll cross slowly."

Indira looked around and there was no one else in sight, and she feared if they were to have an accident no one was there to help. "I'm not going," she insisted.

"Then I will go alone," Nani said. "I'm hungry and we need food." And she set out in her bare feet to cross the treacherous bridge.

Full of trepidation, Indira looked down at the deep, murky water and got even more scared, but she could not let old Nani cross the bridge alone, so she took Nani's hand and, while clasping the hand seine net with the other, she followed nervously. She closed her eyes to prevent herself from looking at the water below as they began feeling their way across the skinny bridge, which was covered by a couple of inches in water, and her legs began to tremble for fear that they would slip and fall into the river. To make matters worse, lightening started flashing just then, and the thunder began roaring, and a gust of wind was blowing. As she and Nani struggled to steady themselves, Indira thought for sure this would be the end of them. She kept her eyes closed and kept on feeling her way along, and suddenly she became so numb with fear that her bare feet could no longer feel the bridge beneath the water, and she felt they had slipped into the river and were drowning.

"Now open your eyes," she heard Nani saying to her.

Indira's eyelashes slowly fluttered open and the numbness in her feet suddenly diminished as she felt the muddy ground, and with a great sigh of relief, she said, "We've made it across the bridge." Then she looked back at the bridge and asked, "How are we going to cross it again with a basket of fish?"

"We'll worry about that when we get back," Nani answered. "Come on, let's go to the seaside and catch some fish." And Nani coaxed Indira until they got to the seaside.

It must have been the gentle coaxing of Nani, or perhaps the smell of the salty sea air that finally calmed Indira, and the feel of the wet sand beneath her sore feet soothed her. And the warm patter of the rain on her face made her suddenly burst out laughing as she felt the taste of the drops on her lips. And she was soon fascinated by the shells on the shore, and the squawking of the seagulls soaring in the rain, and the crashing sound of the waves, and the sea itself, as she watched it churning in the wild wind that was blowing. She let her wet, waist-length hair down and started dancing in the rain in her drenched pink dress, romancing the rain with Indian music in her head, and emulating the film stars from India, thinking she was in the midst of an India monsoon, which for her represented passion and love as portrayed in the movies. Nani looked on for a moment and watched as Indira posed and danced, and she smiled to herself, remembering the days of her youth with her late husband Amar, a long time ago when she had danced for him in the warm rain in her sari.

Riding the boisterous waves were hundreds of *four-eyed fish*, jumping out of the water, and this caught Indira's attention and made her excited, and she playfully plunged into the waves, trying to catch the fish with her hands.

Nani laughed as she watched Indira frolicking, and she said, "You'll never catch one that way for they can see below as well as above the water." And she unfolded the hand seine and said, "Come, hold one side of the seine and let's haul it through the water and catch some fish this way."

Indira did as Nani instructed, and they both hauled the seine across the water. Within moments, the seine felt heavy, and they dragged it onto the shore, and Indira was excited to see all the fish and shrimps they had caught, live and jumping, and she exclaimed, "We have food to eat now!" Then her excitement quickly subsided when she thought they would have to cross the skinny bridge with the load.

Contrarily, as Nani's faith would lead her to believe, she was sure that her God would help them out somehow. In answer to her prayer, she and Indira both noticed a beat-up motorboat coming in their direction. The two fishermen in it, noticing them, pulled up ashore.

The skinny one looked at Nani and said, "What is an old woman like you doing, fishing in the sea in this kind of weather? Have you no fear?"

"We need food to eat," Nani simply said.

The fat fisherman looked at his friend and said, "We better take them back to town."

"But the boat is full of fish and there is no space to take them with us," his skinny friend said.

Indira butted in and said, "Please help us. The bridge across the river is flooded and our basket is too heavy for us to fetch across it. We may slip and drown."

The fat fisherman looked at Indira with empathy, then he turned to his friend and said, "We'll just have to dump out some our fish to accommodate them."

The skinny fisherman was not happy about the idea, thinking of the money he would lose, and he said to his partner, "Let them dump their catch and we'll squeeze them on board."

Nani and Indira had no other recourse or choice, so they dumped the fish and shrimps back into the sea, and they got into the reeking boat. As the fishermen motored on to the estuary of the river near Nani's house, a giant *anaconda* was tailing them; Indira did not know which was worse, being tailed by a snake or having to cross the bridge again. She was greatly relieved when the fat fisherman realised he had a goose on board that he had shot earlier, and he threw it to the snake to divert its focus from following the boat. Not long after, they reached their destination and the fishermen dropped off Nani and Indira by the banks of the river. Before turning to leave, the kind-hearted fat fisherman gave Nani half a basket of *coco-belly fish* he had caught earlier in a swamp, and he also threw in a generous amount of shrimps, much to the chagrin of the skinny one. The fishermen then took off, leaving Nani and Indira to make their way home.

When Nani and Indira arrived back at the house, they cleaned the shrimps and the batch of tiny coco-belly fish, then they got out of their dingy clothes and washed up and went and shared a portion of the seafoods with the neighbours. When they returned, they cooked and had the scrumptious fried shrimps and coco-belly fish mixed with garam masala and curry powder. And they ate until they were satiated, as the rain continued to fall.

* * *

The next day the rain persisted, another inauspicious day it seemed, for Nani and Indira found themselves without food once again and in a dire situation. Nani wanted to go fishing again, but Indira hotly insisted against it, and she won this time. Instead, she waddled through the flood and climbed the trees in the backyard and picked some mangoes and green coconuts and gathered some other fruits, and they had those for breakfast.

Just before lunch time came around that day, Indira, who was now considering resorting to go to her grandfather for help, found Nani sitting in the rocking chair in the sitting room, with her eyes closed and lips moving, repeating a litany. The old woman was communicating with her God, pleading with Him to meet their need and provide food for them once more.

It was not long before that Fazeela, the next door neighbour, now pregnant with her eighth child, was looking out of her kitchen window and noticed that there was no smoke coming from Nani's mud stove and it was now past lunch time. And she found that strange. Then upon pondering the situation, she realised that Nani and Indira had gone fishing in the rain the day before and she figured that Nani must have ran out of food.

Fazeela and family, once destitute, were doing much better now that Shazam was promoted to manager at the movie theatre and was making a decent salary. The children were now well fed and clothed, and she and Shazam could afford to send them to school. Fazeela even had some savings put away so that one day they would move into a better house. And now she always had a bit of extra food on hand.

Happy that she was now in a position to repay Nani for her years of kindness and generosity, she packed a basket of vegetables and meat that she had gotten at the market that day, and she headed over to Nani.

"My Lord has answered my prayer!" Nani exclaimed when Fazeela brought her the basket of food.

"Praise be to Allah," Fazeela responded.

"Praise be to God," Nani said, and she took the basket of food from Fazeela.

And when Fazeela was gone, Nani blessed the food, and she and Indira ate well.

The rain still would not hold up, and in a couple of days Nani and Indira had consumed all the food and were left without any, yet again. And Nani prayed again, and again. In answer, came her friends, all showing acts of kindness and generosity. First came George Williams and Shazam, bringing meat they got from a whale that had washed up ashore. Then came Joan Williams and Francine—who learned of Nani's plight from Fazeela—bringing baskets of food. And soon, others learned of Nani's unfortunate situation; Mr. Jackson and Mrs. Surjeet and Pyari all brought food for Nani and Indira. When the heaven pours it pours, for when Dr. Ramesh caught word of Nani and

Indira's plight, he sent his chauffeur, Sahil, with baskets and baskets of food, as well as money.

And so Nani and Indira were well provided for until the rain dissipated and the flood receded, and even after. Nani thanked her God for His goodness and for making the sun shine on her land again, and she worked alongside of Indira and they plowed the earth and planted seeds. It was not long before that she was back at the market selling and making a livelihood once again.

10

Ling Gets A Whipping In Fifth Form

The sky was sprinkled with twinkling stars in the wee hours of the morning, and a warm, pleasant breeze was blowing. At the crowing of the fowlcocks, some folks in Rose Hall were beginning to stir. Indira opened her eyes and closed them again, relishing another five minutes of sweet sleep beneath the cascade of the mosquito netting. Then, the thought that it was Monday morning, the first day of returning to school in September, woke her fully with a sense of excitement. She had to get the chores done before leaving, so she sprang out of bed and lit the kerosene oil lamp, hung up the mosquito netting, and changed into her work clothes.

She took up the lamp and exited the bedroom and found Nani snoring like a log on her cot in the sitting room. She left her there to sleep and headed down the backstairs to the fowl coop, fed the chickens and collected the freshly laid eggs and placed them in the paint cans. She then took the paint cans and placed them onto the donkey-cart, which had been loaded with vegetable and fruit produce the previous day, with enough for Nani to make a few good dollars at the market. After she milked Rani, she went back upstairs and started the fire in the mud stove and put the milk on to boil to make some porridge for breakfast and, while the pot was boiling, she got out the coal iron and ironed her white school blouse and blue pleated skirt on the kitchen table.

By the time she finished her chores, Nani woke up and they had breakfast together. Right after breakfast, Indira went and bathed and got dressed in her uniform, completing the ensemble with knee-high white socks, a pair of white Yatin sports footwear, and a matching wide-rimmed hat with a blue band. She paused and looked at herself in the mirror to fix her long curls—not realising how beautiful and innocent she appeared—and she made sure her blouse looked neat and the pleats in her skirt were in perfect place. She then got her black leather briefcase and headed out the door and, after seeing Nani off to the market, waited at the bottom-house for Francine. Within moments Francine arrived, looking smart in her school apparel, and without delay, they took off on foot for school, stopping on their way to get Laliwa.

The sky was now clear and blue, and the bright sun was quickly heating up the morning as the three of them made their way down the dirt road, encountering other students who were on their way to school, also. Ladies, carrying large straw baskets of produce on their heads, were on their way to the market at this time, and consumers were shielding themselves from the sun with colourful umbrellas as they also made their way on foot to the market, and shops on the main road. The squeaking of bicycle spokes was heard as others rode along, and an old car bounced by on the bumpy dirt road, making a clattering sound. Some stray dogs and cats and other animals were roaming around in the streets, and a donkey, standing in the middle of the road, started hee-hawing loudly and would not stop. Things got a whole lot louder when the girls passed the market and the fish ladies were hollering at the top of their lungs for people to buy their fishes amid the chatter of voices.

The girls themselves were gaffing—conversing, and laughing as they journeyed down the dirt road, pulling their wide-rimmed, white hats down to block the sharp rays of the sun from their faces. They were all too excited to return to school, especially, Laliwa. She had not seen Afonso since school was adjourned in June, and was looking forward to giving him the letter she had written in reply to his, which she had between the pages of her exercise book, the contents of which was a thrilling topic of their conversation. Equally as exciting, was a recent letter from Sally to Laliwa, keeping the friends abreast of her stay in England. Sally conveyed that her aunt was trying to match her up with an English bloke from an aristocratic family and wanted to marry her off as soon as she finishes high school, and though that sounded very royal, Sally was determined that she would study to become a nurse and return to Guyana to work and settle down.

By the time the girls mulled over the respective letters and got caught up on their personal affairs, they arrived at the school, which was encompassed by a scatter of small, old houses with grassy yards with plentiful flowers and trees, animals, birds, and fowls. The school was a flat wooden building with two sections, one running from the front yard to the back, and the adjoining one running parallel to the street, with no walls on the upper part so that one could clearly see inside the classrooms, and with several posts holding up the corrugated zinc roofing. In front of the dirt-packed schoolyard were two stalls, where

231

ladies were selling sweet and savoury treats, sweet drinks, and crush ice, and in the back, a huge mango tree from a neighbour's yard, copiously loaded with the green fruits, overlapped the schoolyard fence, around which grew crabgrass. Right opposite the vertical section of the school was a sweets' shop, and situated not far from the girls' classroom, at the right end of the horizontal section, was a bakery, and the bakers were already making dough for *tennis rolls*—sweet buns.

When the girls approached the entrance of the school, some boys—all neatly dressed in khaki pants and crisp, white, cotton shirts—were hanging around the stalls in the front yard. Amongst them was Ling, who had grown into a tall and slender young man and was sporting a pageboy hairstyle with limzee—fringe that fell just above his very pronounced Chinese brown eyes. He was accompanied by Afonso, who was now a fine-looking young man with well-groomed, side-parted hair, as black as the night, that accentuated his striking, and notable Portuguese blue eyes.

When Laliwa noticed Afonso her heart started palpitating, and she suddenly had a shyness attack and could not face him. So she quickly handed Francine the letter to give to him and she hurried off to the library, leaving the bewildered Afonso to stare after her. Before he got a chance to ask Indira and Francine about her peculiar behaviour, Francine slipped him the letter, and he took off to read it in private. The girls then gaffed with Ling for a couple of minutes before heading off to join Laliwa.

Laliwa was at the entrance of the library as they were approaching and she was waving her hands frantically, beckoning for them to hurry up and pointing inside as if to show them something. The something happened to be Albert Briggs, who was not in uniform attire but was wearing casual shirt-jack and trousers, and he was displaying a stylish Afro hairstyle. He was busy at the moment sorting books on a shelf.

Francine dropped her briefcase when she saw him and the question, "What's Albert doing here?" escaped her lips.

"What's Albert doing here?" Indira echoed.

"I'm not in the least bit surprised to see him here," Laliwa said, and with her diffidence now subsided, winked at Francine and added, "I told you before that if he likes you he will come after you. Didn't I?" She then picked up Francine's briefcase and as she was handing it to her, asked, "By the way, did you give my letter to Afonso?"

Francine took the briefcase but did not reply because Albert came strolling over to them just then and she suddenly lost her tongue. Indira spoke up and asked, "Have you failed your exams, and is that why you're back at school, Albert?"

Albert smiled, stealing a glance at Francine, and he answered, "No, I haven't failed my exams. I've passed all my subjects with flying colours. I'm back at school because I've volunteered to assist in the library until a suitable teaching position comes up." But Albert failed to tell that his motive for volunteering was Francine, though the girls instinctively suspected.

Indira and Laliwa then intentionally walked away, leaving poor, dumb-founded Francine alone with Albert. It must have been ten minutes that Albert stood there talking to Francine—who eventually found her tongue—before the school bell began ringing, and Francine hurried off to her

233

class and took her seat beside Indira and Laliwa in the very first row.

The class consisted of about twenty-four students, the girls and boys seated separately in benches that held about three each. Sheltered by the zinc roofing held up by posts but with no walls on the upper section of the classroom, a warm breeze was freely blowing through from the right end of this horizontal section, and you could clearly see outside, the trees and bushes that surrounded it, except, for the part that was obscured by the blackboard. Another class was also being held in this section of the building, and with an open concept, you could clearly see that adjacent classroom.

Francine was bursting with excitement to tell Indira and Laliwa about her conversation with Albert, but she had to refrain from doing so because Teacher Sanjay, a tall and bulky Indo-Guyanese, was standing right in front of them, with his black-rimmed spectacles pulled way down his nose, surveying the class with dark, suspicious eyes.

Right away Teacher Sanjay noticed that someone was missing. Afonso, who was seated in the back row of the class, was thinking the same thing, too. He had read Laliwa's letter earlier and could not wait to tell Ling about it. But where was Ling?

Ling, who had not grown out of his skylarking ways, came strolling into class a few moments later with a big grin on his face, and everyone turned to stare at him. He had long given up his boyish pranks of bringing creepy, crawly creatures into the classroom to scare the girls, but his shenanigans were not altogether over. In fact, he simply could not stay out of trouble. Though he arrived early for school, he purposefully showed up late for class just to enjoy the attention from his classmates, and to get under Teacher Sanjay's skin.

Teacher Sanjay had taught him from Forms one to four and had to put up with all kinds of trouble with him, and he did not expect him to be any different in Form Five. But seeing it was the first day of school, Teacher Sanjay did not want to make a spectacle of things over his lateness, so he simply said to him, "Take your seat, Ling."

Ling, still grinning, took his seat next to Afonso in the back row, and Afonso, knowing that Teacher Sanjay would be eyeing Ling like a hawk, decided he would tell him about Laliwa's letter a little later, in which Laliwa promised to dance with him.

Class then commenced, and after a succinct introduction, Teacher Sanjay started outlining the history studies for the semester. As he was doing so, Ling started acting bored and distracted. Teacher Sanjay kept eyeing him as he toyed with his fountain pen and kept looking over at the other class, clearly not paying attention to him. Then when Ling stretched and opened his mouth and let out a loud yawn, that irritated Teacher Sanjay, and he shouted at him, saying, "Pay attention, young man! You're testing my patience!" And though he tried to restrain himself, he felt a whipping was imminent on the first day of school.

Ling paid somewhat of a perfunctory attention for that moment, but soon he started thinking about what mischief he could get into next. In spite of his bad behaviour, he was a brilliant student who scored nothing less than A pluses, but he had no tolerance for the less fortunate. One of the less fortunates in class was a boy named Prajit, who was slow in learning, and for the most part, the students helped him out and did not bother him, but Ling would always pick on this poor boy. And so his attention was now on Prajit, who was sitting in the row in front of him. Ling fished in his pants pocket and got out a miniture slinging shot and a tiny pebble he was carrying, and he shot the pebble in the back of Prajit's head, and the boy screamed.

Well, Teacher Sanjay caught Ling red-handed in the act, and he shouted at him, "Get in the principal's office at once, Ling! I will give you a whipping you will never forget!"

All the students, including the adjoining class, instantly fell silent, so silent that you could hear a pin drop, and they watched as Ling made his way into the principal's office, followed by Teacher Sanjay. And the office door was slammed shut. The students heard the six wild cane lashes struck across Ling's bottom, but they heard no sound coming from him. In fact, when Ling emerged from the principal's office, walking behind Teacher Sanjay, he was smiling. And he was smiling because, in the event of a bamboo cane whipping, he would always wear a thick bukta—underwear, that he padded, and he did not feel even a slight sting of the six wild cane lashes Teacher Sanjay had given him.

Some of the students in class were amused by Ling, and some clearly were not. For one, Devika was not, and was exasperated by his impudent behaviour. Devika was a clear-skinned Indian girl of whom Ling was enamoured, and he wanted to marry her someday after he hopefully becomes a famous cricket player. Ling made Devika laugh and she loved him and liked some of his clowning around, but what he did to Prajit made her very upset that day.

During recess, as Ling was standing in the front yard of the school, laughing and telling the boys how he did not feel the wild cane lashes because he had on padded underwear, Devika went up to him and pulled him aside, and her beautiful brown eyes indicated the anger and hurt she felt when she said to him, "What you did to Prajit is wrong, Ling. If this is who you are, then I want nothing to do with you. Don't talk to me anymore!" And she started walking away.

Devika's threat to stop talking to him shocked Ling, and for the first time he realised that, besides being whipped, there were other consequences for his behaviour, and he ran after Devika and said, "Please, don't stop talking to me. I just meant it as a joke."

"Well, I didn't find that funny!" Devika snapped, and she kept walking away.

"Wait!" Ling pleaded, contritely. "I'm sorry. And I'll never do that again."

"Go and tell that to Prajit," Devika said and walked away, leaving Ling standing there, almost at the edge of tears now.

It was easy to say sorry to Devika because he loved her so much, but Ling wrestled with the thought of having to make an apology to Prajit. Humility was something he never knew of until now and it was difficult to deal with. But when he thought of the hurt and anger he saw in Devika's beautiful brown eyes, he humbled himself and mustered the courage and approached Prajit and apologised to him.

When class resumed, Ling took his seat beside Afonso and sat quietly, without the wheel of mischief turning in his head for the first time. Devika now dominated his mind. She was sitting in the row beside him and would not even look at him the way she used to. And there was not even a smile on her pretty face. Now he was worried that, indeed, she would never speak to him again. And a fear gripped him. He feared that he had lost her love and all the dreams he had of her. Actually, he was now convinced of this. And he was suddenly consumed by pain, a pain that he had never felt before; a fearsome heartache that burned his heart and chilled him to the bone. Even within those few moments, the pain was unbearable enough to make him think of changing his skylarking ways. In fact, out of deference to Devika, he vowed right then that he would start doing so from that moment on. He could not easily efface his love for her from his heart, and thought that he would rather change his ways than lose her love and have to endure a heartbreak.

When his 'pal in mischief', Vijay, asked him that day to slip out to go and steal the neighbour's mangoes, Ling refused. Vijay excused himself from class, however, fibbing that he had to use the toilet, and he went and picked some green mangoes from the neighbour's tree that was hanging over the schoolyard fence. He sliced up the sour fruit and put it in a plastic bag, with salt and hot pepper he got from the ladies at the stalls, and he snuck the bag into the classroom and passed it around, sneakily, without Teacher Sanjay knowing. But Ling refused to partake of that, either. The heartache had Ling so intent on changing his ways that when Afonso tried to tell him about Laliwa's letter during

238

class, he refused to listen, also, and, instead, paid full attention to Teacher Sanjay.

That was the turning point for Ling. It was as though a veil had been lifted from his eyes, elucidating his problem, and he could clearly see himself for the prankster he was, who derided other students and caused them unnecessary trouble, and teachers a great deal of consternation. His love for Devika made him see this and changed him almost entirely in the course of time. Sally's precocious words to him when they were in kindergarten came back to him: "*If you stay out of trouble and instead practise the game you may become just that*," referring to him expressing an interest in becoming a professional cricket player. Given his affinity with the game, he started channeling his energy into pursuing the game of cricket in his available time, instead of thinking of pranks, endeavouring to make it into the professional league someday. Eventually, he would regain Devika's love and would become the epitome of a model student with an impeccable character that everyone would grow to respect, including, Teacher Sanjay.

That same day in class Teacher Sanjay noticed the difference in Ling, and he thought the wild cane lashes had done the boy good, not knowing that Ling never even felt a sting, and for that matter, the love story behind his changed behaviour. And Teacher Sanjay went on to teach that day without further troubles from Ling.

It was nearing midday now, and a hot breeze was blowing through the classroom, bearing the smell of tennis rolls baking next door at the bakery. And that got everyone thinking of hot tennis rolls and cheese, and cold cream soda. It was not long before the school bell rang and class was dismissed for lunch, and some of the students immediately took off to the bakery, while others stayed in the classroom and had their lunch at their desks.

Indira, Francine, and Laliwa were some of those who stayed in the classroom for lunch. Laliwa's mother dropped off a hot dish of pepperpot for her, and Joan brought fufu and parched shrimp chutney that she made for Francine, and she also brought a steaming dish of curried squash and shrimps and rice which Nani made for Indira. While the girls shared and ate their lunch, a neighbour was playing Bob Marley's *No Woman, No Cry*, a song that brought a sweet, nostalgic mood to the torrid day, and that was followed by the Indian love song, *Kabhi Kabhie Mere Dil Mein*, that evoked such deep melancholy and passion that lingered in the air and, like an aphrodisiac, had students dreaming of romantic love.

After a hearty lunch, captured in a moment of enchantment, the girls went to the front yard where the ladies were selling treats, and they bought balls of crush ice —shaved ice with cherry syrup, and they stood around in the hot sun and ate them while they talked.

Francine had told Indira and Laliwa earlier at recess that Albert had asked her to the matinée that afternoon, and Laliwa asked her, "Have you decided if you're going to the matinée with Albert?"

"I want to go," Francine answered, "but I don't have an excuse to skip class."

"You have a bad headache and had to leave in a hurry," Laliwa said. "Teacher Thompson will be teaching geography this afternoon, and I'll tell him that for you." Teacher Thompson was a young and affable Afro-

Guyanese, fresh out of high school, who once played the same tricks his students now played, and he was lenient and let them get away with lame excuses at times. And the students knew this and took advantage whenever they could.

And so Francine snuck off to the matinée with Albert.

Laliwa had plans of her own, too, and, as soon as she delivered the message to Teacher Thompson about Francine, she snuck away, also, leaving Indira to wonder where she disappeared to. Afonso was no where to be seen, and Ling had taken off to play cricket with some other students.

With all her friends gone and still twenty minutes before class resumed, Indira was to join a few students who were playing rounders in a field nearby, but she changed her mind and decided to take a stroll around the neighbourhood by herself. She started down the narrow, dirt-packed school street and passed little, old houses, where ladies were napping in hammocks at their bottom-houses. Curls of smoke rose from mud stoves as others were cooking lunch, the smell of spices drifting through the wind, which rustled the plentiful fruit trees in yards in which chickens roamed about, pecking at the dirt ground. A dog was heard snarling at two cats that were having a fight, and the gobbling of turkeys and the chirping of birds added to the sounds of the day. Indira stopped to marvel at the colourful feathers of a beautiful peacock that was crossing the street, then she continued on and came to a small, secluded, luxuriant garden of roses and hibiscus and jump & kiss flowers, the perimeter lined with swaying palm trees.

It was here that it suddenly started to drizzle as the hot sun was shining brightly in the blue sky, creating an atmosphere conducive to being amorous. And it was here that Indira saw Laliwa and Afonso under a palm tree, holding on to each other and dancing in the beautiful garden in the light rain to *Killing Me Softly With His Song*, that was playing on someone's radio. Afonso finally had his dream come true to dance with Laliwa in a beautiful garden, Indira thought, and she looked on furtively for a moment and was vicariously thrilled by the mystique of the slow dance. And then she turned away and left unnoticed and returned to school.

Laliwa and Afonso returned a little later, in time for class, and after class was dismissed, they took off together, again. And Francine was with Albert at this time, so Indira had to walk home alone.

That night after she tucked Nani in bed, Indira laid in her bed as a languid breeze was blowing through the old wooden window facing the backyard. Through the mosquito netting, she could see the lit mosquito coil repellant on the bedside table, and she watched as the smoke from it curled upwards, the tip of the coil glowing red like the colour of love. And she fantasised about meeting someone and falling in love and dancing in the rain. Soon the sound of the ocean in the distance lulled her into a sweet, deep sleep, carrying her far away to a place of innocent dreams.

11

Celebrations, Ravi And Tarak

A late September night brought the sound of the beating of drums as a group of people in the town of Rose Hall were engaged in the *Kumfa* spirit possession dance, while, simultaneously, others were having a *Kali Mai Puja* or Hindu ritual at the temple, worshipping the goddess Kali, and sacrificing fowlcocks, some lost in altered states of consciousness. In the shadows of that night, a desperate woman was secretly meeting with an *Obeah Man* in his shack, seeking sorcery in trying to bring back her lover to her.

On the darkest night of the year, at the end of October, Indira was standing by the old wooden bedroom window overlooking the backyard, feeling the warm breeze on her face while looking over at Pyari's house as Pyari and a young man were lighting ghee-soaked cotton wicks of diyas and arranging the little earthen lamps in rows on the window sills for the Hindu Festival of Lights, Diwali. She watched for a while as they also placed the diyas on the outdoor steps and lit incense in the home, then she turned away from the window and started to get ready to go out into town with Francine to see the lit houses. Observing the Hindu custom, she got dressed in fresh new clothes, wearing a shimmering dusk-blue sari. Francine also got dressed in new attire, all spruced up in a pale pink chiffon dress. After promising Nani they would not be out too late, the girls headed out into the night.

There were no stars or moon out in the black sky tonight, and the town was brightly lit with hundreds of ghee-lit diyas, placed on window sills and outdoor stairways of freshly cleaned stilt houses, even front yards and walkways were lined with the little clay lamps. It seemed magical as the flames from the lamps flickered in the tropical breeze, illuminating the pathways for the Hindu Goddess Lakshmi to enter and bless homes with prosperity and wealth. The sweet scent of incense sticks burning scattered about in the warm night air, mingled with the scent of food cooking for the celebration. Adding to the mystique of it all, the silky, melodious voice of Lata Mangeshkar rang out into the night as she was singing a tune on a radio somewhere. People in fresh new clothes were hanging around their verandahs, talking and laughing, while others were walking the streets, looking at the beautifully lit stilt homes.

Indira and Francine strolled up the dirt streets and were also admiring the illuminated houses, and they stopped in at various neighbours, who shared their sweets with them. They had mithai and *jalebi* at one house, *prasad* and pera and gulab jamun at another, and they had *barfi* and *kheer* at yet another. When they had their fill, they continued on in the little town of lights.

It was the kind of night that was conducive to romance, Indira thought, and said to Francine, "I envy you and Laliwa for having boyfriends. I wish I could meet someone and fall in love myself."

"Someday you will."

"Someday? I hope it's before I become an old maid!"

"It's not like you haven't met anyone," Francine said. "I can count all the boys in school who are interested in you, but no one has been able to capture your attention so far, Indira. I hope someone does soon."

Just then, as they were lingering in the diya-lit front yard of a neighbour's home, Indira saw him; a handsome young stranger, tall and slender, sitting idly on his bicycle across the street, under the pale yellow of the streetlamp, his shoulder-length hair, as black as coal, slightly tossed by the wind. He was dressed in white cotton shirt, that accentuated the dark brown of his Indian skin, and sleek black pants, with matching shoes. The night did not reveal the fiery brown of his dreamy eyes, but his image alone transfixed Indira.

"Ravi! Ravi!" she heard a group of boys calling out to him as they brought their bicycles to a stop a little ways up the dirt road, waiting for him.

Ravi ignored the call of the boys for he was taken by the vision of the young woman in the shimmering dusk-blue sari surrounded by a pool of flickering diyas, her midnight-black ringlets falling about her delicate shoulders, and her skin glowing light golden-brown. For a moment he thought it was the Goddess Lakshmi herself and was stunned by her beauty. It was not until his friends called out to him for the third time that he tore his eyes away from her and took off on his bicycle.

Francine, who was standing by quietly observing Indira's reaction to this Ravi fellow, teased her, saying, "Looks like someone's finally captured your attention,

Indira. Maybe you wouldn't become an old maid, after all." And then she asked, "Who is he, anyway?"

"I don't know," Indira answered, taking in a deep breath in trying to quell her racing heartbeats. "I've never seen him around before. And I didn't see the others because they were further up the road, so I don't know who he was with."

The girls both thought that he was from out of town and possibly visiting relatives, and for all they knew, he could be visiting from abroad, maybe Canada or America or England. When he disappeared out of sight, their attention reverted to the dancing lights of the diyas and he was soon forgotten. More neighbours invited them into their homes and they were given brown paper bags full of sweets to take home. By now it was nearing midnight and the little clay lamps were still burning and were expected to do so all night long, but Indira knew that Nani would start worrying about her, so she and Francine started heading back home.

And sure enough when Indira reached the gate, she saw Nani looking out the window as she was sitting in her rocking chair, the dim light of the kerosene oil lamp falling on her face and silver hair. Indira bid Francine a quick goodnight and hurried upstairs to join her.

"I'm glad you've come home, child," Nani said to her as she walked through the door.

"You should have gone to sleep, Nani," Indira said affectionately. "There was no need to stay up and worry."

"I wouldn't have been able to sleep while you were out at this hour of the night," Nani said. "I kept myself busy trying not to worry by soaking some fruits to make Christmas cake."

"You're talking Christmas already," Indira said with a glint of excitement in her eyes, then she moaned, "But this means that I have to start studying for my tests."

"Before you know it, school will be all over for you, child," Nani said.

"I know, and I'm counting down the few months left to go," Indira said as she got out the cot and made up Nani's bed. She placed the posey beneath, and tucked the old woman in, then she kissed her on the forehead, and said, "Goodnight, Nani. Sleep well."

"Goodnight, my dear child," Nani exchanged.

Indira then took the kerosene oil lamp into the bedroom and changed into her nightie. It was already too late for her to do any school work tonight, so she blew out the lamp and went and sat by the window and watched the diyas still burning over at Pyari's house, her gaze momentarily falling on the candleflies flickering around the bushes in Nani's backyard, and her ears tuned in to the nocturnal sounds of the chirring crickets and croaking of the crapos in the pond below.

The night was truly enchanting, and she could have sat there for a while longer and feel the gentle breeze on her face, but she decided to get some sleep before the fowlcocks started crowing. She lit a mosquito coil and placed it on the bedside table and let down the mosquito netting and tucked it beneath the coconut fibre mattress, then she crawled into bed and lay her head down on the soft feather pillow and closed her eyes. And the vision of Ravi appeared.

She found herself wondering who he was and where he was from. And she wondered if she would ever see him

247

again. Then she realised she was thinking too much of him and tried to get him out of her mind, but he kept appearing again and again, until, eventually, slumber overpowered her, carrying her away into a land of dreams.

* * *

It was the day of Eid-ul-Adha, the Muslim Festival of the Sacrifice, and the early December sun was bright and blazingly hot, and on this mid-afternoon the air was motionless without sound. In Nani's fowl coop, a few of the chickens were pacing around restlessly, while others were roosting on the ladders. The tilapias and hassars were splashing about in the pond as though to cool themselves, and the branches of the fruit trees in the orchard were hanging limp, exhausted from the heat, and thirsty for a sprinkle of water.

Nani and Indira were now in the backyard, raking the dried grass and bush that they had cut a few days ago and left to dry.

"This should be easy to burn now," Nani said to Indira as they piled the dried grass into a heap in a clearing in the middle of the yard.

"Yes, it's dry enough," Indira agreed, and she got a bucket of water and poured it around the heap so that when they start the fire it would not spread beyond the circumference.

Suddenly, Raj was heard spewing curses, and Pyari shouted at the parrot, saying, "Stop that bloody cursing!"

Nani let out an agitated sigh and said to Indira, "If she would stop cursing herself then Raj would do so, also."

"Never mind Pyari and Raj," Indira said, "let's get the fire started."

Nani tightened her faded brown headkerchief around her head and sighed again, fed up with Pyari and Raj and their cursing. "Never mind them?" she said. "I have a feeling to go over there and give them a piece of my mind!"

"You would do no such thing," Indira said. "They would both start cursing at you if you did."

"They both need to disinfect their mouths with some good salt soap washing!" Nani said.

Indira burst out laughing at this, and Nani started laughing after her. Then Nani reverted her attention to what they were doing and got out the box of matches from her dress pocket and handed it to Indira and said, "My back is too sore to bend down to light the fire, child, please help me with it."

Indira took the box of matches and got a matchstick and fired it up and she went around the high heap and lit the grass and, while the fire was catching, Nani got her peerah and sat a little ways away. Indira then took off momentarily and returned with two green coconuts, and she sat on a log beside Nani, both in the sunshine, and they drank the sweet coconut water and cooled their thirst as they watched the flames flicker and crackle, spouting dark smoke high into the air.

"Fazeela and Shazam have just finished observing Ramadan and they're celebrating Eid today," Indira said to Nani, "and they have invited us to share sweets with them this evening."

Without the slightest hesitation, Nani said, "We will go." And she added, "Fazeela never misses our religious celebrations."

With that, Nani and Indira lapsed into silence and looked on as the heap of grass was burning, filling the air with the sweet smoky smell. They were immersed in the tranquility of the hot day, lost in its pleasant loneliness and dreaminess.

Their quiet moment was soon interrupted by Francine, who came bouncing over with a big smile on her face. "Good afternoon!" she greeted.

"Good afternoon," both Nani and Indira reciprocated.

"Mom sent some *cocorite* and wara that she got at the market today, and some *fat top* and *cassava pone* she baked," Francine said, and handed Nani the cloth bag containing the fruits and cakes.

"That's nice of her," Nani said and took the bag and, when Francine took a seat on the log next to Indira, she shared the fruits and cakes with the girls.

As the dried grass continued to burn down to ashes, the three of them gaffed for a while as they ate, and then Francine said to Indira, "My Afro hairstyle is getting too long and unruly, can you braid my hair for me?"

Indira suggested, "Let's sit over by the back steps in the shade and do that."

Francine clued in that Indira just wanted them to be private so that they could have their personal girl talk. "Okay," she said and followed Indira over to the backstairs, leaving Nani to douse the ashes with a bucket of water.

When they sat down on the steps, beneath the shade of the protruding zinc roof, Solomon, who was standing beside Rani at the bottom-house, suddenly started hee-hawing, showing his big, white teeth and looking funny, and the girls burst out in a sudden fit of laughter. They laughed even harder at Rani as she was chewing her cud with her big, old mouth, making a clapping sound like a man with no table manners.

Once Indira settled into braiding Francine's hair into shoulder-length braids, things turned from laugher to sadness when Francine said, "I miss Jacko." Jacko the monkey had suddenly died just last week.

"I miss him, too," Indira said, and she patted Francine's head to console her, but in the effort of doing so that only made Francine burst out crying.

Indira stifled backed tears that welled up in her own eyes, and she said, "Maybe you should get another pet monkey."

"I can't think of that now, Indira. I'm too sad over Jacko."

Thinking of a way of cheering up her friend, Indira then said, "I can mention someone who would put you in a happy mood instantly."

"Albert," Francine said and smiled right away, and at that moment Jacko left her mind and she dried her eyes and composed herself. "He already wants to marry me, you know."

"Don't think about that now," Indira said. "Wait until you're finished with school. We have only a few months left."

"But I love him so much and want to be with him," Francine said. "Laliwa, too, she can't wait to be with Afonso."

"They're so in love, too," Indira said. "I caught them dancing in a garden one day."

"Laliwa's parents would never consent for her to marry Afonso. Her father has already picked out a husband for her from their tribe she told us. But Laliwa's so in love with Afonso and all she talks about is eloping with him someday."

Just then, Nani snuck up on the girls and caught the end the last sentence, 'eloping with him someday', and she asked, "Who's going to elope with whom?"

The girls were startled and they looked at each other nervously, and Francine said, "Eloping? Oh, we were talking about a girl in a book that we read."

But Nani did not buy the story, and she looked at Indira accusingly and asked, "Have you met a young man, child?"

"Me? Met a young man?" Indira asked, expressing astonishment. "No, no, Nani, I haven't."

"You must tell me about it before you think of eloping," Nani went on to say.

"I haven't met anyone," Indira insisted.

Nani then turned to Francine and said, "Then it must be you, Francine. Who is this boy with whom you're planning to elope?"

"No boy, Francine said," with a straight face. "And I would much prefer the consent of my parents instead of eloping."

Just then the girls were saved by the call of a fish lady at the gate, who was carrying a basket of live, fat hassars and jumbo tiger shrimps on her head, and Nani turned her attention to her and invited her in to the bottom-house. The lady came in and laid out a rag on the earthen ground and

252

made a generous parcel of a dozen of the hassars and a big parcel of shrimps for a good price, and Nani purchased both for dinner.

When the lady left, Nani thought of making some *saijan bhaji*—fried saijan leaves, and she said to the girls, "Go and pick some saijan for me to cook with the shrimps, and, also, pick me some of the saijan drumsticks for me to cook with the hassa curry." Nani paused for a moment and thought she would also like to pickle some mangos, and she added, "Pick some green mangoes, also, so I can make some *achar*."

The girls agreed quickly to do so, relieved that Nani did not bring up the subject of eloping again. As soon as Indira finished braiding Francine's hair, they went in the backyard and climbed the trees and started picking the green leaves' vegetable along with the drumsticks, and the green mangoes, and as they were doing so they resumed their girl talk.

"I wish I had met a young man as Nani had accused me of," Indira said to Francine as she was up in the saijan tree.

From the mango tree, Francine said, "You sort of met someone."

"Who?"

"Remember the fellow you saw back in October on Diwali night?"

Indira remembered him too well. "Ravi?"

"Yes."

"We really haven't met," Indira said. "I haven't seen him since then. He's definitely not from Rose Hall."

"I've never seen you react to anyone like that, Indira. He really did capture your attention," Francine said. "I hope he shows up again."

"I hope so, too."

The conversation continued to revolve around the subject of boys and love until the girls finished picking the saijan and mangoes. They then went up to the kitchen with the loaded straw baskets and found Nani busy with cooking the hassar curry and straining the pot of rice in the dish sink. Nani took a green mango the girls picked and sliced it up and peeled the saijan drumsticks and chopped them up and added them to the curry. While the carahee of curry was boiling, she stripped the tiny saijan leaves from the leafstalks and chopped them up and started frying them with the shrimps. A melange of mouth-watering spices floated about as the dishes were cooking, and the burning wood in the mud stove heated up the kitchen, making the place even hotter than it was.

As the food continued to cook, Nani sat on the peerah and ground up spices on the masala brick for the mango achar, while the girls sliced the green mangoes and ground them up in a manual grinder and squeezed the juice out with a cotton cloth, all the while whispering to each other. By the time Nani finished mixing the ground up mangoes with spices and mustard oil, the food was finished cooking, and the three sat down and had scrumptious hot plates, filling their bellies with saijan bhaji with shrimps and curry hassar with saijan drumsticks, and rice. Right after dinner, Francine left, with some food Nani dished out in a steel lunch box for Joan and George, and she went to bathe and get dressed to go over to Fazeela for the religious sugar feast.

By now, the red sun had just slipped below the horizon and flocks of birds were flying to their evening roosts, and darkness was beginning to settle in, bringing a slight breeze that made the place feel a little less hot. Indira lit the kerosene oil lamp and assisted Nani to bottle the mango achar, then when they were finished, they got washed up and dressed, and they headed over to Fazeela's home.

Fazeela's house, though appearing to be run-down from the outside, was kept clean and was beautifully decorated on the inside. An orange sofa set enhanced the gold, floral-patterned wall paper, and sheer red curtains and a vase of fresh flowers added a splash of rainbow colours to the sitting room, which was also brightened with glass ornaments and painted sea shells arranged on a centrepiece table, beneath which was a mat made of strips of fabrics. The rest of the floor was bare but polished to a shine in a dark mahogany tone. And a copy of a Quran was on a side table, evoking an atmosphere of sacredness to the home. The two small bedrooms were neat, and decorated with fresh flowers, also.

When Nani and Indira arrived, Fazeela was in the lamp-lit kitchen, and she was holding her eighth child on her hip, a curly-haired baby girl. The seventh child whom she had given birth to when Indira was only five years old, now a young lad, was hanging on to her arm. The rest of the family, including, Shazam, were there, also. Two of the older girls, now around Indira's age, were busy making *sawine*, kheer, mithai, and gulab jamun sweets. Shazam and the eldest son participated in setting out the sweets on the

255

small kitchen table, while the others sat around on the bare floor, looking on at the scene.

Nani and Fazeela discoursed about the latest gossips in town, and it was not long before that Francine, Joan and George Williams joined them, followed shortly after by Pyari, who brought with her a few children from the town. And, after the consecration of the food, the sugar feast began. They all loaded their plates with the sweets and started eating. And the children must have thought they were in sugar heaven!

There was much fun and laughter on that warm night as the neighbours and friends celebrated Eid-ul-Adha with Fazeela and her family. It was not until late that the baby girl started crying from being tired and wanting to sleep, and so Nani and Indira and the others left, with brown paper bags full of sweets.

* * *

The sharp rays of the December sun was shining down on Rose Hall this afternoon, and the folks were busy with Saturday chores, scrubbing and cleaning and beating clothes and cooking, and some were putting up Christmas trees and decorations, while carols were playing on radios and turntables. The atmosphere was buzzing with joy and excitement as Christians and non-Christians were preparing to celebrate the Birth of Christ in the quaint little town.

Indira was as busy as everyone else, scrubbing and cleaning the old house with special attention for the occasion, and she daubed the earthen ground of the bottom-house and left it to dry. She then went and joined Nani on the side of the fowl coop, where the old mud oven was situated on layers of stone. Nani was busy with cleaning and preparing the oven so she could bake Christmas cake the following week.

"It would be easier if we do our baking over at Auntie Joan's this year," Indira suggested. "She has a nice electric oven, and I know she would be happy to let us use it."

"I've been doing my baking in a mud oven since I was a girl and I'm not going to change my ways now," Nani responded, adamantly.

"I just think that it's getting too tiresome for you to do now."

"Hush, hush, my child" Nani said. "I know it brings you much joy when I bake with the mud oven."

Indira could not deny that, in fact, she had many precious memories of watching Nani bake fruit and sponge cakes in the mud oven on the hot days of December, and that was a part of what made Christmas so special for her. So she gave up trying to persuade Nani to do otherwise, and she helped her to daub the oven with a mixture of water and clay and left it to dry. She then started rubbing— washing clothes on the washboard, and as she was hanging the clothes out to dry on the clothes line in the backyard, she came across a pumpkin vine and traced it to a ripe pumpkin, which she picked and cooked with fried fish and roti for dinner. After dinner, she and Nani washed up, and she went about putting up the Christmas tree and decorating the old greenheart wood house.

The late afternoon sun was now streaming through the sitting room window, casting a golden glow in the room, from where the sound of the birds chirping in the trees outside was heard, as though they were singing along to the vinyl record of José Feliciano singing *Feliz Navidad* that a neighbour was playing. Indira was singing along, also, as Nani was humming as she rocked back and forth in the rocking chair and looked on at Indira. Indira got out the three-foot, artificial Christmas tree and placed it on a table in a corner and decorated it with colourful bulbs and ornaments, placing a silver star on top. She now wished they had electricity for blinking lights, but they had to do without, so she improvised by brightening up the tree with gold and silver and red and green tinsel garlands that glittered in the sunshine.

"Your grandfather, Dr. Ramesh, is not traveling this Christmas and he has invited us to spend Christmas Day with him," Nani said. "And your Uncle Ram has sent word with bus driver Manil that he would not be coming down for Christmas because he's very busy with work."

"So then we'll be spending Christmas Day with Grandpa?"

"If that's where you want to spend Christmas, then we will," Nani said.

"Yes, Nani, oh yes! I would love to spend Christmas with Grandpa."

"Then I will send word to him with George Williams that we accept his invitation," Nani said. "Your grandfather has also asked if you could visit with him on Christmas Eve for a special dinner."

"I would love to," Indira said without hesitation, excited about the thought. But, after considering, asked, "What about you? Hasn't he invited you, also?"

"No, child," Nani said, "this is strictly for the two of you. You spend all of your time with me, so I'm happy that you will be spending some time alone with him."

Indira had a suspicious feeling that Nani was leaving out something, but she did not persist further, instead, asked, "What will you do?"

"I will need to rest my old bones so I can wake up early for Christmas morning service, which, as you know, starts at seven o'clock, so I will be retiring early to bed."

"Okay, then, send word to Grandpa that I will be there for Christmas Eve dinner with him."

"I will," Nani said. "Now, have you thought of what you would wear on Christmas Day?"

"I'd like to wear a red taffeta dress," Indira said, having thought about it beforehand.

Nani got out her green cloth money bag and untied the string and took out some money and said, "Here, take this money and buy some fabric and give it to Auntie Joan to make your dress."

Indira took the money and thanked Nani, then asked, "How about you, Nani, aren't you getting a new dress also?"

"I have some green silk fabric stored away. I'll give it to Joan to make me a dress with a matching headkerchief."

Nani wasted no time in getting her green silk fabric over to Joan Williams, but Indira waited until all of her school tests were over with before she got the red taffeta fabric. And she instructed Joan to make a full-skirted, knee-length dress, with a v-neck bodice and short puff sleeves, which she would wear for both Christmas morning service and the Christmas Day get together with her grandfather and Nani.

Indira also needed a new dress to wear for Christmas Eve dinner with her grandfather, so she also got some fine white cotton fabric and asked Joan to make an A-line, short-sleeve dress, with a round neckline trimmed with delicate lace.

Just a couple of days before Christmas Eve, Nani decided to do her baking, and it turned out to be a whole day process. She and Indira were up early in the morning and there in the enchanting coziness of the kitchen, in a celebratory Christmas mood, they were sifting flour and preparing the mix for fruit and sponge cakes. Indira had the tedious task of washing the salt off the butter, and there she was sitting on the peerah with an enamel bowl of butter, stirring it with a pot spoon over and over again in some water, and draining the water, and repeating the task again and again until the butter tasted of no salt and was soft and fluffy. And just when she thought she was through with that task, Nani gave her another slab of butter to do, for Nani was making extra cakes to share with the neighbours, like she always did. When Indira was finished with that, Nani gave her the eggs to hand beat, then Nani started making the cake mix, the buttery, fruity, vanilla essence, and flour and egg scents filling the air and enhancing the Christmas mood. By the time they had finished making the cake mix and greasing the pans, it was already past noon.

It was another sweltering day in town, and the neighbours all around were playing Christmas music as children were out in the streets playing in the hot sun. Nani and Indira went down to the backyard and put some coconut shells in the mud oven and started the fire, and while Nani waited for the oven to be ready, Indira went up to the kitchen and fetched the pans of cake mix and placed them on a nearby table. And soon Nani started baking.

Nani and Indira sat on their peerahs under the tamarind tree nearby as the cakes were baking, filling the place with the aroma of the coconut shells burning and the sweet vanilla essence. It was a charming experience, even though the place was hot like fire, making Indira thirst for some Christmas ginger beer.

Right at that moment, Mr. Jackson came calling at the gate in his loud voice, and Indira rushed up to let him in and found that he brought a few bottles of cold ginger beer, which he made himself and boasted that it was the best in town. He also brought a pan of black cake, loaded with rum, which he made himself, and he bragged about that, also. Indira ushered him in the backyard and he joined her and Nani under the tamarind tree, and as they watched the wavering heat rising from the mud oven, they drank ginger beer and quenched their thirst and ate some of the black cake. Indira admitted it was the best ginger beer she had ever had, and the best black cake, also.

Not too long after Mr. Jackson came over, Mrs. Surjeet dropped in with her pan of Christmas cake, then came Joan Williams and Fazeela with theirs, and Pyari came over to join the gathering with a bottle of rum. Shazam and George Williams dropped in next and suggested they do a bush-cook, and they caught a couple of Nani's fat chickens and curried them. Francine and Fazeela's children were called over then and they all sat around and had a good feed.

It was not until the birds started flying to their evening roosts that Nani finished her baking, and she shared her Christmas cakes with the neighbours, after which, they

261

went on their merry way back to their homes, all except for Mr. Jackson, who dropped in on other neighbours who were also cooking and drinking and playing loud reggae Christmas music and dancing, having a good old time in the tropical night under the moon and stars.

The music was still playing by the time Nani and Indira were ready for bed. Nani was tired and exhausted, though she would never admit it, and she went out like a light.

* * *

The Eve of Christmas was now here, and dusk had just fallen. The stars began to appear, sparkling like diamonds in the sky, and the moon emerged to cast its silvery rays over the quaint little town of Rose Hall.

Indira was in the lamp-lit bedroom getting ready to visit her grandfather, putting on the pretty, white cotton dress with the lace neckline that Joan had sewn for her. She curled her night-black hair into ringlets, just like her grandfather liked it, and she smiled at the thought of seeing him. He was sending his chauffeur, Sahil, to pick her up, and with a pleasant warm breeze blowing, she thought it was a perfect night to go cruising up the main road in the blue Studebaker to his big, yellow house. She hurriedly finished dressing and patted some translucent powder on her face and dabbed on a bit of perfumed cream that Nani had gotten her, and she slipped on a pair of white, high-heeled sandals.

Nani came in to see her in the new dress, and she smiled admiringly and thought the only thing missing was jewellery, and she got out her grandmother Chaaya's bag of jewellery and selected a gold chain and matching earrings and put them on Indira, and she gave her two pairs of gold bangles to wear. They both then went in the sitting room, and Indira sat by the window and waited for the Studebaker to arrive, feeling as excited as she had been when she was a little girl going to her grandfather's pig roast.

While she was waiting, Nani made up her cot and was getting ready to settle in for the night. The car arrived promptly at seven o'clock, and Indira kissed Nani goodnight, then she hurried downstairs.

The liveried Sahil ushered her in the back seat, and as he made his way down the bumpy dirt street, she rolled down the window, taking in the sights of the stilt houses along the way, adorned with colourful, blinking Christmas lights and glittering decorations. The night was warm and the moonlight was bright, and merry people were out on their verandahs laughing and gaffing, raising their voices above the sounds of Christmas music, while others were eating and drinking and dancing in their homes. Some were strolling up and down the streets and on the main road, men and women, beautifully dressed in brand new clothes, having a good time romancing the night and enjoying the lights and the spirit of Christmas Eve.

Indira was enjoying herself as much, sitting in the back seat of the luxury car as the breeze was gently blowing, anticipating seeing her grandfather, and observing the people going by on the narrow main road, where the shops and houses were lit up and the streetlamps shed a faint glow. A few other cars were cruising by, also, and cyclists meandered their way through the sparse crowd. Then suddenly Indira saw him again. Coming up the road on a bicycle was Ravi, the obscure young man whom she had seen on Diwali night. And her heart started racing. Ravi slowed down as he approached the blue Studebaker to take a look at it, and he brought his bicycle to a screeching stop when he looked in the back and saw Indira, looking beautiful and mysterious in her white cotton dress and gold necklace, a whiff of her sweet perfume awakening his senses. For a moment they locked stare, Indira mesmerised by his handsome visage under the silvery moonlight. Then the car drove past him, and when she turned back to look at him, he made a turn in an alleyway and disappeared out of sight.

Indira did not know why her heart raced when she saw him both times. She just did not understand the strange feeling that had so suddenly come over her, an uncontrollable feeling that almost took her breath away. Ravi consumed her thoughts for the rest of the drive, leaving her to wonder once again as to who he was. It was not until she caught a glimpse of her grandfather's tall iron gate and big, yellow house that her thoughts shifted back to seeing her grandfather, and she became more and more excited over that as she drew closer.

Dr. Ramesh was sitting on the Christmas-lit verandah waiting for her, full with anticipation of seeing her, and when he saw the Studebaker pulling through the tall iron gate, he hurried down the stairs and met her as she alighted from the car, and he exclaimed, "My beautiful granddaughter!" And he hugged her and kissed her cheeks.

"And my handsome Grandpa!" Indira returned, for Dr. Ramesh was indeed as handsome as he had been ten years ago, his brown skin nearly wrinkle-free, with only his distinguished crop of silver hair revealing his age.

He adjusted his black-rimmed spectacles and took Indira by the hand, and said, "Come upstairs, my dear Granddaughter. I'm having dinner prepared for just the two of us. We will eat and drink and be merry!" And he led Indira upstairs.

Indira was always impressed with the big, yellow house, but tonight her grandfather had his housekeeper Aaja deck the place with Christmas decorations especially for her, and it was dazzling. A live Norfolk Island Pine Christmas tree was in the sitting room, and from it cascaded silvery-white angel hair, and it had numerous bulbs and ornaments, and dozens of colourful, blinking lights that reflected on the immaculately polished mahogany floor, and this fascinated Indira. She could have just sat there and stare at the angel hair and the blinking lights but her grandfather led her to the dining room, where the long table was laid out in sumptuous silver and fine china and set up for just two under the bright chandelier. And, coming from the kitchen, the smell of pork roasting in butter and fresh thyme filled the air.

"Sit, my dear girl," Dr. Ramesh said as he pulled out a chair for Indira. "Dinner will be served in just a little while." When Indira sat down, he poured her some *sorrel* drink, and he said, "I think I'll fix myself a hard drink and have it while we wait." And he fixed a shot of strong drink on the rocks and took his seat at the head of the table, right next to Indira.

The two of them chatted, Dr. Ramesh getting caught up on how Indira was doing at school and at home, and they joked and laughed about this and that. Then Dr. Ramesh's smile dissipated and he suddenly became serious when he said, "I've asked you here tonight for two reasons, Indira. Number one is that you are my only granddaughter and grandchild, and what a pleasure it is for me to share this special evening with you."

"Likewise, Grandpa," Indira responded, affectionately. "And what is the second reason?"

Just then the obsequious Aaja brought in a platter of roasted pork, among other things, and they wasted no time in digging into the hot foods.

Once Indira had a few mouthfuls, she said to Dr. Ramesh, "What's your second reason for having me here, Grandpa? You've got me really curious now."

"How is the food, my dear?" Dr. Ramesh asked. "Does it suit your taste?"

"Delicious, Grandpa, very delicious," Indira said. "Now, would you answer me?"

"Yes, dear," Dr. Ramesh said, "I'll get to it. But I must tell you it is a very important matter."

"Does this have anything to do with Nani?"

"No, dear," Dr. Ramesh said and shook his head. "I've thought long and hard about this before broaching the subject with you, and, I will tell you it is for your own good."

"For Pete's sake, Grandpa, just tell me what this is all about," Indira said, getting a bit impatient with grandfather's long-windedness that he carried on with at times.

Dr. Ramesh wiped the sides of his mouth with his napkin, then finally said, "The second reason for having you here is to discuss your future."

"My future?"

"Yes," Dr. Ramesh said. "You will soon finish high school and it's time you think about getting married."

Indira instantly dropped her fork and burst out laughing, then she said, "So this is what the second reason for having me here is all about. I should think of getting married!"

"I'm very serious, my dear," Dr. Ramesh said, with a stern look behind his spectacles.

It was not often that Indira would get a stern look from her grandfather and she knew she had overstepped her boundaries by laughing at his idea of her getting married, and she composed herself quickly and said, "I know you're serious about this, Grandpa, and believe me, I do think of marrying. But I haven't met anyone, as yet." And, oddly enough, right then the vision of Ravi popped into her head.

"Don't you worry about that because I have some plans laid out for you," Dr. Ramesh said. "I will arrange a good marriage for you."

"An arranged marriage for me!" Indira blurted out, totally caught by surprise.

"Yes," Dr. Ramesh answered. "You know the bank manger, Mr. Jajal—"

"He has a son name Tarak. And you're trying to set me up with him."

"He is a good match for you, my dear, believe me," Dr. Ramesh said assuredly. "The Jajal family is well respected and affluent, and they hold certain cachet in our town. Tarak is a fine-looking chap, twenty years old, and he has a

267

job now, working at the bank himself. If you marry into this family your future will be secure and you will get a job working at the bank, also."

Most young women would have jumped at the opportunity of such a good catch but Indira was apathetic, and she said, "But I don't love Tarak, Grandpa. How can I marry someone who I don't love?"

Dr. Ramesh waved his right hand and said, "Don't worry about that, my dear, for in time you will fall in love with him. I know that because my marriage to your late grandmother was arranged, and we fell in love in time." Dr. Ramesh then went on, with finality, to say, "I will arrange an introduction at my place right after you finish school."

Indira was not exactly the docile type, she did not agree with the whole notion of arranged marriages and was ambiguous about betting on one's future of happiness or unhappiness, but she did not argue with her grandfather out of respect for him, for she knew he was only looking out for the best for her. So she left the conversation at that.

They then finished dinner and went in the sitting room and sat on the bright-red leather sofa by the Norfolk Island Pine Christmas tree, and Dr. Ramesh reached over to the radio and tuned into Radio Demerara. While Christmas carols were playing, he told Indira stories of his childhood Christmas memories and how he grew up in the lap of luxury and, being the only child, was showered with gifts from his parents, who were both non-religious but took the opportunity to feast at the time of every religious celebration. With a glimmer in his eyes, he recounted the lavish Christmas banquets his wealthy parents used to host when they lived in New Amsterdam in a big, concrete house; the tables would overflow with foods and drinks and gifts, and there was much dancing on the polished floors and out in the yard under the moonlight. Then a sadness overtook him when he started talking about his late wife, Shanti, and how he missed her terribly. He went on to tell Indira stories about her grandmother from the time he married her up until he lost her a few years ago.

Dr. Ramesh could have gone on telling stories all night about the love of his life but the radio host soon announced that it was eleven o'clock; time to send Indira back home. So he told her he would continue his anecdotes the next day and for her to expect a feast at his house, and he bid her goodnight. And Sahil drove her back home.

Indira saw no sign of Ravi on her way back. When she arrived home, Nani was snoring, and she retired to her room for the night. She tried to assimilate the conversation her grandfather had with her, about arranging a marriage for her with Tarak, which she was now sure Nani knew about but did not mention when she told her about the dinner meeting with her grandfather. But she did not dwell on that for long, for Ravi entered her head and she just could not get him out.

It seemed she had just fallen asleep when the fowlcocks started crowing and woke her up. And it was now early Christmas morning in the town of Rose Hall.

* * *

At the crowing of the fowlcocks, the millions of stars in the sky and the full moon were shining brightly on this balmy Christmas morning. Indira got up and lit the kerosene oil

269

lamp and went and woke Nani with a kiss and a cheery "Merry Christmas, Nani!" Nani got out of bed and greeted her likewise, then they both headed into the kitchen to prepare breakfast before getting dressed for the early morning church service, which was to commence at seven o'clock. Fazeela, Shazam, Pyari, Francine, Joan & George Williams all planned on attending the service, along with Mr. Jackson and Mrs. Surjeet, the genuine camaraderie amongst this disparate group of friends, with diverse religious backgrounds, revering each other's faiths instead of being sanctimonious. They were all to meet at Nani's bottom-house, from where they would be heading to church on foot.

Indira hung up the oil lamp in the kitchen and opened the window overlooking the backyard to let in the pleasant early morning breeze, then she shoved some wood in the mud stove and lit it and went about making *sada roti*. While she was doing so, Nani put on a pot of water to boil to make tea and she was softly singing *Away in a Manger*. The soft crackling of wood and the sweet scent of the smoke, along with the warmth of the fire, brought about an air of serenity to this special morning, and Nani and Indira were lost in thoughts of The Divine Baby who was born in Bethlehem so long ago. In silence, they had the sada roti with melted butter, and they sipped on their tea and reverently observed the sacred morning.

While the moon was still shining brightly in the sky, Nani went downstairs and bathed, and she came back upstairs and oiled her skin with fresh coconut oil and got dressed in her green silk dress with matching headkerchief, leaving her feet bare, as usual, and she smiled, flashing her gold teeth, for it was indeed a joyous morning. Indira got washed up, also, and she put on her red taffeta dress and black high-heeled sandals, and she did her hair in an updo coiffure and patted her face with powder, all the while humming Christmas carols.

By the time they were ready to leave, the early morning sky had turned a deep shade of cobalt-blue and the stars were fading as dew began falling softly on the green grass. Francine first arrived at the bottom-house, and she was dressed in an identical red taffeta dress as Indira's, which Joan had also sewn. Shortly after, Joan and George Williams arrived looking sharp in their new clothes. Even Fazeela and Shazam afforded new clothes for the occasion, and, also, Pyari, who had a stiff drink before she left home. Mrs. Surjeet arrived next with the gregarious Mr. Jackson, who had a bit of a hangover from partying all night, and they, too, looked impressive in their brand new clothes.

The merry bunch made their way up the dirt street to the road, and on their way encountered a few other church-goers, and everyone stopped to effusively wish each other merry Christmas with affable hugs and kisses. When they reached the church, people were hanging around outside, all in beautiful, fresh clothes and cheerful smiles, and there were more jolly wishes.

The soft morning light created a dreamy and sacred ambience in the beautifully decorated church, which was packed full of exuberant people on this special day. As a gentle wind was blowing through the windows, the Christmas service commenced with a number of carols, followed by a succinct sermon by Pastor Delford, on the birth of Christ. Then there was more heart-felt carolling.

271

When church was dismissed, the people hung around for a while and talked and laughed and wished each other merry Christmas again, and again. By the time they began dispersing to their homes to begin the celebrations, the sun was up, bright and glorious, an indication that it was going to be a very hot Christmas Day in the quaint little town of Rose Hall.

When Nani and Indira returned home, they opened their presents around the Christmas tree in the sitting room. Nani bought Indira a brown-eyed brunette doll, and she got her an authentic gold wrist watch band, much to the thrill of Indira. Indira got Nani a white headkerchief, a comb, and a nice piece of floral fabric for a dress. They both purchased gifts for Dr. Ramesh; a fine fountain pen and a silk necktie from Indira, and a shirt-jack and trousers outfit from Nani, which they placed in a bag to take along to Dr. Ramesh.

By now, the town folks were blasting Christmas music on their radios and turntables, and as Nana Mouskouri was singing *Old Toy Trains*, the children were out on the streets playing with their gifts of toy trains and cars and trucks and machine guns and dolls, while there was a flurry of activities as the adults went about chasing chickens, ducks, goats, pigs, and cows for the Christmas feasts. Some had already taken to the bottle and were having hard drinks, talking and laughing out loudly in the shade of their verandahs and under the fruit trees in their yards.

Nani and Indira did not have to wait long before the blue Studebaker came to pick them up, and they were taken straight to Dr. Ramesh's big, yellow house. The day spent there was in abundance of food, music, and gifts.

At some point, Dr. Ramesh had a chance to have a private conversation with Nani and updated her on the meeting he had with Indira last evening and her reaction to the proposed marriage plans. He and Nani had been in communication concerning this all along. Nani had long expressed to him that her desire was for Indira to marry someone who works at the bank and he had been keeping his eyes and ears open and found the right opportunity. And Nani agreed that the marriage arrangement between Indira and Tarak would be a suitable one. Dr. Ramesh told her that he made it clear to Indira that the introduction between her and Tarak would take place at his house only after her schooling, and very shortly after.

The Christmas celebration went on way into the night, with added enjoyment for Dr. Ramesh and Nani over the auspicious occasion of the marriage plans for Indira, and it was not until midnight that Nani and Indira returned to their humble abode down by the river.

* * *

Besides New Year's celebrations, nothing else eventful happened in the month of January, and Indira had no more sightings of Ravi, neither was there any more talk about Tarak. Then in February people were out in town celebrating the Birth of the Republic of Guyana, Mashramani, dancing in the streets to steel bands playing hot calypso and reggae tunes, and there were masquerade parades and spectacular costume competitions, and lots of cooking, eating, and drinking happening. There was more celebration in March for the Hindu Festival of Colours,

Phagwah or Holi, bringing amity amongst all people, with Hindus and non-Hindus out on the streets throwing *abir*—colourful liquid or powder dyes—perfume, and water at each other. Indira and Francine were also out getting soaked and having fun in the hot sun. They thought they saw Ravi that day, but the fellow was camouflaged in so much red dye that they were not certain of this.

April brought Easter, the celebration of the resurrection of Christ for the Christians, and the bright, blue sky was filled with colourful kites flying high in the sunshine, kites of all shapes and sizes, their frills fluttering in the wind. People in town everywhere were flying kites, both Christians and non-Christians. They were out on their verandahs and outdoor stairs, and front and back yards, and the happy children were out on the streets, trying to raise their kites in the sky. Indira and Francine were participants, also. They sat at Nani's bottom-house and made their own kites with colourful crepe paper and pinta—the spine of coconut leaves, and flour paste. And while Nani was busy baking hot cross buns in the mud oven in the backyard, the girls stood on the backstairs and launched their kites and had fun flying them, as whiffs of hot cross buns drifted about.

On Palm Sunday, Nani, Indira, their neighbours and friends attended church, which was decorated in a profusion of palm branches. And what a joyous service it was. Then they all attended more of a somber Good Friday service on a sweltering mid-afternoon, and what sadness and lamentation that brought about in remembering The One nailed to a cross with wounds bleeding, a crown of thorns on his head, Christ demonstrating His profound love for mankind by dying to save man from the immorality of the world. But there was much gladness at Easter Sunday service, celebrating His resurrection.

On the evening of Easter Sunday, Indira and Francine went to a local school to see the movie *The Cross And The Switchblade* with Erik Estrada and Pat Boone, and after the movie, as they were walking back home under the moonlit sky, strolling along the narrow main road with others, Francine suddenly whispered to Indira, saying, "Look across the street."

When Indira looked, she saw Ravi towing a local girl on his bicycle, Padmini as she was known by, and they were both laughing and seemed totally engrossed with each other, so much so that Ravi did not even notice Indira, and a pang of disappointment took hold of her.

"Looks like Ravi's got a girlfriend," Francine said, sounding let down herself.

"It seems that way, doesn't it?" was all Indira said to that.

And Indira went home and put Ravi out of her mind. Then she started thinking about the arranged marriage with Tarak that her grandfather had proposed, and she thought perhaps Grandpa, old and prudent as he was, knew what was best for her future. For now, though, she put that out of her head, also, and concentrated on studying for her GCE— General Certificate of Education.

So she buried herself in her studies and started counting down the weeks to her exams and her final days in high school.

12

The Rum Shop Incident

Indira woke to the crowing of the fowlcocks in the dark of the early morning, and feeling lethargic from being up late the previous night studying, rested for a few minutes longer before she hauled herself out of bed and changed her night clothes. From the bedroom window she could see the light from the kerosene oil lamp streaming through the upper part of the back door of the kitchen, and she went to the kitchen to find Nani stirring a pot of porridge on the mud stove, her face wet with tears dripping from her eyes, obviously not caused by the swirling smoke from the wood burning hotly because she was softly sobbing.

"Why are you crying, Nani?" she asked, as she went and put her arm around Nani's frail, old shoulders.

Nani wiped away the tears from her faded brown eyes with her apron, and she said, "It's nothing, child. You go and iron your school clothes and get prepared for school."

"Don't tell me it's nothing you're crying about," Indira said. "Tell me what's troubling you, Nani. Has it anything to do with Uncle Ram?"

"No, no," Nani said.

"Then what is it?"

Nani then broke down and, with a heartrending cry, said, "I'm feeling terribly sad that you will soon leave me and go and live with your husband and you would not be around to

276

keep my company anymore. I will miss you so dearly, my dear child."

"Oh, Nani," Indira said and hugged her tenderly. "No need for you to be sad and cry over this, for wherever I go you will come and live with me."

"You are too kind, child, but I don't know if the Jajals' would agree to that. When you're gone I would have no one to help me with the gardening and the house chores. What will I do then?" And Nani wept even more pitifully.

"You will come and live with me," Indira said again. "I will make sure Tarak agrees to this before we get married. Dry your eyes for now. I can't bear to see you cry like this, Nani."

Nani dried her tears then went on to say, "Tarak is a good match for you, though. He's a good-looking fellow, only twenty years old, and he works at the bank, and so will you." This was a dream Nani had for Indira ever since she was a little girl, for her to marry someone who works at the bank, and for her to also work in the shade of the cool bank and not break her back hoeing and tilling the earth and have her soft hands grow callouses or have the sharp rays of the sun burn her tender skin and have it become as leathery as hers. The opportunity for Indira to work at the bank was more important to her than the wealth of the Jajal family, or their reputation for that matter, which as far as she knew was impeccable for she had never heard a bad word about them, particularly, about Tarak. It was paramount to her, though, that the young man love her granddaughter, and she felt sure that he would be captivated by Indira and fall in love with her, and she was convinced that Indira would be taken by the handsome,

277

light-skinned young man and fall in love with him, also. She was feeling very confident about things, and she flashed her gold teeth and said, "I think that your grandfather has made a very good choice for you. He will be introducing you to Tarak as soon as you finish school, so be prepared to meet him."

With her trusted grandfather thinking that the match between her and Tarak was a suitable one, and now Nani, the dear old woman whom she trusted, also, thinking the same thing, Indira was becoming more convinced that marrying Tarak might be the right thing for her, and she was beginning to feel more and more certain that she would fall in love with him. She started building hope to meet him and was actually getting excited now, and she was beginning to envision herself working at the bank and was getting excited about that, also. "I will prepare to meet Tarak when the time gets closer," she said to Nani. "But for now I have to focus on my studies so I can pass my exams."

"I agree with you, child," Nani said. "Put your head on your studies for now and on passing your exams, so that when you marry Tarak you would be qualified to work at the bank with him."

Indira took Nani's wise advice and continued to study diligently for her GCE. She met up with Francine and Laliwa at the library after school everyday and they shared their notes and studied, and the three girls burned their lamps late into the long, warm nights, cramming their text books as the moths were drawn to the flame and the mosquitos buzzed about and the crickets chirred loudly outside.

It just happened that sports day at school fell on a Friday and the students had a respite from studying. That afternoon, the teachers and students gathered at a nearby field, and while they were playing cricket and rounders and high jump, Francine and Laliwa stole away to the matinée with Albert and Afonso. With her friends gone, Indira decided she would also skip sports day, and she excused herself and left.

The rays of the afternoon sun were searing hot and beating down on the dusty streets of the town as Indira started walking home by herself. She decided to take a short cut that day and it just happened that a little rum shop was on this route, and it was crowded with men drinking and getting drunk and loud. Indira pulled down the brim of her white school hat as she was passing by to protect her eyes from the glare of the sun and the sand the hot breeze was swirling about in the dirt street, so she could not see the inside of the rum shop—not that she dared look—but she imagined it was dim and clouded with cigarette smoke and smelled acrid of liquor. She could hear the shuffling of cards and the clashing of dominoes sliding across the surfaces of tables, slamming from time to time, as the voices of the men rose above the cricket match that was playing on the radio, the West Indies verses Pakistan.

A few drunk men were hanging around in front of the rum shop as Indira was passing by, and one of them called out to her, saying, "Hey, *coolie gal*!" The term 'coolie' meaning Indian in Guyanese.

Indira did not answer nor turn to look, but kept on walking with her hat brim still lowered.

"Hey, coolie gal!" the drunk man called out again as he looked her over lasciviously. "I love the way you walk." And the others started wolf-whistling at her.

Indira still kept on walking, saying nothing in reply, but feeling uncomfortable and nervous now.

The drunk man continued on with saying, "Hey, coolie gal, I love you. Talk to me, coolie gal. Tell me you love me, too." And with that he walked out onto the street and came up behind her. He was so close to her that Indira could smell the liquor on his breath as it drifted in the warm wind, and she became afraid of him and hastened her footsteps. "Hey, coolie gal, I said to talk to me," the drunk man went on to say, and he reached and pulled one of Indira's ringlets in the back.

"Leave her alone!" a strange voice shouted at the drunk man just then.

"Who are you, her man?" the drunk man turned to ask the stranger. "If so, then you'll have to fight for her!" And he launched at the stranger to punch him.

Indira turned around in time to see Ravi getting off his bicycle just in time to avoid the punch, and Ravi wrestled the drunk man to the ground and shook him up, and he said to him, "Don't let me catch you harassing this girl again! Do you hear me?" And Ravi left the drunk man whimpering on the ground.

When Ravi got up Indira turned away, she did not know why, except, that she was shy, and she was shaken up by the incident and seeing Ravi. She pulled her hat brim down and began walking away, quietly saying, "Thank you for rescuing me—"

"Ravi," Ravi said, not knowing that Indira already knew his name, and he dusted the sand off his white shirt and khaki pants and picked up his bicycle and rode up alongside of her. "I can escort you home safely if you would like," he offered in a voice more controlled and youthful, the sensuality of it causing Indira to blush.

"My Nani wouldn't like that," she said apprehensively, and kept on walking, with her head down, still avoiding looking at him or even giving him a cursory glance.

"Your Nani wouldn't like a drunk man following you home, neither," Ravi retorted. "Let me see you home part way, at least."

Indira turned around to see the drunk man getting up just then, and afraid he would attempt to follow and accost her again or get into another fight with Ravi, she conceded, saying, "Okay, you can accompany me just part way home."

Ravi was taken by the sound of her voice, soft and alluring like a gentle morning rain, he thought, and he wanted to hear more of her, but he sensed she was demure, so he rode alongside of her quietly at first. As he did, the scent of her—the sweet chameli lotion she rubbed on her skin drifted about enticingly, inebriating his senses. He stole glances at her from time to time and could not help but thinking of how pretty and neat the girl was in her school uniform, and he secretly admired her cute figure and swaying gait and her light golden-brown skin—the colour of honey—that glistened with a dewy sheen in the sunlight, and was smooth as silk. She had the prettiest, long, black ringlets he had ever seen, and he could not help but noticing from her side profile her deep dimple, but the brim of her hat was concealing her eyes. Wanting to look at her fully in the face in the daylight, having only seen her a couple of times at night, and becoming more and more curious about her, he now said, "Tell me about yourself. Who's your Nani, and what's your name? And how old are you?"

Indira still kept her head down when she answered him —shying away like a shame-baby weed, Ravi thought— and she told him her name and that she was fifteen years old. That was all she said because she suddenly lost her breath because her heart started racing, like it did the other times she had seen him. To make matters worse, she was feeling nervous that he was riding beside her, afraid of being seen walking home with a boy in broad daylight, a scandalous thing to do in the small town. Like him, her curiosity got the better of her, though, and when she caught her breath, she turned to look at him and asked, "Where are you from?"

"Skeldon," Ravi replied, and got a look at her pretty, oval-shaped face and dreamy, pearl-black eyes, and small, sensual rose-brown mouth; a picture of an Indian goddess, he thought. After being briefly struck by her looks, he quickly composed himself and went on to say, "I'm visiting Padmini my cousin here in Rose Hall."

At first, what he just said did not sink in because Indira found herself being momentarily enthralled by Ravi's striking fiery brown eyes and finely chiseled handsome face, contoured by his shoulder-length black hair. His dark brown complexion and tall and slender physique did not go unnoticed by her, either. Becoming shy again, she turned away and realised that he had just mentioned Padmini—the girl he was towing on his bicycle that Easter Sunday night, the same she and Francine assumed was his girlfriend—and she let out a quiet sigh of relief that she was just a cousin. But why should that matter now that she would be marrying Tarak? And why was she reacting and behaving like this? She was too captivated by Ravi to even think.

"Ever since that time when I saw you on Diwali night in your blue sari I have been coming down more often to visit my cousin, hoping to see you," Ravi said. Upon hearing this, Indira turned again to look at him and gave a tremulous smile, and he now noticed her deep dimples and complimented her, saying, "You've got the cutest dimples I've ever seen."

Indira found herself blushing again, not from the compliment, but because he was, overtly, enamoured of her, also, and she wanted to tell him she was hoping to see him again, too, but she was too inhibited to say so. Instead, she said, "Tell me about your life in Skeldon. And how old are you? And do you work at the bank?"

Ravi laughed, and exclaimed, "And do I work at the bank?!" Ravi did not know that Indira was instilled by Nani to believe that to be a qualified suitor for her one must work at the bank. "No, no, I don't work at the bank," he answered. "I'm a poor man who dropped out of high school to assist my father with his farm because he was sick. There are four of us in the family; my parents, myself, and my sister, Radhika, who's twenty years old, three years older than me, and we plant rice up in Skeldon."

A man who was only seventeen but was endowed with the build of someone in his mid-twenties, Indira thought, a farmer, and a poor man, not by his looks and the way he

283

dressed—not that being poor mattered to her—but she knew Nani would not look at him favourably as a suitor for her because he did not meet the criterion of working at the bank, and her grandfather would most certainly frown on him. Indira suddenly caught herself getting far too carried away with this stranger, and she abruptly said, "I will now walk home alone the rest of the way."

"As you wish," Ravi said, respectfully. "I wouldn't want to get you into any trouble with your Nani by going any closer." And he added, "And, Indira, take the long way home from school the next time to avoid the drunk man at the rum shop."

With that, Indira hurried along. Ravi saw two boys following her home on their bicycles, and he followed behind and watched as she turned into a street and got to the end, and he took note of the ragged gate she entered.

The boys on the bicycles did not ride away but stopped in front of Nani's house and were looking at Indira as she was walking up the front stairs. They lingered there until she—now changed into a pink cotton dress—came back downstairs and was watering the flower plants in the front yard, and they started tossing her flowery words of love.

"Your skin is as radiant as the golden sunshine, my love," the one named Rish said. "Looks like you're using lots of Ambi, gal." Indira kept on watering the plants and did not even toss him a perfunctory glance.

The other one, Robi, said, "Your face is like an angel, my sweetheart. You look like *them* nice coolie gals in the Indian movies. What's your name, gal?" Indira did not answer but kept her eyes lowered.

"Come over here and let me look into your black and shiny eyes, my darling," said Rish, "and I will tell you how much I love you." Still no response from Indira.

"Your black hair is like a curling river, my light golden-brown maiden, allow me to caress it," said Robi. Indira still remained quiet.

Rish then said, "I love your pretty body, baby gal—" And that was as far as the boys got with Indira.

Nani, who was sitting on a peerah behind the donkey-cart at the bottom-house and was hidden from view of the boys, had been surreptitiously observing them since they arrived and heard their flowery words of love they were tossing at Indira. She knew that they wanted Indira but she would make damn sure that neither of them would ever touch her. Her anger ruffled like the feathers of a hen protecting her chick, and she came out from behind the donkey-cart and, standing with arms akimbo, shouted at the boys, saying, "You good-for-nothing bad boys, *loongeras*! You want a girl, but do you know how to wash your own dirty drawers? And do you have a job at the bank? No. No." With one arm still planted on her hip, and flailing the other in a gesture of chasing the boys away, she went on to say, "Then get away from here and don't let me catch you lingering around anymore! You beasts!" The boys, sorely embarrassed by Nani, said not a word in defence but immediately took off on their bicycles and fled, never to return again.

Ravi, who had been observing the scene from a distance, heard all that Nani said to the boys, and he was disheartened, feeling like a good-for-nothing himself for being a man with no bank job, though he could certainly wash his own dirty drawers. He had never been in love before and had become so attracted to Indira since the first night he saw her, but he was left to think that he had no chance of wooing her and he should leave the girl alone before she gets into trouble over him with her Nani, and tarnish her character. But, on the other hand, he could not suppress his budding feelings for her and wanted to pursue her. He rode away that day feeling torn, not knowing what to do.

Indira was afraid that Nani would become incensed and admonish her if she only told her about Ravi, so she refrained from doing so. Nani would think that she was being brazen for talking to a boy on the street in broad daylight, causing ignominy, even though Ravi was being protective of her, and she would cry and say that she was bringing shame upon her poor old head, also. And if she learned that Ravi was interested in her but was not working at the bank, she would think that he was a good-for-nothing, and if he were to come around, she would most certainly flail her arm and chase him away.

Nani had her mind set on Tarak, the epitome of what she thought of as a future husband for Indira, and Indira had gone through the emotions of convincing herself that both she and her grandfather knew what was best for her, and she had begun to get excited about meeting Tarak, but after encountering Ravi, she was suddenly thrown off course by the power of attraction for him, and inexorable thoughts of him now overrode any thoughts of Tarak. She found herself now secretly thinking incessantly about Ravi, of his handsomeness, and the sensuality of his youthful voice and fiery brown eyes. Their encounter triggered a deluge of sweet emotions, and when she thought of him she felt like she was floating on a cloud, she would become so euphoric. Inherent emotions that were dormant were now awakened for the first time in her youthful teen age. Her heart, that some thought was impregnable, was broken into. No boy had ever made her feel this way before, nor had any boy rescued her so bravely. She was so grateful to Ravi for saving her from the drunk man and thought that he was her handsome and valiant knight in shining armour, and not just a poor farmer with no bank job.

All that weekend, as her amorous young feelings were budding, he was a constant distraction from her studies as she was fantasising about seeing him again, counting the hours before the next day of school and planning to walk home by herself again, hoping that he would come riding up to her again.

13

Young Love

The following Monday Indira purposefully walked home from school by herself again, but, much to her disappointment, Ravi did not show up as she had hoped. Tuesday and Wednesday went by and he still did not show up. And the longing to see him was building up inside of her. Thursday went by with no sign of him, either, and just when she was reaching the point of utter disappointment, he showed up on Friday afternoon as she was walking home from school alone, and he rode up beside her on his bicycle. Her heart started racing again, skipping beats this time, and her face evinced her excitement, though she said nothing from being shy.

Ravi explained to her, "The reason I've stayed away for the past few days is because I'm afraid of your Nani. I'm afraid someone might see us together and tell her and you'll get into trouble with her." Ravi paused then to look around to see if anyone was passing by and, luckily, the road was clear at the moment. "I'm also afraid that if I get caught that your Nani would think of me as a good-for-nothing if she finds out that I don't work at the bank—"

"You heard—"

"I stuck around that day and heard when the two boys on their bicycles were troubling you, and I heard every word your Nani said to them." After a pause, Ravi went on to say, "I risk coming here today because I couldn't stay away from you any longer. I just had to see you, Indira."

Upon hearing this, a thrill spread throughout Indira, from her head down to her toes, but she was too inhibited to tell him she was longing to see him, too. Instead, she looked down and fluttered her eyelashes demurely.

"I want to continue seeing you," Ravi said, "but for me to do so we will have to find another route to take where no one would see us."

The thought that he wanted to see her again, and secretly, sent another wave of excitement through Indira, but her diffidence impeded a response.

Ravi went on to suggest, "Maybe we can walk through the savannah."

Indira kept her eyes lowered but gave a perfunctory nod in agreement.

"Then I'll meet you after school on Monday under the calabash tree at the savannah," Ravi said and, when Indira gave another quick, affirmative nod, he rode away before anyone could spot them together.

As agreed, the following Monday they met under the calabash tree at the savannah in secrecy, both nervous and yet consumed with a fresh and sweet excitement that neither of them had experienced before. Being young, and both virgins, their innocence and purity brought about a natural shyness and, finding themselves alone, they did not know what to say to each other at first or how to act.

As they were walking through the luxuriant field of green grass, side by side, Ravi kept glancing at Indira's pretty hands, and having the natural instinct to hold them and wanting badly enough to do so, he eventually mustered the courage and asked her, "Would you let me hold your hand?" Indira was bashful about this but, being propelled by the power of attraction, she held out her hand for Ravi to clasp and, instantly, that aroused a tingling sensation throughout her fingers, the same feeling awakened in Ravi at the touch of Indira's soft hand, a feeling that they both were experiencing for the first time.

Once they got over some of their initial inhibitions, the two of them walked hand in hand all that week through the lush fields of the florescent green grass as though in a mysterious dream, basking in the hot sun, with the warm breeze blowing through their hair. And the cows grazing there paid them no mind. They laid in the soft grass and looked up at the blue sky and watched the white, fluffy clouds float by as they talked and laughed—Indira's laughter sounding like the melody of a sitar, Ravi noted— and they listened to the whizzing sound of the breeze blowing across the lush grass, both lost in the magic of the moments and thrill of a budding, tender love. Their first embrace happened as they were leaning up against the calabash tree in the savannah, the sweet fragrances of musk cologne and chameli lotion mingled, and like magnets they were attracted to each other and both were locked in a hug in a rush of new and exciting feeling, youthful exuberance, the passion of which caused the rhythm of their breaths and heart rates to accelerate to an almost uncontrollable speed.

Their attraction for each other made Indira think of the conversation Nani had with her about not mistaking attraction for love. Just within that week, she became more and more convinced that she was experiencing both.

Ravi wrote her a poem, and as they were sitting under the calabash tree in the savannah, on the fourth day of their rendezvous, he read it to her:

Nightfall

Night would fall and in the silent darkness of my mind she would appear. Is it the innocence of her face like that of the ethereal beauty of an untouched Victoria Regis Lily that haunts me, or the soft, sensual purr of her voice like that of a young jaguar, or her lips like the rose-brown flesh of a succulent sapodilla fruit, or could it be her long, curly hair, black and shiny like that of a wara seed, or her shyness like that of a shame-baby weed, or her melodious laughter like that of a sitar? Is it the silkiness of her pretty hands, her velvet soft skin, her alluring gait, the charm of her youthful innocence, or her chameli fragrance? It is all that, and her cute dimples that haunt me. If her dark, dreamy eyes were pools of water, I would drown myself in them and be with her forever. We will walk through the meadows and laugh and love under the torrid sun. And I will sing to my sweet with my six strings, songs of love to her in the morning, noon, and night.

And that was how Indira learned that Ravi played the guitar, and sang, also. The following day he brought his guitar along, and as they were sitting under the calabash tree in the savannah, while a soft, pleasant breeze was blowing as the sun was setting, casting a golden glow upon them, he charmed her by singing, in a youthful and sensual voice, the Sonny James song *Young Love*. It was a song that

291

sparked emotions and Ravi stopped and touched Indira's face, and he whispered to her, "I'm falling in love with you, Indira. And all I want is to win your love and marry you." Indira did not have to tell him she loved him, too, for in her dark eyes he saw the flame of love burning for him.

Indira rested her head on his shoulder and thought if the feelings of passion and pleasure that were consuming her was love, then she was falling in love with him, too. But she was afraid, afraid of playing with the flame of love and the dangerous consequences it could bring, as Nani would always warn her about, and afraid because they might never be together. But, still, she found herself submitting to his tender, amorous embrace, and she trembled in his arms when she said, "I think I'm falling in love with you, too, Ravi, but—" She wanted to tell him about her grandfather's marriage plans for her but she could not bring herself to doing so.

"But what?"

"Never mind," she simply said. "I should be on my way home before it gets dark."

The next week she did not go to the savannah and purposefully walked home from school with Francine and Laliwa to avoid Ravi, worried about the repercussion if caught, of being branded a young woman of ill repute. She was feeling inundated by her emotions for him and was now conflicted about her grandparents decision to marry her off to Tarak, and she was in a real dilemma over this. Besides, she was feeling like she was walking on pins and needles now, becoming more and more scared and nervous that she would be caught seen with Ravi, and Nani would find out and she would get into trouble. A Guyanese proverb that Nani would sometimes mention to others kept running through her head over and over again: *Moon ah run till daylight ketch am*, meaning, you may think that you are getting away with your wrong doings, but you will be caught eventually. That now applied to her and was a deterrent. She confided in Francine about Ravi and her dilemma, and Francine emphatically discouraged her from seeing him, not because she was afraid that Indira would get caught, but because she was in agreement with Indira's grandparents that Tarak was a good match for her, given that he would be able to provide her with a financially secure future, a beautiful home, and a chance to work at the bank. And Francine had no doubt that Indira would fall in love with the dashing Tarak, whom all the young girls were dreaming of and wishing they could be the one to marry him.

The last day Indira spent with him left Ravi perplexed over why she told him she was falling in love with him and left him hanging with a 'but' before she suddenly left for home. He racked his brains trying to think of what she was withholding from him but he never would have guessed it had to do with an arranged marriage with someone else. For the first couple of days of the next week, he waited for her at the savannah and was left in more of a quandary when she did not show up. The thought that she might have changed her mind about seeing him kept ruminating in his mind, or maybe she really did not fall in love with him, or maybe he was not good enough for her as he did not meet the career expectation of her Nani, and the fear of rejection and hurt started creeping up on him over those thoughts. He wanted to find out the truth of the matter but he was not so optimistic that she would show up the next day and, besides, he did not have the time to stick around for much longer to find out because he had to hurry back to Skeldon to assist his father with the farm. But when he got there he was in so much love pain that he was not much help, and his father had to rely mostly on the other men he had employed.

Ravi had confided in his sister, Radhika, about Indira ever since he had seen her on that Diwali night. Radhika had never before seen her brother enamoured of any girl and knew he had never been in love before, and now it seemed as though he was obsessed with Indira. She had been encouraging him all along to pursue her, but when she heard of his present predicament and the story about Nani and the boys and the bank job, she was frank with him and told him that he would not be a qualified suitor for Indira, and she tried to dissuade him from pursuing her any further. But all of Radhika's deterring only made Ravi want Indira even more, and he swore to Radhika that he would marry Indira someday and that Radhika would have a *bouji*— sister-in-law that she was always looking forward to. There was little Radhika could do now to console her brother and she watched as he went through the process of a broken heart, eating and sleeping very little, and being cooped up in his bedroom, playing his guitar and singing sad love songs to the walls.

It was now the third day since Ravi returned back home to Skeldon, and on that Friday night, a bright moonlit night, after drowning himself in melancholic Indian love songs and going out of his mind for Indira, he made an arbitrary decision and set off on his motorcycle for Rose Hall, intent on seeing her.

It was now midnight and Indira had just finished her studies and she blew out the kerosene oil lamp and crawled under the mosquito netting and laid her head on the feather pillow, the coconut fibre mattress feeling firm against her. Through the mesh she watched as the moonlight crept over the window sill and fell on the bare wooden floor, and she looked up blindly at the glittering stars, her mind as far way.

She was no less torn over Ravi and Tarak over the past days. There was the man with a bank job whom her grandparents approved of, who was from a wealthy family and that was a promise of happiness, a life of a bed of roses as some would claim, and there was the bona fide love of a poor man with whom she had fallen in love, but with whom she would have to struggle to build a material life. Even if she followed her heart and wanted to be with Ravi, though, she had no choice in the matter. Her Nani and grandfather had their minds made up about marrying her off to Tarak. They were so sure that she and Tarak would fall in love, but her predicament was that she was already in love and she could not be with the one she loved. Because of his low social standing, Ravi would be dismissed as a husband. But if she were to marry Tarak out of deference to her grandparents, that would make them happy. She was really in a dilemma that brought about a lot of confusion and frustration, which only complicated her young life.

At the present moment, as she was laying in bed, she was immersed in her feelings for Ravi. The days spent with him at the savannah left her with indelible memories; his handsome face, his sensual eyes, his youthful and resonant voice, the song he sang to her, the poem he wrote of her and read to her, running through the green grass of the savannah hand in hand were all vivid in her mind. His musky scent she could almost smell. His touch, his embrace, she could almost feel. She could only describe her feelings as being showered by the waters of Kaieteur Falls, flooded and drenched by sweet emotions of love and passion, feelings that made her so high as though she was standing on the top of Mount Roraima. With no hope of ever being with Ravi, though, she felt that she was running blindly through the Iwokrama Forest, lost in love, and that she was drowning in a sea of love with the Georgetown Lighthouse shedding its beam on her, but she could not be rescued.

As the seed of love germinated in her heart, growing more intense with each passing day, she became more and more preoccupied with Ravi in spite of her dilemma. At the moment she was listening to the little, round, red transistor radio she had recently acquired as it was playing soft and low the song Ravi had sung to her, *Young Love*, and she dreamt all along about Ravi and spiralled deeper and deeper in love with him. A soft tap on the old wooden window overlooking the backyard startled her and made her jump up suddenly, and she escaped the mosquito netting and rushed over to the window.

From the back steps, Ravi looked up and saw her, looking angelic in the alluring full moonlight in her sleeveless, violet nightie, her skin glowing light golden-brown, her long, black ringlets falling softly about her bare shoulders, her face the picture of innocence, and even her dimples were visible in the brilliant moonlight.

"What are you doing here?" she whispered, surprised, and scared that Nani would wake up and find him there, yet, so happy to see him that she let out a soft, melodious giggle.

"I just had to see you," Ravi said. "Climb over the window and I'll take you for a motorcycle ride."

"But Nani—"

"I can hear her snoring."

"I can't do this," she protested, "I'm too scared and nervous that Nani would wake up and find me gone."

"By the sound of her snoring, I doubt she would wake up any time soon," Ravi said.

Indira thought for a moment. She did not have to worry about Nani getting up at the crowing of the fowlcocks to go to the market to sell, for Nani rarely did so on Saturdays anymore, only on week days. But she might get up to use the posey. Sneaking off in the middle of the night with a young man was a risky thing to do, and if she were to be caught by Nani, Nani would rake her over the coals and cry that she was bringing shame on her poor old head.

"We'll go just for a short ride," Ravi said, trying to coax her.

It was not Ravi's coaxing that made Indira make up her mind, but as she stood there looking down at him, a sudden yearning to be with him took hold of her and she quickly climbed over the window, too exhilarated to mind that she was still in her nightie and that she was barefoot. Ravi helped her down onto the steps and the two of them immediately took off down the street, where Ravi had parked his motorcycle.

The neighbours were sleeping, and the little town was silent at the moment, except, for the barking of a dog and the rhythmical chirring of the crickets and the croaking of the crapos. Ravi swiftly kicked the motorcycle into gear and Indira hopped on behind him, and as Ravi took her for a ride on the dirt road along the river, their hair whipped about in the soft night breeze. The millions of stars were shining down on them, and the moon was smiling as Ravi started singing *In The Misty Moonlight*, trying to imitate the gentle voice of Jim Reeves. For the two young lovers, the night was truly enchanting and romantic.

After they passed the pump house, Ravi stopped at the riverbank and they sat on the grass and listened to the gushing flow of the river and reminisced about the week at the savannah. Then Ravi said, "The last day I saw you, you were going to tell me something before you left, what was it?" Indira remembered too well what she was going to say to him then, and, again, she wanted to mention the arranged marriage with Tarak, but, again, she just could not bring herself to doing so, and she remained silent. Ravi realised that she did not want to talk about whatever it was and he did not ask again but posed another question, "Why have you stopped meeting me at the savannah?"

The inscrutable expression on Indira's face did not give her secret away, and she answered, "I stopped because I'm feeling overwhelmed and, besides, I'm scared that we might get caught."

"But you love me, don't you?"

She answered, "I do, Ravi." Just then Ravi leaned forward and planted a light kiss on her face, and Indira was gripped by feelings of sensuality that made her nervous. She became even more apprehensive when, as they were locked in an embrace, she looked up at the sky and saw the moon racing by and she could almost hear Nani saying, *Moon ah run till daylight ketch am.* Her feelings were now compounded with the thought that she could be caught, and she pulled away from Ravi and said, "Please take me home."

"Are you scared of me?"

She shook her head. She was not scared of Ravi but the feelings he had awakened in her. And she was scared of playing with this kind of fire that Nani would sometimes warn her of. But all she said was, "I just want to go back home before Nani wakes up and finds me gone."

"Okay, I'll take you home as you wish," Ravi said, respectfully. "But can I see you again?"

Indira did not answer, but she clung tightly to Ravi as he was taking her back on the motorcycle. When she arrived home, she found Nani still snoring much to her profound relief, and she crawled quietly back into bed.

The next morning as they were in the kitchen having breakfast, Nani said to her, "I thought I heard the sound of a motorcycle late last night." A bout of guilt and anxiety took hold of Indira and she froze and could not speak—not that she dared to—failing to tell Nani of the secret moonlight tryst and that she could not sleep all night because of the owner of the motorcycle. To her relief, though, Nani did not pursue the subject any further, but went on to say, "Your grandfather is trying to work out a date for you to meet with Tarak at his house and he wants to know when you'll be finishing up with your exams."

"I don't know the exact date, as yet."

"As soon as you know tell me and I'll let him know."

Indira was even more overwhelmed now. She wanted so much to tell Nani about Ravi but she knew if she did she would regret it instantly. Nani had her mind set on Tarak. Indira recognised that her intentions, as well as her grandfather's, were all good, but that eliminated any chance of her marrying the man she really loved. Nani kept on constantly impressing upon her that Tarak was a good match for her, and at Indira's susceptible age, this brought about more confusion to her than anything else. Her grandparents' wishes and her heart's desire conflicted. In spite of trying to convince herself that they were looking out for her best interest in matching her up with Tarak, she could not stop herself from wanting Ravi. But she had no choice but to follow their wishes and not her heart.

The following Friday night, after a week of not seeing Indira and being cooped up in his bedroom in Skeldon dreaming about her and their moonlight tryst, Ravi suddenly had the itch again to see her and took off on his motorcycle once again for Rose Hall. Indira was up late that rainy night trying on a pink sari that Nani had bought her when she heard the tap on the old wooden bedroom window. This time she and Ravi secretly met in the orchard in Nani's backyard in the middle of the warm night, and neither of them cared that it was raining even harder now, in fact, that only added to the mystique and excitement of the night. Coincidently, Pyari's gas lamp was out at the time and no one was up to see them. The two clung to each

300

other and danced to the rhythmic pitter patter of the rain and the rhapsodic flow of the nearby river, the symphonic churn of the ocean in the distance adding an orchestral effect of harmony in natural music. And the rain dripped copiously from the leaves of the mango tree they were standing under, drenching them both and causing Indira's pink sari to cling to her like a second skin, as did Ravi's white cotton shirt and pants. Their sweet breaths and fragrances of musk and chameli mingled, and the electricity between them was as intense as the strike of the lighting, setting ablaze their desire for each other, and they were both lost in the thrill, revelling in the bliss of a young and innocent love.

"It's not the right thing for us to do, Indira, meeting like this, but this feels so good," Ravi whispered to her.

"I've never felt like this before, but we can't be meeting like this, Ravi. We're playing with fire as my Nani would say." And Indira thought of her proposed arranged marriage, yet again, but kept quiet about it, yet again.

"Tell me that you don't love me, Indira, and you'll never see me again."

Indira could not answer, but she suddenly withdrew from him, and he grabbed her hand and kissed her fingers tips before she ran back upstairs.

After she dried her drenched skin and changed into dry clothes, Indira sat on the chair by the window overlooking the backyard and she let the breeze dry her hair. She felt guilt-ridden that she had snuck out again to see Ravi behind Nani's back, but her guilt was soon overridden by the tingling sensation that lingered in her fingers tips from Ravi's kiss. The sensation stayed with her until the rain dissipated and the sun started creeping up the window and long after the beautiful rainbow appeared in the early morning sky, and even as she walked in her bare feet on the dewy grass of the flower garden, basking in the feeling of pure love, her heart singing like the birds in the trees, *Young Love*.

After their dance in the rain and feeling the enticing warmth of Indira, Ravi was also revelling in sweet first love, inebriated with desire, walking on air, lost in the dark, dreamy eyes of Indira. The rain fell, the sun shone, the moonlight glowed, and all he could see was the lovely face of Indira. The Victoria Regia Lily bloomed pink, the river sparkled like white diamonds, the sky was the clearest blue, but it was she who coloured and decorated his world. The patter of rain sounded, the wind whistled, the ocean churned, but all he could hear was the sound of her soft voice. She was his addictive love opiate, his voracious appetite, and his compulsion to see her again was now even more overpowering. The following Friday he took off on his motorcycle to visit her, yet again. On this hot, pitch-black night, this time he climbed over the window and entered her bedroom as Nani was sleeping soundly.

They were two shadows in the dark embracing by the window and their feelings were like the tip of the mosquito coil, glowing red. Just the slightest movement from them caused the old wooden floor to creak, and the nervousness that they might be caught only added to the intensity of the moment. They did not talk for a while but held each other in silence as they listened to the Indian love song *Kabhi Kabhie Mere Dil Mein* playing low on the red transistor radio, seducing the tropical night with its sweet sadness.

After standing for a long while, they tip-toed over to the bed and Indira pulled aside the mosquito netting in one corner and they sat at the edge, close to each other, arms around each other's waists. And they continued to be silent, listening to the radio and the sounds of the night creatures outside and an almost audible sound of their hearts beating.

"You're right, meeting like this is playing with fire," Ravi broke the silence, speaking softly, as he felt Indira's warmth and softness against him. "I want to kiss you and make love to you, Indira."

Indira remained quiet but tightened her arm around his waist and snuggled closer.

"I want you real badly, but the only way I would take your virginity is to marry you," Ravi whispered, keeping the tone of his voice low so as not to wake Nani. "I would never spoil you and bring shame to your name or upon your Nani's poor old head. You're as pure as I am and we'll stay this way until we get married. Let me meet your Nani and ask for your hand in marriage. I don't work at the bank and I've dropped out of high school to help my sick father with his farm, but maybe I can convince her that I love you and I will work hard to provide and take care of you."

Indira still remained quiet.

Ravi then went on to say, "After we're married, I'll leave my parents home and move in with your Nani to help her out with her work in the garden so you wouldn't have to spoil your pretty hands. I'll also take another job and save up money and build you a house with electricity and buy you a turntable and records, and a gas stove. As for your old lady, she wouldn't have to sell at the market anymore. I'll take care of you both."

Still no response from Indira.

"And when we have our first child, hopefully a girl, we'll name her Mumtaz after the film star from India." And as Ravi was now caressing Indira's face, he felt it wet with tears and said, "You're crying. Why are you crying, Indira?"

Indira started sobbing softly now, and she whispered, "We'll never be together, Ravi. My grandfather has other marriage plans for me. He's arranging a marriage for me with someone who works at the bank, Tarak Jajal, the son of the bank manager, and the marriage will take place right after I finish school."

The news felt like a stab to his heart, and Ravi fought to control the tears that were suddenly threatening to fall, not wanting Indira to see him as a weak man, and he was glad that it was dark so she could not see the pain that distorted his face. "When did you find out about this?" was the first thing he found himself asking.

"A while ago, before I met you the day you rescued me from the drunk man."

"And that was what you were going to tell me the day at the savannah but withheld it. And when I asked you later what you were going to say, you still didn't tell me." At this point, Ravi felt himself becoming agitated that Indira kept that away from him all along. "Why didn't tell me about it earlier?" he asked.

"I was afraid if I told you that I would never see you again."

Ravi then withdrew his arms from Indira and sat there on the edge of the bed in silence for a long time, staring blindly at the mosquito coil on the nightstand as the smoke dissipated and the glowing red tip slowly died. He then got up and went over to the window and stood there looking out into the black night. After the long silence, he returned to the bed and sat down and put his arm around Indira, and when he eventually spoke, with a tremor in his voice, he said, "I don't want to stand in the way of your happiness, Indira, for you will have a good future marrying into the Jajals' family. I heard of the family, they're well-off and respectable, and you'll have a financially secure life with them. Tarak has a lot to offer you, but, me, all I have to offer you is my love, and I can sing you a love tune and write you a poem."

"It's you I want to be with, Ravi," Indira cried. "But I have no choice in the matter. Grandpa and Nani and Tarak's parents have made up their minds about the marriage."

"Then I should stay away from you, Indira, though it would hurt real badly. If we're caught seeing each other that would ruin your reputation and probably your chance to marry Tarak and have a wonderful life. I love you too much to let that happen to you."

Indira was terribly sad and devastated about Ravi's decision, and she wanted to tell him she would risk her reputation and keep on seeing him, but the Guyanese proverb, *Moon ah run till daylight ketch am*, kept ringing in her ears, a warning to her that they might be caught if they continued to meet. So she rested her head on his shoulder and, as the leaves in the trees were gently rustling outside in the dark, they sat in silence holding each other, cherishing their last moments together with broken hearts and hot, fervent tears.

Their impassioned farewell might have lasted all night but, at the crowing of the fowlcocks, they were interrupted by Nani, coughing and calling out to Indira to get her some Buckley's cough mixture. And Ravi jumped over the window and took off in a hurry as if the bush devil, the Bush Dai Dai was chasing him. And so ended their secret affair.

The Bush Dai Dai may have had her way with Ravi had he been in a gold mine somewhere in the jungle of Guyana, but Ravi raced back to his parents home in Skeldon that dark night and stood out on the verandah and cuffed the railing and cried. He had fallen in love with Indira deeper than he had thought, and though he was brave in parting ways with her for what he thought was best for her, the thought of her marrying another man was killing him. He felt he did not want to live anymore if he could not be with her. The soft sound of her voice, her melodious laughter, her dark eyes, her beauty, the softness of her body, her cry in the dark were all now haunting him on this black night. And he cuffed the railing again and again, and cried.

Radhika heard her brother's lovelorn cry and came out to the verandah, and all she could see was his silhouette in the dark. Using the endearing term for a brother, she asked, "*Buddy*, what's wrong?"

Ravi did not answer but kept cuffing the railing, and he held back his cries in front of his sister.

Radhika grabbed his arm and asked, "Does this have anything to do with my future bouji, the girl you're going to marry?"

"Indira will be someone else's bouji," Ravi then said. "Her grandfather, Dr. Ramesh, is arranging a marriage for her into a well-to-do family, the Jajals', and I'm sure Tarak's sister will be happy with her as a sister-in-law."

"Oh, buddy," Radhika said and pulled her brother to her and hugged him, "I feel your pain, for the one I love, too, is now married to someone else, but he is now happy. If Indira's grandfather, a doctor, has made a choice for her, then it must be the best thing for her. You will learn to live with that in time, just as I have. Don't cry anymore for it breaks my heart to see you like this, buddy. Come, sit with me in the kitchen and I'll light the fireside and make you a hot cup of coco tea."

And Radhika's sisterly consolation soothed her brother for the meanwhile.

After Indira attended to Nani's cough that same night, she went to bed and laid in the darkness and wept even more. For the brief time she and Ravi met under the sun and the moon and the stars and the rain, their tender love had blossomed and the feeling that it brought was one of pleasure, but now she was in so much pain over the demise of their affair that she thought she could not bear it. Images of Ravi danced in the darkness and haunted her. His Indian film star looks, his smile, his laughter, his manliness, wit and charm and sensibility, she could not obliterate from her mind. She was infatuated with him and it was painful to think that she would never see him again and, worse yet, she would never marry him. And she wanted him even more.

In the wake of the early morning, as the wood in the mud stove was softly crackling, spouting curls of smoke and emitting a warmth as a pot of lime leaves' tea was boiling, Nani caught her standing by the kitchen window in a state of preoccupation and, mistaking that she was thinking about Tarak, she smiled broadly, showing her gold teeth, and said to her, "You must be happy that the time is soon to come for you to meet with Tarak, my child. Your grandfather and I will plan the introduction for the Saturday right after you finish your exams." Indira had her back to Nani as she was looking out into the backyard at the early morning mist that was hovering about the fruit trees, and Nani could not see the sadness and confusion in her dark eyes as she went on to say, "I will get Joan to sew you a nice dress for that evening, and I will also talk to her about your wedding dress."

Indira was tempted once again to tell Nani about Ravi, but, again, decided against it. Telling Nani that she had been clandestinely seeing Ravi and that she had a transient but sultry love affair would cause her a great deal of consternation, in fact, Nani would admonish her, saying that she was bringing shame upon her poor old head. And Nani would most certainly choose Tarak over Ravi as a husband for all the reasons she was impressing her with. So to spare herself the quarrels and putting herself through humiliation, Indira acquiesced, simply saying, "Okay, Nani, do as you wish."

And so Nani, misconstruing Indira's preoccupation with Ravi for Tarak, was happy for Indira, and she went about making wedding plans for her, while Indira kept sinking deeper and deeper in love with Ravi.

14

Birthdays' Celebration

On this late afternoon the sky was slate grey with heavy rain clouds, and fat drops of rain were pounding the corrugated zinc roof of the outdoor bathroom as Indira stood under the pipe letting the refreshing water wash all over her and enjoying the sound of the rain as the thunder crashed and the lightening flashed momentarily. She could have stood there for much longer lost in the ecstasy of the tropical downpour but she heard Nani calling from the kitchen window, saying that it was getting darker and that she should come in from the storm. Reluctantly, she turned off the pipe and wrapped a towel around herself and hurried up the backstairs, dripping with rain when she entered the kitchen.

"Dry yourself at once before you catch a cold," Nani said to her and handed her a couple of dry towels.

"I wouldn't want that to happen because tomorrow is my sixteenth birthday and I want to be well to enjoy it," Indira said and wrapped a towel around her and sat on the chair at the kitchen table and dried herself as the heat from the mud stove warmed her while a pot of *metemgee* stew was simmering in the old iron pot, giving off wisps of steam and flooding the place with the delicious aromas of coconut milk, ground provisions, meat and saltfish and dumplings.

Nani lit the kerosene oil lamp and hung it up on the hook from the chain dangling from the corrugated zinc roof, saying as she did, "I know that Francine's birthday is also coming up this month, do you have anything planned?"

"We made plans just today at school. Our school friends are coming over tomorrow to celebrate both our birthdays. Laliwa and Devika will be here, and the boys, also. The boys wish to do a bush-cook in the backyard if that's all right with you."

"And who are these boys?" Nani asked suspiciously, raising her eyebrows as she turned to look at Indira.

"Just Afonso and Ling, whom you know," Indira answered, "and Albert."

"Is Albert the young man who has asked Francine's parents for her hand in marriage?"

"The same one," Indira said.

"As long as Albert behaves himself around Francine then it's all right for the boys to have a bush-cook," Nani said.

Nani would not have allowed this, though, if she knew that Afonso and Ling would be there with their love interests, Laliwa and Devika, for she would not allow any such thing as 'courting' or romancing in her backyard, so Indira left her to believe they were all only school friends and, to avoid further questioning, she got up and went to the bedroom to get dressed.

When she returned to the kitchen, Nani dished out bowls of the steaming metemgee stew, and they sat down to dinner, Nani in her usual place on her peerah and Indira at the table, and they ate while the embers in the mud stove were burning on this rainy evening.

"Is Joan making new dresses for you and Francine for your birthdays?" Nani inquired as she spoon-fed herself a hearty portion of the metemgee.

"Auntie Joan is making us dresses exactly the same style and colour, yellow chiffon shift dresses," Indira answered.

"And is she baking a cake for you this year?"

"She's baking one cake for both Francine and I."

"I will get up in the morning and make some treats for the celebration," Nani said, "then I will go to the store and get you and Francine your gifts. What would you like me to get you, dear child?"

Indira thought for a moment and then answered, "I would be happy to receive a pair of white high-heeled slingback shoes."

"Anything else?"

After giving the thought some more consideration, Indira said, "Yes. I have been wearing home-sewn drawers all my life, and now that I'm all grown up, I wish to have some 'store-made' seersucker panties, also."

Nani smiled and said, "As you wish, dear child." Then she asked, "And what would Francine like to have?"

"She would be happy to have the same things," Indira said. "And we wear the same size as you know."

"Then it is set that I will buy you both white high-heeled slingback shoes and store-made seersucker panties for your sixteenth birthday," Nani said.

Nani then fell silent and looked at Indira as she was sitting at the kitchen table lost in thoughts and hardly eating any of the metemgee. Over the past few days she noticed that the girl had eaten very little and seemed to be always preoccupied in thoughts, and she did not laugh or smile like

311

her usual self. The faraway and sunken dark eyes of Indira seemed like a young woman pining away from love, but that could not be possible for, as far as she knew, the girl had not experienced the love of a man, as yet. After all, she had not even met her future husband. After mulling things over, she concluded that Indira's demeanour had to do with her being nervous over her meeting with Tarak and his parents, and she comforted her by saying, "You seem very anxious, my child, and I know it has to do with your meeting with the Jajals. Let me assure you that there's no need to worry yourself about anything because Tarak's parents are nice people and you will feel quite comfortable with them. I have no doubt in my mind that they will like you, so will Tarak. So try not to work yourself up too much and get too nervous. Now, pull yourself together and have some metemgee."

Indira did not say anything in response to Nani's misunderstood words of encouragement, but she made an effort to eat. When they were both finished having dinner, Nani decided she would turn in to bed early, so Indira made up her cot in the sitting room and tucked her in and placed the posey under the cot, and she kissed Nani goodnight on the forehead. Indira then carried the kerosene oil lamp to the bedroom and placed it on the night table, and as it was a rainy night, the kind of night to curl up in bed and read a novel, she thought she would do just that. Besides, reading got her mind off Ravi momentarily and distracted her from her heartache.

It was cozy inside by the soft flickering light of the kerosene oil lamp and the glow of the green, incense-scented mosquito coil, while, outside, the thunder was still rumbling and the lightning flashing and the wind whistling, and the heavy raindrops pelted the corrugated zinc roof in loud spatter and was incessant. Indira got changed into her nightie, and she left the mosquito netting up and curled up in bed and began reading, the kind of 'worldly' books that if Nani knew about she would take a fit, for she would think they were the kind of books that would corrupt and lead any young woman astray.

Mills & Boon are romance novels that Indira would borrow from the library and she would wrap the covers with brown paper before she brought them home so Nani would not see the images and decipher what the books were all about. She did that also with the ranch romance of Louis L'Amour westerns and the more risqué James Bond spy novels, so as not to raise Nani's suspicions as these were also taboo. Nani had no problems, though, with the adventures of Enid Blyton and Nancy Drew and The Hardy Boys, stories that Indira would often tell her while sitting in the kitchen by the mud stove.

Indira just loved reading, and the secular books did not deprave her, contrary to what Nani believed. Reading gave her insight into a world beyond her tiny space. She was intrigued with the settings of faraway lands, particularly, Canada, America, and England, and was fascinated with the white characters on their portrayal of love and life. She was even more fascinated with the Native Indians of North America in the period of cowboys and Indians and tipis and igloos and totem poles. She admired the peacekeeping Canadians and the ambitious Americans pursuing their American dream, and the sophisticated culture of the British with their monarchy and lords and ladies and their upper class society and proper ways. She tried to imagine these foreign people living in lands of skyscrapers and varied seasons, and she found it difficult to grasp that people actually live in winter, below zero degree temperatures, where snowflakes fall and people literally walk on ice. It was all a marvel to her.

After reading a romance novel, Indira took to studying for her exams and burned the wick of the lamp up until midnight, then she blew it out and lowered the mosquito netting and nestled under the cozy quilt as the rain continued to bombard the zinc roof. A week had gone by since she and Ravi said goodbye to each other and since then she had cried herself to sleep every night. Tonight she made up her mind that she would not cry and she settled in to listening to the little, red transistor radio, and she dreamed of Ravi. She thought of his handsome face, the smouldering look in his sensual brown eyes, the passion in his voice when he sang her *Young Love*, and the stimulating warmth of his touch. She remembered every detail of their rendezvous, at the savannah on the hot days, the moonlight tryst in the night breeze, their sultry dance in the warm rain, and their sad farewell in the blackness of the night. She had promised herself that she would not cry tonight, but Bobby Bare was then singing *I Hate Goodbyes* on the radio and she broke down and cried and, by the time the glow of the mosquito coil was extinguished and the curls of smoke dissipated, she drifted off to sleep with tears still in her eyes, and she met Ravi somewhere in her dreams that rainy night.

Indira slept through the crowing of the fowlcocks this morning, too deep in sweet dreams of Ravi, and it was not until she heard the sound in the kitchen of a pot spoon scraping against the carahee that she woke up to the delicious aroma of fried saltfish and roti and coco tea, mingled with the sweet scent of wood burning in the mud stove. She sprang out of bed and went straight to the lamp-lit kitchen and found Nani busy with making breakfast, a joyous look on her face.

When Nani saw her she smiled broadly, exposing her gold teeth, and she greeted her with: "Happy sweet sixteenth birthday, my granddaughter." And she reached for Indira and hugged her, tenderly kissing her on the forehead. "I should call you a young lady now, but you will always be my dear little girl. Happy birthday, child."

"Thank you, Nani," Indira said and smiled sweetly. "But you shouldn't have troubled yourself and get up so early to make me breakfast."

"Hush, hush," Nani said. "It's your birthday and you deserve to be treated in a special way. Now, sit down and I'll serve you and we'll eat together at the table this morning."

Indira took a seat and Nani served breakfast and sat beside her at the table, something she rarely did as she much preferred sitting on her peerah in a corner. And while the soft misty light of dawn was just beginning to emerge and a fresh breeze, after the night's rain, began to blow through the open window, they began to eat as the embers in the mud stove created a soft veil of blue smoke and warmed the kitchen, creating an atmosphere of enchantment.

As they were eating, Nani recounted all the years that Indira had lived with her, remembering every one of her birthdays, and she said to her, "You have brought me a lot of joy and happiness in my old age, my dear child, and I wouldn't know how to repay you for all your help and kindness and love, and for taking such good care of me. Thank you for your company my dear granddaughter." And Nani reached into her apron pocket and pulled out a blue velvet pouch and handed it to Indira. "Take this," she said, "the time has now come for you to have it. Happy sixteenth birthday, my child."

Indira took the pouch and opened it and found a glittering gold ring with a delicate floral design, and she exclaimed, "Oh, Nani, it's beautiful!"

"Ma Raajee gave it to me when I had turned sixteen, and I had given it to your mother, Geeta, when she had turned sixteen, and it's now your turn to wear it."

Indira put the ring on the middle finger of her right hand and said, "I swear only to take it off for my first daughter when she turns sixteen."

"I hope you make many daughters for you'll have all of Chaaya's jewellery to pass on, also."

A sudden sadness took hold of Indira then when she realised she would have no daughters with Ravi, but Tarak, instead, but she brushed aside the feeling as quickly as it came when Nani started singing, in a sweet high-pitched Indian voice, *Baar Baar Din Yeh Aaye,* singing Happy Birthday to Indira instead of Sunita, as the song goes, and Indira joined Nani in singing the Indian tune.

The birds in the trees in the orchard and the bushes were also singing on this now bright and early morning as though wishing Indira a happy birthday, too, and, though Indira's heart was broken and hurting, she wore a smile on her face this day, more so for Nani, for Nani was so happy for her. The old woman flitted around with the energy of a youngster this day, busy with making preparations for the occasion, and Indira soon picked up her enthusiastic vibes and began assisting her. They made savoury treats of bara with tamarind sauce and pholourie, then they scrubbed and cleaned the little, old house and daubed the earthen ground of the bottom-house and tied bunches of balloons on the stilts and strung streamers. After, Nani set up the stones for the bush-cook in the backyard under the tamarind tree and, as the boys were planning on making cook-up rice, she grated a coconut and squeezed the milk from it and placed it, along with the other ingredients, on a side table nearby. It just happened that a lady was passing by then with a basket on her head of live hassar fish, and she purchased a couple of parcels and fried some up for the cook-up rice, and she curried some for lunch.

After lunch, Joan brought over Indira's yellow chiffon shift dress which she had just finished sewing for her and, while Nani went to the store to get the high-heeled slingback shoes and store-made seersucker panties, Indira washed up and got dressed and put on a pair of delicate white slippers. That day she did her hair in a *hassar plait* coiffure, and she dabbed on a touch of Chantilly perfume that Nani had gotten her, and she thought all she needed now was a touch of makeup. But makeup was something Nani prohibited her from wearing. If she were to put on a conspicuous amount, Nani would definitely notice and say the Guyanese proverb, *Monkey dress e pickney till he spoil*, meaning, try not to overdo something as you may end up spoiling it. Nani would prefer her to stay natural. But if she were to put on just a touch, Nani might not notice because of her dim eyesight. Ordinarily, she would not defy Nani on this, but today was special because she was now sixteen and wanted to feel grown up and glamorous and look like the Indian film stars of India that she would see in magazines. So, she made up her face with a touch of foundation and pressed powder and put on a dab of pink lipstick ever so subtly, and she took a pinta, and with the tip collected some blackpat—soot gathered at the bottom of a pot from the flames of the mud stove, and she lined her eyes ever so slightly and, lastly, she polished her nails with pink Cutex as pale as the pink of her nails. And she hoped that Nani would not notice any of it.

By the time she finished getting dressed, Nani had returned from the store, and when she entered the bedroom and saw Indira she thought Indira looked especially lovely, but her dim eyes did not notice Indira's subtle makeup as Indira had hoped. She thought some gold jewellery on Indira would make her look even more flattering, especially against her light golden-brown skin and the sheer, yellow chiffon shift dress. Now that Indira was sixteen, she would let her wear Chaaya's most beautiful gold necklace. She got the bag of gold and chose the glittering necklace with the gold leaves' fringes and a matching pair of earrings and, to complete the ensemble, she gave Indira a couple of pairs of Chaaya's thick gold bangles to wear. While Indira stood enjoying the jingling of the bangles, Nani admired her and

318

told her that she no longer looked like a schoolgirl now but, rather, a beautiful young woman, and Indira smiled and really did feel all grown up that day.

Nani then went to bathe to get dressed, also, and, as she was doing so, the other birthday girl, Francine, came over, looking resplendent in her yellow chiffon shift dress against her deep brown velvet skin, and she had on white slippers, same outfit as Indira's, and was all made up in pronounced glossy makeup that Joan allowed her to wear as it was her sixteenth birthday. She had her hair done in braids with beads, falling past her shoulders, and was wearing a black velvet choker necklace. Like Indira, she no longer looked like a schoolgirl that day, but quite a blossoming young lady.

Nani looked impressive that day, as well, in her white polyester dress and matching headkerchief, and, as usual, her feet were bare. She sat in the hammock at the bottom-house and was oiling them with coconut oil as she waited for the youngsters to arrive. Indira and Francine, also waiting for the others, were lingering upstairs on the front verandah in the sunshine where a warm breeze was blowing on this hot, blue-sky mid-afternoon, scattering the scents of the chameli, roses, hibiscus, and jump & kiss flowers in the garden below.

"I can't wait to see Albert," Francine said and giggled.

"I'm sure he can't wait to see you, too," Indira said with a naughty smile, for now her heartache was overridden by the excitement of seeing her other friends and the anticipation of the birthdays' celebration.

Francine's wait did not turn into an impatient one, for soon Albert came strolling up the dirt street, looking

319

handsome in a big Afro hairstyle and a colourful tropical shirt and white bell-bottoms with matching platform shoes. And, no doubt, he was smelling sweet of musky cologne.

As soon as Nani saw him she got up from the hammock and rushed to the ragged gate in her bare feet, paying no mind to the heat of the sun on the narrow dirt pathway. She greeted him with a smile, flashing her gold teeth, and nicely said, "So you are Albert."

"The one and only," Albert said with a dashing, pearly-white smile that stood out against his dark chocolate-coloured skin, and he added, "The soon-to-be husband of Francine Williams, soon to be Francine Briggs." Francine, who was still standing on the verandah with Indira, blushed darker than the rouge on her cheeks when she heard that.

Nani then suddenly ceased her smiling and she tightened the knot in the back of her crisp headkerchief and, with a stern look in her old eyes, she warned Albert, saying, "Now, you behave yourself while you're here, young man, for I would have no courting in my backyard."

Indira was secretly dreading this, that Nani would start acting strict with her friends, and her temperature was just about to rise with discomfiture when Francine cupped her hands over her mouth and started giggling, and when Indira looked at Albert's response to Nani's warning, she started laughing, also, for Albert had his lips pressed tightly together to stop himself from cracking up with laughter.

When Albert straightened out his mouth, he, rather seriously, said, "No courting in your backyard, I promise, Nani."

Francine and Indira then came downstairs to greet Albert, and Nani then noticed Francine's conspicuous rouge and red lipstick, and she took off on Francine, asking her, "Does your mother know you're wearing that thing on your face?"

Indira was starting to get embarrassed again, but that was quelled when Francine coolly answered, "It's called makeup, Nani. And Mommy bought it for me to wear as it's my sixteenth birthday."

Indira was expecting Nani to say, *Monkey dress e pickney till he spoil*, but, to her relief, Nani hushed up then. But not for too long. She was by the gate when Afonso showed up in a car with Laliwa sitting beside him in the front seat, and Ling and Devika in the back, Laliwa in a blue mini skirt and tight-fitting blue blouse, and Devika as scantily clothed in a white halter top with a plunging décolletage, and red hot pants, which accentuated her clear skin, and both girls were in high-heeled slippers and glossy makeup. Nani immediately looked askance at them and, while Indira, Albert and Francine were at the bottom-house looking on, she said to the youngsters, "I must warn you before you enter my gate that there will be no courting in my backyard!"

Indira just about had it with Nani by now, acting austere with her friends, and she was about to step up and call her aside and have a talk with her, but her friends were all taking it in good humour, and she refrained when Ling affirmatively said to Nani, "I will keep an eye out and make sure there's no courting in your backyard, Nani." And the friends looked at each other and smiled surreptitiously, behaving decorously in front of Nani.

Nani then went on to say, "I've set out everything you need for the bush-cook, even some treats. You will find it

321

all on the table in the backyard under the tamarind tree. I've even laid out the stones for you, and there's wood you can chop yourselves, boys. Now go on and start the bush-cook. I will now go and have a quick nap myself and will be up to join you very soon. And, remember, no courting in my backyard while I'm asleep."

Much to Indira's relief, Nani then went to take a nap in the hammock to rest her old and tired and bothersome bones, and as soon as she was fast asleep and snoring, the young men tore off their shirts and got down to the bush-cook in the backyard.

The heat of the sun was at its peak now, its sharp, shining rays casting a blinding brightness upon the town. In Nani's backyard, the hens in the fowl coop were clucking as the fowlcocks were crowing, while the fishes splashed about in the pond of lilies and shame-baby weeds, and the fruit trees stood motionless with not even a rustle of leaves. Albert took to chopping some wood for the fire, flexing his bare biceps in the sun in trying to get Francine's attention, while Afonso stuck out his glistening chest to show off on Laliwa before he took off to climb the fruits trees to pick guineps and star apples and some green coconuts. Ling, not as self-conscious as Albert and Afonso, tied his shirt around his waist and went about chasing after the lizards and salamanders and crapos, only now he did not scare the girls with them but amused himself. The girls, except for Indira, were fully aware of their beaus and they flaunted their pretty selves at them in their red hot pants and blue mini skirt and short chiffon dress as they went about assisting Indira—who was wishing Ravi was there, also—with chopping up the ingredients for the cook-up rice, gaffing away as they did and listening to reggae and calypso music playing on the cassette player Francine had borrowed from her father, which was turned down low so as not to wake Nani.

As soon as Albert was finished with chopping the pile of wood, Afonso and Ling joined him and the others under the tamarind tree and the boys started the fire and put the large iron pot on the stones and got the cook-up rice boiling in no time at all. As the fire crackled and sparked, spouting smoke about, the friends gathered around the boiling pot and drank coconut water and ate fruits and the treats Nani had set out on the table for them, and they gaffed away.

"'*I must warn you before you enter my gate that there will be no courting in my backyard,*'" Ling laughed and said as he tried to mimic Nani.

"Shucks!" Albert exclaimed. "No courting!"

"Dammit!" Afonso said, and the girls all laughed it off. Afonso then began reminiscing about their childhood days and said to Ling, "Remember when we were in kindergarten we used to stop by the field after school and watch the men bush-cook when they were playing cricket, and one day you said we could do a bush-cook ourselves? And I said we would get into trouble if we did. Then you argued that we wouldn't and it was Sally who hushed you up. Boy, you were such a prankster then."

"He isn't completely cured from skylarking," Devika butted in. "I'm still working on him. But, at least, now he knows better than to pull any mischief at school, especially, after the one with Prajit when he got a whipping from Teacher Sanjay and I threatened to stop talking to him."

323

Ling laughed and said, "What can I say, she's got me wrapped around her pretty little finger."

The group laughed, and Afonso went on to say to Ling, "I remember you said on that same day that you wanted to become a famous cricket player when you grow up. Remember?"

Ling nodded and said, "And Sally said if I stayed out of trouble and instead practise the game I would do just that. I still want to be that's why I took her advice and have been practising. My father is working on getting me drafted in the professional league. And when I do become famous then I will marry Devika."

Devika did not react with excitement to this, for she was not happy that Ling would keep her waiting while her friends were all planning to marry right after school, and, with displeasure in her big, brown eyes, she said, "I may not be single by the time you're ready to marry me, Ling."

"If you truly love me, you'll wait for me," Ling responded. "Before I marry I want to be somebody so you can be proud of me, and, more importantly, I want to be able to provide you with a good life that I think you so deserve."

Devika's attitude then softened at the sincerity in Ling's voice, and she said, "I'll wait for you as long as I know you'll marry me, Ling."

Afonso then said to his friends, "I will have to steal my little Amerindian girl in order to marry her." And Laliwa lowered her eyes shyly at this and pulled on her pigtails as she blushed.

Ling, who would not pass up on the chance of partaking in something so daring, said to Afonso, "I'll help you to steal her," and he added, "but she may want to go to America to become a film star as she wished as a little girl."

Laliwa spoke up and said, "I no longer want to go to America to become a film star, for I will be starring in the film of my life with Afonso wherever we end up."

"And once I steal Laliwa and marry her, I will work on becoming a policeman and ride a motorcycle like I've been dreaming of since I was a little boy," Afonso said.

Albert then chimed in, saying, "And I will teach at school while Francine stays home and sews clothes," and he laughed when he added, "and make babies." Francine's cheeks burned darker than her rouge upon hearing this, and the friends laughed, all except for Indira, and Albert turned to her and asked, "And what about you Indira?"

When Indira hesitated in answering, Francine cut in and said, "Indira will be marrying a well-to-do man who works at the bank, and she will be working at the bank, also."

"You are one lucky girl," Albert said to Indira. "You must be so happy about this."

Indira gave a cursory smile to please her friends, but she wanted to say that she wished to marry Ravi and live with Nani and work in the garden with Ravi. Instead, she said, "Most girls would be happy about that." And then she diverted the conversation from herself and asked Laliwa, "Have you heard from Sally?"

"Sally now has a boyfriend!" Laliwa blurted out.

"What?" Francine said. "I thought she was determined to finish her studies then return to Guyana to work as a nurse and then settle down."

"That is still her plan, only now she's found the someone she wants to settle down with," Laliwa said. "Apparently, she met a Guyanese dougla in England and she fell head over heels with him. His name is Neville and he's also interested in taking up nursing. They both plan to study in England, then they will return to Guyana to work here and settle down."

The youngsters carried on talking more about their plans after school and their dreams for the future. Nani still had not joined them as she had promised to do soon after a quick nap, and Albert went to check on her and found her still snoring in the hammock. With no one there to supervise their behaviour, the friends joked and laughed their heads off freely under the hot afternoon sun while the pot of cook-up rice was bubbling away over the fire, and they poked fun at Nani, saying that their chaperone must have fallen under a sleeping spell, lucky for them. They laughed even more when Solomon the donkey trotted by and started 'skinning' his big, white teeth at them as though joining them in jesting, and Rani the cow made things even funnier when she came around chewing her cud with her big, old mouth hanging down, looking at them cross-eyed and mean as though she was not too thrilled about the goings-on behind her Nani's back. Pyari's parrot, Raj, was heard cursing at her just then, calling Pyari so and so, and saying that he wanted some rum to drink, and the youngsters roared with laughter over this. Pyari was also a source of laughter, an eccentric old woman in her red headkerchief and noticeable gold nose ring, sitting by her window and responding to Raj's barrage of curses with curses of her own, saying that she was fed up with Raj and his impudent behaviour.

As Pyari was sitting by the window she had been observing the youngsters all along as they were bush-cooking and, noticing that Nani was deeply asleep in her hammock, she packed a little surprise in a bag for them and came over and entered Nani's yard through the back gate, and she joined the gathering under the tamarind tree and said to the young men, "Boys, I've brought you something to quench your thirst on this hot day." And she opened the bag she was carrying and pulled out three bottles of cold beer.

The boys reacted with excitement as none of them had ever tasted beer nor drank any kind of liquor before and they thought it was a grown-up thing to do at a sixteenth birthday party. Ling, as was expected, immediately said, "I'll have the first one!"

Indira, who was nervous about the idea, interrupted Pyari, saying, "Nani doesn't mind older men drinking but she wouldn't be happy with the boys for doing so, and if she catches them drinking beer she will break up the party and send everyone home."

"Never mind your Nani," Pyari said, "she's just a laughingstock, sleeping when she should be watching over you all, and snoring, and blowing wind, I'm sure." And Pyari handed Ling a cold bottle of beer, saying, "Go on and have it, boy. Young men should have some fun and have a drink from time to time."

Before Indira could object further, Albert said, "Pyari's right, young men should have some fun and have a drink from time to time." And Albert grabbed the second bottle of beer. Afonso needed no further inducing and grabbed the third.

Pyari went on to inveigle the girls, saying, "Young women should also have some fun from time to time." And she pulled out a small bottle of red wine and wine glasses from the bag and placed them on the table near to the boiling pot of cook-up rice, and she said to the young women, "Take a sip of wine and celebrate for it will not harm you, for a little wine is good for the body and the spirit!"

"But Nani wouldn't—" Indira began to raise an objection again.

"Never mind your Nani," Pyari said. "She used to drink wine in her younger days and Nana used to drink rum. So don't tell me about your Nani." And before Pyari turned to leave she left the youngsters with: "Drink and be merry, and love and be happy. You are all young and love is in the air, so take advantage of it while you can." Contrary advice to Nani's 'no courting in the backyard' rule. And with that, Pyari went back over to her house and placed a few more bottles of beer to cool in the ice bucket for her young male companion she was expecting, and she took her seat by the window and waited for him to arrive.

Right after Pyari left, Laliwa said, "Pyari's right, a little wine is good for the body and the spirit. My father gives my brothers and I a few sips of piwari all the time." And Laliwa unscrewed the bottle of wine and poured it into the glasses, and she first handed a glass to Devika, who willingly took it, and Francine took hers with hesitation, afraid she would disappoint Indira, and then Laliwa handed a glass to Indira.

Indira hesitated at first, then realising that all her friends were for it, she accepted, saying, "Let's keep a close eye on Nani. If she wakes up, we'll have to get rid of the drinks real fast."

And so while Nani remained in her sleeping spell and was closely watched, the youngsters had a few drinks under the sun as the pot of cook-up rice was simmering over the embers, filling the air with a mixture of mouth-watering flavours, and the sweet smoke of the wood burning only added to the melange. It took the youngsters no time at all to get tipsy for it was their first time drinking, all except for Laliwa, and their experience seemed dreamy and their bantering was even funnier, causing them to cover their mouths to silence their laugher so as not to wake Nani. Laliwa lost all of her shyness by now in her tipsy state and she got down to doing the wine dance, winning to the low calypso music, and soon Francine, Devika, and Indira felt less inhibited and joined her, and the boys had much fun watching the girls wine under the tamarind tree.

Fortunately, the friends finished their drinks without being caught by Nani, for she slept all through it. By this time the red sun was setting, casting its golden glow on the tree tops, and the cook-up rice, with fried hassar, was finished cooking. Indira dished out some in a bowl for Pyari and her young companion, and Albert took it over to her. When he returned, the friends stood under the tamarind tree and ate with their fingers from calabashes, mixing the cook-up rice with mango achar and ball-of-fire peppers. By the time they were satiated with the scrumptious meal, the pot was empty, and just a portion remained in a calabash for Nani.

Darkness soon gathered and large flocks of birds were seen flying across the sky to their evening roosts. But tonight there were no jumbies anywhere around. Blame it on the emerging stars, twinkling all over the sky, or the flickering of the candleflies near the bushes, or the seductive warmth of the wind, or it may have been Pyari's prompting, or it may have more likely been the amorous aura of the full moon casting its silvery rays on the forbidden fruits in the orchard—the girls appearing alluring, but this was the kind of propitious night that was conducive to courting in Nani's backyard!

Ling, who had promised Nani that he would keep an eye out for such a thing and make sure it does not happen, was the first to lead Devika under a jamun tree from which hung bunches of the juicy purple fruit, and then Afonso took off with Laliwa and went under a fragranced guava tree. Francine, who would have loved to spend this magical moment with Albert, but who did not want her friend standing around by herself, hung around with Indira. And Albert was officially assigned the task of watching over Nani, something he was not exactly thrilled about because he would have much preferred courting Francine. However, in spite of wanting to abdicate his responsibility, he went over to the backstairs and took a seat on the steps and quietly watched Nani as she was still snoring. Ling and Afonso had told him to signal them if Nani only made a move, and he was to start coughing out loudly. And there Albert was wondering whether Ling and Afonso would even notice him when he does cough. He suspected not.

Indira and Francine took to strolling about the yard on this enchanting moonlit night, and they both marvelled at the fact that they were now sixteen. Their school years were almost over, and their married lives would soon begin.

"Mom has already bought the fabric for my wedding dress and she has started sewing it," Francine told Indira. "She wants to know when you'll get yours so she can start making your dress."

"Nani will take care of that," Indira said in a blasé manner.

"I meant it when I said to you before that I want us to get married on the same day," Francine went on to say. "And I'm waiting for you to set your date."

"A date will be set after my introduction to Tarak," Indira said, still with a lack of enthusiasm.

Francine, sensing Indira's indifference, took her friend by the hand and, assuredly, said, "Tarak is a good match for you, Indira. Trust me. With him you'll have a well-off life and a good career working at the bank."

"But it's Ravi that I love, Francine," Indira responded.

"Put Ravi out of your mind and think of Tarak," Francine emphatically advised. "When you meet Tarak you will be smitten by him, like all the other girls. Nani and your grandfather are doing the right thing by securing a good future for you with him. Don't miss this opportunity."

With Francine now firmly on the side of her grandparents, Indira did not pursue the conversation further but reverted to thinking that her grandparents were doing the right thing for her. Francine went on to talk about how she envisioned her wedding day and that she wished to be married at St. George's Cathedral, but it was not practical for everyone to go to Georgetown for the occasion, so she settled for a local church in town, and she carried on talking about every detail of the wedding, down to the lace underwear she would be wearing on her wedding night.

"Oh shucks, man!" Albert exclaimed suddenly. He did not get a chance to cough out loudly to signal his friends that Nani was up because he was in deep fantasies of Francine and Nani woke up suddenly and jumped up from the hammock and startled him.

Nani was sorely vexed with herself that it was already nightfall and that she had fallen asleep and left the youngsters by themselves all that time with no supervision, and when she noticed Albert sitting on the back steps she straightaway asked him, "Is there any courting going on in my backyard?"

"I'm sitting here alone and I'm not courting," Albert said. He could not cough out loud now to signal his friends, afraid Nani might get suspicious, and if he tried to cook up a story Nani would immediately figure so. Thinking fast of finding a way to notify his friends that Nani was up, he quickly said, "Nani, you wouldn't be able to see much of what's going on in your backyard now, why don't you light the kerosene oil lamp and we'll go and check on the others."

And as Nani was lighting the lamp at the bottom-house, Ling and Afonso immediately noticed the light. And that brought an end to the courting game in Nani's backyard that night. Before Nani went searching for them, all the youngsters came and gathered at the bottom-house, and the boys began telling Nani about what a good cook-up rice they made, some of which they saved for her, throwing her off course from asking any courting questions. Nani did not have another chance to broach the subject again because

George and Joan Williams came over just then, bringing a black cake with icing and sixteen candles, and next came Shazam and Fazeela and their family, followed by Pyari, who came with a sly smile but with no liquor this time.

And the cake was then lit and *Happy Birthday* was sung to both Indira and Francine, and together the girls blew out the sixteen candles to much clapping and laughter and well wishes. There were many gifts presented to both of them, from perfume to talc powder, body cream, dress fabrics, hair bandos, and panties. The girls had fun opening them all, and they sat on the back steps and tried on their white high-heeled slingback shoes which Nani got them, feeling all grown up in them. Behind Nani's back, the boys teased them to try on their store-made seersucker panties, only to have the girls blush.

Once the gifts were all opened, Afonso and Ling would have loved to linger around in Nani's backyard for some more courting in spite of the mosquitoes that were now out in swarms and biting them, and the flying cockroaches and bats were about, but Nani warned them to take Laliwa and Devika straight home and she sent them away. The others then left, all except for Albert, who went over to his future in-laws' and finally had the chance to court Francine.

When Indira settled in to bed that night she did not cry over Ravi, but she stayed up late that night pondering Francine's advice to put him out of her mind and think of Tarak, the one she will inevitably be marrying.

15

The Thrashing Of Indira

It was now the last week of school before writing her GCE exams, and Indira was making her way home after school this day, walking alone, for Francine and Laliwa were at the matinée with Albert and Afonso. Like a typical day in the little town of Rose Hall, it was sizzlingly hot and the shimmering waves of heat were rising from the dirt road which gave the optical illusion of a tempting lake of cool water in the distance, a mirage that was out of reach. Indira pulled down the brim of her white school hat to shield her eyes from the glaring sun and squinted as she walked on, taking the usual route and not the one that had the rum shop along the way. She paid no attention to the odd person passing by and did not even notice the donkey along the way or the hen and her brood of chicks crossing the narrow road, not even the occasional car and bicycle going by caught her attention, she was so engrossed in her thoughts. She was busy memorising the lessons she had learned today in school on various subjects and testing her knowledge on all she had learned over her years in high school, for she had just a few more days to cram for her finals, which was due to begin the following week.

She became aware of the moment, however, as she came upon a sweetie shop on the way as it was her habit to stop in on her way home from school and purchase some treats for Nani. She made her way into the little shop and got some sugar-coated blood-drop and Bulls-Eyes sweetie and put them in her briefcase, then she treated herself to a cold bottle of lemonade and a *blackeye* cake before she continued on her way. She lapsed back into testing herself on her studies, and as she was passing by the market she did not pay any attention to the fishmongers hollering at the top of their lungs for people to buy their fresh fishes, nor did she tune in to the chatter of the shoppers. She did not even hear the humming of the electricity generator as she passed by it, her eyes fixed on the dusty road in deep concentration.

She was so absorbed in thoughts that she did not hear the squeal of the wheels of a bicycle riding up behind her, but she heard a familiar voice say, "Hello, Indira." She turned to look and there was Ravi riding up beside her, dressed in a white cotton shirt and trousers that was flattering to his smooth brown skin, and he was looking so handsome. One look in his sensual brown eyes took her breath away and her heart immediately started racing and, being caught off guard, she was dumbstruck.

"Well, aren't you going to say hello to me?" Ravi asked, smiling all over his face from being so thrilled to see her, and immediately taking in her delicate chameli fragrance, her appealing beauty, and her pretty, dark eyes and cute dimples.

Indira composed herself quickly and tossed him a perfunctory glance and said, "Hello," and she averted her head and kept walking with her eyes cast low from being shy and shocked from seeing him.

"Forgive me for taking this risk," he said, "but I just had to see you one last time." He wanted to tell her how he would stay up at nights thinking of her and languishing away, longing to see her and filling his nights with pages of poems of her and drowning himself in tears, playing the guitar and singing sad love songs, but he knew that would only make things more difficult and confusing for her, and leave her torn, so, instead, he said, "Once you're married, I wouldn't stand a chance of ever meeting you again."

"I'm happy to see you, Ravi," she said, with a slight tremor in her voice, not just from the excitement of seeing him, but feeling nervous that someone may see the two of them together. "I apologise if I seem nervous, though," she added, "it's just that I have a feeling that someone is watching us."

Ravi, fully aware of the risk he was taking, and afraid of this, also, quickly looked around to check and see whether anyone was looking, scanning the dusty dirt road up and down, but at that moment there was no one around, except, for a few innocuous children playing banga on the side of the road. "Nothing to worry about right now," he said assuredly. There was a moment of silence between them then, both aware of each other's presence and the deep, dark sadness that emanated from them both, a tacit regret of a love that was never to be fulfilled. Ravi then broke the despondency of the moment by asking, "When are you writing your exams?"

"Next week," Indira said. "It's a lucky thing you caught me this week because my schedule next week is different, and I will be walking home from school with my friends."

"I imagine you must be busy with your studies, but how are you doing otherwise?"

336

Indira wanted to tell him of how she had been crying since they said goodbye and how she was pining for him up until Francine advised her to put him out of her mind, and that she was just beginning to do so, but all she said was, "I'm doing fine now."

Ravi then asked the inevitable question, "Have you met with your future husband, as yet?"

"No," she simply answered.

"That means you haven't set a date for your wedding, as yet."

"No."

Ravi got the hint that she did not want to talk about her future husband or her wedding plans, and an awkward silence fell between them then. He kept on riding alongside of her, however, stealing just a few more precious moments with her, looking over his shoulders ever so often to check that no one was around to see them, and he could see no one.

But, just as Indira feared, someone was watching them from a distance behind, surreptitiously hiding behind a lamp post. And that someone was no other than the cantankerous Uncle Ram! He was on his way to visit Nani and had spotted Indira quite a while earlier and was tailing her as though to catch her in the act of committing something wrong. And when he saw a young man pulling up beside her on a bicycle, he said to himself, "Ah ha, I knew I would catch her someday with a man!" And he turned livid with anger and came out from behind the lamp post and hurried up the road to confront Indira.

With his back now turned and too preoccupied at the moment with relishing the last few moments by Indira's side, Ravi did not see Uncle Ram coming up from behind, neither did Indira as she continued walking with her eyes lowered. And Ravi went on trying to make conversation with her, but he could sense her discomfort and said to her, "I can see my riding beside you is making you too nervous. I'm sorry. I think I should just leave you alone now before someone sees us. I don't want to get you into any trouble."

But Indira was already in trouble. Uncle Ram came up briskly from behind and started shouting at her, saying, "Is this why the old lady is sending you to school, for you to talk to a man in the middle of the road in broad daylight? You shameless thing!"

Both Ravi and Indira swung around simultaneously to see Uncle Ram, his face black with rage and his breath smelling of rum, and Ravi asked him, "Who are you? And how dare you talk to this girl like that." He thought he would have to defend Indira against another drunk man.

Uncle Ram gave him a baleful look and said, "I'm her Uncle Ram." And, still seething with ominous anger, shouted at Ravi, saying, "And I will talk to her however I want to! You get your backside out of here! Now!" When Ravi did not move, he belligerently challenged him, saying, "Do you want to fight, man?"

Ravi clutched his bicycle handle tightly to subdue the provoked anger and, in defence of Indira, said, "This is all my fault. I rode up to her. Listen, she hasn't done anything wrong but speak to me. I'll take the blame for this."

Uncle Ram ignored Ravi this time, redirecting his attention towards the real object of his anger, and ordered Indira, saying, "You march your tail straight home right now!"

Indira obeyed, not just out of embarrassment, but to obviate a disaster, for she was afraid that Uncle Ram would get into a fight with Ravi if they stayed there any longer and things could turn even more nasty, so she hurried along, with Uncle Ram following close at her heels. Ravi was left with his mouth open in the middle of the road, unable to do anything about the situation but spar and fight with Indira's uncle, and he certainly did not want to do so. He did not get out of there, though, but after Indira and Uncle Ram disappeared down the road and turned into the street where Nani lived, he followed cautiously and stopped close enough to Nani's house without being seen, and close enough to overhear the thrashing of Indira.

Once they entered Nani's gate, Uncle Ram grabbed hold of Indira's arm and hauled her to the bottom-house, where Nani was sitting on a peerah on the earthen ground, slicing off the leaves from some coconut branches with a knife to make a broom with the spine of the leaves, and Uncle Ram said to Nani, "I found her in the middle of the road talking to a man in broad daylight!"

Nani immediately dropped the knife to the ground, flabbergasted by the news, and she rose to her feet and asked Indira, "Is that true, child?"

Uncle Ram let go of Indira's arm and shoved her towards Nani, and when Indira did not answer, he said to Nani, "Yes, it is true. I've seen it with my own two eyes! And if she can be seen in the middle of the road with a man in broad daylight, then who knows what else she is doing in secret!"

Nani, not wanting to believe such an egregious thing and, wanting to give Indira the benefit of the doubt, faced

Indira and asked again, "Is that true, child? Were you talking to a man on the road in broad daylight?"

Indira felt naked in her school uniform, like Nani was looking right through to her heart and could see everything in it; all her secret rendezvous with Ravi. She was too nervous and afraid to say or admit to anything, though, and she just stood there with her eyes cast downwards, her demeanour one of confusion and guilt. And when she did not answer this time, Nani got cross, and she raised her voice and shouted at her, saying, "So it is true! Now I know why you've been daydreaming lately. You're in love with a man and you're brazen enough to talk to him on the road in broad daylight!"

"You should pull her out of school and make her stay home and scrub blackpat!" Uncle Ram yelled, meaning that Indira only deserved to be 'washing the soot off pots', a euphemism for degrading her, and leaving her bereft of her dignity. Continuing his tirade of abuse, he said, "She's nothing more than a *phaglee*, a crazy girl, who should not be going to school because she's disgracing the family by talking to a man in the middle of the road in broad daylight!"

"You have betrayed me, Indira," Nani said bitterly as she sat back down on the peerah on the ground. And she removed her headkerchief and held her head down in shame and started crying out loudly, saying, "I never thought, not even for an instance, that you would bring shame upon my poor old head. I trusted you so much. I noticed that recently you looked like a woman pining from love, but I chose to believe otherwise. And all the time you have been seeing a man behind my back." And, as Indira expected, Nani did say, *Moon ah run till daylight ketch am.*

Indira had stopped seeing Ravi for fear she would be caught one day, and she thought she had gotten away with her misdeeds, but, by the inauspicious risk Ravi had taken to see her, she was caught in broad daylight. She had gone through the terrible emotion of feeling guilty all along for committing a wrong against Nani by not telling her about Ravi because she felt Nani would oppose a match with him, but, now, seeing Nani so frail and weeping so heartrendingly, it made her feel a lot worse that she was causing her so much hurt in bringing shame upon her poor old head. It did not help that at the moment the place was stiflingly hot and still, making her school uniform cling to her with a sudden burst of perspiration, and making her feel nauseous, and, to make matters worse, the derogatory thrashing coming from Uncle Ram were all too much for her to bear, and feeling denuded of her dignity, she broke down and started crying, also, the deluge of tears dripping down her face and falling on her white school blouse.

Nani had never heard Indira cry as a young woman and Indira's tears touched her, and she wiped away her own tears with her hands and turned to Indira and asked, "Who's this young man, Indira?"

Uncle Ram cut in then, saying, "Don't ask her who the man is. You should pull her out of school right away before she causes a scandal in town!"

Well, Nani then turned on Uncle Ram and shouted at him, saying, "You just shut up!"

That started a row between Uncle Ram and Nani, and Uncle Ram accused Nani, saying, "You're a slack woman and very one-sided. You favour Indira like I've always known." And he got even more incensed and shouted, "You can't condone such a behaviour and let Indira get away with this. She's a wild wretch and a disgrace to the family! You should punish her by pulling her out of school right away!"

"I wouldn't pull her out of school," Nani said adamantly.

Ravi, who had been listening all along, overheard the thrashing of Indira from Uncle Ram and, unable to bear it, he rode up to Nani's gate and called out, "May I enter your gate, Auntie?"

"That's the man this little wretch was talking to in the middle of the road, so don't let him in!" Uncle Ram ordered, his fury now diverted to Ravi.

But Nani did not listen to him. She was taken by the immaculately dressed, handsome young man at the gate, and she rose from the peerah and went to the gate and let him in and escorted him to the bottom-house, much to the chagrin of Uncle Ram. In fact, Uncle Ram started cursing at Ravi and began challenging him again to fight. This made Nani quite angry and, having no other resolve to placate his pugnacity, she resorted to picking up the wild cane and began brandishing it at Uncle Ram. Being sorely afraid of the whip, Uncle Ram bolted to the gate and jumped over it instead of unlatching it, and he ran down the street, still cursing as he did, and swearing he would never return to visit Nani for not punishing Indira by pulling her out of school for the indecent act of talking to a man on the road, and for going against him and letting the man in question into her yard.

Nani then took her seat back down on the peerah at the bottom-house, near to the hammock where Solomon the donkey and Rani the cow were hovering about, and she asked Ravi to take a seat on the donkey-cart right opposite her. Indira, meanwhile, remained standing beside Nani and kept her head down, not lifting her eyes even for a moment to look at Ravi, and even more nervous now not knowing what to expect, except, for a serious questioning by Nani, which she knew would be directed at Ravi.

Nani picked up the knife she had dropped to the ground earlier and resumed slicing off the coconut leaves from the spines—the fresh grassy scent of the leaves spreading about the bottom-house—and, while doing so, she began her interrogation by casually asking Ravi, "What is your name, boy, and where are you from, and do you work at the bank?"

Ravi told her his name and that he was from Skeldon, but suspecting that Nani would immediately dismiss him if he were to straightaway tell her he does not work at the bank, he prevaricated and went on to tell her how he had rescued Indira from the drunk man at the rum shop when he first met her. His initial intention was to clear Indira's name after she was thrashed by Uncle Ram, but now realising that he had an opportunity to appeal to Nani to be considered a husband for Indira, he seized it and poured his heart out to Nani, pleading his case and telling her how he fell in love with Indira and wanted only to marry her.

Nani listened intently, trying to assimilate what Ravi said, though the pensive expression on her sun-beaten brown face was enigmatic and not easy for Ravi to decipher. Then, after a while, she voiced her paramount concern, without even looking up at him, asking, "Have you spoiled my granddaughter, boy?"

"I wouldn't dishonour Indira and take her virginity before marriage because I love and respect her too much," Ravi answered. "She's a precious jewel and I would only have her if I were to marry her. I know a marriage is being arranged for her to a banker's son and I hope you would consider my deep love for her and consider letting me marry her, instead."

"Do you work at the bank?" Nani brought up the question again as she kept working away at the coconut leaves.

Ravi began beating around the bush again and, instead, said, "I attended high school and am educated." But he did not mention that he had to drop out of school to assist his sick father with his farm, a vocation that would not be pleasing to Nani, he feared.

Nani persisted with the question and, for the third time, she asked him, "Do you work at the bank, boy?" And she lifted her sunken brown eyes and looked directly into his and said, "Answer me now."

"No," Ravi finally answered, and thought if he told her he was a farmer, his sudden glimmer of hope would be dashed, so, instead, endeavouring to impress Nani, he said, "But I'm a poet." And, truthfully, he was a poet and had written numerous poems of his love for Indira.

"A poet? You mean like the great Shakespeare?" Nani asked.

Ravi nodded, thinking that he had managed to impress Nani by the pleased look on her face.

Nani was quiet for a moment as she kept on slicing off the coconut leaves, but upon pondering his answer, she became skeptical and asked, "But who has heard of one being a poet around here? And how much money do you work for as a poet?"

Ravi thought this old woman was a little too smart for him, after all, she knew of William Shakespeare—obviously through Indira—and he scratched his head, and said, "I'm an unpublished poet."

Nani looked him straight in the eyes and bluntly asked, "And how would you provide for my granddaughter if you're not earning a living?"

Indira, who remained quiet all along, with her hope beginning to rise, now felt it being dashed. And Ravi was now breaking out in sweat, not only from the intense heat of the mid-afternoon, but because he felt his opportunity slipping away. At this point, though, he had no choice but to reveal his work to Nani. "My father has a rice farm up in Skeldon and I help him to farm for a living," he admitted, then added, "I love your granddaughter and I promise to work hard to provide comfortably for her."

"So you're a farmer just like me," Nani said disdainfully. "Well, I will tell you right now, boy, I do not want my granddaughter to struggle like me, for the farming life is a very hard one."

"I'm young and strong and I can handle hard work, and I would not let Indira work and struggle in life," Ravi said. And he went further and revealed his full intentions: "If you agree for me to marry your granddaughter, I will leave my parents' home in Skeldon and move in with you and straightaway take care of tending and cultivating the garden so Indira wouldn't have to do so anymore and spoil her pretty hands. I will also take a second job so I can earn enough to care and provide for you, also, so you would not have to struggle to sell at the market in your old age." In response to this, Nani narrowed her eyes and stared at him suspiciously, and when she did not respond, Ravi, in a final attempt to appeal to her, desperately said, "I will be a good husband to your granddaughter, Auntie. And I will serenade her with my guitar and sing to her and write her poems. I promise to do my best to make her happy and to be faithful to her and love her forever."

"And I will love him forever, too," Indira chimed in.

Nani put the knife down and shoved the coconut leaves aside and she got up and began pacing the earthen ground in her barefoot in deep contemplation, while Ravi and Indira waited anxiously for her to respond. After a few moments that seemed like an eternity, Nani came and stood in front of Ravi, who was now standing up against the donkey-cart, and she finally said to him, "I will not let my granddaughter marry a farmer and struggle in life. She will soon be marrying a man who works at the bank and she will be working at the bank, also. So I will ask you to leave right now, boy, and to never see her again."

Indira's heart sank then, as did Ravi's. He had deluded himself into thinking that he could persuade Nani. But Nani had made her decision and had disapproved of him, as Indira thought she would, mainly because Ravi was a farmer and she did not want Indira to struggle in life like she did herself, but she overlooked the fact that the two of them were deeply in love. And there was nothing neither of them could do now.

Expressing deference to Nani, Ravi bowed out graciously. He took one last look at Indira and left with uttering just one word: "Goodbye." And that brought a cessation to Ravi's impromptu meeting with Nani, and a definite demise of his love affair with Indira.

Nani never brought up the subject of Ravi after that and Indira knew it was futile to do so herself. Nani had more talks about Tarak, though, and kept repeating an old Guyanese proverb to her, *When rain ah fall ah roof yuh put barrel fuh ketch am*, meaning, when opportunity knocks you must try to seize it. It was not just Nani who was instigating her to seize the opportunity with Tarak. Francine, her best friend, had also said so on the night of their birthday celebration, and she kept telling her that over and over again, reinforcing it, and urging her to put Ravi out of her mind and to start thinking of Tarak. So, after a struggle in trying to let go of Ravi and the dejection she felt, she resigned herself to thinking of marrying Tarak, which would be in the very near future. For now, however, she had little time to think about that for Nani let her continue her final phase of her schooling, contrary to what Uncle Ram wanted, and her exams were coming up and she threw herself into her studies. And when she wrote her GCE the following week, she was confident she would make excellent marks.

She attended her farewell school party and spent the last day in school with her classmates, a happy, yet, sad affair for her as she would be moving on from her carefree school days straightaway to a more committed life. That night, she sat by the old wooden bedroom window overlooking the backyard and looked out into the dark, starless night, and what lay ahead of her was as unilluminated as the night itself; a married life that she just could not see into.

She really did not know what to expect of Tarak. All she knew of him was that he was a banker's son and he worked at the bank, also, and all the young girls who knew him were charmed by him and fell in love with him. Surely, with him she would have fine clothes, jewellery and perfume, but, she already had all those things, only in a lesser extent, and she cherished and valued the little things she already had in life and was content and happy now. There was a certain prestige that came with marrying a man with a bank job who would provide her with a house and fine things, but that was all Nani's dream for her. Indubitably, it would be nice to have all that, but cachet and material gains and a good career would not ultimately make her happy, for she yearned most of all for true love and someone to truly care for her—even if she had to continue living a humble existence—and she just could not envision that with Tarak at the moment.

But maybe Tarak would turn out to be a good match for her, after all, she told herself, and maybe she would fall in love with him, just like her grandfather, Dr. Ramesh, told her he did with her grandmother, Shanti, after their arranged marriage. She was now hoping that would be the case with her, also, for that was all she could do now; hope she would find true love again.

With just a couple of days left before the weekend, she gathered herself together and started preparing for the introduction at Dr. Ramesh's big, yellow house.

16

The Introduction At Dr. Ramesh's Big, Yellow House

Indira parted the colourful strands of beads in the kitchen entrance and entered the kitchen to find a pile of coconut husks scattered on the bare wooden floor around where Nani was sitting on the peerah, beads of perspiration settling on her wrinkled brown face as she was bursting coconuts with a hammer and collecting the water in a jug. "You're making coconut oil today," she said to Nani as she took the jug and poured some of the cool coconut water into enamel cups for Nani and herself to quench their thirst on this blistering day.

"Yes, child," Nani said as she took the cup from her and guzzled down the cool drink, and after wiping her mouth with her apron, she then started digging out the coconut from the shells with a knife, placing them in an enamel bowl. "When you're finished with your drink, gather the coconut husks and take them in the backyard and leave them out on a rice bag in the sun to dry, for I will make a new mattress with them."

Indira finished drinking the coconut water and then began doing as Nani instructed. And while in the backyard a woman called at the gate wanting to know if she was interested in buying some fresh shrimps, which she was carrying in a basket on her head. Indira got a large parcel to cook for lunch and, after she finished spreading the coconut husks out to dry, she cleaned the shrimps by the pipe at the foot of the backstairs, then she picked some chorai callaloo vegetable from the garden and returned to the kitchen to join Nani. Nani, by now, had finished grating the coconuts and had squeezed the milk from them and poured it into the carahee, and the milk was now boiling on the mud stove.

"I just bought some shrimps and picked some chorai callaloo to cook for lunch," Indira said to Nani as she got a few potatoes from the basket under the kitchen counter. "I'll fry those up and also make some *aloo curry* with the potatoes, and cook some rice."

"I'll put the rice on to boil right away," Nani offered and went about putting the iron pot on the stove as Indira got the masala brick and sat on the floor and began grinding up curry spices. After Nani put the rice on, she left it to boil and pulled up a peerah and sat beside Indira. Then, unexpectedly, she asked, "Have you ever seen the boy?"

"I just caught a glance of Tarak once when I was passing by the bank one day," Indira answered.

"Well, he has been secretly watching you for a while now, child," Nani revealed. "As you know, the Jajals' live on the main road, and the boy told your grandfather that whenever you go shopping there on Saturdays, he would stand by the window and admire you."

Indira became flushed, not from the heat of the day or from the warmth the mud stove was emitting, but she found herself feeling flattered by this. "I didn't have a clue that he has been watching me," she said. She had to admit, Nani's constant cajoling was effective; she was now actually looking forward to meeting Tarak, which would be only hours away, and the thought brought a smile to her lips.

As she went about peeling the potatoes to make aloo curry and preparing the chorai callaloo to fry with the shrimps, the smile did not leave her face. She kept thinking of the time she had seen Tarak entering the bank, and she remembered him being tall and light-skinned, and at just twenty-years-old, his physique was slim, and she had also noticed his crop of wavy, black hair. She had to acknowledge that he was of *starboy* quality, flashy and attractive like a film star, and she now realised how girls could become easily attracted to him. She continued to think about him as she went about cooking, with that same smile on her face, and the smile remained with her after she was finished and the coconut milk boiling on the mud stove had turned to oil, and even after she and Nani had lunch.

Late that afternoon, when she went over to Auntie Joan's house to pick up her new royal blue silk dress, which Joan had sewn specifically for her introduction to Tarak, she was still smiling up until she found Francine laid up in bed with a swollen foot. "What happened?" she asked her.

"I was stung by a *marabunta*," Francine said. "Those wasps have a wicked sting. But never mind me, it's your big night tonight. And I can't wait to find out when your wedding with Tarak will be, so I can set mine with Albert for the same day."

Indira's smile returned, and she said, "I will come by as soon as I get home tonight and let you know when that will be."

"I will be eagerly waiting."

Back home in her bedroom now, before getting ready, Indira paused by the window and looked out into the backyard. It was a beautiful tropical night, alluring with a

351

full moon casting its shiny rays over the little town, and magical with the millions of silver stars sparkling as a pleasant breeze was blowing about. It was the kind of night that was conducive to falling in love, and Indira could not help but dreaming of that happening to her that very night. The prompting from Francine and cajoling from Nani, and with her grandfather, Dr. Ramesh, telling her that she would fall in love with Tarak, all made her believe that could really happen. The fact that Tarak was so good-looking and that he had been secretly admiring her, only made her belief tangible. And she was now feeling optimistic and truly getting excited to meet him.

Nani was getting excited, also, thrilled that her granddaughter was finally going to meet her husband-to-be and was going to be married soon. And she was pleased that Indira was smiling and had finally come to her senses that Tarak was a good match for her, a young man with whom, she had no doubt, Indira would fall in love. Nani sang as she went about bathing, and, after, oiled her skin with the fresh coconut oil that she had made that day, and she got dressed in a floral cotton dress and matching headkerchief, which Joan had sewn for this special occasion. Nani even broke her custom of going barefoot and put on a pair of brown sandals, for she did not want to embarrass Indira in front of the man she would soon be betrothed to and her future in-laws.

Indira also went about bathing and getting dressed in her new above-the-knee royal blue silk dress, and she did her luxuriant dark hair up in an elegant coiffure, and slipped on the white high-heeled slingback shoes Nani had given her for her sixteenth birthday, selecting a matching beaded purse to go with the outfit. Nani let her wear one of Chaaya's gold necklaces and matching earrings and bangles to finish the ensemble. And Indira then powdered her face with a light dust of pink powder, leaving her naturally beautiful dark eyes and rose-brown lips to accentuate her looks, and she dabbed on a touch of cream perfume Nani had given her. Nani took the time to examine her to ensure every hair was in place, and she exclaimed how Indira looked like a ripe young woman ready for marriage, with innocence that made her face glow.

Within moments after they were finished getting dressed the blue Studebaker arrived at the house, promptly at 8:00 p.m. The liveried Sahil ushered them both in the back seat, and after a bumpy ride on the dirt road they came to Dr. Ramesh's big, yellow house that was cast in brilliant moonlight on this warm, breezy evening.

Dr. Ramesh was at the gate when the car pulled in, and when Indira emerged from the back seat, he greeted her with a broad smile and exclaimed, "My young and beautiful bride-to-be granddaughter!" And he hugged and kissed Indira. Then when Nani came and stood next to him, he looked down at her feet and said, "Nani, you're wearing shoes! I'm very impressed. This is indeed a very special occasion that calls for appropriate dressing, after all." He then turned and began walking up the pathway to the front stairs, saying as he did, "Come, let's go up to the sitting room and wait for the Jajals' there. They will be here shortly."

The three of them headed up to the opulent sitting room and ensconced themselves on the bright-red leather sofa set, with Indira sitting beside Nani on the love-seat and Dr.

Ramesh in the armchair, leaving the three-cushioned couch for Tarak and his parents. The aura of the place was as such to make one comfortable, with the warm yellow light of the chandelier bouncing off the polished mahogany floor and the glass windows wide open, letting in a balmy breeze. The playful breeze picked up and scattered about the piquant aroma of the delicacies of fried watrash and bush-hog wild meats and savoury treats, that Aaja had laid out on the marble coffee table, making the place seem very enticing. Adding a sweet sadness to the ambience, an Indian classical compilation, composed of the sitar and tabla, was playing softly on the turntable, and an aromatic incense was burning on a side table, beside which a bunch of lotus flowers was arranged. With everything in place, the scene was set with the promise of a provocative night ahead, it seemed.

Indira's excitement was building by the moment and the smile on her face was now permanent, though she was now beginning to feel a slight tingling of nervousness over the built-up anticipation of meeting Tarak. She sat there looking innocent and demure—as was expected of a young bride-to-be—with her hands on her lap and her fingers interlocked, eagerly waiting for the starboy and his parents to arrive. Dr. Ramesh and Nani took this opportunity to caution her on how she should behave in their presence, saying she should act with decorum and sit quietly and let the families make the necessary preparations for the wedding. It worked in Indira's favour to be quiet, she thought, for she simply did not know what to say under the circumstance. The whole setup seemed so surreal to her.

The rumbling of wheels at the gate indicated that the Jajals' had arrived. Indira could hear the car doors slam and the faint voice of Aaja welcoming them as they were escorted up the front stairs. She could hear their indistinct chatter as they were making their way up, and she was now bursting with excitement as they walked through the door.

Mr. and Mrs. Jajal, a middle-aged couple, were the first to enter. Mr. Jajal was a stout, brown-skinned man with black hair streaked with grey, and he was in a beige shirt-jack and khaki trousers. Mrs. Jajal, a slim and pretty, light-skinned woman with long, black hair which she wore in a single braid down her back, was dressed in an elegant gold and yellow sari and gold slippers, and decked out in extravagant gold jewellery. The couple emitted an air of amicability, with sweet smiles on their faces that immediately put Indira at ease. The starboy, the tall and handsome twenty-year-old Tarak, followed behind, fastidiously dressed in all black, from his fine cotton shirt to his pants and leather shoes, even his well groomed wavy hair was black, a contrast to his light skin. And he smelled fresh with a touch of cologne. A debonair young man of ebullient nature, he wore a presence of flair and flamboyance that Indira was immediately attracted to.

Dr. Ramesh got up and greeted Mr. and Mrs. Jajal cordially with hugs and kisses, and he shook Tarak's hand, then said, "I want you all to meet my beautiful granddaughter, Indira."

Indira's knees felt weak as she rose to her feet, and she reached out and shook Mr. Jajal's extended hand and softly said, "Nice to meet you." And she said the same to Mrs. Jajal, who smiled sweetly at her and kissed her cheeks. And when Tarak came up to her she nervously shook his outstretched hand and was speechless, for she found him to be incredibly charming.

Tarak did not let go of her hand but he squeezed it tightly, and he flashed a winsome smile and, in a resounding voice, said, "My very-soon-to-be wife, Indira. I'm happy to meet you." And, flattering her with his silver tongue, added, "Your face is as beautiful as a lotus flower, my love."

Beguiled by his flattery and boldness, Indira blushed and lowered her innocent dark eyes and withdrew her hand from his and sat back down, aware that the others were scrutinising them, and feeling a bit awkward about it. Nani then got up and shook hands with Tarak, and as she turned to greet his parents, Tarak took Nani's seat beside Indira on the love seat, already claiming his place, and there was nothing Indira could do about that but sit there and be very aware of his charming presence.

After Nani took a seat beside Mr. and Mrs. Jajal, Dr. Ramesh poured the ladies some *mauby* drink and then fixed three shots of strong drink on the rocks, and he handed a glass to Mr. Jajal and one to Tarak, and took the other and sat back down, and then he invited them all to savour the delicacies on the marble coffee table.

As they were all eating and drinking, the men gaffed briefly about business and sports and the latest news in the Guyana Chronicle Newspaper. Then the subject changed to the real purpose they were all gathered there when Tarak said to Dr. Ramesh, "I'm going to make your granddaughter the luckiest wife in Rose Hall." And he turned to Nani and went on to say, "No more washing blackpat for this princess. I will build her a big house and I will hire servants to cook and clean for her. And I will buy her beautiful clothes and jewellery and anything she desires. And she will work with me at the bank as my personal secretary."

Before Nani could respond, Mrs. Jajal smiled sweetly and said, "Look at Tarak, he's already in love with the girl."

Tarak returned his mother's smile, then he turned to look at Indira and said, "Yes, I'm already in love."

Everyone then turned to look at Indira as if expecting her to profess love for Tarak, and she found herself blushing again but said nothing, behaving with decorum as she was instructed to do by her grandparents.

"She's just shy to say she loves my boy, too," Mrs. Jajal said sweetly.

"You would just have to work on her shyness," Mr. Jajal then said to his son.

"That I will do," Tarak responded as he looked amorously at Indira, who had her eyes lowered. "But I have a feeling there's another side to her, which I hope to find out real soon." He then suddenly pulled out a ring box from his trousers pocket and opened it up and, to Indira's surprise, he took out a diamond ring and boastfully held it aloft for all to see before putting it on her finger and exclaiming, "Now, we're officially engaged!" Then, turning to Dr. Ramesh, he went on to say, "Let's set the wedding date for two weeks from now. My sister, Anika, can no longer wait to have a bouji!"

Dr. Ramesh responded happily with: "You mean *you* cannot wait to marry my beautiful granddaughter! Yes, two weeks will be fine, young man. I have been making preparations for a while now."

"So have I," Mr. Jajal said.

Mrs. Jajal then said, "We are in favour of a Christian wedding and we will have the celebrations at our house."

Nani consented with an affirmative nod of the head, smiling and showing her gold teeth, then saying, "I will get Joan Williams to sew my granddaughter the most beautiful wedding dress."

"For my boy," Mr. Jajal said, "I will have a custom-made suit of the finest quality."

Indira just could not believe this was happening. It all seemed dream-like to her. She was suddenly engaged and a wedding was being planned for her to a total stranger and she had no choice but to go along with it. But, luckily, she was finding her betroth to be a charming starboy. When Tarak turned and asked her, "Is two weeks enough time for you to prepare for the wedding, my love?" she lifted her pretty, dark eyes to his and nodded, still wearing that smile on her face.

Then, in spite of her grandparents warning her to remain quiet, she broke her silence, taking the chance of trying to clarify one important thing before the wedding, and asked Tarak, "Can my Nani move in with us right after the wedding?"

There was a suspenseful moment of silence as Dr. Ramesh scratched his head and Nani sat at the edge of her seat, then Tarak answered, "I don't think so. We will need our privacy as newly-weds." And, flashing an irresistible smile, he went on to say, "You know what I mean." And he winked at her with his alluring black eyes.

Indira, being innocent and never before exposed to the wiles of a man like Tarak, was seduced by his smile and eyes and the implication he made, and she was persuaded not to pursue the subject further—not that she could have with her grandparents giving her the 'eye' warning to be quiet. However, before the wedding, she planned to have Tarak agree to let Nani live with them, like she had promised Nani she would do.

The sweet melancholic twang of the sitar and soulful beat of the tabla were still softly playing in the background, and wisps of smoke from the aromatic incense were floating about as preparations for the wedding continued to be candidly discussed by both families. Indira remained quiet as she listened to them talk about how many goats and sheep they would buy, and all the roti and *puri* they would cook, how many bags of rice and flour were required, and how many bottles of rum and wine they would have, the fancy wedding cake they would design, and the music they would choose, etcetera, etcetera. They even talked about preparing a bridal room at the Jajals' luxury home for the wedding night.

Feeling flushed from all the talk about the wedding night and, also, over Tarak's burning stare, Indira excused herself, saying that she had to powder her nose, and she went to the boudoir of her late grandmother, Shanti, and did so. Then she thought she would slip outside for a few moments to collect herself.

She went in the backyard and, from the cluster of fruit trees, sought out the big guinep tree—now laden with bunches of the ripe, fragranced fruit—to stand under. Unlike her experience just a couple of nights ago when she looked out into the dark night and could not see into the marriage with Tarak, tonight the bright rays of the auspicious full moon and the silvery stars, and the charms of Tarak illuminated things. She could now envision a glimmer of life with him. A big house and all the material things he offered her were embellishments for her, but she could now see the possibility of falling in love and finding true love again. She was so lost in her thoughts of dreaming of falling in love with Tarak that she did not hear someone walking up behind her until she heard a twig snap, and she turned around to find no other than Tarak.

"I was hoping I would find you out here," he said.

Caught off guard and feeling shy to be suddenly alone with him, she said, "I should get back inside right now."

"Don't be in such a hurry. We should start spending some time alone with each other as we will soon be married," he said audaciously.

Indira then seized the opportunity to broach the subject of Nani again, and said, "I would really like for Nani to move in with us soon after the wedding." And in an effort to persuade him, added, "She's getting too old to live by herself, and when I'm gone she would have no one to take care of her, or the garden, which she depends on for a living."

"She would be an inconvenience," Tarak said, dismissing the subject. "I'm not here to talk about that. What I would really like to do now is to test you to find out if you're really as innocent and shy as you appear or if there's another side to you."

"What do you mean?" Indira asked, taken aback by his answer about Nani and his brazen approach, and now looking askance at him.

With the shadows of the thick foliage of the guinep tree obscuring his lower face and the moonlight shining on the upper part, she could see his dark eyes roving over her as he answered, "Why wait until we're married, let's have our first kiss and some fun tonight. After all, we are engaged." Before she could respond, he blatantly grabbed her and roughly pulled her towards him and tried to forcefully kiss her. Shocked by his amoral behaviour, accosting her like that, and repulsed by the liquor on his breath, she instinctively reached out and slapped him across the face, her nails scratching his right cheek as she did. And she broke loose from his grip and took the ring off her finger and threw it at him and ran and hid in the dark behind a huge tamarind tree, shaken up by the unpredictable fiasco, the smile she had on her face all day long now diminished. He came searching for her, calling out her name, but she did not answer and he could not find her. Eventually, he gave up and went back upstairs, but not before she heard him say that she would soon be his.

Tarak went straight to the bathroom and washed his face, but he could not wash away the scratch marks which looked as red as abir dye. As soon as he joined the others, Dr. Ramesh immediately noticed his right cheek and asked, "Where did you get those scratches from?"

"Oh, the cat just scratched me," he answered, with a presumptuous smile on his face.

"But I do not have a cat around here," Dr. Ramesh said.

"Oh, yes, you do. A light golden-brown jaguar in a royal blue silk dress!"

"Where is she now?"

"Somewhere in the backyard, I presume," Tarak said. "She is a wild one as I suspected." And, noticing the embarrassed look on Dr. Ramesh's face, he added, "But don't worry, Dr. Ramesh, once I marry her, I will tame her."

"Mrs. Jajal was just like that before I married her," Mr. Jajal interjected. "And look at how tame she is today."

Mrs. Jajal fluttered her eyelashes and smiled sweetly and said, "The girl will learn how to be submissive once she marries my boy."

Dr. Ramesh and Nani went along with the Jajals' in thinking Indira needed to be tamed. They agreed that the girl needed some advice on how to behave properly with a man, and all of them, including, Tarak, went looking for her in the backyard to bring her back to discipline her. But Indira eluded them. They then went back upstairs and, hoping she would return to join them, they waited for her. When she did not, they proceeded with the wedding plans and settled on a firm date.

Tarak, finding Indira to be a real challenge—unlike the other girls who were like putty in his hands—was now even more eager to marry her and, with utter conceit, said out loud, "I will soon be the owner of one of the prettiest girls in Rose Hall!"

* * *

After the Jajals' left that night Nani was driven home by Sahil, and she went upstairs to find Indira laying in bed in the dark, and she could hear her crying. She lit the kerosene oil lamp and held it up and found her still in her royal blue silk dress, and being sorely vexed at her now, she hollered at her, saying, "You have caused your grandfather and I a great deal of embarrassment! You should not have scratched Tarak's face. He's a nice boy."

"He's not a nice boy, he's a massacooramaan!" Indira exploded.

"He's not a monster," Nani argued. "The boy loves you and he's a good match for you."

"He does not love me, Nani. All he wants is to own me like a piece of property!" Indira shouted. "And his parents want a daughter-in-law who is submissive!" She knew this because she had snuck back in her grandfather's house before she ran back home and while hiding in a bedroom overheard the entire conversation.

"I wouldn't tolerate you talking like that about your future husband and in-laws!" Nani shouted back. "You're full of passion! And you need to be tamed!" And Nani went on to quote the Guyanese proverb, *When rain ah fall ah roof yuh put barrel fuh ketch am,* and she went on to say, "You have a great opportunity to marry a decent boy who works at the bank, so don't play the fool, seize it. Don't be hard ears!"

"I'm not being stubbornly disobedient, and Tarak is not a decent boy!" Indira snapped, but, at the moment, she just could not bring herself to telling Nani why she thought Tarak was not decent, that she was accosted by him, for she was still shaken up by the incident, feeling denuded of her dignity. "And I don't care that he works at the bank and

363

that his parents are well-to-do! I don't love Tarak and I wouldn't marry him!" she cried adamantly.

"Oh, yes, you will," Nani said. "If I have to drag you to the altar, you will marry the boy!"

Laying on her side, Indira clutched her pillow and sobbed more, saying as she did, "You said once, Nani, when you told me about your love story with Nana Amar, 'to not mistake attraction for love.' Well, I think Tarak is only attracted to me. You also said to me 'if someone professes to love you then let him prove it, only then give your heart to him.' Tonight Tarak has proven that he doesn't really love me. But Ravi has proven that he does, and I've given my heart to him. You also told me, Nani, to 'then accept him in your heart,' which I've done. After that, you said to 'zip up your heart and let no other man enter.' I want to do so, so help me, Nani. I want to marry Ravi, not Tarak." And Indira shook with tears.

Nani did not respond to Indira this time for she could not bear to hear her passionate, melancholic cry, and her plea for help was more than she could take, so she took the kerosene oil lamp with her and left the bedroom and went into the kitchen. She hung up the lamp and went about lighting the wood in the mud stove and she put on some katahar—jackfruit seeds to boil, and then tossed them in the embers to roast. As the seeds were roasting she took a seat on the peerah and, above the crackling of the roasting seeds, she could hear Indira still crying in the bedroom.

As she listened to her she absent-mindedly watched the smoke rising from the mud stove, and she quietly pondered the conversation that she once had with Indira on love and attraction that Indira reminded her of. She had indeed instructed Indira that if a man professes to love her to let him prove it before giving her heart to him, like she had done with her late husband, Amar. It became clear to her now that Ravi had proven so to Indira, and Indira's passionate cries made her realise that the young girl had gone too far, that she had fallen deeply and madly in love with the boy, also, and Nani knew what that felt like at that tender age for she was around the same age when she had fallen in love with Amar.

Nani became torn at this point on what to do. She thought of how embarrassing it would be to call off the wedding with Tarak, and how disappointing it would be for him and his parents. But, on the other hand, she now could not ignore Indira's love for Ravi and her plea to her to let her marry the boy. Nani started to perspire now, not just from the heat of the mud stove, but because of the dilemma she was in, and as she wiped the sweat from her face with her apron, she wrestled with what to do, thinking of only the best life for Indira. She believed that the heart finds its own match, but in this case she believed that Tarak was a good match for Indira, and that Indira could learn to love the nice young man.

While Nani sat there on the peerah contemplating what to do, the katahar seeds were finished roasting, and she got up and started extracting them from the embers. As she was doing so she heard the jangling of the strands of beads in the kitchen entrance, and when she turned to look she saw Indira standing there, her face stained with tears and her dark eyes dull with sadness, and her royal blue silk dress was now soiled. Moved with compassion for her, she said, "Come and sit, child, and have some roasted katahar seeds with me." And she pulled up a peerah beside hers and brought the enamel bowl of hot katahar seeds and placed them on the floor, and she sat down.

Indira took her seat beside Nani, and at first they shelled the katahar seeds and ate for a while without saying anything, the kerosene oil lamp casting a soft golden light on them and the lingering smoke from the mud stove emitting the nutty aroma of the roasted seeds. Then seeing how sad and heartbroken Indira appeared, Nani said to her, "You really truly love the boy, don't you, child?"

"Yes, I do, Nani."

"And you're sure he loves you."

"He loves me more than anything in the world, Nani. So much so that he even promised to take care of you, also, because he knows how much you mean to me. Tarak doesn't care that I love and care about you. He wouldn't let you move in with us. He told me you'd be an inconvenience if you did."

Nani was quiet for a moment, pondering what Indira just said and remembering the promise that Ravi had made to her to take care of her, then she asked, "Do you think the boy would treat you with respect?"

"Ravi cares for me and has shown great respect for my feelings and wishes and values. He has never forced himself on me, like Tarak did."

"What do you mean Tarak forced himself on you?"

"He tried to kiss me against my will, Nani. That's why I slapped him."

That now explained the scratches on Tarak's face, and, appalled by his disrespectful and unscrupulous behaviour, Nani exclaimed, "The boy is *manish*!" Meaning the boy is

366

bad. "How I've been deceived, blinded by his charm, and not being able to see past his job at the bank. How selfish and foolish I have been!" And without further ado, she went on to say, "I will have a talk with your grandfather tomorrow and call off the wedding with him. And I will, as well, summon Ravi here tomorrow to set a wedding date for the two of you to get married as soon as possible."

The brilliant shine immediately returned to Indira's dark eyes, and she asked, "Do you really mean that, Nani?"

"Yes, I do, my dear child. I would not let any man take advantage of you and disrespect you. Besides, I should not stand in your way of true love, child."

Indira reached out then and hugged her old Nani and she broke down and cried, this time out of sheer joy, and Nani also wept with tears of happiness, then they both burst out laughing at the thought that a wedding of true and deep love was soon to take place.

Indira then thought of something that may deter the plans and said, "There's just one thing I must mention, Nani, and that is Ravi and I are not of the same religious faith. He's Hindu and I'm Christian."

Nani was silent for a moment, then prudently said, "It is not religious faith that brings two people together, but, rather, love. Remember, I was a Hindu once before converting to Christianity. If Ravi and his parents have no problem with the difference of your faiths, then there is no problem."

"He's already told me that is not a problem."

"Then we will go ahead with the wedding."

Indira hugged and kissed Nani again, then she ran out the back door and rushed over to tell Francine.

She found Francine sitting on her outdoor front steps—the swelling from the marabunta sting on her foot now diminished—eagerly waiting to hear about the happenings of the evening. She was shocked to hear of the outcome of things and was glad that Nani was going to call off the wedding with Tarak, and she was happy to see Indira so happy that she was going to marry the man with whom she truly and deeply fell in love. That night the two of them sat down on Nani's back steps and planned their weddings under the moonlight and stars, and they did so until the sun rose the next morning.

17

Weddings And Afonso Attempts To Elope

Ravi was in the rice field with his parents and the hired workers and they were busy planting rice on this sunny morning when his cousin, Padmini, pulled up on the side of the road in her jeep with his sister, Radhika.

Ravi dropped the bundle of the green blades of rice from his hands and waddled through the water in his tall boots to meet them, his trousers and thin shirt clinging to his tall and slender physique, and his dark brown complexion glistening in the sun. Thinking something was wrong, he straightaway asked, "What brings you to Skeldon, cousin?"

"I'm here to deliver a letter to you," Padmini said, with an inscrutable expression.

Ravi wiped his wet hands on his trousers and with a puzzled look on his face took the white envelope, which had only his name written on it in a feminine style written with a fountain pen, and he tore it open. A faint scent of chameli flowers emanated from the letter, giving away the identity of the author, and he hurriedly unfolded it and began to read the contents:

Dearest Ravi,

It is with great excitement that I'm writing to you. My wedding arrangement with Tarak has been called off and I am now eligible. If you are available yourself and still in

love with me, come quickly and meet Nani and my
grandfather, Dr. Ramesh, at my home. Please bring along
your parents, and, sister, also, and your cousin, Padmini, is
also welcomed.

Affectionately yours,

Indira

It took Ravi a few moments to assimilate the lucid
contents of the letter, pressing the letter to his nostrils and
inhaling the delicate scent as he did, and then he burst out
laughing, saying, "Radhika, you will soon have a bouji!
Oh, Padmini, you have borne me such great news!"

Ravi read the letter to them as well as his parents, who
could not be happier for him, and straightaway they left the
rice field—leaving the workers to carry on the task at hand
—and went to get ready to leave for Rose Hall. Ravi took a
dip in the nearby river and then got dressed and took off on
his motorcycle at top speed, leaving Padmini to transport
his parents and Radhika in the jeep.

When they arrived at Nani's house in the afternoon, Dr.
Ramesh was already there. Nani had told him about the
fiasco with Tarak and Indira, and they had called off the
wedding with Tarak, and she convinced him that Ravi was
the right person for Indira to marry because, unlike Tarak,
he was a decent boy who loved and respected their
granddaughter, and, as importantly, Indira was in love with
the boy, also.

Dr. Ramesh was made to understand that Ravi was not a
scion of a well-to-do family but a boy from a poor family

of farmers, who was a farmer himself, something that, initially, Dr. Ramesh was disappointed about, for he had high expectations for Indira to marry someone with social status and wealth and academic achievement. He did, however, came to terms with it through Nani's example. Over the years he had come to admire Nani for she was living proof that one can attain happiness and peace and richness of spirit without formal education and a lack of material riches—something some of the educated and wealthy and those of social status themselves have difficulty finding, he thought, for he knew that firsthand. He admired Nani's sagacity and trusted her with the welfare of his granddaughter—Indira being a testimony to Nani's astute mental discernment in the way she was properly brought up, both morally and spiritually—so, he went along with Nani's decision to let Indira marry Ravi.

Dr. Ramesh instantly took a liking to Ravi when he met him, and he took him into his heart. He quickly found the young man to be genuine and intelligent, and he had empathy that he had dropped out of high school because his father was sick and could not take care of his rice farm, a responsibility that Ravi had to assume, and he thought it was an honourable thing to do for a sick parent. He was impressed with Ravi, and found him to be an ambitious young man. He learned that Ravi's intention was to move in with Nani and help her out with her business of farming in the interim until he was settled, but his desire—especially in wanting to provide comfortably for Indira—was to become a businessman someday and own a chain of fabric stores across the country, something Ravi thought to be a viable choice of business because of the demand of

371

fabric as most people had their clothes sewn by local seamstresses and tailors. Dr. Ramesh was impressed with Ravi's sound business sense and reacted with serious consideration upon learning of his intention, unlike how he had been with his own son, Indira's father, Sameer, now deceased. He realised how controlling he had been in trying to push Sameer into becoming a medical doctor, something his son never wanted to be, a disagreement that led to the demise of their relationship, which after his son's death had caused him years of regret and suffering. He now had another chance of having a son and swore he would not make that mistake again and let pride come in the way and destroy this relationship, so he acted with understanding and respect for the young man and offered to financially assist Ravi with pursuing his own dreams.

The meeting of the families and the plans for the wedding went over very well that afternoon, and a compromise was made to have a Christian wedding in favour of Nani's religious belief, and a private, partial Hindu ceremony to appease Ravi's parents. Mr. and Mrs. Singh were struggling to get by in life and could not afford much for the wedding and Dr. Ramesh willingly offered to cover all the expenses for his precious granddaughter and the son he was looking forward so much to having. It did not matter to Ravi and Indira, however, what religious ceremonies were to be conducted, nor were they concerned about having celebrations, for they were content just to sign the papers and be married just to be together, but in deference to their family, they agreed to go along with their plans. So, the almanac was perused by the families and the wedding was set to take place in a matter of a couple of weeks, not soon enough for the two young lovers.

* * *

A couple of days before Indira and Francine were to marry, Afonso met up with Ling and a plan to steal Laliwa was hatched. They were now seated in a blue Chevrolet sedan that belonged to Afonso's father, which was parked up the street from Laliwa's house, allowing a view of the sight of the elopement.

True to his word, Ling would assist Afonso in this daring attempt, a thrill he would not allow himself to pass up on. "Tell me your plans and I'll help you in any way I can, my friend," he offered Afonso with eagerness.

"Laliwa and I plan to elope this Friday night," Afonso said.

"You mean tomorrow night. But Indira and Francine are getting married this Saturday."

"It was Laliwa's idea. She's feeling sorry for herself that her best friends are getting married and she's not, so she thinks it best to elope then."

"But that means we'll all miss the weddings," Ling said, which, incidentally, he would prefer to do rather than miss out on a good prank.

"She told both Indira and Francine about the plan and they're now excited for her. They'll have their dreams come true in marrying the ones they love, and they want the same for Laliwa and myself, also."

"Then I'll go along with the plan, also," Ling said, as though he needed any convincing. "When and where do we start?"

"I am to arrive here tomorrow at midnight and park the car and wait for Laliwa," said Afonso. "She wouldn't be able to make her escape through the front door because her two brothers sleep in the sitting room, and her mother usually weaves baskets in the kitchen at nights and often falls asleep there and Laliwa wouldn't take a chance of using that exit. So, she'll climb over her bedroom window using a string of knotted sheets. She plans to do this at the strike of midnight and then meet me here at the car. And we will then make a quick escape."

"And what part do I play in all this?" Ling asked, almost feeling disappointed that so far he was not included in the plans.

"You will meet me tomorrow night down the street from my house. Be there exactly at 11:30, and we will come here together and wait for Laliwa. Once she escapes, you will drive us to the Guyana-Suriname border and leave us there. From there, Laliwa and I will take the ferry over to Suriname and stay in Paramaribo."

"And once you get there, what would you do then, my friend?" Ling asked, with sincere concern.

"I'll marry Laliwa as soon as we get there, and then we'll rent a place and live on the money I have until I find a job."

"Where did you get the money from?"

"It is money Dad gave me over the years, which I saved up."

"Does your father have any idea that you're planning to elope with Laliwa?"

"None at all, neither does Mom," Afonso said, and tears started building up in his blue eyes. "I feel so terrible to have to do this to them. But I'm so crazy in love with Laliwa and want to be with her so badly." And Afonso broke down and cried.

Ling patted his friend on the shoulder consolingly and said, "Don't cry, my friend, you'll be back to see them."

"I plan to return as soon as I see it possible," Afonso said as he wiped away the tears.

"I would advise you to write a nice letter to them explaining the situation, and tell them you'll be in touch with them as soon as you can."

Afonso heeded Ling's advice and went home and started writing a letter to his parents straightaway, crying all through it. '*Love can make one do strange things*', he heard an old man say once, and he thought of how true that was as he was propelled to elope with Laliwa only by his feelings for her, not mindful of the consequences that may cause, because he was so blinded by love. He could not see beyond eloping with Laliwa and spent the time ruminating on it every moment he was awake. She was the only girl of his romantic dreams since childhood, and she had loved him as long, she admitted, and if all went as planned, they would have their dreams come true and be together, forever in love.

And, so, with much impatience and anxiety, Afonso started counting down the hours until the elopement.

That same day while Afonso was busy making plans with Ling to steal Laliwa, a bedroom was being built for Nani at her bottom-house. Ravi was expected to move in to her place on the night of the wedding, so Nani relinquished the upstairs to give the two love birds their privacy. This day, Ravi brought a few of his belongings from Skeldon, consisting of his motorcycle and bicycle, guitar, his favourite books and Indian film stars' magazines, a fountain pen and a bottle of blue ink, along with writing pads, and he also brought his clothes and toiletries.

Ravi, along with Albert, George Williams, and Shazam set out to build Nani's bedroom early that morning, and between the four of them had the job done late that afternoon. The room they built was tiny and smelled fresh of the greenheart wood it was constructed with, which was left unpainted. The men furnished the place with a single bed, with a coconut fibre mattress and feather pillow, and they brought down Nani's posey and placed the white enamel chamber pot under her bed. They built her a clothes-horse and a small dresser, and they brought down her rocking chair and placed it by the door, by which they hung a kerosene oil lamp. Joan Williams lent a hand and made a pink floral sheet with a matching pillow case and dressed the bed, and she made a mat with colourful strips of fabric and placed it by the door, which had an upper section as well as a lower one—the only opening in the windowless room—when opened allowed a view of the hammock, Solomon, and Rani. The finished room was comfortable and cozy, and provided Nani with her own space.

Nani's other friends and relatives were gathered at her place and were busy with cleaning and decorating the little, unpainted, greenheart wood house for Indira's wedding. They scrubbed the bare floors and front and backstairs and even daubed the bottom-house with cow-dung and clay mixture, leaving the smooth earthen ground to dry, and they hung colourful streamers and balloons both upstairs and at the bottom-house. Over at the Williams', the same fervour of preparing for Francine's wedding was taking place, and the mood was one of great excitement.

* * *

While friends and relatives were busy that day with preparing for the weddings, Nani was having a private talk with Indira and Francine upstairs in the kitchen. It was now late afternoon and the golden rays of the sun were streaming through the old wooden kitchen window as a warm wind was blowing. Nani was sitting on the peerah with the two young women sitting around her, on peerahs, also, and while an iron pot of rice and a carahee of *gillbacker fish* curry—which Nani specially chose to cook for them—were cooking on the mud stove, filling the place with the piquant spices and making the kitchen even warmer than it was, Nani talked to the young brides-to-be about the rudimentary facts of married life.

She began by saying, "A married life is what you make of it, children. You can either make your bed hard or soft,

377

it's up to you to choose, for you will be the ones laying in it."

Francine interrupted Nani just then by saying, "Don't speak to us in riddles, Nani. Speak to us clearly so we can understand."

"Okay, then," Nani said, "I'll explain things clearly by telling you about my life with Nana Amar, and I'll start with the day we got married." And Nani smiled and flashed her gold teeth in remembering. "We had a small Hindu wedding and were married in a tent, and I remember how it rained hard that day. My Ma Raajee told me then it was a good sign, that the deity of the weather was pouring down blessings upon us. However, despite the weather, it was the happiest day of my life. I didn't want that day to end. I wanted it to go on and on and on. And the celebrations did go on until the wee hours of the morning. It never stopped raining throughout, and that night, I remember clearly how Amar lifted me in his arms and carried me through the rain. My yellow silk sari and his sherwani and dhoti got soaked, but that didn't bother us at all. Amar took me that night to live in my parents mud house which was just up the street, which they had given to us as a wedding gift. That was where we started out in life. We were so in love and so happy in our little mud house. How I miss those days!" And Nani had a faraway look in her dim brown eyes as she reminisced of a time long gone when she was young.

Indira attempted to interrupt her reverie and said, "You always talk about how happy and in love you were, Nani, but was life always like that?"

Nani did not answer right away but continued to be lost in thoughts. The girls could hear the gillbacker fish curry and rice bubbling and the wood in the mud stove crackling as she thought, then when she collected herself she answered as frankly as she could, saying, "I wouldn't flower things up and make you believe life was like that all the time, my children. There were good times and bad times. And we faced many challenges. In the very beginning of our marriage, we loved and laughed and enjoyed the bliss of a new married life, but as time went on and the fire in us raged less and the smoke scattered, we saw through the clearing that we had differences in the basic values of our lives."

"And how did you handle that?" Francine asked.

"At first I used to argue with Amar over our differences, for I didn't know better then. But that was not the way to handle things I later realised."

Indira then asked, "Are we not to argue with our husbands if we disagree on something?"

Nani tightened her headkerchief, then replied, "I learned in my life that arguments only lead to more arguments, and the bitterness of words lead to anger, and with anger there is no peace. There is a way to approach a disagreement without having to fight and argue, my children, and that is to learn to speak softly and lovingly to your husbands, and you will find that it would be easier to resolve your disagreements that way."

"And what should we do if we speak softly and lovingly and still we can't resolve our differences?" Francine asked.

"Then agree to disagree and accept your differences, and at all times, show respect to your husbands," Nani simply said. And she went on to say, "If you make your bed soft, girls, life would be wonderful, in other words, give of yourselves and your love and understanding to your husbands, and always strive for peace. Only then you will find happiness. Marriage life is not a bed of just roses, but it's a garden filled with roses with thorns, and if you can avoid the pricks of the thorns, in other words, avoid fighting and arguing, you will feel only the velvety softness of the rose petals." And Nani momentarily lapsed again into a reverie of her late husband and a time when she lived with him in their paradise, and she longed for those days.

When Nani collected herself, she continued by saying, "The two of you are like precious jewels with your love shining like gold, and Ravi and Albert seem genuinely in love, also, so I would predict that you will have good lives. When a man truly loves a woman, he will do anything for her. Likewise, when a woman truly loves a man, she will do anything for him. Don't fuss about little things that can affect your marriage, my children, but focus on loving your husbands, and love will see you through this life. But bear in mind, challenges will arise, and how you respond to them could make or break your marriage."

"What kind of challenges did you face with Nana?" Indira asked.

Nani got up and stirred the pots on the mud stove and she sat back down on the peerah before answering, "Oh, there were different kinds of challenges that Amar and I had faced, some of which were bickering over little things that we differed on. But Amar was a poor farmer and our biggest challenge in life was that we were poor and times were tough for us. I remember that there were times when we had only rice with salt and pepper to eat. At first, we fought over this situation out of frustration and desperation, but we soon learned how to cope. I found a way out of our hardship by working together with Amar side by side in the fields and bringing in a few more shillings that put sufficient food on the table."

"What were some of your other challenges?" Francine asked.

Nani thought for a moment and then she said, "Amar and I had faced a number of illnesses in the family, which only made our poor situation worse then. Both my children, Ram and Geeta, suffered typhoid fever when they were children, and Amar and I must have suffered as greatly over them with grief and worry, for we almost lost both of them." A film of tears then gathered in Nani's eyes as she thought of those times. "I can never forget the time when I was pregnant with Ram and how ill I had become, also, and Amar stayed at my bedside for months and nursed me back to health or I would have died. No greater love can a man show than to care for a sick wife."

Nani got up again and stirred the carahee of fish curry and then added the sac of gillbacker fish eggs that she had set aside while cleaning the fish, and she took the pot of boiling rice and emptied it in the strainer in the dish sink and left the maar—rice water to strain, then she took her seat again and continued her talk, saying, "Oh, there are many challenges in marriage. I will not paint the sky all blue and make you believe otherwise, my children. Dark clouds will gather from time to time. Storms. They can rip you apart, but if you cling to each other and ride them out together, you will come to the silver lining, and you will become closer and stronger in your love. Amar and I learned through trials and errors to never let our problems get in the way of loving each other, and we lived a happy life despite our challenges.

"The meaning of my riddle is explained, thus, if you do not know how to overcome life's problems, then you will make your bed hard, and on the other hand, if you learn how to work with your husbands to face challenges together and resolve your problems, then you will lay in a soft bed. Marriage is like a game and you must learn how to play together to both be winners. But you must play as a team and not as opponents. Become friends with your husbands and share interests that you have in common and explore life together, and don't fuss about little things. Be lovers and live to love, my children, and life would be wonderful." And with that Nani went on to say, "You are both very young and I would advise you to enjoy the first couple of years of your marriages before you think of making babies."

"But I want so much to have a little baby girl right away," Francine said, her baby face radiating the innocence of a baby itself.

"So do I," Indira said.

"Take my advice, children, and wait for a while until you're a bit more mature and until you establish a life for yourselves and build a nest egg. Having a baby is a big responsibility. Enjoy your lives with your husbands and bathe in the sunshine of love in your new marriages, for you both will have plenty of time to make babies later on." And Nani concluded with, "That's all I have to say to you about marriage, young ladies. Now, let's have some supper."

Nani then served the young brides-to-be with plates of steaming rice and hot gillbacker fish curry, and she dished a calabash full for herself, also, carefully dividing the fish eggs amongst the three of them, and she sat at the table with the girls and ate with her fingers while the embers in the mud stove were glowing softly.

* * *

It was planned that both Indira and Francine were to be married at the same Christian church and at the same time, and the venue for the celebrations was to take place in a tent in George Williams's backyard. A private Hindu ceremony for Ravi and Indira was also planned, and that was to take place at Nani's home just before the church weddings, with only a selected few.

The day before the weddings, on this bright and hot afternoon, a whole lot of activities were taking place with everyone in a celebratory mood. Little boys and girls from the town, who had gathered at Nani's bottom-house for the excitement, were having a good belly laugh as some men were dragging in squealing pigs and rebellious goats and sheep that were kicking and screaming as they were brought in and tied to the fruit trees in Nani's backyard, the animals having reason to fight back for they would be the weddings' feast. Amidst the activities, people were fetching in bags of rice and flour and potatoes and baskets of vegetables and all kinds of food and spices to cook, which they stored at Nani's bottom-house, for most of the cooking would be taking place there and in Nani's backyard.

At this time, while Joan was busy fitting the girls with their wedding attires for the last minute alterations, George Williams was in his backyard with his friends, some of whom had flown in from the Caribbean and South America for his daughter's wedding, and they were all busy with cutting down the crabgrass in the backyard so they could put up the tent for the celebrations. As they were working under the searing sun, and drinking rum at the same time, they were all in jovial spirits and were gaffing and bantering around.

George Williams paused from cutting the crabgrass and turned to his Jamaican friend, Kendrick, and said, "You only visit me now when there's a wedding or funeral, Kenny."

"And you don't visit me at all now!" Kendrick shot back as he was sharpening a cutlass.

George Williams laughed and said, "Since you married that coolie gal from my country, you took off with her back to Jamaica and I don't see you anymore."

Kendrick grinned and said, "My wife is upstairs by the kitchen window and I hope she doesn't hear me saying this: The woman keeps me busy, man, if you know what I mean. It's true when they say coolie gals are hot!" There was a burst of laughter from the men, and Kendrick went on to say, "Why don't you come to Jamaica and visit me, man? Now that your girl is getting married there's nothing that would hold you back."

"Next year, I promise," George Williams said. Coincidently, a Bob Marley song was playing on the turntable stereo system that was on full blast at this time, and Marley was singing *No Woman, No cry*, singing about

Trench Town, Jamaica, and George Williams said to Kendrick, "You know, when I listen to this song I always think that Trench Town, Jamaica is Rose Hall, Guyana."

"I don't know what you mean, man, we don't have muddy waters in Jamaica!" Kendrick laughed and said. "When you come to Jamaica, you'll know you're in Jamaica by the white beaches and turquoise waters, and the hospitality. My wife will make you some good *oxtail* and *rice & peas* and *jerk chicken*. The woman is a real Jamaican now; she can even cook *ackee & saltfish*!"

Fareed, who stopped working to take a drink of rum, joined the conversation, and he said, "George, if you want good hospitality, you must come and visit me in Trinidad. I have a big house in Port of Spain. And my wife knows how to cook well, too. You can ask her, she's standing by the kitchen window with Kendrick's wife and the others."

Marvin, who took a break and was sitting around on an aluminium bucket with a drink in his hand, then said, "And don't forget me down in Barbados, George. I don't have a big house like Fareed, but I have plenty of rum. My wife doesn't even know how to boil water, boy, but we can sit by the beach all day and drink with her. And there's no one who would treat you better than the Bajans."

"You mean to tell me, Marvin, that *we* Guyanese don't treat you as well?" George Williams asked jokingly as he paused from cutting the crabgrass to wipe the perspiration dripping from his forehead.

"You Guyanese are a misplaced people!" Marvin said. "You're in South America and you carry on as though you're down in the West Indies. What's the matter with you people, man?"

385

The men erupted with laughter over this, and Eduardo, who was busy with gathering the crabgrass into a heap, paused and said, "In defence of Guyanese, I would say they're not the only Caribbeans who are incorrectly positioned. But, don't let Marvin ridicule you like this, George. Why not do your travels right here in South America? The invitation to visit me in Rio de Janeiro is still open. And my wife not only knows how to cook, but she can dance the *samba* real good, also."

Carlos, busy with driving stakes down in the ground to put up the tent, spoke up and said, "Don't listen to these other fellows, George. Venezuela is the place to be. And not only Eduardo's wife can dance, my wife can dance the *salsa*."

Nani's friend, the gregarious Mr. Jackson was with the men, also, and had one too many drinks so far, and he said in his loud voice, "As for me, Guyana is my paradise and is the place to be," and with a boisterous laugher, he added, "in spite of our muddy waters! But, it doesn't matter what country we're from, we're all one family, man. You all come and visit me at my house and I'll do a bush-cook and show you what Guyanese hospitality is all about with some fine rum!" He then paused before saying, "I don't have a wife to brag about because the woman left me years ago!"

There was another explosion of laughter from the men and the bantering continued as others joined them, including, Dr. Ramesh and the prospective fathers-in-law, and they all worked together to finish building the tent, lining it with electric lights and arranging tables and chairs, and setting up a stage for performers, and decorating the place with colourful streamers and balloons. Before they realised it, the afternoon went by and the sun slipped below the horizon and early evening brought a brilliant full moon, with a starry sky and a pleasant breeze. It was really an enchanting night for the eve of weddings.

This night was not carried out exactly like a typical *cook night* or *sangeet* in a Hindu wedding, with cooking and performers singing songs to entertain guests, and with dancing, and the cutting up of vegetables—which were mostly reserved for the next day and night as the weddings were planned on a smaller scale due to the hasty timing. However, the ladies, including the brides-to-be, gathered at Joan's home and they were having fun cooking and eating and playing music amongst themselves, and the men were gathered in Nani's backyard and were doing much the same.

It was not until the brides-to-be retired for the night that the bridegrooms-to-be showed up—after being forewarned to stay away until then—and they were two very excited young men. Ravi and Albert joined the men in Nani's backyard as they were bush-cooking and drinking and playing music, and under the bright moonlight and the firelight, the experienced married men talked to them about married life, but unlike Nani's candid talk with the girls, the men shared only their happiness and love for their wives. And the boys were teased.

"*Kanyadan brides*!" Mr. Jackson teased, meaning virgin brides.

"Man, aren't you boys lucky!" Shazam added. "I can clearly remember my first night with Fazeela when she was just a shy virgin girl."

Ravi, now eighteen, and Albert the same age, being young virgins themselves, smiled with sparkles in their eyes, Ravi being shy-faced and Albert appearing bold.

Kendrick put his arm around Albert's shoulders and said, "Tomorrow night you will be in heaven, my man." To which Albert said, "I can't wait for Francine to take me up there, man." And Kendrick moved over to Ravi and poked him in the chest and said, "You both will be experiencing what they call 'heavenly pleasures' or 'heavenly delights', my young friends." In response, Ravi just put his head down and smiled again, now getting flushed, and feeling somewhat nervous.

Dr. Ramesh joined in and said, "Kendrick, you shouldn't be teasing the *dulhas* so loudly," meaning the bridegrooms, "the *dulhans* are in bed and they may hear you." And Dr. Ramesh went over and hugged Ravi and said to him, "Son, have my blessings. I'm truly happy for you." Dr. Ramesh then led Ravi away from the men and they went further down in Nani's backyard to the far end of the orchard where the moonlight was shining on the tree tops and, while the men continued to tease Albert around the fire, Dr. Ramesh had a chance of developing a father-son relationship with Ravi.

He gestured over at the log situated near to a loaded mango tree and said, "Have a seat, son." When Ravi did, he sat beside him. In the moonlight, Dr. Ramesh could see the unease in Ravi's youthful face, and he clapped him on the back and said to him, "I can sense that you're a bit nervous, son."

Ravi, who sat bent forward, twiddling his fingers, said, "I feel like the luckiest man alive, yet I have this gnawing anxiety that trickles from my head down to my toes."

"That is a typical thing to happen to the bridegroom-to-be on the night before the wedding," Dr. Ramesh explained nonchalantly. "I myself was a bit nervous the night before I married Shanti. I was as young as you then and she was my first girl and I did not know what she expected of me."

"That's what I'm nervous about, also," Ravi admitted.

Dr. Ramesh patted him on the shoulder and said, "Just relax, son, once the passion in you takes over, your nervousness will subside and you will perform just fine."

"Hearing this from you means a lot to me. Thanks for easing my anxiety," Ravi said, happy that he could have a frank conversation with Dr. Ramesh, unlike his father who was too apprehensive to talk about these things. "I also worry about if I would make Indira happy and what kind of life I would be able to provide for her. I promised her and Nani that I would provide for them both and that's a big responsibility for a man of my age with no money and no job, and I'm afraid if things don't go as promised that would be a strike against my manhood."

"I was also worried whether I would make Shanti happy," Dr. Ramesh said, relating to his own life. "My marriage was arranged and my problem was that I was afraid I may not fall in love with Shanti. But, fortunately, I did, and was able to make her happy. You have an advantage, son, you love my granddaughter and she loves you, and that is the key ingredient for happiness between a couple. With that, things like understanding, compassion, patience, and unselfishness will all come naturally. Just show her you love and care about her and I know that will make my granddaughter very happy." Dr. Ramesh then went on to respond to Ravi's other concern, saying, "As to your worry about what kind of life you would be able to provide for Indira, let me say this, Indira is a very content young woman and she does not need a lot of material things to make her happy. She likes a simple life with simple things and cherishes things of sentimental value." And with a broad smile on his face, Dr. Ramesh added, "And she likes to pretty up herself. You don't have to concern or pressure yourself with providing her extravagantly. Stick to your plans to help out Nani with her work and you will make a living for now and that would take care of them both, and I will assist you with your dreams of setting up your own business of opening a chain of fabric stores in due time."

Ravi said, "You are very kind and generous, Dr.—"

"You can call me Pa from now on," Dr. Ramesh said as he affectionately nudged Ravi in the ribs. "Just don't call me Grandpa. That would make me feel too old."

Ravi laughed and said, "All right then, thanks, Pa." He then paused for a moment then said, "But I would like to provide for Indira by the sweat of my own brows. Only then would I feel worthy of it."

"As you wish, son. But always remember that you can count on me if you're having trouble executing your plans. Think of me as your backup plan."

"I'll bear that in mind," Ravi said. "I know Indira is content with a simple life, but I dream of buying her jewellery and clothes and building her a beautiful house. If only I were Shah Jahan, she would be my Mumtaz Mahal and I would build her a Taj Mahal, only it would not be a mausoleum but an ivory-white marble palace, and built when she's alive! And I'll have her bear me as many children as they had."

"Spoken like a man who is truly in love, bona fide love," Dr. Ramesh said and smiled at the fervour of the young man, happy to know that he so loved his granddaughter.

Ravi then pointed at the candleflies in the nearby bush and said, "My love for Indira would burn like the flame of a candlefly and would not be extinguished until I close my eyes in eternal life."

"Sounds like the words of a poet," Dr. Ramesh commented, and then learned about Ravi's hobby in poetry, and, also, music; playing the guitar and singing.

Dr. Ramesh sat with Ravi for a while longer and listened to him talk about his love for Indira and his dreams for the future. He felt a sense of elation, thrilled to be given another chance of having a son, and this time having the mental discernment of building a compatible relationship, devoid of pride and control, one based on love and caring and sharing, and mutual respect. And he was happy that Ravi was responsive. Ravi felt a fatherly connection with Dr. Ramesh and was glad to have a confidant in him, a man with whom he could have a profound and meaningful relationship. By the end of their talk that night, Ravi's nerves were soothed, and Dr. Ramesh blessed him, once again, with happiness and prosperity.

They rejoined the men around the fire, and the teasing of the bridegrooms-to-be continued way into the night. It was a night for the young men to laugh and be merry, and laugh they did for they could not contain their excitement.

That same night, Afonso was up finishing off the letter to his parents. As he sat in his bedroom by his desk, he tried to fight back his burning tears but he could not control them and a few drops spilled onto the letter as he was writing, pouring his heart out and telling his parents of his love for Laliwa and his plans to steal her away, and promising he would return home when it was fit to do so. And the next moment, Afonso was laughing his head off out of the sheer excitement of eloping with Laliwa. Through tears and laughter he managed to finish the five-page letter, and he did so just in time for him to take his leave.

It was going on to 11:30 now on this Friday night, and all at the white mansion were asleep, even the dogs and cats. Afonso stole into his father's office and left the farewell letter on his desk, then he snuck out to the blue Chevrolet sedan, which he had parked down the street earlier so his parents would not be woken up by the start of the engine.

Ling was right on time when Afonso got to the car and the two of them wasted no time in driving over to Laliwa's home. They got there about fifteen minutes before the appointed time, and Afonso parked the car just up the street from her little, old house, which stood erect on stilts and was in complete darkness within. Laliwa's bedroom window was illuminated by the full moon and stars tonight, giving the boys a clear view of her escape route.

"What should I do with your dad's car once I drop you and Laliwa off at the border?" Ling asked.

"Park it in the same spot where you met me, down the street from my parents," Afonso said. "I left them the letter telling them that I'm borrowing the car and will have it returned to them."

The car was not priority at this moment for Afonso, though, for his eyes were fixated on Laliwa's bedroom window, and he twitched in his seat with nervousness and excitement as he waited for the moment Laliwa would appear. The town around here was fast asleep by now and only the dogs were heard barking momentarily, and the house stood in silence. As planned, precisely at midnight, Laliwa's wooden window flew open, and Afonso could have jumped out of his skin with joy at the sight of seeing Laliwa in the moonlight. "I can't believe this is really happening!" he exclaimed. "Let's jump over the paling and go and get her," he urged Ling.

"She said she'll meet you here at the car," Ling said. "Stay calm and let's wait right here as planned."

Afonso could not stay calm and sat at the edge of his seat and watched as Laliwa lowered the knotted string of white sheets, and after she secured it to the bed, she jumped over the window and started climbing down. Just then, someone in the house lit an oil lamp, and Laliwa scrambled back up and pulled up the string of sheets and closed the window hastily.

All the excitement was instantly zapped from Afonso, and he grabbed the steering wheel to steady his trembling hands as he exclaimed, "Oh, no!"

"This is not the way things should go," Ling said, as his face dipped with disappointment.

"What do I do now?" Afonso cried.

"We'll just have to sit here and wait and see what happens next." They waited for an entire hour but there was no more sign of Laliwa, and Afonso was growing more and more distraught by the moment, wondering whether Laliwa was all right.

What they did not know was that Laliwa was in a real predicament. Ostensibly, that same day, one of her brothers had found Afonso's note in her text book which had a detailed account of the plans to elope, and he informed his parents of this. It did not surprise her father that Laliwa was in love for he had suspected that for a long time by the faraway look in his daughter's eyes, but the plan to elope came as a shock. He was livid with anger over this for he had plans to marry her off to an Arawak man from his tribe, but he purposefully played along with her plan to elope with the intention of foiling it, and he did so by lighting the oil lamp at the precise moment she was to make her escape, which indeed hindered Laliwa from doing so.

Afonso, sorely distressed now, said to Ling, "I have a feeling Laliwa is in trouble. Maybe I should go and knock on her door and find out if she's all right."

"Not a good idea," Ling said. "You'll just blow your plans."

"I have a feeling that my plans are already blown," Afonso said. "What do I do now?"

"We'll just have to wait."

"But Laliwa might be in trouble, and I should help her," Afonso insisted.

"You'll only make matters worse for her," Ling said. "Let's just keep on waiting. Perhaps there's still a chance of her escaping, and still a chance to elope. Let's wait for a while more."

The oil lamp went out in the house, and Afonso and Ling waited, and waited.

After another hour of waiting, Ling succumbed to the realisation that Laliwa's plans were somehow foiled, and he said to Afonso, "I don't think Laliwa has a chance of escaping now. We've waited long enough. Let's go home."

"I can't leave until I find out whether Laliwa is okay," Afonso said and got out of the car and started walking towards Laliwa's house. "I'll take the chance of knocking on her door."

"I'm telling you that's not a good idea," Ling hollered after him.

But Afonso did not heed Ling's advice. He entered Laliwa's gate and headed up the front stairs and, though dreading he may come face to face with her father, knocked on the door.

And indeed it was Laliwa's father who answered the door. He stood in the darkness of the doorway, a silhouette of a figure of medium stature, and, in a deep voice, he said, "I've been watching you from behind the curtain since you got here, young man, and was wondering when you would come asking about Laliwa."

Afonso was dumbfounded at first, realising that Laliwa's father had found out about his plans, then, after collecting himself, he asked, "Is Laliwa all right, sir?"

Laliwa's father stepped outside and closed the door behind him, and he lit his pipe, the flame of the matchstick illuminating his craggy, reddish-brown face and stringy, dark hair, and then he answered, "No need for you to worry about my daughter, she's safe and sound, and will not be eloping with you."

The blind veil of love that had obscured Afonso's sensibility suddenly lifted, and he felt ashamed and terrible about his plans and said, "I'm sorry, sir— "

"You're sorry!" Laliwa's father exploded. "You came here to steal my daughter away from me and you're telling me you're sorry!"

"I love her, sir," Afonso said passionately, "and eloping is the only way I thought I could have her."

"That's a cowardly and foolish thing to do!" Laliwa's father reprimanded Afonso harshly. "Do you realise what kind of suffering and shame you would have caused me?"

The hurt and anger in Laliwa's father's voice jolted Afonso into now thinking of what the consequences his actions would have caused, and again he said, "I'm sorry, sir."

Afonso's remorse only agitated Laliwa's father even more so, and his voice was hard and cold when he said to him, "Go on your way, young man. And don't let me see you anywhere around here again."

Afonso did not move but stood right in front of Laliwa's father, defying him, and he said, "I love your daughter and I want to marry her, sir."

"Laliwa will be marrying someone else. Now, go on your way, young man."

Battling to be the husband to be chosen for Laliwa, an obstinate Afonso persisted with: "But she does not love the man you plan on marrying her off to, she loves me, sir." When Laliwa's father did not respond this time, Afonso went on to make an impromptu case, saying, "I will take good care of Laliwa if you let me marry her. I'm the son of a wealthy man and my father will make sure she has a comfortable life living in his white mansion, and she will never have to work and struggle in life. I, personally, am high-school educated and plan to become a policeman, and I will work hard myself to provide for her." And Afonso resorted to pleading. "Please, sir, allow me to marry your daughter."

Laliwa's father remained silent for a long while as he puffed on his pipe and thought. The man he was planning to marry Laliwa off to happened to be twice the age of Laliwa and was very poor and did not have much to offer her in life, and Laliwa had never met him and obviously was not in love with him. And here was an ambitious young man with whom Laliwa was in love, and by his bravery and persistence demonstrated that he loved Laliwa by battling for her, and he could afford her a good life free of hardship. Besides, the young man was high-school educated, and so was his daughter, and she deserved to be with someone her equal. Some things to seriously take into consideration for his daughter, he now thought. After mulling things over for a while longer, the hard edge in his voice softened and he finally said, "This seems too good to be true. The son of a rich man is likely to pursue many other women. Come back and see me in one year, and if you're still in love with my daughter, I will consider your proposal then." And with that Laliwa's father went back inside and shut the door behind him.

Afonso skipped down the stairs and ran to the car and informed Ling of what had just transpired between him and Laliwa's father, and he said, "I can wait for a year and I'll still be in love with Laliwa then, in fact, I have loved Laliwa since in kindergarten and all the way through to high school and will be in love with her for the rest of my life! I will be marrying Laliwa in a year's time, my friend!"

"Congratulations, my friend!" Ling said with almost as much joy, although he was somewhat disappointed that he could not participate in the prank to elope. "Speaking of marrying, this means that we can attend Indira and Francine's weddings. And I hope Laliwa can make it."

That same night, Laliwa's father had a talk with his daughter and eased her worry and pain by telling her what had occurred between him and Afonso. And Laliwa was now all too content to wait a year if that was all it would take to marry Afonso in the proper fashion. She now had reasons to celebrate at Indira and Francine's weddings.

* * *

Indira and Francine themselves were up early at the crowing of the fowlcocks on this warm, moonlit Saturday morning, and was so Nani. The girls had spent the last two weeks assiduously rubbing copious amounts of Ambi fade cream all over their bodies to make their skin glow on their wedding day—not that they needed it, for their supple youthful skin glowed naturally. Indira talked Francine into also rubbing dye on their skin in her effort to emulate the Hindu *haldi*—tumeric dye ceremony, for she thought this would be pleasing to Ravi and his parents as it is an act done for cleansing before marriage, and it also beautifies in that it gives the skin a golden glow. Indira did not go through the Hindu *mati-kore* or *dig dutty* ceremony, where a puja is done with a bit of earth—prayers to Mother Earth, neither, a *mehendi*—painting of the hands and feet ceremony, but she previously had Ravi's sister, Radhika, and his cousin, Padmini, design hers with the henna. She conscientiously made a compromise to wear a sari for the Hindu ceremony, though she chose to wear white instead of yellow or red, and she planned to wear the same for the Christian wedding instead of a traditional western wedding dress. She decided on these things for she thought these would also be pleasing to Ravi and his parents.

Francine was presently over at Nani's house, in the lamp-lit kitchen. Nani played along with the young brides-to-be to dye their skin, and she ground up some tumeric on the masala brick and made a paste. While the wood in the mud stove was crackling as a pot of chocolate tea with cow's milk was boiling, in the soft glow of the kerosene oil lamp, Nani rubbed the yellow dye on the girls' faces, arms, and legs, teasing them as she was doing so that this should be done by five young virgin girls and not an old woman like herself, a ritual which she had gone through for her Hindu wedding, and she went on to tell the girls about her anecdotes of the haldi, mati-kore, mehendi and other ceremonies, much to the fascination of the girls.

Once the dye was applied, Nani left the girls sitting on the peerahs to let it soak into their skin, and she went about serving them hot cups of the chocolate tea, then she started making them their favourite breakfast; saltfish with tomatoes, and roti. As the delicious aroma of her cooking pervaded the cozy kitchen, the girls gaffed in the soft light of the oil lamp, whispering about their anticipation of the day and talking about their wedding night, Francine being

399

bold to a bashful Indira. Through it all, they did not forget about Laliwa and thought by now she and Afonso must have eloped and were well on their way to getting married themselves; little did they know.

When Nani was finished cooking, she fed the girls, and then she sent them to the bathroom in the backyard for their morning ablutions, to wash the dye off their skin before the peep of the sun, and, in the semi-darkness of the morning, the girls scrubbed down their skin with nenwa loofahs and sweet soap. In the light of dawn, their skin glowed golden and was soft and silky smooth, making them appear as 'glowing brides'.

The rise of the warm golden morning sun brought about a flurry of activities at Nani and the Williams's houses as preparations for the weddings' feast were underway; goats and sheep and pigs were being prepared by the men for currying and frying, which would take place in Nani's backyard in large carahees in bush-cook style, and great iron pots of rice and dhal, also attended by the men, were already boiling over the fires. The ladies took to slicing up vegetables and kneading colossal amounts of dough at Nani's bottom-house to make puri, keeping a borrowed kerosene stove going non-stop with frying the puris, as others kept Nani's mud stove burning nonstop with making savoury victuals. Joan's gas stove and electric oven were also busy with the making of other treats and sweets, and even Fazeela and Pyari's mud stoves were lit for the weddings' feast today.

While families and friends were busy cooking and making preparations for the weddings, the morning progressed, and what a splendid day it turned out to be, for the sky was bright and blue and a balmy breeze was blowing. It was really a fine day for weddings. George Williams already had an eclectic mix of music blaring, from reggae, calypso, Indian, and country, to entertain everyone there, initiating the celebrations.

By now Joan was busy with dressing her gem of a daughter in her fairytale wedding dress, making her up like an African goddess in an updo braided twist coiffure, bejewelled with pearl beads. She adorned her with a classic tiara and veil, and satin shoes, and accessorised her with a precious diamond & pearl necklace with matching earrings and bracelet; heirloom Joan had also worn for her wedding.

Joan paused to admire her baby face daughter and thought what a glowing bride young Francine was in her flawless makeup with her rose-blush cheeks and rich brown glowing skin, and looking resplendent in her wedding dress. She felt she was looking at herself in the mirror some long years ago when she was getting married. Tears sprang to her eyes when she thought Francine would no longer be her baby girl for she would soon leave home, and she wondered how she would take it when she drives away that night.

Over at Nani's house, Indira felt like she was walking through a dream as she was being dressed. Radhika, Ravi's sister, was there to give Nani a helping hand in dressing her, and she curled Indira's luxuriant, midnight-black hair into dozens of long tresses and let them fall softly about her. For this special day, Nani went against her rule and allowed Radhika to apply makeup on Indira, and Radhika painted Indira's face and nails like an Indian doll in rich ruby-red and gold tones. Nani then dressed Indira in a fitted, white choli blouse and wrapped her in a sheer, lily-white sari, and accessorised her with the finest of Chaaya's intricate gold jewellery; a matching set of necklace, earrings, and bangles, and Radhika put on a delicate, pearl-jewelled pair of slippers on her. Lastly, Nani veiled Indira's face with a matching sheer white sari veil.

After Indira was all dressed, Nani took a look at her granddaughter and thought of how innocent she looked at sixteen years old, a child of a woman for a bride, but Nani had no tears of sadness in her eyes in knowing that she would not be losing Indira after the wedding. Tears of joy trickled down her cheeks, though, that Indira was getting married to the man she truly loved, and Nani was happy that she would have an addition to the household, a young man for whom, in her heart, she already had a soft spot.

Nani left Indira in the company of Radhika and went about getting ready herself. For this special day, she dressed in a brand new silk purple dress with matching headkerchief, and she, of course, wore only coconut oil on her feet. Today, her gold teeth were glittering brightly for everyone to see for she could not stop smiling.

As planned, a private, partial Hindu ceremony, the *mangal phera* and the *saptapadi*, were to take place at Nani's house for Ravi and Indira to perform their Hindu vows before taking off for the official Christian wedding. Nani's sitting room was transformed by Radhika and Padmini into an aesthetic wedding canopy—the *mandap*, draped with sheer red and yellow fabrics, and lit by small, luminous red lanterns hanging from the four bamboo posts. A new red and gold rug was laid out on the old wooden floor and was strewn with fragrant red rose petals. The sacred fire for the wedding ritual, the *yajna*, which was lit by the *pandit*—the Hindu priest, was now burning in a brass *havan kund* to evoke the fire god, *Agni*, to bear witness to the ceremony, and beside it was an ornate lotus incense stand, emitting the sweet scent of the Agarbatti incense stick burning. The private gathering included Ravi's parents, his sister, Radhika, and cousin, Padmini, Nani, Dr. Ramesh, and the pandit, and they were all now seated on the floor in Nani's tiny sitting room in this enchanting setting, along with the bride and groom.

Today, Ravi looked like a handsome young Indian prince, dashingly dressed in a sherwani—knee-length jacket and dhoti—pants, wedding outfit of yellow colour, that accentuated his rich brown skin and his sensual brown eyes, and his shiny black hair was arrayed about his shoulders, for he chose to go without a turban.

He had not laid eyes on Indira since the wedding arrangement two weeks ago, and as they were sitting on the rug before the sacred fire, his eyes were drawn to her shy, soft beauty behind the sheer white sari veil, and he noticed the sweeping curve of her kohl-lined dark eyes and her dimples and ruby-red lips, and a thrill went through him. He figured she had worn the sari just to please him, and the henna on her pretty hands and feet did not go unnoticed, neither did her glowing skin, which he guessed was from the dye, things his parents were sure to be impressed with, also, he thought. Indira kept her sari veil on to be unveiled at the Christian wedding, and she was glad she did so, for she stole perfunctory glances at her bridegroom ever so often, and excitement like warm waves washed over her each time she did.

As a sitar was playing softly on a cassette player in the background, the enchanting ceremony began with Dr. Ramesh handing over his granddaughter to Ravi's family in the ritual of *kanyadan*, and the bride and groom exchanged garlands of flowers, then the prayers and circumambulation of the sacred fire—the mangal phera was performed by the bride and groom, followed by the seven steps—the saptapadi, at which time the vows were made. The placing of *sindoor*—red powder on the bride's *maang* or forehead was not carried out as the formal Christian wedding was to take place right after, where Indira would be unveiled and the exchanging of the rings would be done then, also.

Ravi, breaking the solemnity of the occasion in making light of not being able to see Indira's face fully, whispered to her, "Hope I haven't married a little piggy in the bag." To which Indira responded, "Maybe you have." And the two of them cracked up laughing, not only over that, but out of the sheer excitement of them now being husband and wife, a moment that seemed like a dream. With that, they headed off to the church for their Christian wedding, and there they would meet the other bride and groom.

Albert, the epitome of what is tall, dark and handsome, was immaculately dressed in a fine white suit and matching shoes, a contrast to his youthful chocolate brown skin, and he was sporting a stylish Afro hairstyle. He was now standing at the altar displaying his striking, pearly-white teeth, thinking only of the 'heavenly delights' the men had teased him about the previous night as he waited for his princess to arrive. And when Francine walked down the aisle and came and stood next to him, he could just about explode with excitement at how stunningly beautiful she looked. After waiting for what seemed like an eternity, it now seemed dream-like to him that he was about to marry her. He just could not say his vows fast enough and was impatient when Francine took her time in doing so. Francine's face bore no diffidence when he unveiled her, and she was not afraid to kiss him passionately. Indira, on the other hand, blushed when Ravi lifted her veil and kissed her, for the first time, but a thrill raced throughout her, from her head down to her toes.

By the time the young newly-weds, Mr. & Mrs. Singh and Mr. & Mrs. Briggs, arrived back home it was mid-afternoon, and there was much whistling and cheering coming from the ebullient guests as the brides and grooms took their seats in the decorated tent in George Williams's backyard, now in the peak heat of the bright day. George Williams started up the music again, now playing some hot calypso tunes, and in Nani's backyard the men were moving to the rhythm as they were stirring pots of curried and fried meats over the fires, while little old ladies were singing along as they sat on the earthen ground of Nani's bottom-house, busy with rolling out dough and frying puri on the kerosene stove.

The banquet soon began, and everyone was toasting and feasting, and even those in town who were not invited to the weddings, dropped in for wedding food; dhal and rice, and curried and fried meats, and puri, served on *puri leaves* —water lily leaves, which Ravi's parents suggested, being Hindus. A variety of sweets then followed, from kheer to mithai to gulab jamun and prasad. Both Indira and Francine had agreed to share one wedding cake, and after the cutting of the gigantic black rum cake, the music grew louder, and the rum and wine flowed freely, and soon there was a whole lot of wining—dancing taking place in every corner of the tent and under the sun and even in the shade of the trees in Nani's orchard. Nani let her silver hair down and was also dancing that day.

Indira and Francine were surprised to see Laliwa, Afonso, and Ling there. They were told of the thwarted plan to elope and were happy to hear of the conditions of the outcome. Families and friends, including, Mr. Jackson, Shazam and Fazeela and family, Mrs. Surjeet, even the eccentric Pyari and Dr. Ramesh's elite coterie of friends were at the wedding banquet, all except for Uncle Ram, and that was a good thing because the celebrations went on just splendid without him.

Late in the evening, as the celebrations were still throbbing, with performers taking to the stage, singing and dancing, entertaining the guests, the brides and grooms left the tent, momentarily, and went up to Nani's kitchen, and, Radhika, being as considerate and obsequious as she was, bolted the doors to give them a chance to spend some time alone. The newlyweds, filled with bliss, took their seats around the table overlooking Nani's backyard and, as the kerosene oil lamp in the kitchen was burning and the crimson embers in the mud stove were glowing hotly from just being used, the couples bantered around.

The boys immediately started joking around with their brand new young wives, Albert saying to Ravi, "Let's put the two of them to a test and see if they can cook before we take them home."

Francine spoke up, and she laughingly said, "I know how to boil an egg."

"That's all?" Albert asked. "Well, does this mean I have to do the cooking at home?"

"And some house work, too," Francine said, now with a straight face.

Albert gave her an incredulous look and said, "Woman, all I want is some 'heavenly pleasures'. I didn't know I have to work so hard for it. I'm now thinking this is not a good deal. I think I will change my mind and not take you home!"

The group laughed, and Ravi said, "And does my wife know how to cook?"

"I know how to cook very well, and clean, too," Indira said.

"Well, then, I think I will keep you," Ravi said.

"But that doesn't mean that I would do all the cooking and cleaning," Indira said with a mimicked pout.

"Okay, I'll rub your clothes if you rub mine," Ravi said.

"Now, that's fair," Indira said, "I think I will keep you, too."

The bridegrooms laughed, and Francine then went on to say, "Now, let's test our husbands and see what they're good for."

Albert was quick to boldly say, "I'll tell you what I'll be good for; I'll sow seeds so we can have a lot of babies!" And he winked at Francine, who tossed him an amorous look in response.

Ravi, feeling more at ease and confident since his talk with Dr. Ramesh last night, quickly added, "I think I'll be good at that, too." And he looked Indira in her eyes and added, "We can start as early as tonight."

Indira blushed, while Francine led Albert on with a flirtatious look and said, "No babies just yet."

With a disappointed look, Albert said, "Uh, does that mean I have to wait for my heavenly delights?" In reply, Francine cast him another coquettish look.

Ravi then said, "Let's name our wives, Albert."

"My hot Black Goddess is what I'll call Francine," Albert immediately said, already feeling Francine's teasing heat.

"My shy Indian Doll is appropriate for Indira," Ravi said, to which Indira lowered her eyes, too shy to reveal her torrid feelings.

The group sat around a while longer and joked around and talked about embarking on their married lives, then they returned to the tent to continue the celebrations. Sometime after midnight, on this moonlit night, Albert and Francine made their move to leave to go to Albert's parents home to consummate their marriage, a place where Francine would be starting her new life, and as they were in the car and just about to take off, Joan, in spite of her efforts to keep it together, became so overcome with emotions that her baby girl, the apple of her eye, was now leaving home, and she created a bit of a scene, saying, "You can't take her just yet, Albert, because I forgot to pack Francine's hair clips."

"Francine would not need hair clips," Albert said, eager to take off, "she will wear her hair down tonight." To which, Francine added, "Albert's right, Mom, I don't need hair clips tonight."

"But, wait!" Joan said. "I didn't pack Francine's frilly nightie."

"Francine wouldn't need that, either. She'll be wearing her birthday suit," Albert said. To which, Francine added, "Albert's right, Mom. I don't need a nightie tonight."

"Slippers," Joan then said, "Francine needs to take her slippers."

"I will keep her feet warm, she doesn't need them," Albert said. "The only thing she needs is me, mother-in-law. Now, let us go." Francine then said, "I don't need anything else but Albert tonight, Mom." Then realising that her mother was being heartbroken, she added, "I'll miss you, Mom, but I'm not going very far, we can see each other anytime."

George Williams stepped in then and said, "Let her go, Joan. Just let her go. She's just moving right here in Rose Hall, just up the street." Choked with emotions himself, George took Joan in his arms and comforted her. And Albert and Francine were whisked away before Joan could make another attempt to hold back her baby girl.

Soon after the Briggs' took off, the Singhs' left the tent while the celebration was still going on with more music and a whole lot of drinking and wine dancing on this balmy tropical night. Nani left Indira in the care of Ravi's sister, Radhika, and his cousin, Padmini, and she personally took to dressing Ravi for the wedding chamber in her newly built room at the bottom-house.

Indira was escorted up the front stairs by Radhika and Padmini, and she entered Nani's sitting room to find it softly lit by the small red lanterns hanging from the bamboo posts of the sheer red and yellow draped mandap, which was still up, only now it was transformed into a cozy bathroom with a large aluminium tub in the centre of the red and gold rug, and the tub was filled with cool water scented with chameli flowers floating on the surface. For this special night, a fresh terry cloth towel, instead of Indira's usual flour bag towel, was laid out for her. With some coaxing, Radhika and Padmini helped the bashful bride out of her wedding sari and got her into the tub, and they left her there to take a bath while they went to prepare her tiny bedroom, which the two of them transformed into an alluring wedding chamber for the night.

Nani sent Ravi to bathe in the bathroom in the backyard, and when he was finished he returned to her room. There, in the dim light of the kerosene oil lamp, Nani had him dress in fine new bed clothes as she had her back turned, and Ravi sweetened himself up with a touch of musk cologne. When he was finished, Nani asked him to stand in front of her and, when Ravi did, she said, "Let me bless you before you go up to the chamber, boy." And Nani placed a hand on Ravi's head and said, "May the good Lord bless your life with my granddaughter with happiness and prosperity and peace. And may your union with her bring you an abundance of pleasure, and may your love bear a lot of fruits in due time." With that, Nani walked Ravi to the front stairs, and before he headed up, she gave him a solicitous embrace and whispered in his ears, "Be gentle with my granddaughter, boy, she's young like the bud of a flower, and innocent, much like you are a young shoot of a plant, young and tender."

By now, Radhika and Padmini had finished preparing the wedding chamber and had tidied up the sitting room and left. Ravi headed straight to the wedding chamber, from which came the soft sound of classical Indian music;

the seductive melancholic twang of the sitar and the alluring beat of the tabla, playing on a cassette player. When he entered the chamber, he found it softly lit with many diyas, the earthen ghee lamps resting on the windows' sills and night table, which cast a golden glow on the sheer mosquito netting, embroidered with red tassels. And the white satin sheet on the single coconut fibre bed—on which velvety white chameli petals were strewn—glistened, as did the matching feather pillow, embellished with red silk thread. The sweet scent of incense pervaded the room, and a light warm breeze played with the red lace curtain of the window which faced the backyard and was left slightly open, allowing a sliver of moonlight and gust of pleasant breeze to enter, adding to the mystique of the provocative ambience.

Ravi's young wife, his Indian Doll, was standing by the window, dressed in a lily-white silk nightie which depicted her purity, and the wind was gently blowing her long, midnight-black tresses about her glowing face and bare shoulders and arms, scattering the scent of her perfumed, silky-soft skin as she stood there looking demure, with dark, dreamy eyes. Indira took a look at her prince of a husband, dressed in white himself to signify his own purity, his shoulder-length hair tossed by the wind, and unable to hold his gaze with eyes burning like brown desert sand, she lowered her moist dark eyes and shrunk away in shyness. Ravi reached out for her, and when she succumbed to his embrace they held each other tightly, and they trembled as tears of love and passion rained from their eyes, releasing their pent-up desires. Inebriated with her beauty and innocence and her sweet chameli scent, Ravi lifted his wife and took her to the wedding bed and he gently laid her down and lowered the mosquito netting.

By now, the celebrations had ceased and everyone had dispersed and the fowlcocks were already crowing. Nani retired to bed in her room at the bottom-house, the light of her oil lamp now extinguished, and as she laid there in the darkness she could hear the sounds of the crickets and crapos. And the soft sounds of the sitar and tabla drums coming from the wedding chamber sailed through the warm breeze and seduced this enchanting moonlit night. The faint sound of her granddaughter softly moaning caught her ears, and Nani drifted off to a peaceful sleep in knowing that the boy was being a gentle lover to her.

18

Settling Down And Certain Tragedies

The day after the nuptials, Ravi woke up before dawn to the mystique of a rainy morning and the sound of doves cooing in the trees in the orchard. The scent of the earth and flowers in the garden below wafted up in the wind and through the slightly open window, drifting through the mosquito netting. Indira was fast asleep with her black curls spread out on the white satin feather pillow, and Ravi feasted his eyes on her naked beauty, every part of her a gem, even her pretty dimples; all his own treasures, and his heart played like the sound of the sitar, lulling him back to sleep. Shortly after, Indira woke up and found Ravi sound asleep and, for a moment, she was lost in admiring her husband's youthful handsomeness, remembering his passionate eyes the night before, then she quietly slipped out from beneath the mosquito netting and went to bathe in the backyard while it was still drizzling.

When she was finished, she got dressed in a soft pink cotton dress and went to the kitchen and shoved some wood in the mud stove and lit it. For this special morning, she began making roti, pumpkin and saltfish, *float bakes*—fried bakes, and dosea—pancakes, and she fried eggs and boiled chocolate sticks and made tea with fresh cow's milk.

Nani came up the backstairs as Indira took to her wifely duty and was busy preparing breakfast, and she said, "I came up to make breakfast this morning. You should have stayed in bed, child." And Nani noticed the peachy glow of her granddaughter and thought the child was now a woman, that Ravi had brought out the ravishing woman in her.

"I now have a husband to cook for," Indira said softly with her whole face smiling, but too shy to meet Nani's eyes.

Just then, the partition of the long strands of beads in the kitchen entrance jangled, and they both looked in the direction to find Ravi in his bukta and singlet—undergarments. Upon seeing Nani, he quickly retreated to the bedroom and came back out with a towel around his waist and greeted them both politely with, "Good morning."

Both Nani and Indira returned a 'good morning' to him, and after stealing a glance at his shy young wife, Ravi hurried off to the backyard to bathe.

Indira had arranged the hot cups of chocolate tea and enamel plates of steaming breakfast on the old wooden kitchen table by the time he was finished and had gotten dressed and joined her and Nani around the table. The kerosene oil lamp was left burning low this morning as it was rainy dark out, creating an atmosphere of coziness, which was enhanced by the warmth of the embers burning in the mud stove.

"The plants need water and I'm glad it's raining," Nani said as they began eating.

"I'm glad, too," Ravi said, but the rain was not what he was glad about at the moment; at the moment he was giddy with euphoria. He was feeling the impact that he was married to Indira and she was now his wife, and a beautiful one, and he kept glancing at her, furtively, whenever Nani

414

was not looking at him. Indira was also coming to the full realisation that she was now married to him, and she was feeling self-conscious after spending the night with him, aware of his glances and feeling flushed.

Nani was aware of what was tacitly transpiring between the newly married young couple just by observing their demeanour, but she had her business to think of, more specifically, of having to earn extra money to now maintain three instead of two in the household. "I hope it stops raining by tomorrow, though, so I can sell at the market."

"I hope so, too," Ravi said, absentmindedly, as he was thinking of how dark and pretty and mysterious Indira's eyes were in the soft light of the oil lamp, and he noticed how alluring she looked in the pink cotton dress, with her arms bare.

"In fact, I hope it stops raining soon so we can pick some vegetables for me to take to the market tomorrow," Nani went on to say.

"I hope so, too," Ravi said, as images of being with Indira the night before played out in his mind.

Indira then said, "I heard on Radio Demerara that the rain should clear up later this morning."

"I will go to church this morning and leave the two of you alone," Nani said, and looking directly at Indira now, instructed her, saying, "When the rain stops, show Ravi around the garden and give him a rundown on things. Get him to help you to pick some vegetables and collect the eggs in the fowl coop, and show him how to pack them onto the donkey-cart. Ravi?"

"What, you said something about going to church?" Ravi asked as he took his eyes off Indira to look at Nani.

Indira cast a perfunctory glance at her husband and smiled for she knew she was his distraction, and she intervened, saying, "Don't worry, I'll see to things, Nani. You get dressed for church."

When Nani left for church, Ravi thanked Indira for the breakfast she cooked to impress him, and he gave her a peck on the cheek. He had the urge to take her in his arms and love her like he had done the night before, but, Indira was feeling too shy and strange in the rainy light of day and she hurried off and went about doing her daily chores, making up the bed and cleaning and tidying up the old house. She kept herself busy until mid-morning, and around then, a lady stopped by with a basket of fresh, plump shrimps, and she bought a couple of parcels and then began cooking shrimps curry and rice for lunch.

Ravi, feeling somewhat strange himself, and not being able to express himself to his bashful wife, got his bottle of blue ink and his fountain pen, along with writing paper, and he ensconced himself at the kitchen table and, while Indira was busy cooking, he began penning his love for her in the form of a poem, detailing the first night he spent with her in heaven, as he thought. When Indira was through cooking, the rain had stopped, but Ravi was still engrossed in writing, so, like a good wife, she left him at the kitchen table and went about picking the vegetables and collecting the eggs, and she loaded them onto the donkey-cart herself, not heeding Nani's instructions to have Ravi help her.

When Nani returned from church, she found the donkey-cart already loaded for the next day but saw no sign of Ravi at the bottom-house, and when she inquired if Indira had shown him around and whether he had helped her, Indira simply said he was busy and that there would be another time for that. Nani went up to the kitchen and found Ravi at the table, immersed in writing, and she figured that he was occupied with something important and did not take issue with him, but interrupted him to have lunch, which all three of them sat down to.

In the following days, Ravi and Indira indulged in the pleasures of their sweet and innocent love, and Nani was happy to see the two young people riding the waves of pleasure, their love like shimmering waves of heat, their romance sparkling like the golden waves of an ocean in the setting sun. Ravi's heart continued to play the sitar incessantly, playing the melody of love, and what a duet the two of their hearts made. They loved under the rose-pink of the early morning sky, the brilliant white rays of the afternoon sun—in the luminous green grass, the violet of the late afternoon sky, and under the silver stars and pale yellow moon, and even in the jet-black of the midnight, lost in the mysteries and passions of a young and tender love.

Over the next couple of weeks, Indira proved to be not just a doll for Ravi to play with but she executed her wifely duties with efficiency, cooking for her husband and serving him, and taking care of the household chores and, also, the gardening. As a young and inexperienced wife, she took Nani's advice on the talk she had given on marriage and gave of herself and love and understanding to Ravi. His constant writing, which was all he spent his time doing while she was busy with chores, could have been a source of quarrel between them, but she refrained from doing so, in fact, she facilitated his writing by putting out his bottle of blue ink and fountain pen and paper on the kitchen table for him to write in the days. And in the evenings, she would light the kerosene oil lamp in the bedroom and place on the night table his favourite books by authors, Tagore, Shakespeare, Browning, E. R. Braithwaite's *To Sir, With Love*, and his Indian film stars' magazines for him to peruse, along with the daily copy of the Guyana Chronicle Newspaper. She would even leave his guitar on the chair by the old wooden bedroom window for him to indulge in his passionate country & western love songs, and she set out her red transistor radio in the sitting room for him to listen to Indian music. Ravi was not living up to his promise to 'rub' Indira's clothes but she kept hers, and even ironed his clothes with the coal iron. She catered to his every whim, while Ravi continued to write poems of her, lost in the thrill of first love. And he spent all of Indira's free time with her.

Indira was now spending less and less time with Nani, only serving her the three meals a day, and she hurried her chores so she could be with Ravi, and Nani was soon beginning to feel neglected. To exacerbate the matter, Francine was off with Albert, and Nani was missing her, also, and irritability crept in. Adding gas to the spark, Indira was doing all the chores and cooking and serving Ravi, and all Ravi did was sit around writing poems and singing love songs, serenading Indira and listening to Indian music and spending time with Indira; showing no sign of keeping his promise to work and provide for her. Nani was now beginning to wonder whether she made the right choice for Indira. Feeling frustrated, she consulted Dr. Ramesh, who elucidated the matter by saying to her, "My son drank of the elixir of love and has become inebriated," explaining to Nani that Ravi was drunk with the potion of love, an

418

aphrodisiac, and was infatuated with Indira, and being in love had addled his brain, leading him to indulge in his compulsive desires. And Dr. Ramesh urged Nani to give the young man some more time to enjoy himself.

Nani let things play out in the same way for the next week, and soon it was coming up to a month and still Ravi was making no attempt to work, showing only apathy towards it, and that churned in her mind. She was now beginning to feel that Ravi had deluded her with all his promise of working and providing for them, and that was only a façade, and she began to think that Indira had married a lazy bone, a loongera—good-for-nothing bad boy; Ravi was now Nani's bone of contention.

One day, she was observing him as he was sitting in the hammock at the bottom-house, his sensual eyes naked in his erotic thoughts as he was looking at Indira while she was towel-drying her hair on the back steps, and Nani's irritability reached a crescendo. And bam! There went Nani, lashing out at him, saying, "Now that you drank of the love potion, you're dizzy with romance and behaving like a lovesick fool! Look at my disaster!"

Ravi laughed and said, "Your granddaughter has made me sick with love, yes, I'm sick with love but I'm no fool." And Ravi went on to say, "Old Gal, didn't you drink of the same love potion when you were young? And weren't you dizzy with romance yourself? You should know what I'm going through. Don't fret yourself."

The next day as Indira was serving Ravi breakfast, Nani took another fit and said, "Eh, eh, you think you're some kind of a king to have this child cook and serve you and cater to your every need?"

Ravi smiled at Nani and said, "Old Gal, didn't you treat your lover the same way when you were first married? Let me revel in this pampering for a while."

The next day while Ravi was sitting at the kitchen table writing love poems, Nani flared up at him, yet again, over his indolence—just as Dr. Ramesh came over for a visit—and she quoted the Guyanese proverb, *Too much sit down ah bruck trousers*, meaning, people only wear out their pants by sitting around doing nothing. And she said, "You promised to provide for my granddaughter and so far you haven't done a thing. You lazy boy, I now think you're just a *gaff box*!" Meaning that Ravi was all talk with no action. "You're nothing more than a *phagla*, a crazy boy!"

Indira, in defence of Ravi, intervened this time, and she said, "Nani you told me, and Francine, to be loving to our husbands, and here you are picking a fight with my husband. What is troubling you, Nani?"

Confronted by Indira with advice she had given to her, Nani backed down then, and she searched her heart for what was really troubling her. Sure, she was worried that she had an extra mouth to feed and that Ravi was not making an attempt to work and provide for Indira like he had promised to do, but what was causing her all the upset was that Ravi was taking up most of Indira's time, and Nani was not only feeling neglected, she was getting very lonely.

Dr. Ramesh, who had deciphered Nani's problem when she had consulted him a couple of weeks back, took Ravi aside for a stroll in the backyard and had a talk with him. "Nani is feeling neglected and lonely, son," he said, "try and free up some of Indira's time so she can spend some more time with her. And give the old woman some of your attention, also." And Dr. Ramesh went on to say, "Nani is also concerned that you're not working, as yet. She's a poor woman and cannot support three people in the household. There's a time for everything, a time to play and a time to work. Overindulgence in anything is not good—you must learn to balance life. I know you'e captivated with Indira, but man cannot live on love alone. Enough play, it's time to get to work." Dr. Ramesh then got out his wallet and took out a few dollars and said, "Here, take this to cover your expenses until you're able to generate some income, son."

"That wouldn't be necessary," Ravi said, refusing the offer. "I'll get down to work right away. Thanks for the advice, Pa."

Ravi first took care of Nani and freed up some of Indira's time so she could spend more time with her, and he began dividing his time between Nani and Indira, giving the old woman some of his attention, also, in an attempt to win over her affection with his charm and humour.

"Let me take you for a walk," he said to Nani later that same day, after Dr. Ramesh had a talk with him.

Nani was taken aback by his change in attitude and, giving him a stern look, said, "Don't take your eyes and pass me," meaning don't disrespect her, "I'm not your wife, boy."

"You're my gal, too," Ravi laughed and said. "You're my Old Gal, and Indira's my young one."

"Don't be so brazen with an old woman like me," Nani said, still serious.

Later that day, Ravi said to Nani, "Get dressed, Old Gal, I'm going to take you for a motorcycle ride."

"You want some licks for saying that to an old woman like me," Nani said, and broke out in a smile this time.

"Then let me sing you a love song," Ravi said.

Nani smiled again and said, "Boy, clear out of my sight and don't provoke me." Ravi sat down that night and played his guitar and sang Nani some religious tunes.

The following day while an Indian song was playing on the radio, Ravi said to Nani, "Let me dance with you, Old Gal."

"Don't play the fool with me, boy," Nani said, but she went on to dance. Ravi was impressed at how well she did and then learned that she was once a performer in her youth. She taught him a few dance moves and told him stories of her past. After that day, the two of them would sit at the bottom-house alone and she would tell him long time stories of fishing and of jumbies and *bushmaster* snakes and jaguars and alligators, and stories of her parents and grandparents and of mud houses; stories that captivated Ravi and formed a bond between the two of them.

Nani also shared her life of inner peace, contentment, and happiness with him, and he learned many things from the wise old woman. He in turn shared his poetry with her.

Beneath The Sapodilla Tree She Stands

Beneath the sapodilla tree she stands, her lips the rose-brown colour of the fruit
Her long, curly hair flows like the swirls of the black water river upon her back
Her dreamy eyes, sweeping and mysterious, like the pitch black of a backdam night

422

And skin like the shimmer of fresh honey, silky and fragranced with chameli petals

Her love is soft to the touch, like her voice, yet ardent like the rains of the Amazon

She is my moon, the only star in my sky, she is the rays of sun that caress my skin

She has set aflame my mind and turned my love as crimson as a ball-of-fire pepper

And she is now mine and mine alone, to have, to hold, to love forever.

It was difficult to tear himself and thoughts away from Indira, but, after Dr. Ramesh's talk with him, Ravi got down to being serious about working. He first offered to fulfil his promise to Indira—the one he made on their wedding day when they were together bantering with the Briggs' in Nani's kitchen—to rub her clothes if she would rub his, a promise she already kept, but Indira would not let him do so, saying that was a woman's job, so he started out with helping Nani with more manly work; gardening. He insisted that Indira should quit such laborious work, but Indira would not let him toil alone, and, so, together they worked alongside each other, tilling the soil and planting vegetables. Indira, however, let Ravi pack the donkey-cart with the produce they reaped, and Ravi would have also taken it to the market to sell, but Nani insisted in continuing to do so herself.

Ravi soon realised that the small business Nani had would only generate sufficient income to sustain the household of three, and in order for him to execute his business idea of opening a chain of fabric stores, he would have to take a second job elsewhere so he could earn and save up money. He had the experience of working at his parents' rice field and proved to be hard-working, and he soon found a second job in the fields, cutting cane. This required him to be up at the crowing of the fowlcocks in the week days, as he was scheduled to work early mornings until mid-afternoon, after which, he would continue to work for Nani until the setting of the sun.

The first day he was scheduled to cut cane, he was up with Indira by the crowing of the fowlcocks, in the dark of the early morning, and they were both in the kitchen, while Nani was still asleep in her room at the bottom-house. The mud stove was lit, emitting a sweet smoke and warmth, and he was sitting at the table looking at Indira as she was rolling roti dough on the *chowki*—pastry board, with the *belna*—rolling pin, the light of the kerosene oil lamp illuminating her loveliness in a baby blue polyester dress and accentuating the tender beauty of her face, across which a loose strand of curl that escaped her ponytail blew about in the gentle breeze coming from the open window. She was preparing roti for breakfast for them and had curry baigan—eggplant, and saltfish cooking on the mud stove for him to take to work for lunch. She paused to look at him when he said, "You're a good wife to me, Indi. You cook and feed me and wash my clothes and make my bed. I must tell you how thankful I am for your devotion to me."

In the few weeks they had been married, some of Indira's shyness had worn off and she now openly communicated with her husband, in fact, at times she chattered like a little bird. "My pleasure," she said. "But you owe some of your thanks to Nani for preparing me for my duties as a married woman." And she turned to get the hot roti from the tawa on the mud stove, and then clapped it with her bare hands before folding it and placing it in an enamel bowl with brown paper.

Ravi then said, "I will work hard and save up money and build you a house one day, and when I make enough money from my business, you wouldn't have to work in the garden alongside of me. And, someday, Nani wouldn't have to ever sell at the market, either. And someday we will have a cook so you wouldn't have to spoil your pretty hands clapping hot roti."

Indira let out a melodious laughter and smiled, showing her deep dimples, and she said, "You have big dreams, Rav. But for now I will have to cook and work in the garden to make ends meet. Even if you become successful someday, I don't know if I would ever stop doing so."

Ravi then unexpectedly asked, "Do you ever have any regrets for not marrying Tarak? If you had, life would have turned out so differently for you, Indi. You would have had anything you wanted right away, and servants at your feet, without having to live on promises and struggle along with me until, hopefully, I fulfil my dreams."

"As long as you love me I will have no regrets," Indira simply said. She never told him about the reason for the cancellation of the wedding arrangement with Tarak for she simply did not care to do so, or, for that matter, even think about that shameful and humiliating incident.

Ravi got up and took hold of his wife and held her close to him, inhaling her spicy curry scent, and as the wood in the mud stove crackled softly and the early morning breeze coming from the open window scattered the smoke about, with tenderness he assured her, "I will love you forever, my wife, and I will do whatever it takes to make you happy. I will provide you with a house and try my best to give you all the nice things a young woman should have."

"You've already done what it takes to make me happy, Rav, you gave yourself to me, and that's enough for me," Indira said as she held Ravi tightly. "I'm just happy being with you, Rav."

"Wanting to provide you with nice things and build a house for you would be just a token of my love for you, Indi. And I hope to someday fill the house with many children of our own."

"Then I will appreciate the token of your love, my husband," Indira smiled and said. "As to filling the house with children, remember, Nani said to wait a couple of years before we think of making babies."

"I agree, that's wise advice," Ravi said. "For now I will work hard and save up money to set up my own business, and I hope to make a profit and build a house with that and put some aside so we can afford to feed little mouths."

With that, Indira finished her cooking and packed the hot curry baigan with saltfish and rice and roti in a steel lunch container, along with a ball-of-fire pepper and a guava fruit for Ravi to take to work, then they sat down and had breakfast in silence, enjoying each other's company as the embers in the mud stove burned down to ashes. After breakfast, Ravi kissed Indira on both dimples, and off to cut cane he went, on his bicycle in the wee hours of the morning, with a cutlass and the steel lunch container of hot foods Indira had prepared for him, thinking of her only as he rode along the dirt road in the darkness.

The young couple soon settled into a weekly routine. They both got up early on weekday mornings, and Indira would prepare Ravi's breakfast, and lunch for him to take to work, and Ravi would take off to cut cane. While her husband was gone, Indira occupied herself with taking care of Nani and with house work and attending to the flower garden, and she spent her spare time doing her favourite handicraft, crocheting doilies, with her mind always on her husband and his love. When Ravi returned from cutting cane at mid-afternoon, they both would work in the vegetable garden, and, later, while Ravi would prepare the donkey-cart with produce for Nani to take to the market to sell the next day, Indira would cook dinner. Then they would bathe and have dinner with Nani.

After dinner, Ravi would sit at the kitchen table in the evenings and in the light of the kerosene oil lamp he would work for a while on drafting his fabric stores' business plan, and he would also lay out his plans of building a house and attaining his dreams. Both he and Indira would then devote time to Nani and entertain her. Ravi would play the guitar and they would sing Nani her favourite song *Family Bible* at the bottom-house, in the light of the oil lamp and, at times, in the moonlight. Ravi would lull Nani to sleep with singing her other religious songs and Indira would tuck the old woman into her bed in her room at the bottom-house, then the couple would share moments together.

Ravi would often times serenade Indira with country & western love songs on the backstairs, in the moonlight, singing in his youthful and gentle voice, and Indira would sometimes sing along, trying to imitate country singer,

Lynn Anderson, but her soft voice sounded more like sensual whispers, which only amused Ravi. They would then play dominoes at the kitchen table; the winner entitled to a massage at the end of the evening, which Ravi got most of the times, not because of always winning, as Indira played as well as he did, but Indira did so to soothe his aching muscles from all his hard work. The two of them would then take to reading in the soft light of the kerosene oil lamp, especially on rainy nights, laying side by side in bed, Ravi more into great literary works and Indira into mysteries and romance; books they borrowed from the local library. Often times, Ravi would read Indira poems, then he would tell her impossible stories he would fabricate just to see the childlike wonder in her face and hear her soft, melodious laughter when he would reveal he was just making up the stories.

The nights would often proceed with Indira, having a penchant for dressing up, dolling up for Ravi in her finery like a *star gal*—attractive like a film star, and Ravi facilitated this, for Indira made his world picturesque. With the first income he received from cutting cane, he bought her a sheer, shimmering orange sari and she got dressed up in it and even put on Chaaya's jewellery, and she danced for him in the flickering lights of the enchanting diyas to the alluring sound of Indian music. Indira played the game of love as though she knew it all along; naturally, and so did Ravi. They both admired each other's youthful beauty and played with the fire of love and lust; a fever that burns the whole body. And their nights most certainly ended with a massage and making love before going to sleep.

Ravi did not work on the weekends, neither did Indira, and the two of them would take off on the motorcycle and go on long rides, or they would go to the movies, or just sit around at home on Sunday afternoons and listen to the country & western songs' hour on the radio. Sometimes they would both take off and visit Dr. Ramesh, who had long since retired and had a lot of free time on his hands. At times, Ravi would just go alone, and he and the doctor would sit around and have a few drinks and play cards and dominoes, and Ravi would discuss his business plans and dreams with him, and Dr. Ramesh would guide him along like a father would. Quite often, Ravi and Indira, along with Padmini, would take off in Padmini's jeep to visit Ravi's parents and his sister Radhika in Skeldon, and sometimes they would spend the weekend there, and Ravi would assist them with the rice field, with Indira by his side, faithfully toiling along with him.

Ravi did not know what to expect from a wife. Fortunately, Indira turned out to be a great lover, and a hard-working and devoted girl, kind-hearted, and a lot of fun to be with. He soon found out, though, that there was even more to her than that. After a couple of months of working in the cane field, he was bitten on his leg by a snake in the field and was laid up in bed with acute pain, the doctors not knowing whether he would live or die, and his and Indira's fate as a couple was challenged. Indira rose to the challenge valiantly, remembering Nani's talk on the illnesses she and Nana had faced early in their marriage, particularly, when Nani was sick and Nana nursed her back to health. '*No greater love can a man show than to care for a sick wife*', she remembered Nani saying, and vice versa.

Indira stayed up with Ravi day after day and night after night and nursed him, sponge bathing him and cleaning his wound and applying poultice to it, and treating him with antidote. If it was not for Indira's loving care, and her firm faith, Ravi knew he would have died. He would watch her as she would sit on the chair by the bedside, the kerosene oil lamp by her side, and he would see her lips moving in prayers, never giving up hope on him. She not only had faith and attended to him, but she continued to labour in the garden, with tenacity.

Indira's faith was further challenged when, as Ravi was still convalescing, Nani fell and fractured her ankle. Instead of giving up, Indira loaded the donkey-cart with produce and rode it to the market herself, bearing no shame in doing so, but seeing it as imperative—though it broke Nani's heart—and she sold the produce and solely provided bread and butter for the family, for just like Ravi, Indira was quite independent. When Ravi thought that things could not get any worse, a flood came and all the fishes in the pond swam away and the vegetables in the garden perished, but, not Indira's perseverance. Indira and Nani had faced the same kinds of hardship in the course of their lives, and Indira had learned how to deal with this kind of suffering from the wise old woman; tackling it as a challenge to overcome in life. She remained sanguine and did not resort to asking or begging for help, but she sold the chickens that Nani had raised and made ends meet with the paltry amount of money she generated. And when the money ran out and all the food was gone and there were no more chickens to sell, she did not tap into Ravi's immature savings, which he had worked so hard to gain, but she went out fishing with some town locals and put food on the table. It would have broken her heart if Indira had to use up Ravi's little savings, which was his dream, but, luckily, the neighbours soon realised the predicament she was in and, along with Dr. Ramesh, they willingly helped out until both Ravi and Nani—with the ceaseless care from Indira—got back on their feet in the span of a couple of months.

Things then resumed to a normal routine and a year soon elapsed. Soon after Ravi and Indira celebrated their first wedding anniversary, Afonso, who had met Laliwa's father's condition of waiting a year for Laliwa, got permission from Laliwa's father to marry Laliwa, and he and Laliwa signed the papers quickly and Laliwa was now settled into Afonso's father's white mansion, a happy housewife, while Afonso was training to be a policeman, as he had planned on doing. Ravi and Indira would meet up with them from time to time on the weekends, and, occasionally, they would also pay Albert and Francine a visit.

Francine took Nani's wise advice and was enjoying the bliss of her new marriage, being a dutiful wife, also. And Albert was enjoying his 'heavenly delights'. Albert's parents built them a house right there in Rose Hall as they commenced their second year of marriage, and the couple moved in and were busy setting up house and making plans for a family in the near future. George Williams made a connection for Albert to teach at the same school he was still teaching at, and that brought in a steady source of income for the couple, while Francine was busy with establishing a small business at home, working as a seamstress.

Life would have come as easy to Ravi and Indira as it was for Albert and Francine if Ravi had taken up Dr. Ramesh's offer to assist him, but Ravi was determined to make it on his own, by the sweat of his own brows. So far, he had saved up a good sum of money but not quite enough to start up his business, and he had a far way to go before he could afford to build a house. Through rain and sunshine he toiled and toiled, wearing himself to exhaustion. Nani now regretted she ever told Ravi the proverb, *Too much sit down ah bruck trousers*, for now Ravi was doing the opposite, working too hard, and she now wished he would sit down during the week and take a rest. Indira was by his side, working as gruellingly hard in the vegetable garden, and never once complaining of the struggle.

Indira was ridiculed by some in the town for marrying a poor man where she had to struggle in life when she could have had a materially rich life with a banker's son and not have to suffer, as they thought she did. But little did they know. She never considered her life a poor one. As a little girl, she had chosen the mystique of her Nani's mud stove over her grandfather's big, yellow mansion, and this was an indication of who she was, even then. And Nani, the wise old woman, had taught her things that money simply cannot buy; Indira's wealth was attaining contentment and happiness and peace in just *being*, and she only pitied those who did not know better and relied on material gains and conceit to make them happy.

Ravi was hurt over the way Indira was ridiculed but was impressed at how she handled it. She stood firmly by her decision to be with him, and she ignored what she thought of as silly gossips and stuck by Ravi's side, saying that she would rather decline the whole world of wealth for the true love of a poor man than sell herself to a rich man who did not love her or whom she did not love, and a man who saw her only as part of his possessions. Even if she had to live the rest of her life being materially poor, it did not matter, neither did what people had to say about it, for she as well as Ravi realised that no money in the world could buy the love, happiness, contentment, comfort, security and, above all, peace that they had found in each other.

And, so, through hard work and illnesses and, sometimes, ridicule, Ravi and Indira adhered to each together, and they frolicked in the sea of inebriating ecstasy and loved as though there was no tomorrow, happy just to be together.

* * *

It was not long before that certain tragedies came knocking on the door, interrupting the little world of happiness that Ravi and Indira had built. It was now on a Friday evening and what a dark night it was, without even a star in the sky, and the air was warm and still. At this time, Ravi and Indira were sitting upstairs on the front verandah, relaxing after a long week's work, and Nani was sitting in her rocking chair in her room at the bottom-house, with the door wide open and with the kerosene oil lamp, hanging above, burning low.

From where Nani was sitting, she could plainly see Solomon and Rani. Given her affinity with the animals, she noticed that there was something unusual about them tonight; Solomon was lying on the earthen ground and Rani was standing, instead of the other way around, and Rani was circling Solomon and was mooing as though crying. Instinctively, Nani felt something was wrong and she got the kerosene oil lamp and went over to check on Solomon, and she let out a piercing cry on this dark night, for Solomon was as still as a log. "Oh, my faithful donkey!" Nani wailed as she placed the lamp on the earthen ground, "Oh, my faithful donkey, why did you have to leave me?"

Ravi and Indira heard Nani's cry and rushed downstairs to find Solomon lying dead on the ground, and Indira screamed and cried, and she held Ravi and said, "Poor old Solomon. Why did he die so suddenly?"

"Why did you have to leave us now?" Ravi said, as he also started tearing up, for, over the time he had lived with Nani, he had grown attached to the old, faithful donkey.

If Rani could have spoken, she would have also asked Solomon why he had to leave her so suddenly, her companion whom she had known all her life, but all she did was stood there looking down at Solomon and letting out heart-rending bellows to break one's heart.

It was a dark and sad night, for death had stolen the happiness of the moment and brought only sorrow. Nani continued to weep poignantly, like a mother who had lost a child, for though one may think it was just an animal that had passed, for Nani, it was a precious life she had lost. Solomon was her work partner and had carried her from and to the market for many years, in rain and sunshine, always carrying the load, the burden of making a living, and never once braying a complaint, though stubborn at times.

Nani must have spent a couple of hours crying nonstop, and when she dried her eyes, she told Ravi to go and borrow a neighbour's tractor to take Solomon away to bury him in the backdam—back woods. Ravi got the tractor and tied Solomon to the back of it, and Nani and Indira watched with tear-brimmed eyes as Solomon was hauled away in the dark of the night, with only the tractor's tail and headlights' beams lighting the dirt street, and they stood there until the tractor disappeared down the street and Solomon was out of sight. Ravi took Solomon and buried him in the backdam that night as Nani instructed him.

When Ravi returned, he had to console a crying Indira all night, and Nani sat with Rani all that night, for Rani was sorely distressed. Rani paced the bottom-house and mooed and mooed, and over the next few days she stopped eating and would just lay on the earthen ground and would not move. It broke Nani's heart to see Rani grieving that way. Rani missed Solomon and was lonely for him, for the two of them were together ever since they were babes. Rani continued to pine away for Solomon day after day, then one day, Rani's old heart gave away; she died of a broken heart. Rani was buried next to her companion, Solomon, in the backdam. And there they would rest together forever in eternal life.

For a whole week, Nani and Indira mourned the deaths of their faithful animals. To console them and assuage their grief, Ravi went out and purchased another donkey and cow. He named them, respectively, Solomon, and Rani. In time, the happiness of life returned, and things returned to normal, and they once again had fresh cow's milk from Rani, and Solomon was off carrying the load to the market.

And Ravi and Indira continued to work and play as they settled down in life.

19

Radhika Leaves For Canada

Ravi had now nearly saved up the money for his fabric stores' business idea and had drafted a meticulous plan with his innate business acumen, but having to execute the plan was causing him a great deal of anxiety.

He was pacing around the earthen ground of the bottom-house while Nani was laying in the hammock on this late Saturday afternoon, as the luminous rays of the sun were just turning to gold, and he said to her, "What if things don't go as planned."

"Have some faith, boy," Nani said.

"But what if the business does not take off and I end up losing all the money I worked so hard for."

"What ifs' would get you nowhere," Nani said.

"I'm beginning to get cold feet, Old Gal. I'm nervous about taking the risk," Ravi said, evincing the skepticism he felt.

"It is natural to feel this way at this stage, boy, but let me pass on to you a wise old proverb," Nani said, and she went on to relay thc Guyanese proverb, *Turtle can't walk if he nah push he head outa he shell*, explaining that: "You would not get anywhere in life if you do not take risks."

"I agree it is a wise saying," Ravi said. And after Nani went on to tell him stories about the risks she had taken in her own life, coaxing him along the way, the doubts and nervousness he had recently developed left him and was replaced by a burst of what he initially felt; ambition and optimism.

Straightaway, he dashed upstairs to the kitchen and, while Indira was cooking, he sat at the table and went about perusing his business plan in the light of the kerosene oil lamp, checking off every detail, from the very first store he would open, the rental, setting up of the store, hours of operation, to the fabrics and contacts he had sourced out, to setting his prices and even projecting the profits to be made. "No more menial job for me, cutting cane," he said out loudly, "I will take the risk and give this business a great start, opening one store at a time, and someday I will become a successful businessman!"

Indira responded, saying, "I believe in you, Rav. I have the confidence that you will make it happen."

"Thank you for standing by me and my dreams, Indi," Ravi said, and he rose from his seat and hugged and kissed his wife in front of the mud stove.

* * *

Indira supported Ravi in his endeavours as they continued on in their married life, and she embraced his family with love and respect. Mr. and Mrs. Singh reciprocated likewise, in fact, they embraced Indira with the same affection they showered on their own daughter, Radhika, doting on her, for they thought she was God sent for their beloved son. Radhika found a sister in Indira, and though she was four years older than her, the two quickly became friends. Unlike her parents whose obligation to their rice field kept them in Skeldon, Radhika visited Rose Hall often, by bus, to spend time with her sister-in-law and brother, and Nani.

In early August, following Ravi and Indira's first wedding anniversary in June, on this sweltering mid-afternoon, Radhika came calling at Nani's gate, and Indira, who was alone at home working on transplanting palm plants in the flower garden in the front yard, left what she was doing and dusted the soil from her hands and rushed to greet her effusively with hugs and kisses.

Radhika was a petite young woman endowed with very attractive light complexion and luxuriant black hair that flowed down her back way down to her knees. Today, as usual, she was nicely dressed, in a lilac shift dress and was wearing white high-heeled slippers, and Indira could not help noticing that the demeanour of her pretty, round face and limpid, big, brown eyes seemed particularly radiant.

As they were making their way up the dirt pathway leading from the gate, Radhika said to Indira, "Oh, bouji, you don't know how I've been dying to talk to you since last week." She paused then and handed Indira a small, flower-patterned cloth bag. "But before I tell you anything, first open the bag and see what I brought for you."

Indira paused in the pathway and opened the bag to find a small, blue bottle of perfume, and she exclaimed, "What a beautiful blue bottle! Thanks." Then she asked, "But what's the occasion that you bring me a gift, sis?"

"I brought you this just because you married my brother," Radhika said with a benign look on her face. "I will forever be grateful to you for making my brother a happy man."

"Oh, Radhika," Indira said, "you're so sweet and kind and generous to me, and so considerate. Never in my dreams have I thought I would have such a wonderful sister-in-law like you. What have I done to deserve such treatment from you?"

"I just told you; you married my brother," Radhika smiled and said. But, really, that was who Radhika was; a young woman with a golden heart, the epitome of kindness, the appellation she was known as.

Indira smiled at her in return and then took her by the hand and led her to the backyard, saying as she did, "Come, sis, sit with me under the tamarind tree where it's not as hot in the shade there, and tell me why you've been dying to talk to me. I can tell by the glow on your face and the twinkle in your eyes that it must be something good."

A smile swept across Radhika's face again and she widened her big, brown eyes and said, "It is." And she followed Indira to the backyard, past the fowl coop, and pond, which was occasionally disturbed by fishes jumping and splashing water on the water lilies and the open shame-baby weeds, causing the weeds to close up. Both young women went and sat down on the log under the tamarind tree, then, with a tremor of excitement in her voice, Radhika blurted out, "Rohan asked me to marry him!" Rohan was the young man whom Radhika had loved and lost to another woman, about which she had confided in Indira in the course of their friendship.

Indira was taken aback by the news, and she said, "But you told me Rohan is already married to someone else."

"Not anymore," Radhika said, and she went on to explain: "I fell in love with Rohan when I was fifteen, and when he had chosen to marry Sunita, I thought I would never endure the pain of it. But I found the strength and did so. My heart always longed for him, though, and as fate would have it, his marriage didn't work out; Sunita left him and took off with another man. And Rohan realised then she never really loved him as he had thought she did, and he realised how much I love him."

"But does he love you, Radhika?"

Without dithering, Radhika answered, "I know he does, bouji. I can see it in his eyes and hear it in his voice." And Radhika continued on to say, "He visited me just last week and told me that he had made a terrible mistake in marrying Sunita, and he felt sorry that he had hurt me. He said that he had loved me all along, and still does, but was carried away by the lures of Sunita. And he went down on his knees and pleaded for me to marry him."

"And did you give him an answer?"

"Not yet, because there are other things to consider," Radhika replied dubiously. "You see, Rohan's uncle has sponsored him to Canada and he expects to get through soon and move there. Marrying Rohan means that I would have to emigrate to Canada, also, which means I would have to leave Ma and Pa behind."

"But this is a good opportunity for you, sis," Indira said. "You always care for everyone else around you, and it's time for you to think of yourself. Ma and Pa would do just fine. Ravi will be here for them, and they would still have one daughter left here. Trust me, I will be here for them. Getting married to someone you love is a good opportunity in itself, but you're also getting a big chance to go to Canada to live. How many people around here dream of this? Don't pass up on this opportunity, take it, I urge you to do so, sis."

At the prompting of Indira, her confidant, Radhika began to reconsider things, now seriously thinking of her future and, after a long period in silent contemplation, she said, "You know, you're right, bouji, I should take this opportunity, because I'm now twenty-one and if I don't, I'm afraid I will become an old maid!"

The young women both laughed, and Indira asked, "Did Rohan say when he wants to marry you?"

"He wants to marry before his papers from Canada arrive in the mail, which should be very soon."

"Then marry him quickly before he leaves," Indira said.

"He'll drop by the house tomorrow to meet with Ma and Pa and ask for my hand in marriage. It would come as such a shock to them when they learn that I would have to leave them and go to Canada, and I know it will make them terribly sad, but, like you, I'm sure they would be happy for me to take this opportunity instead of staying here and working in the rice field."

"I know they would be happy for you," Indira said, knowing that her in-laws would not condemn their daughter's life to drudgery. "You deserve a good life, sis."

"And a good life is what Rohan promised me," Radhika said. "His uncle has secured a job for him, to manage one of the two clothing stores he owns in Toronto, and Rohan said, if I agree to marry him, I don't have to work if I don't want to when I get there. He said I can sit around and eat apples and grapes all day long while he works to make a living. All he asked of me is to bear him a couple of children."

"That sounds fair," Indira said, "you make babies and take care of them while he works."

"Talking of babies, when are you having your first one?" Radhika asked.

"Rav and I will start trying when he starts building our house," Indira said with a smile, with traces of diffidence still present in her demeanour.

"Speaking of the devil, where is he? I thought by now he should be coming home from cutting cane."

"Your brother is no longer a cane cutter, sis. He's the owner of a business; a businessman," Indira said with a gleaming smile, proud of Ravi's accomplishment.

Radhika looked surprised, and she said, "I didn't think he had enough money to open a business just yet. How and when did this happen? It must have been very recently."

Indira led Radhika to the front yard in the flower garden and showed her about a couple dozens of pots of palm plants she had just transplanted, and she explained to Radhika: "Rav was eager to launch the business but he fell a little short in his savings, so I started growing plants to sell to earn some money to contribute. Nani takes them to the market and sells them for me, and in the first couple of weeks she sold everything I had and I made some good money, and I contributed every penny of it to Rav's business, so he was able to open the first store, which he did just last week. He's renting a small space by the roadside, not far from Grandpa's house."

Just as Indira was breaking the news to Radhika, Nani arrived home from the market and she hugged and kissed Radhika, and having overheard what Indira said, with a proud smile, she added, "The boy used a wise tactic and launched the store with a sale and he's done very well for the first week."

Indira then said, "Our neighbour, Joan Williams, and her daughter, Francine, are both seamstresses, as you know, and they, along with all of their many customers, were informed of the store opening and they all rushed in last week to shop for fabrics. Nani and I have also been spreading the word and rounding up other people to shop at Rav's store, and, now, Rav has a steady flow of customers."

"I'm so happy for buddy," Radhika said with her face emanating the expression.

Nani left momentarily and went to get a couple of green coconuts, and she chopped the tops off with a cutlass and returned and handed them to the girls to quench their thirst on this hot day, then she excused herself and went and sat in the hammock and began counting the money in her green cloth money bag—money she made from selling at the market that day—leaving the young women to continue on with their discourse.

Indira resumed her seat on the tree stump, where she had been working on the palm plants earlier, and she had an aluminium bucket nearby and turned it upside down for Radhika to sit on, and both the girls sat down in the flower garden and finished their coconut water. Radhika then split the coconuts with a cutlass and, while she was scooping the jelly and eating it, Indira returned to transplanting the palm plants. Radhika said she would stay on until Ravi gets home from work, and the two girls gaffed until the rays of the sun turned to a golden hue and it was time for Indira to cook dinner.

Just as Indira was wondering what to cook, Shazam dropped by with a big, live *houri fish*, and fresh shrimps he had just caught. Indira decided she would fry the shrimps with bora, and she and Radhika went to the vegetable garden and picked some, while Nani sat by the stone slab and pipe at the foot of the backstairs and cleaned the shrimps, and the fish to *bunjal*—dry curry, with dhal and rice. As soon as Nani was finished, the three of them went up to the kitchen and lit the mud stove and started cooking.

By now the sapphire-blue of dusk had gathered and Nani lit the kerosene oil lamp and hung it up in the kitchen, which was saturated with the smell of fried and curry spices and the maar from the boiling rice. Just as the cooking was almost finished, the entrepreneur arrived home from work, looking finely groomed in his work attire, with hair he now wore in medium length with a side part.

"Businessman!" Radhika exclaimed as Ravi entered the kitchen from the back steps.

Ravi beamed from ear to ear and hugged his sister and said, "We did it, sis! If it wasn't for Indi's help I wouldn't be a businessman just yet." He then turned and planted a kiss on Indira's forehead and handed her the cloth bag he had in his hand, and said, "I picked this out with love in my heart for you, Indi."

When Indira opened up the bag, she found a piece of shiny, copper-coloured fabric of silk and, affectionately, she teased him, saying, "If you keep fetching me fabric from your store, you would no longer be a businessman, Rav." Ravi pinched her dimpled cheek and just smiled.

Dinner was finished cooking now, and Nani dished out food for the youngsters and she sat with them at the kitchen table and, as the oil lamp was softly burning, they joined Nani in eating the hot houri fish curry with shrimps and bora with their fingers. Dinner conversation now revolved around Radhika. She could not wait to tell Ravi about the recent happenings in her life and broke the news about anticipating marrying Rohan, at which time, Nani learned of it, also, and both Nani and Ravi were happy for Radhika and showered her with many blessings.

Radhika left for home that evening feeling intensely euphoric, and the next day when Rohan met with her parents and asked for her hand in marriage, she happily agreed. Things happened rapidly from there on. The two were married in a fever of excitement the following week in a private ceremony, and within a couple of weeks, by the end of August, Rohan received his landed immigration papers and he booked a flight and left for Canada. There he started his job and sponsored Radhika, who, after filling out the necessary forms and doing her medical examination, had the impatient task of waiting everyday for the postman to arrive with her papers.

* * *

There was no way of expediting the process, and after waiting for an entire year, precisely in August of the following year, Radhika's papers finally came in the mail and the time had now come for her to leave for Canada. She arranged to leave from Rose Hall, and had arrived the day before to stay over at Nani's house, while her parents stayed at her cousin Padmini's home, right there in Rose Hall. That August night, she barely slept. She was up by the

446

crowing of the fowlcocks and was in the kitchen with Ravi and Indira, who were up with her for most of the night, talking and assisting her with packing her suitcases. They were now busy preparing foods to take on the trip to the airport.

As the kerosene oil lamp burned softly, and the wood in the mud stove crackled, clouding the kitchen with the spicy smell of the foods cooking, an enchanting excitement lingered about in anticipation of Radhika's trip to Canada, but there was also a certain sadness that hung in the warm, still air of the dark morning that she would soon be leaving.

As Radhika was standing by the kitchen table, clapping hot roti that Indira was making on the mud stove, Ravi, who was packing a basket with foods and fruits and drinks for the trip to the airport, paused and said to her, "I can't express how terribly sad and heart-broken I am that you're leaving, sis, yet, on the other hand, I'm so happy that you're finally going to be with the man you love and start a new life, in Canada of all places, the land of milk and honey."

"I feel much the same way, too," Radhika said. "I'm sad that I'm leaving and, at the same time, excited that I would finally join Rohan. And I can't wait to see Canada; I think of all the grapes and apples I will get to eat there!"

"And you would actually get to see snow," Indira said. "Oh, Radhika, I'm so happy for you."

"Bouji," Radhika said to Indira, "I will miss you. My heart breaks because of having to leave all of my loved ones behind." And she looked at Ravi and said, "Buddy, I will never forget you. I will think of you always."

447

Ravi got choked up at this, but he fought back his tears as he said, "Radhika, you've been a good sister to me, and I'm sure you have some idea how I'll miss you. Pa and Ma will miss you terribly, also."

Radhika broke down and started crying then, and she said, "I don't know how they'll manage without me, buddy. You left home, now I'm leaving and leaving them all alone. Ma is getting sickly and I don't know how much longer she can work in the rice field."

Ravi took Radhika in his arms to console her, and he patted her head and said, "Stop crying Radhika or you'll make me cry, also. Now, don't you worry about Pa and Ma, I will make sure they're taken care of. Dry your eyes now, sis. Pa and Ma will be here anytime now."

As Ravi spoke, they heard the rumbling of the wheels of Padmini's jeep on the dirt street, and Ravi rushed to the sitting room window, and in the semi-darkness of the early morning, saw his parents and Padmini getting out of the jeep.

Ravi went down to meet them, leaving Indira and Radhika to finish the cooking, and they gathered at the bottom-house. Nani woke up then and they all started discoursing about Radhika's departure, arousing a melange of happy and sad feelings. And as the darkness of night faded and the dawn-blue of this auspicious morning emerged, more relatives, and friends came calling at the gate, all expecting to escort Radhika to Timehri Airport in a bus they rented.

Everyone was spruced up in fresh new clothes for this special occasion; the women in custom-made dresses with some in elegant coiffures and wearing makeup and stockings and high-heeled shoes, and the men were in their shirt-jacks and trousers and were sporting well-groomed hair and polished shoes. Joan Williams sewed new dresses for Radhika, Indira, and Nani, and, Francine, who was also going to the airport and taking along Albert, designed and made her own, and they all got dressed up themselves. The twenty-two-year-old Radhika, the going away girl, looked fit enough to get on an aeroplane, immaculately dressed in a royal blue crimplene dress, beautiful against her clear skin, with her long, black hair flowing loosely down her back, and she was also wearing sheer, dewy makeup and stockings and high-heeled shoes.

The rented bus soon arrived at Nani's home on this early morning, carrying some family and friends who had boarded it in Skeldon, and everyone else embarked, taking along baskets of copious foods, fruits, and drinks, and soon the bus rumbled down the dirt street and took off for the ferry in New Amsterdam. The early morning breeze was blowing through the open windows of the bus as it made its way up the narrow main road, and along the way, it passed expansive fields of sugarcane and rice, tall trees, little houses on stilts, and cows and donkeys and goats and sheep grazing in the lush countryside. There was much chattering in the bus as it journeyed along, and the momentary burst of laughter, but there was also a gnawing sadness that hung about heavily.

Radhika was sitting by the window next to her mother on the right side of the bus, her mother's pallid face contorted with the sadness of her daughter's departure, and her small, frail body feeling drained of all energy. Radhika fought back tears as she clasped her mother's thin hands in hers and looked out at the lush greenery of the countryside as the bus rolled on. She was not only leaving her mother and father, family and friends, but she was also leaving the soil of her land for another, and now her heart was even more torn, oscillating between the dejection of leaving and the excitement of going to Canada to meet Rohan.

Radhika's father, a sturdy, dark-skinned man, who was sitting right behind Radhika and his wife, noticed the sad eyes of his daughter as she was looking out the window. He tried to look brave, but no one could see the tears in his heart over the departure of his only daughter. He reached in front and laid his hand on her shoulder, and with a strong and steady voice, he said, "Don't be sad, child. This is a great opportunity for you. Today you'll cry, but tomorrow will bring you much joy and happiness."

Nani, who was sitting beside Mr. Singh, took out her handkerchief from her dress pocket and started wiping away the tears that had settled in her eyes, and she said to Radhika, "I will miss your visits, my dear, but go in peace. And worry not yourself over your Pa and Ma, for the boy will take care of them."

Ravi, who was sitting beside his cousin Padmini in the seat across the aisle from Radhika and their mother, said, "I assured her of that already. You've been a good and faithful daughter to Pa and Ma, sis, now go and start your new life and make your husband happy. I wish you all the best."

Others then chimed in with their well wishes, but all of that only saddened Radhika even more and she broke down and started crying. Her mother started crying then, and Ravi broke down, also, and his father, who was trying to act brave, succumbed to tears, and Padmini and all the others joined in, all with their handkerchiefs out to wipe their tears. Exacerbating the situation, Albert, who was sitting in the seat in front of Radhika and her mother, had his transistor radio on and John Denver was singing *Leaving On A Jet Plane*, making everyone cry even more vehemently.

The bus driver, a big, fat, light-skinned man with a couple of missing upper teeth, appeared to be the only one not crying. He found the poignant cries of the others to be a distraction to his driving but he endured it for a while, thinking it would stop soon, but the deluge of tears proliferated and soon became an irritant to him, and he stopped the bus and stood up and declared, "If you all don't stop crying, I will turn this bus around and not take you to the airport!"

Francine, who was sitting beside Indira in the seat in front of Ravi and Padmini, said to Indira, "I think he means it. We should stop our crying before Radhika misses her flight to Canada. Let's dry our eyes now, Indira." But no one could help themselves at that moment and they continued to ball their eyes out. At the moment, something like a good antidote of laughter was needed for the terribly sad situation.

Out of the blue, the driver then started to laugh for no reason it seemed, holding his big, fat belly as he did, his missing front teeth conspicuous, and he threw his big self onto the floor of the bus, rolling with fits of laughter.

Radhika was the first to stop crying; she began to laugh over the way the bus driver was laughing and the funny way he looked with his bulk of a body rolling on the floor and his missing front teeth, and then Radhika's mother burst out laughing, and Ravi and Padmini and Indira and Francine and Albert and Nani caught on, then Radhika's father and the others did, also. Soon, everyone on board the bus was laughing over the laughing bus driver, who was laughing over nothing at all, except to alleviate the crying and make the others laugh; an act he would perform whenever he would take a bus load of disconsolate, crying passengers to the airport.

Once he accomplished just that, he returned to his seat and continued on the journey, saying as he did, "If I hear one person crying again, I will turn this bus around and take you all back home. Do you hear me?"

From thereon, it made for a pleasant drive for the bus driver for there was much laughter now. And there was much talk about all the good things about Radhika, for everyone knew her to be a kind and sweet person; a good soul of impeccable character, who made an indelible impression on everyone who knew her. As the bus journeyed on, the group opened the baskets of foods, fruits, and drinks they brought along and they began to eat and drink. Soon after they were finished, they arrived at the New Amsterdam Ferry Stelling where there was a whole lot of chattering and hustling and bustling as passengers and vehicles boarded the Torani Ferry.

There was a certain charm to this warm morning and a sense of strangeness was in the air, for it was the first time that everyone on board the bus was going to the Timehri Airport to send someone off to Canada, and the first time for others to travel the ferry across the Berbice River. A warm wind was now sweeping across the sepia-coloured water of the Berbice River, and the sound of the waves was heard lapping against the boat as it cut through the water and, above, the birds cackled as they soared and swooped down to catch fish in the river.

Indira and Radhika sought out some time to be alone, and they got out of the bus and went and stood by the railing of the boat, in a quiet corner away from the cacophony of chattering of the other passengers.

"Promise me you'll write to me, sis," Indira said as she took Radhika's hand and held it tightly.

"I will write to you, bouji," Radhika promised, "and I'll tell you about Rohan and Canada."

"I'll miss you, sis," Indira said and reached out and hugged Radhika.

"I'll miss you, too, bouji," Radhika said as tears settled in her eyes.

"Don't cry now, sis, or you'll make me start crying again," Indira said. But neither Radhika nor Indira could hold back their tears, and the two held each other and cried. Then, on a happy note, Indira said, "When you get to Canada, eat lots of apples and grapes for me."

"I will, bouji, if you promise me two things," Radhika said: "Keep on loving and taking care of my brother for me, and see to it that Ma and Pa are doing fine."

"I promise I will do so. Now, don't you worry your head about anything. Rav and I will see to it that Ma and Pa are taken care of. You can have my word on it." Both the young women then lapsed into tears again.

When the boat was approaching Rosignol Ferry Stelling, Indira and Radhika dried their eyes as they were walking back to the bus, and it was a good thing they did, for when they re-embarked, the bus driver reminded the passengers

453

again that he would desert them if they start crying again, so there was no more crying on the way.

However, when they arrived at the airport and disembarked, they all took out their handkerchiefs and the crying started up again. It was heart-breaking, especially for Radhika's mother, who held on to Radhika until Ravi parted them so Radhika could board the aeroplane. Through the glass windows in the terminal, everyone watched with tear-drenched face as the aeroplane slowly circled the runway, and within moments, it took off from the ground and soared into the hot August afternoon sky, its silver wings glistening in the sun. And it carried Radhika away, up, up in the blue sky, and then it disappeared.

* * *

The postman delivered a letter from Radhika to Indira a month later, in September, and when Indira opened it she found a picture of Radhika biting into a luscious red apple with a bunch of wine-coloured, plump grapes in the other hand, and along with the picture was another envelope addressed to her parents.

The letter to Indira read:

Dear Bouji,

My flight to Canada was a strange but exciting one as I had never been on an aeroplane before, as you know. The cabin of the aeroplane was nice and cool, and the stewardesses were very friendly. Flying through and above the clouds was quite a dreamy experience. I cried for the most part of the flight, though, out of the sadness of leaving and the happiness of seeing my husband. I arrived in Toronto in the evening, and, my, what a sight it was descending on the city of lights! It was simply dazzling. I have never before seen so many lights in my life.

When I landed, Rohan was right there at the airport to receive me and I can't describe the joy I felt when I saw him. I was thrilled, also, to be in Canada. Everything around seemed to be so new and strange at first. We had to take an escalator at the airport terminal and I found myself in an embarrassing situation because I was actually scared to get on the thing. While getting on, I tripped and made a fool of myself, I thought, but Rohan only found it funny and laughed.

It's summer time in Canada, and it was a hot and humid night when we left the airport. I was amazed by the streaming highways as we made our way to the downtown apartment Rohan rented for us. The city streets are all brightly lit and lined with numerous shops and tall buildings of glass and concrete, and beautiful houses, and the streets are paved and clean. What a beautiful city it is!

I soon settled into our one-bedroom apartment and I'm trying to get use to things like air conditioning and microwave and telephone and television. There's so much to see and learn here in this cosmopolitan city. What a fascinating way of life, with so many opportunities! I stayed home for the first couple of weeks and Rohan took time off work and took me for a tour around the city and showed me the good as well as the bad and seedy side of it, and I ate apples and grapes every day, some especially for you. Rohan wanted me to stay home and be a housewife, but I

455

told him I wanted to work, so he hired me to work as a sales clerk in the clothing store he manages for his uncle. Oh, you wouldn't believe the beautiful clothes they have here, and it's so exciting working in the city, and there're so many stores to shop at and places to eat!

Though I'm having a good time, I do miss home terribly and am homesick at times. I miss Ma and Pa, especially. I cry for them everyday. I've enclosed a letter for them, as you will find, and ask that you read it to them. I've sent along some money for them, also. Tell my brother that I send him my love, and please give my love to Nani and Padmini, also.

Sincerely,

Radhika

Indira wrote back, telling Radhika she was happy to hear about her flight and how things were going with her and Rohan, and that she was thrilled to learn about her experience of Canada in the summer time. She wrote that she and Ravi visited his parents and she read her letter to them, and she said they missed her, also, and sent their love, and gratitude for the money she sent them; a real boon to their livelihood. She also mentioned to her that Ravi was doing well with his business and had just opened up a second store in early September in New Amsterdam, and that he was also assisting their parents financially, and so was she, with the money she was making from her palm plant business. She wrote that Ravi and Padmini said to pass the message on to her that they missed her and sent their love, so did Nani.

The next letter from Radhika came in October of the same year, and Radhika wrote:

Dear Bouji,

It's now autumn in Canada and the trees have changed colours from green to brilliant yellows and reds and rusts. Rohan and I took a walk in High Park just yesterday and I stood under a great maple tree and looked up and the leaves were bright yellow and so pretty, I was lost in their beauty. It's so much fun seeing the leaves fall; it's almost like walking through a fairyland. What a beautiful time of the year it is. Though, it's starting to get cold and I can feel it through my bones. This will take some time to getting adjusted to.

Things are going better than I dreamed of. Rohan and I are having the time of our lives. He's so good to me, bouji. He treats me with such love and respect, and spoils me with gifts.

I've been working hard and, with some of the money I earned, I bought a few clothes and sweet soap and shampoo and other household goods to send home to you all, so you should receive a box in the mail soon.

Give my love to my brother and Nani, and whenever you see Padmini say hello to her for me, and please give her the box of makeup I've sent for her. Please read the enclosed letter to Ma and Pa and give them the money I sent along, and kiss them both for me.

Sincerely,

Radhika

Indira wrote back to Radhika and said she was happy to hear how things were going with her and Rohan, and that she was excited to hear about Canada in the autumn season. She informed her that she received the box of things she sent and thanked her on behalf of everyone, and she wrote that Padmini was pleased to receive the makeup from her and she sent her gratitude and love. She informed her that Ravi had opened up a third store in Georgetown earlier in October and was doing very well, and that they were saving up money to build a house. She also wrote that both she and Ravi were continuing to assist her parents and seeing to it that they were being taken care of. She also mentioned that she passed her messages on to Nani, Ravi, and Padmini, and she promised to see her in-laws soon and deliver the letter and money and kisses to them.

The next letter from Radhika came in the mail in the month of December of that year, and it read:

Dear Bouji,

It's winter in Canada and I've never seen anything like this in my life. I woke up yesterday morning and looked out the window of our apartment and flakes of snow were falling, and the place was all covered in white as though the deities and angels in the heavens had spent the night dumping tons of white flour on the city. I hurried outside for a walk, and the snow was so soft under my feet, though

458

it was cold. Rohan made a fire by the beach, and we sat around and warmed ourselves and roasted marshmallows.

Christmas is soon approaching and already the city is lit up with Christmas lights, and the shops and malls are brightly decorated and bustling with holiday shoppers. Everyone is talking about a white Christmas. It should be quite an experience spending my first Christmas here in Canada.

I shipped a box of Christmas gifts, so you can expect it in the mail soon. Give my love to Nani and Padmini, and give my brother a big hug for me for Christmas. And please read Ma and Pa the enclosed letter. I've also sent along some money for them as a Christmas gift.

Sincerely,

Radhika

Indira wrote to Radhika that she was thrilled to hear about winter time in Canada and said she could only dream of the white snow flakes. She mentioned that she received the Christmas gifts and thanked her on behalf of her parents, Ravi, Padmini, and Nani, and she mentioned that she gave Ravi a big hug for her for Christmas. She also updated her on how things were going at home and told her the nest egg was getting larger and that they plan to start building the house the following May. And she wrote that they all sent their love.

The two in-laws continued to communicate regularly, and it was in the spring time in Canada, in May of the following year, that the following letter from Radhika arrived, and she wrote:

Dear Bouji,

The leaves are budding and some flowers are now beginning to bloom. I took a walk around this morning, and what a magical experience it was. The fragrance of the flowers filled the air as I walked the streets lined with trees, and the fresh smell of spring is in the air. What a wonderful time of the year it is to see the trees spring to life.

Rohan and I have saved up some money and we're planning to buy a little house right here in Toronto. Hopefully, we'll find one with a view of Lake Ontario. I have some other news to tell you, so I hope you're sitting down. I'm pregnant! And you can't imagine how happy I am! I can't wait to hear when you are.

Give my love to Nani, Padmini, and my brother, and enclosed is a letter for Ma and Pa with some money I've sent along for them.

Sincerely,

Radhika

Indira wrote back to Radhika and said it was a pleasure to hear about spring time in Canada, and that she was happy to hear about the progress that she and Rohan were making in planning to purchase a home. She responded that she was very excited to learn about her pregnancy and was now trying to conceive herself, now that Ravi started building their house, their new acquisition which he hoped to complete by their third wedding anniversary in late June. She also wrote that Ravi had stopped her mother from working and had invested in the rice field business and hired a couple more labourers and that things were now going well with that business, and even her father did not have to work as hard. And she wrote that her parents sent their gratitude for the money she sent and that they all sent their love, and that she was looking forward to her next letter in the mail.

20

Triplets And Ravi Builds A House

Early on this Saturday morning, as the twinkling silver stars were fading and the sky was just turning from black to the sapphire-blue of dawn, Francine got up and left Albert sleeping in bed, and she walked up the street and made her way over to Nani's house to visit Indira, who was in the lamp-lit kitchen cooking breakfast on the mud stove while Ravi and Nani were still sound asleep.

It took her less than five minutes to get to Nani's place, and when she got there she passed Nani's room at the bottom-house and made her way up the backstairs and found the top half of the kitchen door open and, as she was about to unlatch the bottom half, she said to Indira, "I knew I would find you cooking this early, Indira."

Indira looked up as she was rolling out roti dough with the belna on the chowki on the kitchen table, and she saw the radiant face of Francine and said, "What brings you here so early in the morning, my friend? By the glowing look on your face it must be something good."

Francine nodded and smiled, and she entered the cozy kitchen as the wood in the mud stove was burning and took a seat at the table, a position which allowed a vista of the shadowy orchard in the backyard, and then she said, "I've got some exciting news to share with you," and she blurted out, "I'm pregnant, Indira!"

Indira reacted with a pleasantly surprised look, and exclaimed, "Congratulation!"

"You wouldn't believe how excited I am," Francine said, her visage evincing the happiness she felt.

"I'm excited for you, also, my friend" Indira said. "This is the second pregnancy news I've received this month of May. My sister-in-law in Canada just wrote and said she is pregnant, also."

"I'm happy for Radhika," Francine said, "she would make a caring mother. And what about you, Indira, what are you waiting for?"

"Rav and I are trying," Indira replied as she stoked the fire in the mud stove before she threw on a rolled out roti dough on the tawa and began oiling it with ghee.

"So I should receive the news anytime now."

Indira turned around and looked at her friend and smiled as she said, "You should." Then she said, "Why don't you stay and have breakfast with us and we can catch up on the news of our friends."

"Sure," Francine said and straightaway went on to say, "I just learned from Albert that Ling is now playing professional cricket. Albert caught a game on the radio just yesterday."

"That's what Rav told me. I'm so glad for him. So he should be marrying Devika very soon."

"That's what he always intended to do after becoming a professional cricket player," Francine said, and paused before going on to say, "Oh, I met Laliwa at the market just last week and she said things are going better than expected with her and Afonso. She's a happy housewife and he's enjoying being a policeman and riding a motorcycle. I can't

463

believe they've been married for almost a couple of years already."

"And our third wedding anniversary is coming up at the end of June, just next month. I can't believe that, also," Indira said, and paused before asking, "By the way, did Laliwa mention anything about Sally? Did she write recently?"

"Yes, she did. Sally is presently in nursing school, so is her Guyanese dougla boyfriend, Neville. As soon as they both complete their studies they plan to tie the knot and return sometime in the near future to Guyana to live and work."

"I'm happy to hear that," Indira said, and she handed Francine the eggplant she had picked just that morning from the garden and said, "Francine, help me to roast this baigan and cut up a piece of onion and make some choka with it while I'm finishing up with cooking this roti and drawing some tea."

Francine took the eggplant and put it on the wire mesh on the mud stove to roast and, as she was cutting up the onion at the kitchen table, she and Indira gaffed a while longer about their friends, then she reverted to her pregnancy. "I'm hoping to give birth to a baby girl, but I'm making plans for either a girl or a boy," she said.

"And what does Albert want?"

"It doesn't matter to him. He's just happy that he'll be having a child," Francine said, and paused before going on to say, "I'll design the baby clothes myself and will be making shimmies and cloth napkins, and I'll crochet booties, instead of buying store-made clothing."

"When my turns comes, I hope you'll do the same for me," Indira said.

"Well, of course, my friend, and I wouldn't charge you for anything. It would be my pleasure." And Francine went on to say, "Albert will get a local carpenter to construct a cradle and a play pen."

"Isn't there anything you haven't thought of, as yet?" Indira asked.

"My mind's been spinning since I learned the news," Francine said and, lost in the excitement, went on to talk about every aspect of her preparation, down to the baby bottles and toys she planned on getting.

Her chatter went on until they were finished making breakfast and, by that time, Nani and Ravi woke up and they all sat down to eat. Francine shared the exciting news to both of them, and Nani shed a tear of joy, happy for Francine, and pleased that she took her advice and waited a while after marriage before embarking on a life of motherhood.

The conversation over breakfast inevitably revolved around Francine, and Nani went about giving her advice on things she needed to know about caring for herself and the expected baby. Nani then initiated thoughts of having her own great-grandchild, hoping for the day when Indira and Ravi would bear a fruit from their love, a wish she had blessed Ravi with on the night of their wedding, in fact, she prayed for many fruits in due time, and the time was now here to make that happen.

All the talk about babies spurred Ravi on and, soon after breakfast, he took off, dreaming of his own family as he went next door to resume working on his house with a renewed vigour to complete the structure as soon as he possibly could.

* * *

Ravi had started building his house that month of May, right beside Nani, on the land where Shazam and his family used to live. Shazam had moved to another rented house right there in Rose Hall, a much better place for his family, and the owner of his former home had torn down the dilapidated house he used to rent and sold the land to Ravi.

Ravi proved to be an astute businessman, and his fabric store business took off and was thriving. He put people in place to run his three stores and now had the time to work on his house himself. He was his own architect and had cleverly designed the home, a three-bedroom house for the family he was anticipating, and with the help of his father, Shazam, George Williams, Albert, Dr. Ramesh, and a professional building contractor he employed, the house was already taking shape, the foundation laid with four sturdy stilts and the frame in place.

The fresh scent of the greenheart wood and metallic smell of the sheets of zinc permeated the air as the structure was being built in the heat of the long days, and every whiff of it excited Ravi, thrilling him after waiting for what seemed like eons to be finally building his own house. Even the cacophony of the hammering of nails and sawing of wood was pleasant to his ears. He worked assiduously and oversaw every little detail of the execution of his plan, working long hours in the day time, and even staying up late in the nights with the watchman who guarded the building materials from thieves. He would sit with the old man in front of the makeshift cabin in the backyard, by a kerosene oil lamp, and while the moths fluttered around the flame of the lamp, he would look up at the starry sky and dream in the dark of the nights when the house would be completed as he slapped the mosquitoes biting into him, counting every moment that went by.

Time seemed to be crawling by as slow as a turtle to him, but by the second week of June, when Ravi's skin had turned darker brown from labouring under the sharp rays of the sun, the house on stilts was finished, built with glass windows, and with upstairs shower and toilet; luxuries Ravi designed for his beloved wife Indira.

Painting then commenced. Ravi chose a lime-green colour for the exterior, including, the verandah, and different shades of yellow for most of the interior. Indira chose the colours for the bedrooms, having one done in pink for the girl baby she was hoping for, a blue for a boy, and her and Ravi's room was painted a tropical turquoise sea colour.

Unlike Nani's little, unpainted, old house which had no electricity, with the only lighting being the kerosene oil lamp, Ravi had electrical wiring done in his house and fluorescent tube lights installed in every room. And instead of a mud stove and mud oven, he got a gas stove for Indira and an electric oven, and a sponge mattress and pillows instead of homemade ones made of coconut fibres and feathers. He even got a turntable stereo system with the latest vinyl records of country, reggae and calypso, and Indian music. By now he had used up his savings and had to take a loan to complete the furnishing of the place until more profits were generated from the business, and he hired a carpenter and assisted him in building beautiful furniture for every room. Unlike Nani's earthen bottom-house which had to be always daubed with cow-dung and clay, Ravi had his paved with concrete, and he had a wooden paling and gate built, which he painted in white. A quintessential modern home in those times.

The house was finished and furnished just in time for Ravi and Indira's third wedding anniversary at the end of June, which Ravi had thoughtfully planned for, and he proudly and joyously presented it to Indira as a token of his love for her, as he had promised he would do when they had gotten married. They moved into it on that auspicious afternoon of that same day, and it took them no time at all to ensconce themselves into the comforts of their new home.

Indira was excited about the modern house and the amenities Ravi had laboured so arduously to provide for her. The first thing she did when she moved in that afternoon was cook. She made fried pork on the gas stove and baked fresh *plait bread* in the electric oven, and she even fried some *gulgula*—banana fritters, and she and Ravi sat out on the verandah and ate and listened to the crackling of the vinyl records playing country & western songs on the turntable. That night, they slept under their new mosquito netting, on their sponge bed and pillows, in their turquoise, sea-coloured bedroom with glass windows, and, as the white lace curtains were flapping in the tropical wind, they made passionate love, hoping to conceive their first child and begin the completion of their home with children.

Ravi and Indira's third wedding anniversary went by, and that year proved to be another prosperous one for Ravi, monetarily. He was off on his motorcycle early in the mornings overseeing his three stores, and with employees running them, he was free to do other things in the afternoons. He reverted to farming, which was an inborn thing for him to do, for his grandparents and parents were farmers and he was brought up in the rice field business since he was a little boy, and farming was in his blood; he loved the earthy smell of the soil, the fresh, sweet foliage of plants, and labouring in the heat of the sun, and, with watering, he loved to see the seeds grow miraculously; it was a marvel to him.

He was not able to retire Nani and Indira just yet because of the debts he had incurred in completing the furnishing of his home, which he was presently working on paying off, but he wanted to fulfil his promise to solely provide for them both and had that in his future plans. For now, he returned to helping Nani with her vegetable garden and raising chickens, and he cut down the crabgrass in his backyard and cultivated that, also, growing a wide range of vegetables; bora, chorai callaloo, baigan, ball-of-fire peppers, and many more, which was a boon to his income. He wanted to hire someone to assist Nani with selling the surplus produce at the market, but Nani insisted that she was very capable of doing so. He also would have bought a truck to transport all of his and Nani's produce to the market or pay a lady to carry it in a basket on her head, but Nani preferred to ride the old donkey-cart, so Ravi let her do things in her archaic way for that kept his Old Gal happy.

Life went on as such and the following year arrived, and in February Indira received a letter from Radhika with the exciting news that she had given birth to a robust baby boy, and Indira wrote back and shared her happiness in her bundle of joy. But, Indira was still not able to conceive herself. Just a couple of weeks after she received Radhika's letter, Francine sent news to Indira as soon as she gave birth in the hospital, and Indira learned that she was the ecstatic mother of triplets, and that the babies were all girls.

When Francine returned home, she took a day to settle in and get hands-on training in caring for the babies from her mother Joan, then she sent word to Indira with Albert as he was leaving for work the next morning, that she was now back home.

Indira rushed over bright and early that morning as soon as she received the news, and she was so overjoyed and did not know which one of the curly-haired, brown dolls to hold, so Francine handed her one of her babies and said to her, "You better start practising how to hold a baby, my friend, for your time would come one day to do so. I can now give you lessons on how to feed and bathe a baby, and even change napkins. I had a whole day experience of it with Mom showing me exactly what to do."

"I need all the lessons I can get," Indira said and smiled down at the baby as she held her tenderly against her bosom.

"Then come over and assist me with them during the week when Albert is off teaching," Francine said. "Three is more than a handful for me to take care of. Mom has her sewing business to look after and she can't always be here to help out, and my mother-in-law is a sickly woman and I can't count on her."

Indira jumped at the opportunity to assist Francine with the babies. She would get up early in the mornings and hurry her chores and, by mid-mornings, she would walk over to Francine and help her. It brought her much pleasure to care for the babies, especially, because they were Francine's. She learned how to mix powdered milk in right proportions to feed the babies, making sure the milk was lukewarm, and she looked upon the babies adoringly when she fed them. She enjoyed bathing them in the large, white basin and then massaging their tender skin with fresh coconut oil and exercising their tiny arms and legs. And after dusting them with baby powder, she would hold them close and sniff their skin and take in the sweet scent of the baby powder. She was extra careful whenever she put on their cloth napkins, careful not to prick them with the enormous pins that were used to hold the napkins in place. And she took her time when she dressed them in the clothes Francine sewed for them. It brought her joy to caress their tiny fingers and toes as she rocked them to sleep in her arms, and she would smile along with them as they smiled in their sleep in their cradles.

Taking care of Francine's babies made Indira yearn even more for a baby of her own. Francine told her she would make a great mother someday. And Indira simply could not wait for that day to come. She welcomed every chance she got to make love to Ravi, and waited anxiously for the signs of pregnancy. But the weeks went by and turned into months and Francine's babies were growing and Indira was still trying to conceive her own.

* * *

Radhika's baby boy was now four months old, just two weeks older than Francine's babies, and it was now in June that Radhika wrote to Indira and said she was pregnant again. Indira did not reply right away this time, but kept procrastinating.

Just a week later, still in the month of June, on one of her visits to Francine, Francine said to Indira, "I have some exciting news to tell you, my friend. I'm pregnant again!"

Instead of Indira reacting with joy at the news, like she had done with Francine's first pregnancy, a strange feeling took hold of her and she froze and her stomach began to feel nauseous. Her reaction to the news surprised her. The next day she went over to Francine, and as she watched Francine cuddle her babies, she found that it bothered her and she left in a hurry, saying she had other things to do, as an excuse. She did not feel up to visiting Francine the following day, but she did, and she found that being around Francine and the babies did not seem as much fun anymore.

She kept up the charade, though, and kept on going over to Francine to assist her, thinking only of keeping her promise to her friend. Then one day in August while the babies were sleeping in their cradles, as she and Francine were sitting out on the verandah on this hot and sunny afternoon, Francine lifted her dress and was showing off her two-month pregnant belly which was just starting to grow, and Indira got up suddenly and bolted out of there, leaving a bewildered Francine to wonder about her friend's strange behaviour.

Indira struggled with the strange emotions she was having, and it soon became apparent to her that she was being envious of Francine's fertile womb. Her visits to Francine now reminded her of her own struggle to become pregnant and she found she could no longer bear being near to Francine and watch her nurse her babies and watch her belly grow again, so she made up excuses and began avoiding Francine, and, within a few weeks, she totally extricated herself from her. Feeling like an arid desert, she soon started spiralling into the abyss of despondency and depression.

After being gone for a whole day, looking after his business, Ravi came home one evening, as darkness was upon the town, and found Indira sitting on the verandah of their home, the sweeping curve of her lashes dripping with tears.

"Why are you crying, Indi?" he asked.

Indira averted her head in trying to brush him off, and she said, "It's nothing, Rav."

"It can't be that you're crying over nothing," Ravi said. "You're crying like someone with a broken heart and it must be that something is bothering you. I'm your husband and you can tell me anything. I can't bear to see you cry like this. Please, tell me what's the matter, Indi."

"Okay, I'll tell you what's the matter, Rav," Indira said. "Francine and Radhika already started a family and they're both pregnant again and I'm getting frustrated that we've been trying and I'm not getting pregnant myself. What's wrong with me, Rav?"

Ravi reached down and pulled her up to his chest, solicitously, and he kissed her softly on the forehead and consolingly said, "Be patient, my love, you will get pregnant."

"Aren't you getting just a little disappointed with me, Rav?"

Ravi wiped the tears from her eyes and commiserated with her, saying, "We'll keep on trying, Indi. Don't get discouraged and get frustrated, but have faith."

With a great deal of concerted effort, Indira pulled herself out of her depression and took Ravi's advice and demonstrated some faith, throwing herself into decorating the pink bedroom Ravi had built for a baby girl. She had Ravi build a cradle and she painted it white and made a sponge mattress and dressed it in frilly bed spread, and she sewed a white mosquito netting and had fun hanging it over the cradle. She even knitted a soft pink blanket and made a tiny pillow, and she made cloth dolls and crocheted yellow ducklings and stuffed them and placed the toys in the cradle. She also had Ravi build a miniature white dresser for the room, and a quaint bench which they upholstered in pink velvet, and she decorated the walls with pictures of cherubims and made fluffy white mats for the floor. Then she went out and bought pink baby clothes and feeding bottles and everything she needed for a baby girl. After she was finished decorating the pink room, she tackled the task of doing the same for the blue room, for a baby boy. And on the long hot days and nights, she and Ravi tried and tried to conceive. But time went by and they failed to do so.

Indira's faith then began to dwindle and she slowly relapsed into a world of despair. Her faith in her God, to whom she had prayed to since she was a child, was now tested. She was repeating the same prayer, day after day, and there was no answer and she was now starting to question her God, though she still kept on praying, devotedly. The equanimity and contentment and happiness she had acquired over the years through Nani's teachings, seemed to have taken wings and left her heart, leaving her feeling bereft and desolate.

Wrapped up by her own distress, she could not see beyond her suffering and had no idea of how Ravi was feeling. All she knew was that he was being comforting and supportive to her, and he appeared to be patient and hopeful under the circumstance. But things were not as they appeared to be, as she would soon find out.

On a torrid mid-afternoon, the dark sky was pouring rain and thundering with lightings, and she had just finished bathing and was wrapped in a terry cloth towel, with her long, black hair hanging loose and wet, and as she was passing the room they had decorated for a baby girl, she found Ravi sitting on the pink velvet bench. He was leaning forward with his elbows resting on his knees and was clutching the sides of his head. She had never before seen him appearing so distraught, and she entered the room and asked, "What's wrong, Rav?"

Ravi kept his head down as he replied, "I don't want to talk about it, Indira. Just go and close the door behind you, and leave me alone."

"I wouldn't leave you alone until you tell me what's wrong," Indira said, adamantly.

"Just go, Indira. I don't want to bother you with my troubles. You've got enough to worry about."

In the semi-darkness of the room, Indira noticed how strained and doleful Ravi's face appeared and, instinctively, she then had a feeling of what was bothering him. She went and sat beside him on the bench and slipped her arm around him and said, "You know, you've been by my side all along, encouraging me and giving me support on my struggle to conceive a child, but you've never talked about how you're feeling. Talk to me, Rav."

"Leave me alone, Indira."

"I told you I'm not leaving until you tell me what's wrong," Indira said, even though she had an inkling.

Ravi let out a sigh of frustration and said, "Okay, okay, I will tell you what's wrong as you insist, Indira, but it will only make you feel worse." Then after dithering for a moment, without looking directly at her, he went on to say, "I've been by your side, telling you to have patience and faith for a child, and though I'm not a religious man, I have been praying to the many gods of my parents for a child myself, hoping they would hear me. But they haven't so far, and I'am now running out of patience and faith and starting to get discouraged and frustrated that you still haven't conceived a child. I have laboured so hard and built a house expecting a big family, and now I'm struggling to come to terms that it may not happen, and I'm starting to feel devastated."

Even in the heat of the dark, rainy afternoon, Indira could feel the blood in her veins turning cold, and she sat still for a moment trying to assimilate what she just heard, not knowing how to respond at first. Learning of Ravi's true feelings hurt her immensely and she started feeling that she was a big disappointment to him and not worthy of his love, for the thing he wanted so much in life, she was unable to fulfil so far. When she spoke, there was a tremor in her voice as she said, "It's my fault for causing you all this devastation. Sorry for not being able to bear you a child so far. It's all my fault, Ravi." And Indira broke down and started to cry.

Ravi now turned and looked at her, her long lashes wet with tears, and the sadness in her pretty, dark eyes was more than he could take, but he restrained himself from crying and said, "Don't blame yourself, Indi. It's not your fault. I don't want you to go around feeling bad about yourself now. That's why I didn't want to talk about it in the first place. For all you know, it could be my fault." And Ravi pulled her close to him and hugged her and felt her warmth and a deluge of emotions consumed him. Attempting to assuage her pain, he then said, "I want you to know this does not change the way I feel for you. I will love you no matter what, Indi."

A feeling of relief suffused Indira to hear Ravi assuring her of his love for her, and, still weeping, she reciprocated, "And I'll love you, too, no matter what, Rav."

"Then love will see us through this life together," Ravi said, and he was so overwhelmed with emotions now that he could no longer control himself, and he broke down and succumbed to tears himself. Even in that state, he was tempted by his wife's beauty, wrapped in the towel, smelling of a fresh bath, and Indira found herself being madly attracted to her husband at that emotional and provocative moment; two people desperately in love.

Outside, the plump raindrops were beating down hard on the corrugated zinc roof and pitter-pattering wildly against the glass window of the room, sounding like a melancholic rhythm and emanating a mystique that semi-dark afternoon, and Ravi and Indira sank to the bare, polished floor and they made love that day like the boisterous tropical rain itself, holding each other until their tears and frustrations subsided, both desperately hoping that they would get lucky this time and their love would bear a fruit.

21

Twins And Nani Becomes Ill

Francine had not seen Indira for a couple of months now since Indira took off in a hurry after the day she showed Indira her pregnant belly. She had sent word with Albert and her mother several times to Indira, inviting her over to spend some time with her and asking her to continue in assisting her with the triplets, but all she got from Indira were messages of excuse. Her peculiar behaviour led Francine to conclude, rightfully so, that Indira was being envious of her because of her predicament of not being able to conceive, as yet. The two of them had been best friends since they were children and, in fact, had made a pact to be sisters, and they had shared many secrets and adventures as they grew into young women, and Francine never thought that anything would ever come between them and impede their relationship. She missed Indira terribly and it bothered her immensely that Indira had withdrawn her friendship. She confided in her mother about it and Joan told her that Indira needed her space to deal with the pain and frustrations of her circumstance and that she should leave Indira alone until she comes around, and Francine had been doing just that.

But one afternoon, now in her fourth month of pregnancy, in October, Francine took the triplets to visit her parents, and as she was sitting on the back steps of their house, overlooking Nani's house, she noticed Indira was hanging out clothes on the clothes line in Nani's backyard, and she could not resist going over to say hello to her.

When Indira saw her approaching, she dropped the tin can of clothes pins she was holding, and Francine said, "No need to get nervous around me, Indira. I'm just your friend."

Indira did not respond but bent down to gather up the clothes pins scattered on the grass.

Francine went on to say, "I miss you, Indira."

Indira still would not respond. She picked up the last sheet from the wash basin and began hanging it out on the clothes line, seemingly ignoring Francine.

"I wish you would talk to me," Francine persisted on. "Tell me how you're feeling. Tell me how you're doing. If you're having a problem, you can talk to me about it. I'll be here for you like I've always been. There was a time when you used to tell me everything, Indira."

The only sound Francine heard in response was the sound of the wet sheets flapping in the warm wind; Indira got the empty wash basin and headed back to the concrete slab at the bottom of the backstairs, and she turned on the pipe and sat down on the peerah and took the rest of the clothes that were soaking in a basin and started beating them with the clothes beater—wooden paddle, splashes of water spilling onto her dress and bare arms and legs.

Francine followed her and turned off the pipe, and she said, "I've figured out why you've drifted away from me."

Indira kept on beating the clothes.

"You shouldn't be envious of me for having children because you don't have any, as yet. This is not how friends should behave, Indira. I understand your frustrations and I

480

would love to share my babies with you until you have your own. Let me bring them over for you to see."

Indira stopped beating the clothes, wiped the perspiration from her forehead with the back of her hand as the hot sun was beating down on her and, with her eyes lowered, she quietly said to Francine, "I don't want to see you nor your babies, Francine. Just go away and leave me alone."

The words, though softly spoken, stung Francine like a painful sting from a marabunta wasp, and she said to Indira, "You know, I never thought that anything would ever come between our friendship, but I was so wrong."

Indira kept avoiding looking up at Francine. She turned the pipe back on and resumed beating the clothes, and above the noise of the running water and the pounding of the clothes beater, she heard Francine say, "Okay, Indira, if you don't want to see me nor my babies, then I will part ways with you from now on." And Francine walked away from Indira that day with eyes brimming with tears.

As soon as Francine left, Indira dropped the clothes beater, gathered up her wet dress and dashed up the backstairs to the kitchen, and she bolted the door, braced against it, and shook uncontrollably with tears.

* * *

"There is a tear in your relationship and if you don't mend it quickly it will fall completely apart. Sew things up carefully, and don't prick yourself or you'll only make things worse." Those were the words to Indira from Nani when she learned of the situation between Indira and Francine.

But Indira did not heed Nani's advice, for she was too immersed in her own worries of still being unable to conceive. In fact, months went by and the following March came and Francine gave birth to twins this time, both girl babies, and Indira still did not come around. She even failed to respond to Radhika, who had written and told her that she had given birth to a baby girl that same month.

While the scenarios between Indira, Francine, and Radhika were playing out, Ravi kept busy and business went on as usual. His business continued to prosper and he was able to pay off his debts. He also built up his nest egg again and was in a position to retire both Nani and Indira in the month of April, nearly five years after he had made them the promise. He remembered it so vividly when he had said to Indira that one day she would not have to work in the garden alongside of him and spoil her pretty hands. Indira loved to have her hands in the soil, though, and had no intention of quitting, for she shared the same sentiment as Ravi in having an affinity with the soil and plants. Ravi also clearly remembered the promise he had made to his wife while she was cooking on the first morning he was going to cut cane, that someday they would have a cook and she would not have to spoil her pretty hands clapping hot roti. Now he could afford to hire someone to cook, but, like planting, Indira loved cooking and refused this offer, also. Things worked out for the best for Indira, Ravi thought, for the work kept her busy and momentarily took her mind away from her worries and depression, so he let her be.

Ravi's Old Gal, Nani, on the other hand, had been complaining recently that she was having aches and pains, so she was happy to retire from selling at the market to rest her weary bones. Her leisure aided in excessive thinking, though, worrying over Indira's troubles. She had tried to mend the tear in Indira's relationship with Francine but to no avail, and she had tried to talk to Indira about her problem of not being able to conceive, as yet, but Indira refused to engage in any such talk with her. Now Nani's hope for a great-grandchild was diminishing, and she was terribly sad for Indira. And Nani wept bitterly for her grand-daughter.

It was within a month of retiring, precisely in the first week of May, that, unfortunately, the path of life took a wrong turn and Nani became ill. Dr. Ramesh quickly learned of this and offered to help her, but Nani emphatically refused to see him and, for that matter, any other doctor. Just as vehemently, she refused to go to the hospital. Nani was now living in the twilight of her life, and she just kept on saying the old Guyanese proverb, *Nah mind how pumpkin vine run, he must dry up one day,* meaning, that you may want to live forever, but life comes to an end eventually. Nani had climbed the ladder of life and it seemed as though she had almost reached heaven, her retirement mansion, and she held out that she wanted to die at home in peace.

Without a diagnosis it was difficult to tell what exactly afflicted Nani or what her infirmity was, though it appeared there were several things happening simultaneously to her. It was obvious that she had a cold and fever, and she complained of dizziness and severe headaches and acute chest pains, and respiratory problems. Indira, who now had more worries to heap onto her already strained nerves, tried to cure Nani, giving her every drug, tonic, medicinal plants, and herbal tea she had on hand. Nani also had Indira prepare lemons and cloves and ginger tea, breadfruit leaves and calabash fruit pulp, and she even resorted to taking senna pod tea, a laxative she used for its cleansing and antibacterial properties that sent her to the latrine often enough with bad stomach aches. It seemed as though all those remedies worked for a while for Nani became better just in time for Ravi and Indira to celebrate their fifth wedding anniversary at the end of June, but, right after, she fell ill again.

Nani still kept on adamantly refusing to go to the doctor, and without knowing exactly what her ailment was, it was difficult to treat her with the appropriate medicine. She grew gravely ill and was debilitated to the point where Indira now stayed by her bedside and took care of her, day after day and night after night, attending to feeding and sponge-bathing her. Having to care for Nani, Indira soon forgot her own troubles, and her fear of losing Nani was now dominant and became all consuming. It grieved her to see Nani's health continuing to deteriorate over the four-week period in July, and it weakened her spirit to see Nani become *maga*—very thin, a decrepit old woman.

On a warm, inauspicious evening, just as the birds were flying across the sky heading to their evening roosts, Indira gave Nani a sponge bath and dressed her in her nightie, and she combed her long, silver hair then tucked her into bed in her room upstairs, which Nani had moved back into when Ravi and Indira moved into their own house. Indira then lit the kerosene oil lamp and placed it on the bedside table, and as she was feeding Nani some barley soup for supper, Nani, in a feeble voice, said, "I don't have much time left here on earth, Indira, and I'm preparing to meet my Maker beyond the blue sky."

"Hush, don't talk like that, Nani," Indira said and, out of desperation, went on to say, "I'll look for a potion, and when I find it, I'll give it to you to drink and you will live on for many more years."

"There's no point in searching for the elixir of life for no such thing exist, my child," Nani said. "When it's time to go, we must go. I know I wouldn't last for long by the way I'm feeling. And you must start accepting the fact that I will die soon."

Indira placed the soup bowl aside and took Nani's frail hand in hers, and she was quiet for a moment, struggling to assimilate that fact as she looked at Nani's thin face in the flickering flame of the oil lamp. Then she asked, "Are you afraid of dying, Nani?"

Nani appeared unperturbed, so content and peaceful in the face of her own mortality when she answered, "No, child. When the snake bites I will leave this world, but I have no regrets because I have lived a good and peaceful life, and I know where my soul will be when I die. In fact, I'm sick and tired and weary, and instead of enduring this pain, I would rather go home to be with my Lord and rest in eternal peace." And a glowing look of euphoria emanated from Nani's face as if she was welcoming life on the other side.

Indira tenderly stroked Nani's silver hair and said, "I don't know what I'll do without you, Nani."

"You'll do just fine without me, my child. You have a wonderful husband to lean on." Nani then paused for a moment before asking, "Is there anything I can do for you now, child?"

"Yes," Indira said, "bless me, Nani, so I can have a child."

A tear dripped from Nani's eye, and she placed a frail hand on Indira's head and said, "I pray that the Lord would hear my prayer and bless you with children." And she withdrew her hand and continued on to say, "But, perhaps, He has already designed another life for you. Accept your destiny in whatever it may be, my child. If Ravi truly loves you, and I know he does, he would love and cherish you no matter what. In the end, we must all walk alone, children or no children." With that, Nani said, "Goodnight, my dear child."

Indira kissed Nani on the forehead and lowered the mosquito netting, and Nani said her prayers and drifted off to sleep. Indira then put out the oil lamp and she went to sleep on the cot she placed alongside of Nani's bed.

* * *

The next morning, Indira found Nani laying still in bed and, like she had done so many times before, she shook Nani and said, "Wake up, Nani. Wake up." But this time Nani would not wake up. And Indira let out a mournful cry and collapsed.

Ravi came over just then and did not take notice of Nani for his attention was drawn to Indira as she was lying on the floor. He realised she had fainted and he slapped her face gently, and when she regained consciousness, he lifted her in his arms and said, "Let me carry you home and put you to bed and we'll leave Nani to rest some more."

"But Nani wouldn't wake up," Indira said and started crying. "Put me down and let me sit by her side. I want to be with her alone for a moment."

Ravi put Indira down and went over to the bed and then took a look at Nani and he then realised what Indira meant when she said that Nani would not wake up. He gritted his teeth to hold back his tears, and said, "Your suffering is now over, my sweet Old Gal. Rest in peace."

Ravi then left Indira alone in the room to sit beside Nani, and from the sitting room he could hear her weeping bitterly, and saying, "I will miss you so, Nani. I will miss your smile. I will miss your laughter. I will miss all your love. And I will miss watching you cook on the fireside. Oh, Nani, why is there such a thing as death? Why should something so cruel part us? My heart is breaking because I will never be able to see you and touch you again or ever hear your voice again." Indira's cries were so pitiful that Ravi broke down and started crying, also, and he went to the bottom-house and left her alone with her beloved Nani.

When Indira emerged from the room some time later, she went to the bottom-house and found Ravi with George and Joan Williams, Shazam and Fazeela, and Pyari, all of whom Ravi had informed of Nani's passing, and they commiserated with her, shedding tears as they did. As the morning heat rose to a stifling pitch, Mr. Jackson and Mrs. Surjeet, and others joined them at the bottom-house, and there was a great deal of wailing as little old ladies held their heads and beat their chests with their fists, with some even collapsing in the heat. Ravi left the women in the care of the men for a moment and went over to Uncle Manil, the bus driver, and asked him to deliver the sad news of Nani's demise to Uncle Ram up in Skeldon.

Indira had not seen Uncle Ram for five years now, since the incident when he had caught her walking home from school with Ravi. He was angry at Nani for going against him and letting her marry Ravi after what he thought was a scandalous thing they did, seen together in broad daylight on the road, and he had kept away since then. Without Nani around to defend her, Indira was full of trepidation that her nefarious uncle would become belligerent and start a row with her, but when he arrived in the afternoon, along with his wife, Nita, and two sons, Ajay and Ajit, he went straight up to Nani's room and closed the door and sat alone in a chair by Nani's bedside. And he poured his heart out to her, a little too late.

" . . . I always thought you would be around forever, Ma. I can't believe you're now gone," he cried as he sat bent forward on the chair, clasping the sides with trembling hands. A bout of poignant guilt then seized him that he had kept away from Nani for so long, the intense heat of the afternoon only exacerbating his feelings, and he sobbed as he apologised, "Ma, I'm so sorry I stayed away from you, and sorry for also keeping your grandsons and your daughter-in-law away from you. How terrible of me!" Uncle Ram continued to cry as he reflected on the spiteful things he had done to Nani, and he confessed: "Since I was a child I was angry at you because I thought you had loved my sister Geeta more than me." Scenes of Nani's love and kindness then played out in the darkness of his mind, of how Nani would cover him with a sheet when he used to fall asleep drunk in the hammock at nights after behaving badly, of how she would bring him a hot plate of food and leave it beside him, of how she would sit by his side and look at him, when she thought he was asleep, and weep because she loved him, and of how she would kiss him tenderly on the forehead. He shook his head sadly as he came to the realisation that she truly loved him dearly, and he went on to say, "I was so consumed with anger and bitterness over my jealousy that I was blind to the love you had shown me, old lady. How foolish and selfish of me!"

Uncle Ram remembered the numerous times he had behaved badly and how Nani would quote him the Guyanese proverb, *Nobody wants dutty powder,* meaning, that people would not want anything to do with you if you have a dirty reputation. And the other proverb she used to say kept ringing in his ears, *Seven years nah too much fuh wash speck off ah bird's neck,* meaning, that years may pass yet some people would not change their ways. He realised his wicked ways had been incorrigible, and, now, as she laid there silently before him, he said, "If I could turn back time I would do things differently and make you proud of me, Ma. I'm so sorry I brought you so much grief and disgrace, old lady. Sorry for being a mean, drunk scamp." Overcome with grief and regrets, he then swore, "If you're looking down from heaven, I promise I would change my wicked ways, and I will never drink again." In his remorseful state, he searched his heart, and buried deep down within him, below all his pent-up anger and bitterness, he now realised how much he loved his mother. Gripping the sides of the chair now, he shook as tears

489

streamed down his face as he went on to say, "How I wish I had told you that I love you, old lady. Now you're dead and gone and I'll never have a chance to tell you . . ."

While Uncle Ram remained in the bedroom crying his heart out and telling Nani all the things he should have told her when she was alive, Indira was in the kitchen, cautious not to get in his way, and Ravi was holding her as she was sitting at the table, crying. Her world had turned black and the pain she was feeling seemed unbearable. She was bereaved and was left feeling like a lost child. Nani was not just her grandmother but the mother who had brought her up with such love and care, and Indira was having a difficult time accepting her death. And she could not stop crying.

"You have been crying non-stop," Ravi said to her as he handed her a handkerchief, "now dry your eyes for a moment and I'll prepare something hot for you to drink." And Ravi went and lit the mud stove and took the pot of milk hanging over it and set it to warm.

Indira did not dry her eyes, though, for the smoke coming from the mud stove and the crackle of the wood and the warmth coming from it only reminded her of the many, many times she had spent in the kitchen watching Nani cook, and she tearfully said, "I will never again have moments with her in the kitchen, Rav. Some of the most wonderful times I've had with her were right here. I'll miss her so much." And Indira sobbed even harder.

Ravi insisted on saying, "Dry your eyes for now, Indi, for if Nani's watching from above, it would make her sad to see you cry like this, just like it makes me sad. Knowing Nani, she would want you to rejoice because she's in

490

heaven with her Lord. Think of it this way, she's now free from suffering and is in a better place."

Ravi was right in everything he had just said, Indira then realised, and she took comfort in his words and composed herself and dried her eyes, but she could not stop the tears in her heart for nothing could assuage her grief at that moment.

Ravi poured her some hot milk in Nani's favourite enamel white cup and said, "Drink this, and pull yourself together. I'm going over to the house to take care of a couple of urgent business matters and I'll be back soon to join you." And he kissed Indira on the forehead before he left.

Indira sipped the hot milk as she was sitting at the kitchen table, and as she watched the smoke from the mud stove curl its way up and scatter about, she reminisced of the good times she had right there with Nani.

She mused on the many times she had watched Nani cook on the mud stove ever since she was a little girl, of Nani grinding spices on the masala brick, and of the spicy smell of curry and the melancholic sound of a sitar sailing through the old wooden window in the golden rays of the late afternoons. She thought of how Nani, from the kitchen window, would keep an eye on Fazeela's kitchen, and when she did not see smoke coming from her kitchen window, how she would pack a basket of provisions and send her to deliver it to Fazeela. She thought of the times when Uncle Ram would come home with a big catch from fishing and how Nani would sit on the peerah right there in the kitchen and clean the shrimps and crabs and mullets. She thought of Sunday mornings and how Nani would hum hymns

491

while preparing breakfast, and smile and show off her gold teeth. She remembered how Nani would tell her and Francine jumbie stories and stories of her life at nights while they would eat roasted katahar seeds as the wood in the mud stove would crackle and burn down to ashes by the time she was finished. She remembered the time when there was a rainstorm and she and Nani sat around right there in the kitchen and sipped hot coco tea while Nani told her the love story of her and Nana Amar. She thought of the times Nani would iron her clothes with the coal iron on the kitchen table and take her time in starching and ironing her headkerchief, and how softly she moved about on her bare feet. And she thought of the time Nani sat her and Francine down right there in the kitchen and cooked for them and gave them advice before they got married. There were so many memories of Nani that she was now left with, that would never be effaced from her mind. Precious memories of Nani, the wise old woman who, at times, had been the object of humour.

Deeply absorbed in thoughts while fixated on the curls of smoke from the mud stove, Indira did not hear Uncle Ram's footsteps on the creaking floor as he exited Nani's bedroom, but the parting of the strands of beads in the kitchen doorway caught her eye and she turned to look and saw him entering the kitchen, his black and handsome face stained with tears, his obsidian-like eyes bloodshot. She was afraid of him, and afraid that he would start a row and blame her for Nani's death, and she got up and made a dash for the backstairs.

But before she got to the door, Uncle Ram grabbed her arm and turned her around to face him. What happened next was unprecedented and came as a total surprise to her. "Indira, my niece, I don't know what to say," Uncle Ram began and paused, searching for words and looking at the orphan child Nani had so loved, her faced stained with tears, and for the first time his heart stirred with pity for her. It was that, compounded with the sorrow over Nani's death, that cracked his convoluted shell of cruelty and aversion he had towards Indira, and he was propelled into saying, "I've treated you so terribly over the years and had put the poor old lady through hell over you. I'm sorry for all the misery I had caused you. Can you find it in your heart to forgive me for my wrong doings?"

Indira looked askance at him, for she could not believe her ears, and she met his eyes and asked, "Are you really being serious, Uncle Ram?"

"Yes, my niece, I am serious as serious can be," Uncle Ram said, and there was no denying of the sincerity and contrition in his voice.

"But why, Uncle Ram, why did you have to treat me that way?" Indira questioned, as all the years of hurt rose up inside of her and threatened to choke her. "What have I ever done to you to deserve such harsh treatment from you?"

"You have never done me wrong. You have never even said a mean word to me, Indira."

"Then why, Uncle Ram? Tell me the truth. I deserve to know."

Uncle Ram had to face the ugly truth of his cruelty, and spitting it out was not easy for him to do, but with a concerted effort, he admitted, "Firstly, I really thought that Ma had favoured you over my sons. And, secondly, I've been jealous of you ever since Ma took you in as a child, because of how much she loved and adored you. I felt that she had to divide her love between you and me."

"Is that why?" Indira said, feeling relieved to hear the truth of the matter directly from the mouth of Uncle Ram. "Nani had never favoured me over your sons, my cousins, in fact, she yearned to see them. And Nani had so much love in her heart for both of us, and for your sons, and your wife, also, and so much left over that it spilled over to neighbours and friends."

"I realise that now," Uncle Ram said. "I was the same way with your mother, my sister Geeta; jealous. I thought Ma had loved her more than me, and I was very angry with Ma over the years. I turned to drinking thinking it would ease my anger, but that never did, only made things worse." Uncle Ram then paused before going on to say, "Ma and Geeta are not here now and you're the only close family I have left. Please forgive me, my niece, for all the pain I had caused you over my own insane jealousy." And Uncle Ram burst into tears.

Indira could have hated him for all the pain and humiliation he had put her through, but she just did not have it in her heart to do so, in fact, she pitied him as he stood before her, crying and looking so helpless and devastated. "Time will heal my wounds and erase all the things you've done and said to me, Uncle Ram," she said, "but it's a pity that it took the death of Nani for you to realise your wrong doings. I will forgive you in time."

Ravi came back and found Indira holding a sobbing Uncle Ram, and he sensed that was a pivotal moment of reconciliation between the two, and he stood back silently and watched as Uncle Ram cried.

When Uncle Ram collected himself, he said to Indira, "From now on I will be good to you, my niece. And I promise you that from this day on I will never drink again and behave badly."

"I'll hold you to your promises," Indira said, and she gave him a big hug before letting go of him, and all the fears she had of him subsided in that moment.

Uncle Ram then turned and saw Ravi, and he said to him, "We'll have to get an ice box for Ma and make funeral arrangements. I'll need your help, man. Let's go—"

Just then, Ravi's acute sense of hearing picked up a faint call, and he asked, "Did you hear that?"

"Hear what?" both Uncle Ram and Indira asked, and they hushed and listened.

"Son, son, Ram, where are you? Come back to my side, my child . . ."

"It's Ma!" Uncle Ram said, flabbergasted, a look of confusion on his face.

"But that can't be!" Indira said in astonishment, perplexed herself, as was Ravi.

All three of them rushed into the bedroom at that moment and found Nani in bed with her eyes open and dripping with tears.

"Ma! You're alive!" Uncle Ram hollered and dropped to his knees at his mother's bedside and clasped her hand in his. "You're alive! You're alive, Ma, you're really alive!"

Indira screamed, thinking Nani was a ghost, and she collapsed in Ravi's arms. Ravi could have fainted himself from the shock of seeing Nani alive.

Uncle Ram pressed his mother's hand to his face and burst into tears. "We thought you were dead," he said, "but you must have been in a coma, Ma." And the next thing he said to Nani was: "I love you, Ma. I love you. I love you. I love you, old lady." And he continued to effusively pour his love out to Nani.

Nani pulled herself up against the pillow and reached out her frail hands and embraced her son as he took a seat beside her on the bed, and they wept, and Nani said to him, "I love you, too, son. I love you more than you'll ever know." Then after a pause, she went on to say, "I heard every word you said earlier at my bedside."

"You did?"

"I must have been in a coma, but I heard everything you said."

"I meant every word," Uncle Ram said. "I will change my wicked ways. I will be a good son to you. I'll do whatever you say. I will stop drinking and cursing and swearing and fighting. I'll do anything for you, Ma."

Indira regained consciousness just then and stared at Nani for a moment then asked Ravi, "Is Nani really alive, Rav? Is she just a ghost or am I dreaming?"

"You're not dreaming, Indi," Ravi said, "my Old Gal is alive. She was not dead but has obviously been in a coma."

"I can't believe this has happened. I feel I'm in a strange dream," Indira said.

"I am alive," Nani said, reassuring her. "I'm not a ghost. Come to me and give me a hug, my child."

But even though Indira heard Nani speaking, she thought she was hearing things in her state of shock, and she pinched Nani's hand to see if she could really feel her, then feeling Nani's warmth, she exclaimed, "It is real! You are alive! Oh, Nani, you're really alive!" Indira then threw herself into Nani's outstretched arms and cried and laughed, simultaneously, showering her beloved Nani's face with kisses.

By now, Nani's estranged daughter-in-law and two grandsons had gathered in the room, and Nani cried for joy at the sight of them, and they embraced Nani and cried themselves. Once the excitement settled a bit, Nani went on to tell them all that she had really died and gone to heaven and had seen the bright and shining city, and the pearly white gates, and that she had walked the golden streets of heaven, and she said she had met her Lord and He said to her that her work on earth was not done, and He sent her back with renewed strength. No one questioned Nani's compelling experience, but they were all thrilled to have her back.

What would have been a funeral then turned into a celebration of life for Nani, with her family and friends gathered around her. The sombreness of the day quickly vanished and the occasion called for a feast and Nani now had an appetite for hot duck curry and rice, and fresh ball-of-fire pepper from her garden. Uncle Ram and Ravi took off in the town and came back shortly with three fat ducks to curry, and everyone assisted in getting the cooking started.

While Nani sat back in her rocking chair in the kitchen and looked on as sweet smoke from the burning wood filled the air as the pots were boiling on the mud stove, giving off a spicy, mouth-watering aroma, Uncle Ram took Indira aside and said, "I know I promised you and Ma that I wouldn't drink anymore, but I really need a shot of rum now. You see, I'd like to celebrate Ma's life, and rum and a plate of hot duck curry also go very well together."

"But you made a promise, Uncle Ram," Indira said.

"All I want is just one shot, my niece. I don't want a whole bottle."

Indira could not help but smile, for the once tyrannical Uncle Ram now looked so docile. "Okay, Uncle Ram, Rav has some over at the house. I'll take you over and give you just one shot this time. But remember your promise to Nani."

"After this shot I will keep my promise, I promise," Uncle Ram said. But Indira was now beginning to think, about this particular promise, that Uncle Ram was somewhat of a gaff box; a person who is all talk with no action. In fact, she could not imagine him giving up drinking entirely, but she believed he was serious about changing his wicked ways in not behaving badly, and being good to her and a good son to Nani, for the anger and bitterness over his jealousy that had driven him to drink excessively were now resolved.

The two of them took off down the backstairs, heading over to Ravi's liquor cabinet, and as Nani watched them go she smiled, pleased to see them on good terms, but not knowing what the two of them were up to.

Whatever illness had struck Nani for the three months had now passed, and she recovered fully in a matter of a couple of weeks and regained her strength as well as exuberance, and she was now in good health and desired to go on living until her Maker was ready to call her home again. Life then resumed: Ravi was off in the mornings taking care of business, and in the afternoons, he worked the gardens, which he and Indira did only for their consumption now, and Nani remained retired from selling at the market, but she continued on with raising chickens and sold them from her home.

22

Radhika Visits And Indira's Tragedy

It was now Christmas time in the little town of Rose Hall, the same year Nani had recovered from her illness, and relatives from abroad were flying in to spend the holiday at home. After being abroad, in Canada, for over three years, Radhika decided she would return home for Christmas this year, with Rohan and their two children, but, because of work obligations, they had to schedule a flight to arrive no earlier than on the eve of Christmas.

In the wee hours of the morning of Christmas Eve, Ravi, who had recently bought a car, left to pick up his sister and her family at the airport, and along with him went two other car loads of relatives, including, Padmini and Rohan's family. Ravi's parents, Mr. and Mrs. Singh, came the day before to spend the night at their son's house, and because Mrs. Singh was not feeling very well, Mr. Singh decided she was not fit to travel to the airport so early in the morning, and he stayed behind to look after her.

Indira also stayed behind. She did so to make preparations to accommodate Ravi's relatives for the day. She was up before the crowing of the fowlcocks, even before Ravi and the others had left for the airport, and while the old folks, Nani and her in-laws were still asleep, she tidied the house and cooked an abundance of sweet and savoury treats, and made a barrel full of strong ginger beer. She and Nani had made fruit and sponge cakes in the mud oven earlier that week, and she made a special black cake just for Radhika. She had been neglectful in keeping up her correspondence regularly with Radhika due to her own worries and having to care for Nani, and, now, after not seeing her sister-in-law since she left for Canada, she was looking forward to seeing her.

Radhika was expected to arrive shortly after dawn. Just before then, Indira had finished making preparations and was making breakfast as the town was just beginning to stir. Somewhere in the neighbourhood you could hear a baby crying as it was waking up, and the sound of neighbours talking low. The squeal of a pig was heard, a dog barking at a bleating sheep, and the exuberant chirping of birds in the trees caught the ear. The occasional rumbling of a car, the reverberating of bicycle wheels, and patter of heels on the dirt streets were heard as marketeers were making their way to the market. At this time, the milkman was already making his way around the town to deliver fresh cows' milk. The sound of someone chopping wood and the clatter of carahees and tawas—pots and pans were heard as folks were preparing breakfast, and curls of smoke escaped the mud stoves of some, and pots of those with gas stoves, floating out of their kitchen windows and saturating the early morning atmosphere with spicy, delicious aromas.

Around this time, Indira's in-laws woke up and Nani came over to join them for a breakfast of roti and saltfish and coco tea. Soon after breakfast, they all bathed and got dressed in fresh clothes and waited on the verandah for the arrival of Radhika.

There is such a sense of excitement in the air when anyone from abroad is coming home for a visit, and that was no exception in this instance. The warmth of the early morning and Christmas music already blaring in the neighbourhood only added to the anticipation. Not long before, Ravi's car came rumbling up the dirt street, followed by the other two car loads of relatives, and Indira, her in-laws, and Nani hurried down the stairs to greet Radhika, as curious neighbours surreptitiously peeped out of their windows to look on at this exciting affair.

The cars parked on the street side and Radhika was the first to alight, and she came rushing through the gate and embraced her parents with kisses and tears of joy. "How I missed you, Ma, Pa," she cried, talking with the twirl of the tongue of a Canadian. "I'm so happy to see you."

"My daughter!" Mrs. Singh cried as she held Radhika. "It's been too long since you've been gone. I can't begin to tell you how happy I am to see you, my child."

Mr. Singh stifled his tears as he said, "I've been longing to see you day and night, my dear gal, and I wonder if I'm now dreaming."

"No, Pa, you're not dreaming," Radhika said, "I'm really here." And Radhika gave her father a long hug. When she let go of him, she turned to Indira and embraced her, and said, "Oh, bouji, I've been looking forward so much to seeing you."

Indira was also caught up in the joy of the moment and her eyes teared up as she said, "Likewise, sis. As Ma said, it's been too long since you've been gone."

Radhika then turned to Nani and, in her Canadian twang, said, "I'm glad to see you're alive and looking well, Nani."

"Eh, eh, what did you say, gal?" Nani asked with a puckered look on her face. "You sound like some kind of

English duck and I can't understand 'what the devil' you're saying. You've been gone for just a few years and you come back talking like a *bakra*," meaning, a white person.

Radhika started laughing, and said, "I'm Canadian now, Nani. When in Canada one learns how to speak with a Canadian accent."

Nani turned to Indira to interpret what the devil Radhika just said in her Canadian accent, then she turned back to Radhika and said, "Well, you're in Guyana now, so speak Guyanese so I can understand what you're saying." Nani then looked over Radhika keenly and noticed her complexion was lighter than usual, and she went on to say, "How come you look so white? What kind of cream are you rubbing on your skin, gal?"

Radhika laughed again and, now speaking in Guyanese, said, "It's winter in Canada and people generally turn paler at this time of the year, Nani."

Nani then broke out in a broad smile, exposing her gold teeth, and she threw her arms around Radhika and said, "I missed you my dear gal. So glad to see you."

All the other relatives had filed through the gate by now and were gathered at the concrete-paved bottom-house, and the focus then turned to Radhika's two young children and her husband Rohan, and there were more hugs and kisses and tears of joy.

The folks lingered at the bottom-house for a while, relishing the special moment of having family visiting from abroad, then they moved upstairs where Indira served up the treats and Christmas fruit and sponge cakes and ginger beer, and she served Radhika the special black cake she had made especially for her. Radhika thanked her and gluttonously ate just about all of the pan at once, and when she had her fill she sent Rohan and Ravi to fetch the suitcases of gifts she and Rohan brought from Canada, and she gathered all of the relatives around the Christmas tree for the sharing of the gifts.

Radhika had been looking forward so much for this moment, so Rohan let her take charge of giving out the gifts. But before she started doing so, she went about opening a suitcase containing something else she brought for everyone there. As she was unzipping the suitcase, the delectable scents of Canadian fruits came seeping out, flooding the sitting room. When she tossed open the case, the sights of luscious red apples and plump red grapes made everyone's eyes dazzle with excitement. They were all delighted to have a chew of the foreign fruits. Radhika then handed out the gifts, from toys to sweet-smelling clothing to costume jewellery, lotion, shampoo, and sweet soap. She brought Indira a bottle of perfume and hair accessories and lace underwear, and a t-shirt with a seaside imprint on it, that Indira said she would cherish. Ravi was given an electric shaver and cologne, and Nani received a piece of fine, white cotton fabric to make a headkerchief for herself. Everyone there got something or the other from abroad, and that was very special for each of them.

After Radhika handed out the gifts, Ravi and Indira took her for a tour around the house, and with a certain pride, Ravi told her he had designed the house himself and showed her the modern kitchen with the gas stove and electric oven, and the upstairs bathroom he made especially for Indira, then they came to Ravi and Indira's turquoise-coloured bedroom.

As Radhika lingered there to admire the beautiful room, she said to Ravi, "You and bouji have done well, buddy. I always knew you would be prosperous one day."

"We've worked hard to have what we have now," Ravi said. "Business is doing well and Indira doesn't have to work in the garden or do her palm plant business anymore, but she chooses to continue doing so. In fact, we can now afford to hire a cook—"

"I can't sit around doing nothing," Indira chimed in. "Besides, both Rav and I love gardening, and I love to cook, especially, for Rav."

Ravi kissed Indira tenderly on the forehead, then went on to say to Radhika, "I've seen to it that Nani is taken care of. I've retired her from selling at the market, but she continues to raise chickens to sell from home. And, as you know, Ma doesn't work in the rice field anymore, and I've hired a couple more people to assist Pa with the business. With your financial help, also, they're both taken care of and are doing well. Yes, we've done well for ourselves, and so have you, sis."

"Rohan and I have also worked hard to have what we have now," Radhika said as they all made their way out of the turquoise-coloured bedroom to the hallway, heading to the other rooms. "We're both still working at the clothing store for his uncle, and with both our income, we were able to purchase a small house in Toronto, with a view of Lake Ontario. I'm grateful that I have a good life and a wonderful husband and two beautiful children." Just then they came to the blue and pink bedrooms which Indira had decorated for the baby boy and girl she was hoping for, and Radhika said, "I see you've made plans to have a family."

505

"We're working on that," Ravi was quick to say.

Judging by Indira's quiet reaction, Radhika quickly realised she had stumbled on a sensitive subject, and she changed it, saying to Indira, "I miss your regular letters, bouji." Radhika did not have the slightest idea that Indira's lack of communication related to her predicament of not being able to conceive, as yet, and her despair over it.

Indira apologised, being as tactful as she could for she did not feel it was the appropriate moment to divulge her troubles to Radhika. "Sorry for not keeping up with your letters, sis," she said, "it's just that I've been sidetracked by other things. I'll try to write regularly, I promise." Indira then diverted to another subject, saying, "Tell me all about Canada, sis. Tell me all about Toronto."

Radhika graciously accepted Indira's apology and made no hesitation in saying, "Oh, bouji, there's so much to see and do there. You just have to come and visit someday. I'll take you up to the CN Tower and take you to see Toronto Centre Island, and I'll take you to the museums and art galleries and theatres and the many parks and restaurants and clothing stores . . ."

Indira and Ravi spent the rest of the day intermittently listening to Radhika and her talk about Canada and her life there with Rohan and their two children. Their boy was now a couple of months short his second birthday, and the girl was just an infant, a lot of fun to play with, and both Ravi and Indira doted on the children.

The day called for a feast, being a homecoming occasion and the eve of Christmas. Ravi caught a couple of Nani's fat chickens in the fowl coop to cook, and he even went into town and bought two hefty ducks, fresh cow and goat's meats. Radhika wished to do a bush-cook, so she and the others hung around in Nani's backyard on that hot and sunny afternoon and cooked, while drinking and playing reggae Christmas music. When the feast was ready, they ate and drank until they were replete. Then, right after, Radhika, her family, Mr. and Mrs. Singh, and the other relatives loaded into the cars and they all left for Skeldon under a moonlit and starry Christmas Eve sky.

* * *

Radhika spent a merry Christmas in Guyana then left for Canada right after the New Year. Having spent the time with Radhika's children, Indira's yearning to have her own resurfaced, even stronger this time. She had been trying to conceive for three years now with no success, and that year she would turn twenty-two and she was now becoming desperate. To make matters worse, she learned that Francine was pregnant, yet again, and was a few weeks on the way, and Afonso was to be a father, for Laliwa had recently conceived herself, and Ling had married Devika in a private ceremony and she was now carrying his child.

Indira had blamed herself for not being able to conceive and, in spite of Ravi telling her it could be either of their faults, she continued to take the blame. Becoming more and more frustrated himself, Ravi urged her to go along with him to the doctor to have them both examined. It was then proven that it was indeed Indira who could not bear a child, for it was diagnosed that she had an ovulation disorder, and both she and Ravi were left to deal with the devastation that they would not have children together.

The same afternoon they learned the news, Indira locked herself up in the bedroom, she was so distraught, and she wallowed in her misery in the stifling heat of the day. Eventually, sometime in the evening, she got up and went to look for Ravi. She found him pacing in the pink room they had decorated for a baby girl, and he was furious, flailing his arms about and shouting, "God has cursed me! God has cursed me! Or is this some kind of a cruel joke?" After having made many attempts to impregnate Indira with only failures over the years, he struggled to digest but had never fully come to terms that he may not have children with his wife, for he had always entertained a glimmer of hope that he would, but the finality of the doctor's results that he would not, jerked him into a harsh reality and left him feeling shattered.

He was so wild with devastation at the moment that when Indira reached out to comfort him, he pushed her out of the room and slammed the door on her. Indira ran back to their bedroom and buried her face in the pillow and cried. It was bad enough that she was infertile, but for Ravi to push her away was more than she could bear. That evening seemed endless, for Ravi stayed away from her. He stayed in the baby girl's room and she could hear him continuing to curse and swear, something not characteristic of him. He had always been patient with her and had been a source of support and comfort and hope, and to see him lose it like that was hurtful beyond what she thought she could endure. She only wanted to love Ravi and would never think of hurting him, but she was unintentionally doing so, causing them both enormous suffering. She was angry at herself for doing so, and now angry at Ravi for pushing her away and causing her even more hurt.

She stayed in the room and continued to cry in bed. At an instance, as she brought her right hand up to wipe away the deluge of tears from her face, the streak of moonlight creeping up the open window shone on the delicate floral gold ring Nani had given to her on her sixteenth birthday, causing it to glitter and catching her attention. She vividly remembered when Nani had given the ring to her and had said, 'Ma Raajee gave it to me when I had turned sixteen, and I had given it to your mother, Geeta, when she had turned sixteen, and it's now your turn to wear it'. And she had put the ring on and said to Nani, 'I swear only to take it off for my first daughter when she turns sixteen'. At that moment, Indira yanked the ring from her finger and pitched it on the floor, knowing she would have no daughter to pass it on to. She then lay there ruminating about Chaaya's gold jewellery Nani had shown her when she was a little girl, when she had said to her ' . . . someday, child, it will all be yours', and, ' . . . someday you will marry and have children and you will pass it on to your children'. Indira cried harder as those memories came alive in her mind, and she did even more so when she mused on the time when Ravi was courting her and had jumped over Nani's bedroom window and had sat beside her on the bed and said to her ' . . . when we have our first child, hopefully, a girl, we'll name her Mumtaz after the Indian film star'. Indira's thoughts then travelled to the time when Nani was ill and she had asked her to bless her with a child, and Nani had said, 'I pray that the Lord would hear my prayer and bless you with children . . . But, perhaps, He has already designed another life for you. Accept your destiny in whatever it may be, my child. If Ravi truly loves you, and I know he does, he would love and cherish you no matter what. In the end, we must all walk alone, children or no children'. All those words kept ringing in Indira's ears over and over again, until, from mere exhaustion, and when Ravi's cursing had subsided and calmness had settled in the house, she gradually drifted off to a disturbing sleep clouded with unfulfilled dreams.

It was around midnight when she stirred in her sleep, and through the mosquito netting, she found Ravi leaning against the bedroom door in the semi-darkness of the room, dimly lit by the glow of a fluorescent tube light in the hallway. And she said to him, "I understand what you're going through because I'm devastated and hurt myself, but by getting angry with me you're causing me more hurt than you can imagine. If you're here to get angry with me then go away and leave me alone, Ravi. Don't hurt me anymore than I am. Just go away."

Ravi walked towards the bed and he lifted the mosquito netting and saw Indira's face, forlorn and stained with tears, and he sat down beside her and, in a voice husky with emotions, said, "I'm sorry, Indi. I didn't mean to hurt you."

"Then why did you, Rav?"

"I was dealing with my own frustrations and shattered dreams, Indi. And I didn't know how to handle myself."

"You're angry at me, though."

"I *was* angry at you. I was angry at God. I was angry at the world. I was angry at the universe. I was angry at my misfortune. But I'm not anymore. I have had time to calm down and think of what you mean to me. You mean the world to me, Indi. Let me lie down beside you and hold you." When Indira did not resist, Ravi laid down beside her and wrapped himself in her softness and inhaled her sweet chameli lotion scent. Then in a voice filled with tenderness, he went on to say, "Please forgive me for my nasty outburst, but in doing so I've let out all my anger and frustrations, and all I'm left with is my love for you. If this is any consolation, with no children, you will have my undivided love, my love. I promised you sometime ago that I would love you no matter what, and I said that love will see us through this life together. I sincerely mean that, Indi."

Upon hearing this, Indira broke down and cried, and Ravi held her close until she ceased, then they drifted off to sleep in each other's arms to the gushing sonata of the river that ran alongside the house, accompanied by the chirring of crickets.

Though Ravi tried to comfort Indira and reassured her of his love for her, Indira was no longer the same after that night. In the following week, she began deteriorating in health and spirit. Ravi thought of when he had first met her of how shy she had been, and when she came out of her shell of diffidence, how she would chatter like a little bird. Now she seemed to have lost her tongue. And her sweet, melodious laugher ceased altogether; there was barely a trace of her dimples for her smiles were now diminished. Her pretty, dark eyes soon shone no more and the sweeping curve of her lashes now drooped with sadness. The fire in Indi died. She did not want to doll up and dance for him anymore, for she did not want to be a toy doll or plaything for him, she said, for the pain of knowing she would never

511

be able to conceive was too great. She now slept in the corner of their bed, cold as ice.

Indira had, likewise, promised Ravi that she would love him no matter what, but now it hurt too much to be with him. Her despair reached a crescendo in the upcoming week and she found herself being nostalgic for the comforts of Nani's old house. In the middle of a dark night, she quietly slipped out of bed and made her way over. That one night in January turned into a week, then a month, and there was nothing Ravi could do to persuade her to return home. In fact, she began avoiding him entirely.

Indira retreated into depression and sequestered herself from the world, becoming a recluse, suffering privately, not telling anyone, even Nani, of her predicament. She stopped watering the flower plants, leaving the garden in a desolate state, neglected her palm plants, did no farming, even stopped feeding the chickens, and fishes in the pond, only confining herself to Nani's upstairs bedroom for most of the time.

One afternoon, Nani entered the bedroom as a warm wind was blowing about the maroon lace curtains and slightly swaying the old wooden windows, and she found Indira laying in bed, withering away like a flower, becoming increasingly maga—thin, for she barely touched a morsel of the meals Nani prepared for her. And there was nothing Nani could do to console her for she could not reach Indira, for she was too far gone. Nothing would cheer her up or give her solace, not even Radhika's letters, which Nani delivered to her but were left unopened on the night table.

Ravi's parents were sad over the breakup, though neither them, nor Nani, knew why Indira had broken off the relationship with Ravi, for neither Indira nor Ravi would talk about it. They tried cajoling Indira into returning to Ravi and his love, thinking that would revive her, but their words fell on deaf ears. No one knew of the pain and suffering Indira was going through.

* * *

Ravi settled down to a life by himself. The house seemed so desolate without Indira, and he was feeling lonely and missed her terribly, but he could not even talk to her for she remained aloof. The only times he would see her were when, as he would sit on the backstairs of what was once *their* home, she would go to the old bathroom in Nani's backyard at dusk for her evening ablution, and he would ache for her, long to touch her soft skin again, smell her sweet chameli lotion scent, hold her in his arms, but she was just a mirage; in sight, but out of reach. She paid him no mind, only kept her head down. He was afraid that he had lost her love and that thought was sometimes more than he could bear, driving him to the edge of insanity at times. The sitar that once played in his heart when she was his, stopped when she left, and his mood was now of a dark complexion. Having lived in absorption of her beauty, his world now seemed unattractive, and insipid. He turned to drinking while alone at nights, and in his drunken stupor would often play his guitar and sing the song by Percy Sledge, *When A Man Loves a Woman*, a hundred times, but nothing would ease his pain of a heartbreak.

He succumbed to ennui and despair, languishing away in his sorrows. Without Indira around to cook for him, and also having a lack of appetite, he ate very little, debilitating him further. He was so distraught that he started neglecting his fabric store business and farming, and, like Indira, he began withdrawing from everyone. After not seeing him for sometime, Nani went over to his house to check on him and found him as maga as Indira. She started taking hot meals over to him, morning, noon, and night, trying to nourish him back to health, and she commiserated with him. Dr. Ramesh also stepped in and gave him a shoulder to lean on, encouraging him and giving him some sound advice.

Taking the wise advice of the doctor, Ravi soon got back on track and he thrust himself into working, and even harder. He would rise before the break of dawn and take off on his motorcycle to oversee his business in Rose Hall, New Amsterdam, and Georgetown, and he would return late at nights. He even expanded his land, bought another plot and tilled the soil and planted even more vegetables, but in spite of trying to keep busy, he could not get his beloved wife off his mind. Indira was the only love he had ever known and he could not see beyond that love, for to him there was no other love but hers. She was a good wife and lover and all he had ever dreamed of, the epitome of a faithful woman, except she could not bear him children, but he had come to terms with that and now he would do anything just to have her back.

Sad and lonely and intoxicated, he staggered over to Dr. Ramesh one dark midnight, seeking consolation, which he had often done since Indira left him.

All the lights were on in Dr. Ramesh's big, yellow mansion that night, for the doctor had company earlier and they had just left, and he said to Ravi, "Come in, son, and have a seat." By the pained look in Ravi's eyes, he knew his son was lovelorn, still suffering from a broken heart, and he was also feeling sad and lonely tonight over his deceased wife. "Let's have a drink and wallow in our misery, for misery loves company, as we all know," he said, and went about decanting a couple of shots of El Dorado Rum.

He served Ravi a glass as Ravi sat back on the red leather sofa, and after a swallow of the hard drink, Ravi said, "Let me ask you something, doctor, is there a cure for a broken heart?"

Dr. Ramesh scratched his head and smiled as he took his seat in the armchair with the drink in hand, and he said, "I haven't found a medicine for that, as yet, son. If I had, I would be prescribing it to myself." He took a drink and placed the glass down, then unloaded a box of dominoes on the marble coffee table and began shuffling them, and he went on to say, "But you know, you don't have to fetch your pain around with you all the time, it would only weigh your heart down. Set it down for now and lets enjoy some good memories of our wives."

"I thought we are supposed to be wallowing in our misery," Ravi said as he selected the seven dominoes from the pack.

Dr. Ramesh picked his seven tiles, and said, "I take that back. Let's wallow in our *memories* of our wives. No need to torture ourselves with misery."

"It is the wise thing to do," Ravi concurred, "for God knows I've been through enough misery just tonight." And both men went down memory lane as they drank and played, amid the clattering and slamming of the domino tiles on the marble coffee table, talking about their wives with laughter and tears in their eyes.

Dr. Ramesh started way back in the beginning, saying, "My marriage to Shanti was arranged by my parents and due to circumstances I didn't get to see her up until the day we got married. Man, I tell you, I was worried sick that I would end up with a pig in the bag!" They both laughed then, and Dr. Ramesh continued on by saying, "But, luckily, she turned out to be a pretty one."

"I vividly remember the first time I saw Indi," Ravi said, "she was in a shimmering dusk-blue sari. It was on a Diwali night and I came down from Skeldon to visit my cousin Padmini right here in Rose Hall, and while I was lingering on the street corner with some other boys, I saw her standing in front of a neighbour's yard, lit by a sea of diyas. And, man, I thought I was struck by lightening, died and gone to heaven! In fact, I thought she was the Goddess Lakshmi herself."

"My granddaughter has an ethereal beauty," Dr. Ramesh proudly said. "She does have some features like her grandmother Shanti. Nani, of course, would say Indira resembles her mother Geeta, but I see a lot of Shanti in Indira." Dr. Ramesh had a faraway look behind his spectacles as he went on to say, "Shanti, my dear wife. She was quite a woman, I must say. Carried herself graciously, spoke well, dressed well, was a loving, caring woman, and so devoted to me."

"I can say the same for Indi," Ravi said. "She must have gotten her attributes from Shanti."

"I would say so, though I wouldn't want to take any credit away from Nani, for she raised her properly," Dr. Ramesh said and took a swallow of drink then reverted to his late wife. "Shanti left me with so many memories of her. I can spend the rest of my life telling you things about her." He paused briefly before continuing on to say, "I remember the time when I had a pig roast when Indira was around five years old, how sick Shanti was that time, but in spite of that she braved it and got out of bed, determined not to ruin the occasion for me, and she played the part of a wife so well that day, never once complaining of her illness. What a woman!"

"I wish I knew her," Ravi said.

"Knowing, Shanti, she would have taken to you and treated you just like a son."

There was a brief pause then, and Ravi went on to say, "Speaking of a woman of determination, I can see how Indi has taken that trait from Shanti. I remember when I was sick from a snake bite, how Indi nursed me back to health with such perseverance. And when I couldn't work then, she shouldered the responsibility and put food on the table, even when things got worse with a flood and Nani had a fractured ankle. And she never once complained about the hardship. She is quite a woman herself."

"It makes me proud to hear you talk about my granddaughter like that. You really do love her, and very deeply I can tell. Just like I had loved my dear wife."

The two men continued to talk non-stop about the love of their lives way into the wee hours of the morning, commiserating with each other, as they continued to play dominoes, on equal footing, and by then alcohol-induced sadness set in and Dr. Ramesh, with tears in his eyes, said, "How I miss my Shanti. It's over a decade since I lost her and I still feel her around me at times. Wish I can have her back."

"I can say the same thing about Indi, Pa," Ravi said as he choked back tears that were threatening to fall, "wish I can have her back. Our sixth wedding anniversary is coming up in a couple of months, in June, and that is my wish, that she would come back to me."

"That is my wish for you, also, son," Dr. Ramesh said. "Have some faith, and hope that she would return then, my boy."

The domino game ended with Ravi beating Dr. Ramesh just by one round that night, and Ravi ended up sleeping over at the big, yellow mansion.

Ravi took Dr. Ramesh's advice and began building his hope that Indira would return to him. He pined for her for another couple of months, and soon the day of their sixth wedding anniversary arrived. He took the day off and tidied the house, hoping Indira would return that day. In fact, he had convinced himself that by the end of the night she would, and he had even gone out and bought her a gold bracelet for a present, he was so sure she would not miss their wedding anniversary.

All that day, he saw no sign of her, though, but he remained hopeful. Then as the sapphire-blue of dusk started to set in as the birds were flying across the sky to their roosts on that hot evening, while sitting on the backstairs, he saw her heading to the bathroom in Nani's backyard, beside the fowl coop, a towel draped over her shoulder. She did not appear to be aware of his presence.

He watched as she entered the bathroom and bolted the door. Through the slit at the top of the bathroom, he saw as her hands went up as she pulled off her dress, and a moment later the gushing of the pipe water was heard as she turned it on. In his mind's eye he could see her, and his thoughts ran to the many times she had loved him; intimate thoughts etched in his mind that he now savoured and hoped to relive that night.

Moments later, she emerged wrapped in the towel with her hair hanging loose and wet. She appeared to be absorbed in thoughts as she made her way up Nani's backstairs and disappeared out of sight. He thought that she was going to get ready then to come over that night, and he went and washed up and got dressed, and even splashed on her favourite musk cologne. Then he poured himself a hard drink and sat and waited for her on the verandah.

The hot night was pitch black, except for a copious sprinkle of stars in the sky, and behind the mass of black clouds, hid a sliver of moon. As Ravi sat in silence, he could hear the dogs barking in the neighbourhood, and somewhere in a distance, the electricity generator hummed faintly and incessantly. The flow of the river that ran alongside the house, the chirring of the crickets, buzzing of the mosquitoes, the flapping wings of the bats, and other sounds of the nocturnal creatures, as well as the rustling of the leaves of the many fruit trees around added to the night sounds. And the wings of a night owl fluttered and halted as it perched on the ceiling of the verandah. Curls of smoke from a glowing mosquito coil burning in a corner of the verandah scattered about, emitting a sweet incense scent.

Nani had gone to bed in her room at the bottom-house for the room was in darkness, and from Ravi's view from the verandah, he could tell that the kerosene oil lamp was lit upstairs, which meant that Indira was probably still getting ready, he hoped. He fixed himself another hard drink and waited but did not see even a shadow of her behind the curtain. But he remained sanguine for now and kept on waiting. However, as his watch kept ticking away, to half past eleven now, his hopes began to dwindle. At the stroke of midnight their sixth wedding anniversary slipped by, and the kerosene oil lamp was extinguished, so did what was left of his hopes of Indira returning that night.

"Bloody fool!" he shouted at himself in his intoxicated state, angry that he had deluded himself, that his act of hoping was nothing but sheer folly. "How could I be so foolish to think she would return to me tonight!" And he took up his drink and stood up and looked out into the thick darkness of the night. Tilting his head to the sky, he cried, "Mother Star, from where she came, bring her back to me. Can you hear me, Star? Or have you died and taken her with you, leaving your light behind to deceive a foolish man like me!"

He then hurried inside and turned on the fluorescent tube light above his desk in the sitting room, and he sat down, filled his fountain pen with ink, and began scribbling a poem:

Mother Star

Mother Star, from where she came, bring her back to me. Can you hear me, Star? Or have you died and taken her with you, leaving your light behind to deceive a foolish man like me! My soul has fallen into the abyss of pain, my tears as inky as the black water river, my heart so torn as though whipped by a thousand bamboo wild canes. Bury me not in my sorrows and let the wild crabgrass take over my grave. Bring her back to me, I implore you, oh Star of the Universe!

The soft voice and the melodious laughter of Indira and her beauty and dark, dreamy eyes haunted Ravi, appearing in his mind and thoughts and vision, and he wanted her so badly that night that he broke down and started crying. Then, after grappling with the idea and suddenly coming to the realisation, he said, "But she's not coming back. No, she's not coming back to me because you've taken her away, oh Star, and she doesn't love me anymore!" And he tore up the poem he wrote and scattered the pieces of paper about, then pelted the glass of drink against the wall, shattering the glass to pieces and spilling the drink onto the polished floor.

That very night, Ravi's drinking exacerbated things and his suffering reached a crescendo. He then swore to extricate himself from his pain, and he picked up his fountain pen again and started scribbling another poem:

I Am The Cliffs Of Mount Roraima

I am the cliffs of Mount Roraima. Puff and howl you dangerous wind, push and shove me, I will not move. For I am strong. I am rock.

I am the cliffs of Mount Roraima. Pelt me with your drops you vicious rain, hit me again and again, I will not wash away. For I am strong. I am rock.

I am the cliffs of Mount Roraima. Sear me with your rays you merciless sun, scorch me again and again, I will not burn up. For I am strong. I am rock.

I am the cliffs of Mount Roraima. Smother me you ominous clouds, envelop and stifle me, I will not die. For I am strong. I am rock.

Right there and then, Ravi, now feeling as strong as the cliffs of Mount Roraima, resolved to move away from Indira and obliterate her from his mind. He decided he would sell the house and move far, far away, away from the sights of her who only now tormented his heart, for he could not endure another night of pain without her.

23

Coco For A Gift

It was a bright and sunny Saturday morning in the little town of Rose Hall, and folks were going about their weekend activities, scrubbing floors and cleaning their homes, rubbing clothes, and running errands at the local market, banks, and shops. The sounds of people chattering, children playing in the streets, and animals braying, mooing, barking, bleating, and squealing were heard. Despite the cacophony all around, Indira was still in bed, oblivious of the happenings. Nani had been up by the break of dawn when Mr. Jackson came calling at the gate to buy a couple of fat chickens. Since then she had a steady flow of customers, all wanting fresh meat for lunch that day, and crisp callaloo and bora and hot ball-of-fire peppers, and other vegetables from her garden, as well as an assortment of ripe mangoes and guavas and star apples, and other fruits from her orchard. After currying a carahee of fresh chicken for lunch, Nani took off on foot to the market to shop for a few things. By the time she returned home, it was just past mid-afternoon and the place was now as hot as an oven, making her feel too tired and exhausted to cook dinner. She took the provisions she had purchased up to the kitchen and asked Indira to make some roti, and *guruma*—sweet mango curry for supper, and she went to her room at the bottom-house to take a nap.

She tried sleeping but slumber evaded her eyes. Since Ravi broke the news to her a couple of weeks ago of his plans to move back to Skeldon with his parents, she was distressing over it and losing sleep. Though she had her suspicion, she still did not know for sure what caused Indira to leave Ravi, for neither of them still would not talk about the separation. Up until now, she had been entertaining the thought that Indira would patch up things with Ravi, but now that he was planning on moving away, her hopes had dwindled to none at all. She had tried cajoling Ravi into staying but to no avail. He had his mind firmly made up. In fact, he already procured a buyer for the house, namely, Shazam, who jumped at the opportunity without hesitation, and they hoped to close the deal at the end of that same month of July. Nani informed Indira of this and made several more earnest attempts to have her patch up things with Ravi, but Indira did not utter even a word in response, only told Nani to leave her alone. Nani grew so desperate and thought of asking Francine to intervene in the matter and have a talk with Indira, but she quickly realised that was not a viable idea as Francine and Indira were still not on terms.

Francine had not seen Indira since Indira told her she did not want to see her nor her babies. Nani had told Joan about the situation between Indira and Ravi, so Francine was aware that Indira had left Ravi and that Ravi was now planning to move back to Skeldon, but she was not privy to the reason Indira had broken up with Ravi in the first place, for not even Nani knew of the reason for sure. In spite of the profound hurt Indira had caused her in breaking off their friendship, Francine was sad for both Indira and Ravi, but there was nothing she could do to assist them in reconciling, for she and Indira were still estranged from each other.

Francine had been cautious in keeping her distance from Indira and had been refraining from going over to her parents just to avoid her, and, instead, had been encouraging them to visit her. But, recently, Joan started insisting for her to bring the children to spend time at her home, and Francine acquiesced and had Albert drop her and the children off, not only to spend Saturday afternoon, but, also, the night and next day with her parents. Albert had the chance of having that afternoon off and took off to play cricket with the boys, and he was glad that he would also have the night off from crying babies waking him up in the middle of the night; a break he really needed. Francine was also happy to have a break and have her parents look after the children, for she had not been feeling too well for a while now and could use the help.

Joan and George could not be happier to have their grandchildren at their home. They doted on them and gave them treats of Bulls-Eyes and sugar-coated blood-drop sweetie, sugar cakes and Fudgesicle ice cream bars, and Joan got out the soft balls and skipping ropes and she and George took the triplets and twins to play in the backyard, under the torrid mid-afternoon sun. Not feeling as energetic as they were, Francine left them to enjoy themselves and she sat in the shade of the verandah with her newborn baby in her arms, and was quenching her thirst with a cold drink of mauby.

As she was sitting there on the verandah, Francine casually scanned Nani's place. There was no sign of anyone at the moment, and the place remained the same as she had last seen it, for what seemed like eons ago. The old, unpainted greenheart wood house appeared even more sun-bleached than she remembered it, the silver corrugated zinc roof shining in the sharp sun, and the earthen ground of the bottom-house looked grey and smooth as though it had recently been daubed with cow-dung and clay. The hammock was still in place, tied to the stilts, and the donkey-cart, which Nani no longer used and was now an archaic means of transportation in the town, was where it was usually parked at the bottom-house, and on it was a heap of coconut leaves and a bunch of pinta, which Nani had been working on to make a broom. The upper part of the door of Nani's room at the bottom-house was wide open at that moment, but the inside was too dark to make out whether Nani was there or not. Rani the new cow was grazing on the grass alongside the house and Solomon the new donkey was beside her, thirstily lapping up a drink of water from a trough. The chameli and hibiscus and jump & kiss in the flower garden in the front yard were drooping from the heat of the day, and the bora and chorai callaloo in the vegetable garden in the backyard appeared to be wilting, even the crabgrass around the edges of the yard looked limp. The fishes were playing in the pond in the backyard as the chickens were clucking away in the old fowl coop, and a fowlcock was crowing loudly at the moment. The mango and tamarind and guava, and other fruit trees in the very back were at a standstill for there was not even a slight play of breeze. Even the sheets hanging on the clothes line in the backyard were at a standstill. Waves of heat were rising from the dirt ground, and a neighbour down the street was burning dried grass and the sweet smell of the smoke drifted about in the searing afternoon air.

Just as Francine was wondering where Nani was, the old lady emerged from her room at the bottom-house and went and laid back in the hammock. Francine had not seen her since the time she last saw Indira, and she had not even visited her when she was ill, and she felt bad about it. The sweet old lady had been so kind to her and had always treated her as her own child and she really missed her. She suddenly had the urge to go over to say hello and show Nani her newborn baby, but she was afraid that Indira may show up, so she hesitated. It was not long before, though, that Nani looked up at the verandah and spotted her sitting there, and she made a gesture with her hand for her to come over. Francine felt she would come across as being insolent in ignoring Nani, so, for the moment, she put aside her trepidation of encountering Indira and headed over to visit Nani.

When she got there, Nani sat up in the hammock and her eyes lit up like a candle, and she said, "I always wondered if I would ever see your sweet smiling face again, my child. I missed you." And tears of happiness trickled from Nani's eyes.

"I missed you, too, Nani," Francine reciprocated, and her eyes brimmed with tears, as well, as she bent down and kissed Nani on the cheek. "I often think about all the good times we had together."

"So do I, my child. You are like a daughter to me and it makes me terribly sad not to have you around." Nani then directed her eyes to the bundle of joy Francine was holding in her arms, and she said, "I see you have another baby."

"Another girl," Francine said with a smile. "Now I have six girls and no boys." And Francine lowered the baby to show Nani. "She'a already a week old, and we haven't even named her, as yet."

"Why not?" Nani asked as she stretched out her arms to hold the baby.

"Albert and I just haven't come up with a name, as yet."

"How's Albert doing?"

"Being a teacher, he's off work until school reopens in September, but with six children he has no time to rest at home. He has a break while I'm visiting my parents and is off playing cricket with his friends, and he even has tonight as well as the day off tomorrow."

"Are you still sewing clothes?"

"I sew occasionally now, usually when the children are asleep at nights. That brings in some extra money to feed all the little mouths we have now. And how are you doing, Nani?"

"I'm doing well by the grace of God. From time to time I have slight pain in my old bones but I'm doing better than expected for my age," Nani said. "I don't sell at the market anymore but I keep myself busy raising chickens and knitting cast-nets to sell from home."

Francine was hesitant to ask the next question, but, contrary to her feeling, she found herself asking, "How is Indira doing?"

Without dithering, Nani said, "I think you should find out from her yourself, child," and she added, "she needs your friendship more than she knows."

"But—"

"I know the two of you have not been on terms for a while now, but it's high time you make up as friends. Indira is upstairs in the kitchen cooking. Go on up and say hello to her."

"But, Nani, the last time I saw her she said she did not want to see me nor my babies."

"Just go on up and see her, my child," Nani urged.

Francine thought for a moment, debating within herself whether she should do so or not, then she said, "I don't think it's a good idea, Nani."

"Go and say hello to her," Nani urged on. "The worst that could happen is that she may tell you to leave her alone. That's what she says to me these days. Take the chance and drop in on her. Go on. Go on now, child."

With Nani coaxing her on, Francine gave in, saying, "Okay, Nani, I'll take your advice and go up and see her. But I'll leave the baby with you because it may only irritate Indira that I have another baby."

"No, child, don't leave the baby with me, take her with you," Nani insisted and handed the baby back to her.

Francine did not bother resisting for she knew Nani would only persuade her to take the baby along, so, with her newborn in her arms, she started up the front stairs as the kitchen door in the back was closed. When she entered the sitting room, she could smell the tangy mango aroma of guruma cooking, mingled with the buttery scent of ghee, used in making roti. She walked over to the kitchen entrance and paused before parting the long strands of beads in the doorway, which revealed a shaded kitchen tinted misty-blue with the smoke rising from the burning wood in the mud stove. She found Indira sitting at the old wooden kitchen table with her head down, and, immediately, she noticed how gaunt and worn and despondent she appeared.

At the sound of the jangling of the beads, Indira lifted sunken eyes to see who it was, and when she noticed Francine, she looked away and stared out the open window into the backyard, a blank look on her face.

"I've come to say hello," Francine said softly.

Indira did not respond but sat with her hands crossed on her laps and remained impassive as she continued to stare out the window.

"We cannot go on forever not being friends, Indira," Francine found herself saying.

Still, no response from Indira.

Francine then went on to say, "Remember when we used to play with our dolls when we were children, Indira? Remember when we used to share our sweetie? Remember when we used to play hopscotch at the bottom-house?" Francine paused when Indira shook her head as though she did not want to be reminded, then she persisted with, "Remember when we used to walk hand in hand and go to school? Remember when you used to braid my hair on the back steps?" Francine paused again, long enough to let the memories play out in Indira's mind and, when Indira still remained silent, she continued on, saying, "Remember the night when the thief man was found in Nani's fowl coop how we played Chinese Checkers and Snake and Ladder in the bedroom that night, and made a pact that we would be sisters? I'm still your sister. Remember how we used to giggle as little girls and laugh together as teenagers? I miss those times, Indira. Don't you?"

A tear then fell from Indira's eye and she broke her silence and said, "You have no idea how I miss those times, Francine." But Indira still would not look at Francine.

"Then talk to me like you used to, Indira. Confide in me. Tell me what's going on in your life now."

With tears now pouring down her cheeks, and still looking out at the backyard, Indira said, "I'm a barren woman, I cannot have children, Francine. That's what's *not* going on in my life now. And I've left Ravi because of it. I feel so inadequate as a woman not being able to bear him children. You're the first person I'm talking to about this because I feel so ashamed to tell anyone." She feared ignominy, public shame she felt she could not survive, so she kept her infertility to herself all those months. As it was, it was bad enough that she had to suffer over it privately. "I haven't even told Nani about it for fear she may mention it to someone out of seeking sympathy, but it may spread in town and some people's tongues may wag with ridicules," she explained. "Don't mention anything to Nani. I will tell her in time."

Francine knew Indira had been having trouble to conceive but never thought it was conclusively infertility, and upon hearing of her friend's plight, she was moved with great pity and teared up as she felt Indira's deep pain. And all she could say at that moment was: "I'm so sorry to hear this, Indira. I wish I could wave a magic wand and make things turn out differently. But all I can do for you is offer you my children. My children are your children if only you would let it be." Indira then turned to face

531

Francine and her eyes fell on the baby Francine was holding, and Francine said, "Hold her for just a moment, Indira." And Francine held out her baby for Indira to hold.

Francine was afraid that Indira would turn her away again, but, as Indira remained seated, she held out her hands and took the baby in her arms. And the instant she rested her eyes on the baby's face, a smile broke out on hers, for the baby was the prettiest baby she had ever seen, having rich brown skin the colour of coco and a head of little black curls, large almond-shaped brown eyes and long curly lashes set in a little round face with the cutest formed lips. As Indira held the cooing brown baby against her breasts, the name 'Coco' escaped her lips.

Francine heard her and was quick to say, "Coco is what I'll call her! Albert would love that name."

"You haven't named her, as yet?"

"We've been thinking about names for her ever since she was born a week ago but haven't settled on one. You've just named her."

"Coco just suits her," Indira said as she looked down at the deep brown face of the smiling baby. "Oh, Francine, she's so adorable. She's the prettiest baby I've ever seen."

"I happen to think so, too," Francine said and laughed, and seeing how happy Indira suddenly seemed, she said, "You can keep on holding Coco and I'll finish the cooking for you, Indira."

Indira stood up then and threw an arm around Francine's shoulders, and she started crying again and said, "I'm so sorry for the way I mistreated you, Francine. It's just that I was frustrated that I couldn't conceive, and being around you and your children and your fertile womb only reminded me of my predicament, so I only wanted to stay away. I didn't mean to hurt you."

"I understand," Francine said.

"I was too wrapped up in my pain to realise how awful I was, and I'm now realising how much hurt I must have caused you. Forgive me, please."

"You don't have to ask me that a second time, my friend, I forgive you," Francine said as she broke down and started crying, also, letting out the many months of tears that had accumulated in her heart.

"I'm so sorry, Francine," Indira said again, and the two of them held each other and had a good, long cry of relief. When their tears finally stopped flowing, Indira pointed to the tray of roti dough sitting on the kitchen table that she had portioned and folded with ghee, and she said, "Yes, I'll keep on holding Coco if you want to finish the cooking for me, Francine. All you need to do is put the tawa on to heat and cook them up."

"All right," Francine said and washed her hands and put the tawa on the mud stove, and she stoked the fire and began rolling out the roti dough on the chowki with the belna, right on the kitchen table, and she began cooking.

Indira sat back down, relishing cradling Coco in her arms, and as she was doing so, she asked Francine, "Where's Albert?"

After informing Indira of Albert's whereabouts, Francine went on to bring her up to date on the news of their friends as Indira had been out of touch for some time now. "You must have heard by now that Ling married Devika in a private ceremony," Francine said.

"That was a while back," Indira said. "The last I heard was that both Devika and Laliwa were to be mothers."

"They both have baby boys."

"Hope to see them soon to congratulate them," Indira said, then asked, "Has Laliwa heard from Sally?"

"Laliwa told me that Sally got married to Neville."

"Well, that's wonderful news. When are they returning home?"

"They're both working temporarily as nurses and are planning on returning home in the near future to work and live. When exactly, I don't know. They've been planning this for a while now, as you know." The friends were then quiet for a moment, Indira caught up in playing with the newborn baby, while Francine was wondering whether she should mention Ravi. Testing the waters, she went ahead and said, "I wonder how Ravi's doing these days."

Indira gave no response to that but was caressing Coco's fingers, and she said, "How little and delicate her fingers are." Just then Coco clasped Indira's pinkie in her tiny hand.

"Ravi loves you, Indira."

"She's now sucking on her thumb. I think she's hungry."

"I think you should patch up things with him."

"Does she drink from the bottle, Francine?"

It became obvious to Francine that Indira did not want to talk about Ravi, so Francine then dismissed the subject. Besides, Indira was too involved with Coco at the moment and her maternal instincts were taking over. "Yes, she drinks from a bottle, she doesn't breastfeed at all," Francine said. "Look in my handbag and you'll find a bottle of milk already prepared. It should still be warm." Having had experience with Francine's triplets, Indira took to feeding baby Coco. And Francine went on to ask, "How do you spend your days now, Indira?"

Indira answered to this, saying, "Not doing much, just wasting away in bed. Not even caring for the gardens or my palm plant business."

"Maybe you should start up your palm plant business again," Francine encouraged her.

"I'm so depressed over my situation that I've lost interest in everything for some time now, Francine," Indira said as she continued to feed the baby.

"If you continue to lay around in bed doing nothing you would continue to feel depressed," Francine said. "You need to do something to work your way out of it. Nani always wanted you to work at the bank. What about taking up a typing course."

After a long pause, contemplating the idea, Indira said, "I'll think about it." She then lapsed into silence and finished feeding the baby, then she lifted Coco to her shoulder and began gently rubbing the baby's back until Coco burped. "It's time for a nap now, baby," she said, "guess I'll have to change your napkin before putting you to sleep. Did you bring any napkins, Francine?"

"They're in the handbag," Francine said. "Just remember to be careful with the pin."

Indira laid Coco on a towel on the floor and changed her wet cloth napkin, carefully folding and pinning on the clean one, then she placed the baby on her shoulder and rocked her to sleep with a lullaby.

By now, Francine had finished cooking the roti and the red sun was beginning to set, and very soon the sapphire-blue of dusk fell over the little town and the birds were flying in flocks across the sky to their evening roosts. While Indira continued to hold the sleeping baby, Francine lit the kerosene oil lamp and hung it up in the kitchen, and Indira said to her, "Can you take some dinner down to Nani?"

Francine dished out some guruma in a calabash and placed a roti in an enamel plate and carried the dinner to Nani, who flashed her gold teeth in a pleasing smile, happy to see the two friends spending time together again, something she had gone over and shared with Joan, who was also happy for the girls. When Francine returned to the kitchen, she and Indira sat at the table and ate like they used to, while the embers in the mud stove glowed, Indira still holding Coco in her arm.

By the time the embers burned down to ashes, it was getting late in the evening, and Francine said, "I must go now, Indira. Let me have Coco."

Indira looked down at the baby, still sleeping peacefully in her arm, and she found herself not wanting to part with her. "Can I keep her for just one night, Francine?" she pleaded. "I've taken good care of the triplets and I'll care for Coco just the same."

Francine looked at her friend as she was holding the baby, and thinking of her plight that she would never have the opportunity to experience motherhood, she was moved with empathy for Indira. She had no qualms in letting Indira keep the baby for one night, for she knew that would bring Indira much pleasure and, besides, she had been feeling overly fatigued for a while now and could use a little help, even for one night. But she was hesitant to say yes because Albert was upset with Indira for the way she had treated her, breaking off their friendship, and Francine was not sure how he would react to her leaving the baby with Indira.

Indira noted Francine's hesitation and in an effort to persuade her, she said, "I have a room already prepared for a baby girl over at the house and I have everything she needs. I have powdered milk, clothes and napkins, and even a cradle for Coco to sleep in."

"Then you'll be moving back in with Ravi tonight if I let you have Coco?"

Indira nodded and said, "Just for the night."

"What would Ravi think?" Francine asked, to which Indira lowered her eyes and did not respond, her facial expression giving no indication of what she was thinking. Francine then went on to say, "I haven't been feeling too energetic for a while now and can use the help with the baby, but I don't know what Albert would say about leaving the baby with you." And just as Francine uttered those last words, she felt another surge of pity for Indira and her unfortunate situation. She knew it would mean the world to Indira to care for her baby even for just one night. After spending just hours with the baby, Francine could not help but noticing how Indira's demeanour had changed from when she first saw her earlier that day, looking utterly despondent to now smiling and looking cheery. After taking all things into consideration, she said, "Okay, Indira, keep Coco for the night. I'll deal with Albert. Fortunately, I'm staying at my parents for the night and I wouldn't see him until tomorrow night, as you know, so I'll explain this to him after the fact and hope he doesn't get upset with me.

But I'll be back here first thing in the morning to get Coco."

"Oh, Francine, you don't know how much this means to me."

"I do, Indira," Francine said, "that's why I'm doing this. And I know you'll take good care of my baby."

"I will," Indira said. "But before you go, hold her for a little while so I can bathe and get dressed."

By the time Francine left, Nani had retired to bed and had no idea about the arrangement between Indira and Francine, and that Indira was planning on spending the night with Coco over at her former home; Ravi's residence.

* * *

Over the last few months, Indira had been severely depressed, but her mood changed drastically after she reconnected with Francine. As Nani mentioned to Francine, she needed Francine's friendship more than she had realised. Not only was she happy to reconcile with her friend, but she was also relieved to unload the weight of suffering and shame she had been carrying all alone for months, in confiding in Francine about her unfortunate situation. She did not deserve Francine's compassion towards her after the way she had treated her, she felt, and for Francine to share her baby with her for the night, in spite of her concern about how Albert may react, only proved the love and sincerity of a loyal friend. She was delighted in being given the chance to care for her friend's baby, so much so, that she did not put too much thought as to how Ravi would react to her returning home just to ask him to use the baby girl's pink room for the night to take care of Coco, nor, did she consider how he was feeling about her at the moment, for all that mattered to her right now was the baby.

It was pitch black outside when, fresh in an immaculate pale green crimplene dress and hair still wet from just finished bathing, she left Nani's house with sleeping Coco in her arms, and the candleflies shed some light on the dirt pathway as she made her way over to what was once her home, and up the front stairs, walking silently as a cat. When she reached the top of the stairs, she made out Ravi's silhouette as he was slouching shirtless on a chair on the verandah, a bottle of liquor on the side table, and just then he picked up the bottle and took a swig from it.

In an intoxicated slur, she heard him muttering to himself, "I can smell you, Indira. I can smell your sweet chameli lotion scent."

"That's because I'm right here, Ravi," she said quietly in the dark.

Ravi turned and looked in her direction, at the outline of her in the dark, and, as though talking to a fantasy, he said, "Is this some kind of a grandiose dream in which I can even hear your soft voice now and smell your sweet chameli scent? I've spent endless nights drinking and thinking of you, so much so that I've had visions of you. Is this another vision of you, my love? Play no more tricks with me, mind, and tell me this is not a dream!"

"Sounds like you've had too much to drink, Ravi. No, this is not a dream. I'm really here. Turn on the verandah light and you'll see."

Ravi got up and felt for the light switch inside and turned on the light, and when he turned to look at the beautiful face that had haunted him for drawn-out days and endless nights, his heart leaped for joy, but only for a moment, for his eyes fell on the bundle Indira was holding in her arms. Rubbing his eyes, he said, "Don't tell me this is not a dream. What the bloody hell do you have in your arms, a brown doll?"

"A baby."

"A baby? Have you been with another man, Indira?!"

"No, Ravi, I've only been away from you for—"

"Six months and five days, precisely," Ravi finished. "So the baby could be premature? Perhaps you have another lover and you're meeting him at the savannah?"

"Don't be absurd, Ravi. The baby is Francine's—"

"Oh, so you're back on terms with Francine. And why have you come to me so late in the night with her baby?"

Indira explained that she asked Francine if she could have the baby for one night, and she went on to say, "Since we have a room already prepared for a baby girl, would you let me stay here for the night to take care of her?"

Ravi was bewildered for a moment, and incensed at her indifference towards him, and he said, "You want to move back in with me for one night just because of a baby?! Don't you love me anymore, Indira? For a moment, I've made a fool of myself in thinking you have returned to me. But, man, was I ever wrong!" And he shook his head in disbelief. "To do this to me only proves that you don't love me anymore! Bloody fool I am!"

Indira looked at Ravi and could not help but noticing how handsome he looked with no shirt on—wearing just black cotton trousers—and with his shoulder-length, jet black hair and dark brown skin, and he appeared lean and with a certain maturity now that he was in his mid-twenties, his fiery brown eyes as sensual as she remembered them, except, sunken with sadness. "I've never stopped loving you, Ravi," she admitted softly.

"But you have returned only to stay for one night because you want to take care of your friend's baby in my home. Is that what you call love?" Ravi said, much to his chagrin. "Don't you miss me? Don't you ache for me the way I ache to be with you? You left me without even saying goodbye and left me to drink myself to sleep over you. How can I believe that you still love me?"

"I didn't come here to argue with you, Ravi. But, believe me, my love for you has never changed. Now, would you let me spend the night so I can take care of the baby?"

"I don't believe you just like I wouldn't trust a thief with a $20.00 bill!" Ravi said with an ironic sigh. "But I cannot refuse you because I'm still in love with you, Indira. Come on in. You'll find the home still looks the same."

Indira entered the house and noticed that things were just as she had left them, except that there were many empty bottles of liquor laying around on Ravi's writing desk, and she felt a sudden sense of guilt that she had driven him to drinking, but, for the moment, she obliterated the thought and why it happened in the first place, because, at this moment, she had a baby to take care of, and just then Coco woke up and was cooing and smiling.

She took the baby straight to the pink room she had furnished with everything for the girl baby she had been hoping for, and Ravi followed her and stood by the

541

doorway and watched as she held the baby against her breasts, someone else's baby and not theirs. He was reminded of the reason Indira left him in the first place, because she could not fulfil his dream of having children and was feeling inadequate and devastated. As he watched her, it made him sad that she would never be able to have a biological child. She would have made a good mother if they had children, he thought, as he observed her looking at the baby so lovingly and holding her so tenderly. But it did not seem to matter at the moment whose baby it was to Indira, for she was being a mother, and for the first time in the longest while, he could see her dimples as she was smiling down at the baby. The happiness she exuded only aided in dissipating the anger he was feeling towards her.

He left Indira alone to absorb the joy of the moment and went and got his bottle of liquor and, with it in hand, stretched out in bed in what was once their bedroom, which happened to be situated just opposite the baby girl's pink room. Tonight, he turned out the lights and deliberately left the mosquito netting up and the bedroom door wide open. From there, he watched Indira as he continued to drink. She stood below the fluorescent tube light, the white light softly illuminating her ethereal loveliness in the pale green crimplene dress she was wearing, making her light golden-brown skin glow and her black, wet curls glisten, and her rose-brown lips tempting like the flesh of a sapodilla fruit. In his intensified inebriated state, he was aware of her being so close and he wanted her badly, but, at the moment, his pride would not let him go to her for fear of rejection. Indira was unaware that he was laying in bed in the dark looking at her and lusting after her, she was so engrossed with the baby.

Ravi silently looked on as she cared for the baby, giving her a bath and dressing her, then she fed the baby from the bottle and put her on her shoulder and rocked her gently as she sung her to sleep with a lullaby. She then put the baby in the cradle and, after carefully placing the blanket over her, drew the mosquito netting around the cradle. Still unaware that Ravi was silently observing her, she tidied up the room and then she went over to the open window and stood there looking out at the black night as the warm July breeze was blowing about the white lace curtain, her back to him, dripping with provocative appeal in her pale green dress which clung to her, making her look like a ball-of-fire pepper.

Having had a few more swigs of liquor, Ravi desired Indira more than ever now as he laid there watching her, and he became so desperate that he wished she were a Bush Dai Dai, a succubus at the moment. But that she was not, more like a shy Kanyadan bride, and he figured that she would not come to him tonight and that he would have to go to her. Unable to control his lust for her he let down his guard for the moment, forgetting his fear of rejection, and he got out of bed and staggered over to her. Acting impetuously in his drunken stupor, he swung her around and tried to kiss.

Indira pushed him away, and said, "Don't be manish, Ravi. You're drunk. Go to bed and sleep off the liquor."

"You call me manish! I'm not being bad. I'm still your husband and have every right to come to you!" Ravi exploded. "But you would not have me because I was right in thinking that you do not love me anymore, Indira." Having his manly pride hurt over Indira's refusal, and feeling insulted, he did not persist further, but staggered out the door and went to his room and flopped down onto the bed, and he went out instantly, like a fluorescent tube light. Indira went and closed his bedroom door and returned to the baby's room, and she stretched out on the pink velvet bench in the corner of the room and fell asleep just as quickly, also.

Even before the break of dawn, still in the dark of the early morning, Ravi woke up to the sound of Francine's voice, gaffing with Indira about the baby. He jumped out of bed and got dressed, but by the time he emerged from the bedroom, both Francine and Indira were gone, along with the baby. Indira never even said thank you or goodbye to him, leaving him to feel the awful sting of rejection, yet again. Sober and alert now, he woke up to reality and felt foolish for letting the liquor induce his lust for Indira and control his actions last night and made him ambivalent in the decision he had made. He had made up his mind to leave her and was in the process of selling the house and moving back with his parents in Skeldon, he emphatically reminded himself. He remembered her telling him that she had never stopped loving him, but he was now convinced she had. She had the audacity to show up with someone else's baby and asked to spend the night for the comforts of the baby, he thought, and then she slipped away in the dark of the early morning, like she had done before in the middle of a dark night. He was now certain that she had no intention of returning to him. Her only motive was to care for the baby. And she left him feeling used. He had no tolerance now to toy with the ambiguity of the situation, and he decided to adhere to his plans to move away from her. This time, he had no intention of vacillating. He hurriedly bathed and got dressed that early morning and speedily took off on his motorcycle to meet with Shazam to work out the financial details of the sale of his house, the sum of which he planned to divide equally with Indira.

A glimmer of hope dawned on Nani's mind when she learned that Indira had spent the night over at Ravi's residence. By the happiness registered on Indira's face, something she had not seen in months, Nani surmised that she and Ravi were patching up things. Indira was indeed happy, it was the only night of happiness she had since she left Ravi, but, contrary to what Nani was thinking, that had everything to do with baby Coco. To experience being a mother, even for that one night, was exhilarating for Indira, something that she had been dreaming about for the longest time. She was so engrossed with Coco, though, that she failed to think beyond anything but the baby. She spent the next day with Francine and her children, especially doting on Coco. Joan and George, happy to see the friends reunite, gave them space to rekindle their friendship. The occasion called for a cook up, and George wanted to do a bush-cook in the afternoon, so Nani offered two of her fat chickens and they made a huge pot of cook-up rice in Nani's backyard, much to the excitement of the children.

While everyone was eating in the shade of the fruit trees, Francine, who was sitting beside Indira on a log, whispered to her, "So, did you and Ravi, you know . . . make up?"

Indira was eating from a plate set on the log and Coco was in her other arm, and she did not respond but was caressing the baby's fingers at the moment.

"Am I being too inquisitive?"

"You are, Francine," Indira said dismissively, leaving Francine to wonder how Ravi handled Indira's sudden return just for the sake of the baby.

Nani was also thinking about Ravi. She noted he had taken off on the motorcycle very early in the morning and she kept looking out for him to return, hoping he would join them for the bush-cook, but the afternoon went by, and by the time the flocks of birds were flying across the sky heading off to their evening roosts, there was still no sign of him. It was not until late that evening that the revving of the engine of his motorcycle was heard, and Ravi parked the vehicle at his bottom-house and went straight upstairs, leaving Nani to question her guess that he and Indira were patching up things.

Thick darkness had long enveloped the town and it was now time for Francine to return home after a time well spent. As she was upstairs at her parents place getting ready to leave, Indira, who had Coco in her arms and had difficulty parting with the baby, asked, "Would you let me have Coco for one more night, Francine?"

Francine thought for a moment then answered as candidly as she could. "You've taken good care of Coco, Indira, and I trust to leave her with you for another night, but Albert might get upset with me. Come over at my place and you can spend all the time you want with her." Francine pitied her friend and felt bad that she had to refuse

Indira another night of enjoyment of being a mother, and she added, "I hope you understand."

"I understand, Francine," Indira said and handed Coco over to Francine.

But as Francine was getting into her father's car to take off for home with her children, her compassion for Indira escalated, making her feel worse for refusing Indira a pleasure she would not otherwise have, and she handed Coco back to her and said, "You can have her for one more night, Indira. I'll handle Albert."

Nani started building her hopes again when she saw Indira heading over to Ravi's place again. Ravi was at the verandah again when Indira showed up with the baby the second night and, before she even asked, he said, "Yes, you can spend another night here with the baby."

Indira was so taken up with the baby that she did not even thank him, which only made Ravi vex, and she held up Coco and said, "Isn't she adorable, Ravi?"

"How can one not think she's adorable?" Ravi said in spite of being annoyed. "Use the room while you can. The house wouldn't be available for much too long."

Indira hurried inside without even responding to the latter part of what he said, in fact, it went straight over her head and did not reach her ears, for the only thing that mattered to her at the moment was the baby in her arms.

Ravi intended to reciprocate as indifferently to Indira, but his intoxicated mind dictated his actions and he found himself laying in bed again, in the dark, watching her as she bathed and fed and put the baby to sleep. Knowing what Indira was like, an ardent wife and lover who had taken him to the depths of erotic pleasures, he could not help lusting for her, but this time his heart was impregnable and he would not let his lasciviousness control him tonight. In fact, he was more firm in his plans to move away from her. When she switched off the lights and went to sleep on the pink velvet bench in the baby's room, he turned his feelings off just as easily and drifted off to sleep himself.

Not too long after he had fallen asleep, there was a loud banging on the front door and he jumped out of bed and rushed to answer it. It was Albert, saying, "I've come to get my baby." And Albert barged inside the house and demanded, "Where's my baby?"

Indira woke up then, startled, and she rushed to the sitting room and said to Albert, "Shhhh! She's sleeping in the cradle. Don't wake her now, Albert."

"I want my baby now!" Albert shouted at Indira.

"Calm down, Albert," Ravi said, intervening for Indira, who shrunk back at the sound of Albert's angry voice. "Come sit with me and have a drink and let's have a talk, man."

"What's there to talk about?" Albert asked. Then he turned to Indira and, again, demanded, "I want my baby now!"

"Francine said to Indira she can have the baby for one more night," Ravi said.

Albert was now even more livid when he said to Ravi, "Indira had stopped talking to Francine and didn't want anything to do with my children, and Francine should have never left my baby with her!"

"Indira was going through her own struggles with not being able to conceive herself and being around Francine and the children only brought her more pain because it was a constant reminder of her predicament. That's why she withdrew," Ravi tried to explain. "The most important thing, though, is that they've made up as friends, and Francine has empathy for Indira and cares enough to share her baby with her."

"Francine should have never done this!" Albert hollered to the top of his voice.

"Listen, Albert," Ravi said, "Francine and Indira grew up like sisters, and all families have their ups and downs. Take it easy on Indira. She's been through a lot over the years. Taking care of Francine's baby means the world to her now. And it's her way of paying back Francine for her bad behaviour towards her." Indira stood back and listened as Ravi was sticking up for her. She understood why Albert was angry with her, but she was afraid of saying anything that might upset him even more. "Leave the baby with her for one more night," Ravi pleaded on her behalf, and he patted Albert on the shoulder and urged him, saying, "Come on, man, let's have a drink together. It's been a long time since we've spent time together."

Albert then let out a heavy sigh and tried to shake the anger he had towards Indira, which he found difficult to do, but with the help of a couple of drinks which Ravi poured him as they were sitting out on the verandah, he managed to relax, and he started mulling over Indira's plight of not being able to conceive. By the time he had a couple more drinks, he started to feel bad for Indira as well as Ravi when he learned from Ravi that Indira would never be able to bear Ravi any children, consequentially resulting in the demise of their relationship, and he felt even worse to hear that Ravi was planning on moving away sometime in the near future.

When Albert later went back inside the house with Ravi, he saw Indira holding Coco like her own baby, and he was now moved with compassion for her and said, "Okay, Indira, you can have the baby for a week. I'm sure Francine would have no objections to that. God knows we have our hands full with all the others, and, besides, Francine has not been feeling well for a while now and she can use the help. I'll caution you, though, that by the end of the week you'll get tired of taking care of the baby, changing napkins and waking up constantly in the nights to feed her." And as Albert was making his way out the door, he commented, "By the way, I do like the name Coco."

"Francine said you would," Indira said. She then apologised, saying, "I'm sorry for upsetting you, Albert. I didn't mean to cause any friction in our relationship."

"Don't worry about it, Indira. I now understand."

"You have a big heart to let me keep Coco for a week."

"Just promise me you will take good care of my baby."

"I promise."

With that, Ravi said, "The baby's room will be available for a little while longer, so you can stay the week to take care of the baby, Indira."

Indira did not get tired of taking care of Coco as Albert indicated she would. On the contrary, she treasured every moment. Ravi stayed up late at nights and watched as she took care of the baby and he still could not resist desiring Indira, but as soon as she put the baby to sleep and turned off the lights, he would exercise control and will himself to sleep. Early in the mornings, even before Indira and the baby would wake, he would get dressed and take off to oversee his business. In the middle of the week, he met up with Shazam, at Shazam's rented home in town, and Shazam told him he was working on coming up with the finances to purchase the house, and they left off that they would reconvene on the weekend.

With Indira around, Ravi found himself regaining the sense of comfort he used to have before she left him, and certain normalcy began returning to his life. The ache in his heart began easing and he did not feel the need to drink himself to sleep at nights. He now spent time sitting out on the verandah playing his guitar in the evenings, or he would recline in bed and take to reading books of his favourite authors, and, at times, penned poems at his desk. Indira returned to doing what she would naturally do; cook and clean, and rub and iron his clothes, though she would not interact much with him, but spent most of her time doting on the newborn baby.

Ravi soon began to notice certain changes in Indira, also. The sweeping curve of her lashes perked up and no longer seemed to droop with sadness like they used to in the months before she left him, her pretty, dark eyes were shining once again, and her dimples were more pronounced, the lustre of her beauty returning day by day. Ravi wished it was him who brought about all that, but he was not to make a fool of himself and believe so. Indira gave him no indication of wanting to become intimate with him, not a coquettish batting of the eyelashes, or a seductive smile, not even an alluring sway of her hips, nothing at all, leaving it seeming obvious that the joy of having to care for the baby was what was stimulating her.

The week went by, and night after night Ravi found himself longing for Indira in spite of trying to exercise control, but she kept up her distance, showing no interest in patching up things with him. So he persisted with his plans to move away. On the last day of Indira's stay, sometime late in the afternoon, he met up with Shazam as planned, at Shazam's home, and Shazam told him that he would come up with the money the following week, at which time they would seal the deal.

Ravi stayed at Shazam's home for dinner and went home late that evening. Indira was busy with the baby in the baby's room, enjoying the last night with Coco, and he went and bathed and then went straight to bed. That night, he closed the bedroom door and lowered the mosquito netting, and he laid shirtless in bed, silent in the dark, and completely sober. He found himself worrying that Indira would be gone the next day, gone completely from his life this time. An uneasy feeling took hold of him and he feared that he would be thrust into the dark abyss of pain and misery and he would have to drink himself to sleep again. He dreaded spending endless, lonely nights again, going out of his mind. At the moment, his body and his heart were in conflict with his mind, and his mind with his mind. His heart started aching and his body was burning up for Indira and he wanted to go to her and take her and tell her how much he wanted and needed her, but his mind was telling him it would only be an act of folly, for it had convinced him that Indira did not love him anymore. His mind was confused at some point, wanting him to procrastinate the selling of his house to give him time to work things out with Indira, but then his mind dictated that she would not have another opportunity to reject him and hurt his manly pride, leaving him even more steadfast in his plans to move away.

Tonight, a Kali Mai Puja—Hindu ritual was taking place down by the river and the beating of drums and invocations were heard in a distance. In the heavy darkness of the bedroom the glowing red tip of a green mosquito coil repellant was burning in a corner, letting out curls of scented smoke. Ravi laid behind the mosquito netting with his eyes closed, in acute torment, his heart encumbered with pain. He was thinking only of Indira as the crickets outside chirred and the crapos called their mates and bats fluttered their wings, and mosquitoes buzzed outside the netting. He started breaking out in sweat from the heat of the night and his racing thoughts.

He was so engrossed in thoughts that he did not hear her enter the turquoise-coloured room that night, and when she lifted the sheer white mosquito netting, a gust of wind swayed the white lace curtain aside and he opened his eyes just then and saw her face in the silver streak of moonlight coming in from the window. For a moment, he thought he was dreaming, yet again, but when he smelt her sweet chameli scent and she touched him, he realised it was not a fantasy. He pulled her down beside him and felt the softness of her skin and a deluge of lust and emotions spilled over and consumed them both.

For a long time, they laid in each others arms in silence, saying not a word, two people obviously still deeply in love, locked in a passionate embrace. Then Indira broke the silence in her soft and seductive voice, saying, "I want to move back in with you, Rav. I don't want to spend another lonely night without you."

Her words were like the sweet sound of the sitar to Ravi's ears, and he realised how wrong his mind had been in thinking that Indira no longer loved him. "I've been desperately and secretly waiting all this week for you to say that, Indi," he admitted.

Ravi and Indira made love to the beating of the drums from the Kali Mai Puja, and to the colour of crimson, and they floated away in the exuberant winds of love that torrid night, setting the night on fire, loving not with the intention of conceiving this time, but out of the pure pleasure of desiring each other. After they were all spent they laid in each other's arms, relishing the moment of reconciliation and committing themselves to love to see them through life, promising each other that nothing would ever keep them apart again. If Francine were to see them together, she would be so happy that her baby Coco played the part in the making up of two people who loved each other so passionately and genuinely.

Ravi and Indira's love did not bear fruits of children, but, rather, a fruit of love. Their love for each other ripened into a golden fruit. The sitar in Ravi's heart started playing again and Indira found the thrill of life again.

Ravi wasted no time in withdrawing from the deal of selling his house to Shazam. It worked out that Shazam could not come up with the finances to purchase the house, anyway, but, fortunately, he found something more affordable and ended up happy in closing that deal. Dr. Ramesh was not the least bit surprise to hear the news that his granddaughter had moved back in with Ravi, for he was confident that would happen sooner than later. Ravi's parents were thrilled to have their beloved daughter-in-law back. And Nani was beside herself, so happy to see Indira back to normal. Indira, feeling more at ease now, then divulged to Nani the reason for leaving Ravi in the first place, which Nani sort of suspected all along, and Nani was happy to see Indira accept her fate as she had prayed she would. Though, initially, Nani had the innate desire to have a great-grandchild, and Ravi's parents, grandchildren of their own, they accepted their fate, also, as destiny would have it, and Nani felt blessed for having Coco in her life. As expected, Francine and Albert were glad that Indira patched up things with Ravi and moved back in with him, and that Coco aided in their reconciliation.

The following week after Indira returned Coco, Francine was down visiting her parents again on the weekend and she let Indira have the baby for a couple of nights. Albert made no fuss about it this time around but was grateful for the assistance. Unfortunately, though, on that very visit, Francine took down with a cold and became very sick. The years of having to care for her children as a young mother left her feeling rundown, compounding her condition. She was so fatigued and stressed that her mother Joan told her to stay on with her for a while so she could take care of her and assist with the children. Joan would have been happy to care for Coco, also, but Francine thought she would have her hands full with her and the other five children, so they decided to ask Indira to keep Coco for a while longer, which Indira gladly accepted.

Francine was bedridden for a week, at which time Indira not only cared for Coco but helped her friend out with the triplets and twins. Over the following week, Francine showed no signs of improvement, only deteriorated daily, so Albert decided to take her to the doctor. After a series of test, it was diagnosed that Francine not only had an acute cold, but was also suffering from iron deficiency anaemia, thus the lack of energy she had been experiencing for sometime.

Francine stayed with her mother for the next few weeks and, altogether, Joan, Nani, and Indira tried to nurse her back to health. To elevate her iron level, Nani picked fresh callaloo from her garden and Indira cooked it up with shrimps for Francine everyday. Nani even had George select the most hefty chickens in her fowl coop and Indira also made chicken soup for Francine everyday. Indira even caught some tilapia fish from Nani's pond in the backyard and fried that up for her friend. Joan spared nothing for her precious daughter and often bought fresh beef and liver from the local butcher and cooked that up for Francine, also.

By the time Albert and George were ready to return to their teaching positions at school in September, Francine, in spite of all the nutritional and personal care she was given, had only recovered somewhat and was still feeling weak and fatigued. She asked Indira to continue caring for baby Coco until she was well enough to do so herself, and she returned home with the other children. Both Joan and Indira took turns to visit and care for her, and they assisted with the children. Albert's mother would have assisted, also, but she was a sick woman stricken with severe high blood pressure who needed help herself. Nani walked over to Francine as often as she could and helped out in whichever way she could, always taking her fresh vegetables from her garden, and herbal remedies.

While Francine was still trying to convalesce, Indira worked out a routine for herself. She went over to help Francine a couple of days during the week and spent most of the time with her on the weekends, except, for when she and Ravi would take off the occasional time on the motorcycle for a ride to Number 63 Beach where they would meet up with Uncle Ram and his family, or they would just stay home and go to the matinee, or visit Dr. Ramesh, or Ravi's parents up in Skeldon, during which time she would leave baby Coco with Nani, who delighted in taking care of the infant. Indira acted upon Francine's advice and took a typing course at a business school in town with the intention of procuring a bank job, as was Nani's lifelong dream for her, and, in time, she indeed secured a part-time job at a bank right there in town, something that made Nani flash her gold teeth, she was so pleased, and she gladly took care of Coco while Indira was at work. Indira also returned to her palm plant business and she started taking care of the flower garden again, and she resumed farming, with Ravi by her side, cultivating Nani's vegetable garden as well as theirs. She even resumed cooking regularly, something she had lost interest in doing during her period of illness. She also eventually got around to opening the pile of letters from Radhika, which she had left unopened during her separation from Ravi, and she took the time to reply to each.

It was not long before that Indira started looking round and healthy again, and she glowed with love for Ravi. Her sweet, melodious laughter returned. The peace and happiness and contentment that had taken wings and left her heart, also returned, in full force. Baby Coco brought life back to her. The ring she had yanked from her finger when she had learned that she would never be able to bear children, the one that Nani had given her on her sixteenth birthday and had told her to pass on to her first daughter, she slipped back on her finger.

She did not know how long Francine would let her take care of Coco, only hoped for her friend to recuperate fully, but for now she cherished being a mother to the baby, as Nani did in being a great-grandmother. Ravi, however, was put in a position of having someone else's baby around and he appeared aloof. But he amply provided for Coco. He gave Indira whatever amount of money she needed to get whatever she so desired for the baby and all that the baby needed, and that was all he did. Indira sensed his lack of interest in getting anywhere close to Coco but she never brought it up with him and assumed the responsibility of nurturing the baby on her own. After all, Coco was not his baby and she did not expect him to act and embrace her as his own. The first week she had Coco, he used to watch her care for the baby, but soon after he became occupied with other things.

Weeks turned into months and Francine's health did not improve fully and Indira continued to care for Coco. And as the months went by Ravi kept up his distance from the baby. When he was not working and was at home in the evenings, he would leave Indira alone to take care of the baby and he kept busy at his desk with shuffling business papers, or he would take to having a drink on the verandah, or choose to play his guitar, or write poems. It was only after Indira put the baby to sleep in the cradle at nights that he would join her.

After putting the baby down one night, Indira joined him in their bedroom and she fell into a deep sleep after a long day's work. She was so sound asleep that night that when Coco woke up in the middle of the night and was having a hunger cry, she did not hear her. When she woke up some moments later, while still laying in bed, she noticed Ravi was in the baby's room holding Coco and was feeding her. She remained silent and watched as he burped the baby afterwards and rocked her to sleep in his arms. The next night, at the slight cry of the baby, he jumped out of bed before she could and took the initiative again of caring for Coco. From then on, Ravi started getting off work early and the first thing he would do when he got home was rush to hold the baby, and he would smile so broadly just to hear her cooing.

One night as he was rocking Coco to sleep in his arms, Indira was in the baby's room beside him, and he looked down at the baby and said, "A baby, no matter whose, is a gift from God." And they watched as the baby grew and took her first steps, and Ravi read to her and sang her to sleep every night.

Indira had prayed for a baby and had no answer and she had questioned her God, but she had kept on praying though her faith was tested. She had even asked Nani to pray and bless her with a child. Now, she thanked her God for blessing her with baby Coco, even though she would only have her until Francine was well enough to take care of her, as Francine had specified, and Ravi thanked the Universe for his luck of having the opportunity of holding a baby in his arms and caring for it. Life was not designed exactly as they wanted it to be, for they both wanted a houseful of children of their own, but not only were they blessed with having Coco for a while, their house, as their destiny would have it, would oftentimes be filled with Francine's children and the children of their other friends. Their house now overflowed so much so with children that Dr. Ramesh would, at times, open up his big, yellow mansion to accommodate them all for sleepovers.

One hot afternoon, when Coco was one year old, Francine and Albert were over at Ravi and Indira's place and they had brought the triplets and twins along. Laliwa and Afonso and their boy child were also there, so were Ling and Devika and their little boy. Sally had returned home with her husband Neville and they were there, also, and they now had a newborn girl child. That day, as the children were playing in the backyard, Indira made blackeye cake, *turnover, pine tart,* and cheese roll pastries, and she baked plait bread and took the fresh, hot bread down with sweet, rich condensed milk, along with the pastries for the children to eat, and a jug of Kool-Aid for them to quench their thirst. Ravi had a bag of toys and sugar-coated blood-drop sweetie and bubble gum and was sharing them out at that time. Nani was there churning ice cream for the children and was happy to play the role of a great-grandmother. She recalled when she had blessed Ravi on the night of his wedding, when she had told him she hoped that his and Indira's love would bear a lot of fruits in due time; it did not happen the way she had expected it to happen, but they now had more children around them than she could count.

560

As Ravi and Albert were standing around in the backyard enjoying a couple of ice-cold bottles of Banks Beer, they were watching the children play in the white light of the afternoon sunshine, and Ravi commented to Albert, "Look at them all. We have interracial offsprings between an Amerindian and a Portuguese, Chinese and Indian, English European and a dougla—Indian and African descent, and Coco and her five sisters. Man, what a mixed pot of people we are, just like a good pot of cook-up rice!"

Indira was sitting in the shade of the back steps at the moment with Coco on her lap, feeding her a bottle of milk, and Francine, who was feeling much better these days, was sitting on the step behind Indira and was braiding Indira's hair into a hassar plait, and Francine said to her, "I told you a long time ago that you would make a great mother, Indira. Now you have proven that. You're taking good care of my baby. Is there anything I can get for her?"

"Coco has everything she needs, Francine. Ravi sees to it that she does. How much longer would you let me keep her for? Or would you let me keep on raising her?"

Francine was quiet, causing Indira to look up at her, and all Francine did was give her friend a smile but did not give her an answer.

* * *

It was a warm and enchanting night in the little town of Rose Hall and, as people were sound asleep in their shacks and colourful stilt houses, a crescent moon was brightly shining and the millions of stars were sparkling like diamonds in the sky, and candleflies hovered about the dark corners of the bushes, their yellow lights blinking. The chirring of the crickets, croaking of the crapos, and the barking of a dog, as well as the symphonic gush of the nearby river composed the sounds of this tropical night.

A balmy wind was blowing in through the old wooden windows of Nani's upstairs bedroom, tossing the maroon lace curtains about and spreading the incense-like-scent of the burning green mosquito coil—set on the bedside table —across the room, in which Nani and five-year-old Coco were fast asleep on the feather pillow, on the single coconut fibre bed, behind the white veil of the mosquito netting. Nani had been up that night telling Coco jumbie stories and folklore by the mud stove while they were eating roasted katahar seeds, and it was quite late when they had retired for the night.

In the wee hours of the morning, Coco woke to the crowing of the fowlcocks and laid in bed. Through the mosquito netting, she could see the glowing red tip of the mosquito coil on the bedside table, and as she watched as the smoke from it curl upwards, she thought of the stories Nani had told her last night. After a while, her thoughts shifted to something she always found exciting, and she turned to Nani and gently shook her and said, "Wake up, Nani, wake up, it's time to get up and light the fireside."

Nani opened her eyes and rubbed the sleep away with the back of her hands. "Yes, *bab*," she said, using the endearing term for a special child, "I will get up and light the fireside." Coco drew the mosquito netting aside to let her old Nani pull herself up and sit at the edge of the bed, then Nani said to her, "Find the matches and give them to me so I can light the kerosene oil lamp."

Coco foraged through the bedside table drawer and found the box of matches and handed it to Nani, and Nani took a matchstick and fired it up and lit the kerosene oil lamp then held it up to Coco and smiled at the child, exposing her gold teeth, for the child made her happy. Even with her eyesight as dim as it was, Nani could see what a pretty little girl Coco was, a little doll in a pink cotton nightie. The child had a small round face as innocent as an angel, wide almond-shaped brown eyes lined with long curly lashes, jet black hair now done in adorable ringlets, and tender skin the colour of rich brown coco. It was her smile that could melt Nani for she had perfect little teeth as white as lily. The beauty of the child and her happy ways gave Nani vigour in her old age, and a reason to keep on living.

Nani pinched Coco adoringly on the cheek, then she rested the oil lamp back on the bedside table and asked the child to bring her their home clothes hanging on the clothes-horse in the corner, and when Coco did, Nani helped her to change her nightie and put on her favourite sky-blue dress. Coco buckled on her brown sandals as Nani also got changed and tied on her faded brown headkerchief.

While Nani took some time to oil her bare feet with coconut oil, Coco said to her, "Before you light the fireside, can we milk Rani and get the eggs from the fowl coop, Nani?"

"Yes, bab," Nani said; she would do just about anything for little Coco.

"And can I play with the yellow ducklings for a while?"

"Yes, you can, bab. And what else would you like to do?"

"Help me up onto the donkey-cart so I can have a look at the baby birds in the nest on the roof of the bottom-house."

"Okay," Nani said, "I will do that for you."

Coco then spotted the white enamel posey under the bed, and she said, "I can take the posey and empty it in the latrine for you, Nani."

"I would not let you do such a thing, bab," Nani said. "Besides, it's too dark to go that far in the backyard now. I will take care of it after breakfast. Come, let's go downstairs and brush our teeth." And Nani took the kerosene oil lamp and made her way out of the bedroom.

Coco followed her across the sitting room and out onto the front verandah into the darkness of the morning, the sweet scents of the jump & kiss, chameli, and hibiscus flowers in the garden below drifting about in the early morning air. They made their way down the stairs and across the bottom-house—the earthen ground appearing grey and smooth from being freshly daubed just the day before with cow-dung and clay—and they passed the swaying hammock and stopped at the pipe by the foot of the backstairs where Nani cleaned her teeth with a black-sage chew stick while Coco used a toothbrush, then they headed straight to the old fowl coop in the backyard.

While Nani held up the oil lamp in the fowl coop, Coco went around searching for eggs beneath the chickens sitting in the nests of hay, and she collected a paint can of warm eggs. She then wanted to pick green tamarind from the tree in the orchard in the very back of the yard, salivating to eat

564

it with hot pepper sauce and salt, but Nani told her the mosquitoes there would eat her alive. It was not the mosquitos that made Coco change her mind, though, she suddenly thought that the jumbie man might be lurking among the fruit trees and she became scared. She cheered up when Nani distracted her by leading her to the edge of the pond to play with the yellow ducklings sitting there with their mother, and when a fish jumped in the pond, she said, "Would you let me catch some fish with you today, Nani?"

"We already have some live hassa in the green barrel in the kitchen, remember? And shrimps, also. But I will let you catch some fish with me next week. Now, come on, let's go to the bottom-house and milk Rani."

Coco helped Nani to milk Rani, collecting the thick, rich milk in an aluminium bucket. After, she headed over to Solomon, who was laying around on the earthen ground, and she patted the donkey's ear. Then she said to Nani, "Now help me up onto the donkey-cart so I can see the baby birds, Nani." Nani helped her up and Coco looked up at the nest on the roof of the bottom-house and said, "I can't see them now, Nani. They must be sleeping."

"Wait until it gets bright when their mother is feeding them and you'll see them then for sure," Nani said. "Come, now, let's go back upstairs and I'll light the fireside."

Once they were in the kitchen, Nani hung up the kerosene oil lamp on the hook of the chain dangling from the ceiling, then she shoved some wood in the mud stove and started the fire, much to the excitement of Coco, and she asked Coco, "What does your little heart desire for breakfast, bab?"

"Curry hassa and saijan bhaji with shrimps, and rice," Coco was quick to say, and she pointed at the green barrel where Nani had the live hassars and shrimps.

"Okay, if that is what you want for breakfast then I will cook it," Nani said as she opened the old wooden window overlooking the backyard, letting in the early morning warm air. "But before I start cooking, I'll warm you up a cup of fresh cow's milk."

"Can I have some *guava jelly*, also, Nani?"

"Sure, bab," Nani said, and got the jar of guava jelly she had made just the day before, especially as a treat for Coco, and she took a spoonful and gave it to the child, who clapped her little mouth in savouring every bit of it. Nani then got the black iron milk pot hanging over the mud stove and warmed up some milk and poured it in Coco's favourite white enamel cup and served her at the table.

Coco dipped a little finger in the milk and scooped up the layer of cream and ate it, and as she went about sipping on the hot milk, she looked on fondly at Nani as Nani started preparing breakfast, enjoying the old lady's company as much as Nani was enjoying hers. As the wood in the mud stove crackled, emanating a soothing warmth and flooding the kitchen with a sweet veil of smoke, Nani sat on the peerah and ground up the spices for the curry on the masala brick, with ball-of-fire pepper, and she chopped up the saijan leaves, which she had picked just the day before, to fry with the shrimps, and she cut the saijan drumsticks for the curry then fished out some of the hassars and shrimps from the green barrel and cleaned them in the dish sink. She then started cooking, the mouth-watering spices now permeating the kitchen, and as the pots were boiling, Coco looked on at the dancing flames, fascinated by the mud stove—fireside.

A tinge of violet-blue was painted across the semi-dark sky by the time Nani was finished cooking, and the birds were now chirping exuberantly in the trees. Nani served Coco a hot plate of curry hassar and saijan bhaji with shrimps, and rice, with mango achar and ball-of-fire pepper, and Coco sat at the table and ate with a spoon while Nani took her seat in the usual place, on the peerah, and ate with her fingers from the calabash. After the scrumptious, spicy meal, Nani scrubbed her fingers with a nenwa loofah in the dish sink and dried them on her apron, and she put some more wood on to burn and put on a carahee of vermicelli and milk with raisons and brown sugar to boil to make *vermicelli milk pudding*, Coco's favourite sweets, then she left the kitchen and came back with a faded brown cloth bag.

"What's in there?" Coco asked, inquisitively.

"You'll soon see," Nani said, and she took a seat at the table beside Coco.

As Coco looked on with great anticipation, Nani untied the string from the bag and opened it and tossed the contents onto the old wooden table, and the light from the kerosene oil lamp and the flames from the burning wood in the mud stove caused the gold jewellery to glitter brightly. Coco was dazzled by the sight and she exclaimed, "Gold!"

Nani went on to explain the heirloom: "These were all given to me by my mother, Raajee. And my mother got it from my grandmother, Chaaya. My grandmother, Chaaya, got the jewellery from a rich Englishman who was an overseer for a sugar plantation . . . And so you see, the

567

jewellery has been passed on from generation to generation, and someday it will all be yours, bab."

End

www.ingramcontent.com/pod-product-compliance
Lightning Source LLC
Chambersburg PA
CBHW051929020726
47501CB00001B/36